Gently, but firmly, Rafe Pendragon tugged at the sheet and blanket. Julianna bit her lower lip as he pulled the bedclothes slowly from her grasp and folded them back to expose her body. Her cheeks warmed as she waited.

"What are you doing?" she demanded.

"I've only now realized I have yet to kiss you. You wouldn't let me before as I recall."

A small shiver rippled through her. "No," she murmured in soft reply.

"Seems I shall have to rectify that, now that we are here together. Alone."

When they met hers, Rafe's lips were silky, almost feather-light, they played over her own—skilled, certain. He groaned, the sound vibrating against her mouth before he angled her head and slanted his lips over hers to take their kiss to the next level. . . .

Also by Tracy Anne Warren

The Husband Trap
The Wife Trap
The Wedding Trap

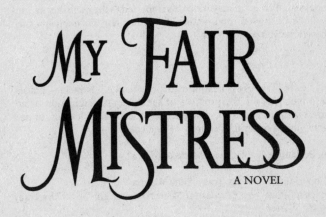

MY FAIR MISTRESS

A NOVEL

TRACY ANNE WARREN

BALLANTINE BOOKS • NEW YORK

A Ballantine Books Mass Market Original

Copyright © 2007 by Tracy Anne Warren
Excerpt from *The Accidental Mistress* copyright © 2007 by Tracy Anne Warren

Published in the United States by Ballantine Books, an imprint of The Random House Publishing Group, a division of Random House, Inc., New York.

BALLANTINE and colophon are registered trademarks of Random House, Inc.

This book contains an excerpt from the forthcoming mass market edition of *The Accidental Mistress* by Tracy Anne Warren. This excerpt has been set for this edition only and may not reflect the final content of the forthcoming edition.

ISBN 978-0-345-49539-6

Cover illustration: Chris Cocozza

Printed in the United States of America

www.ballantinebooks.com

OPM 9 8 7 6 5 4 3

For Mama
with love

Acknowledgments

WITH GRATITUDE TO my editor, Charlotte Herscher, for believing in the stories I have to tell and for helping me bring them so vividly to life.

My sincere appreciation to Signe Pike and Lindsey Benoit—thank you both for all your hard work and support.

To my fabulous agent Helen Breitwieser for the thousand and one things you do. Big hugs for always being in my corner!

A special mention to Carol Essen, Christine Finch, Megan Bell, Chrissy Dionne, Valarie Pelissaro, Cybil Solyn, Debbie Kepler, and Michelle Buonfiglio.

My appreciation to the unfailingly generous Mary Jo Putney for her advice and for giving me just the right nugget of inspiration.

Love to my comrades-in-arms, Mary Blayney, Dorothy McFalls, and Ruth Kaufman. Hugs for being there to let me cheer and whine.

And finally, to all my wonderful fans—nothing would be possible without you!

Chapter One

London 1812

THE RENTED HACKNEY rolled to a stop.

Lady Julianna Hawthorne leaned forward and stared out the carriage window, surprised by what she found. Instead of the average, unremarkable row home she'd been expecting, an imposing townhouse rose upward, its three stories nearly blocking out sight of the cloudless blue sky above. Clean and genteel, the Georgian residence boasted an elegant stone façade, a fine green iron railing, and a bright white door that appeared recently painted.

Perhaps the driver has mistaken the address, she mused. Surely this beautiful home could not belong to the man she had come to see. Hand trembling, she reached into her silk reticule and drew out a small square of paper inked with the financier's direction.

36 Bloomsbury Square.

Her gaze flashed back to the townhouse—the numbers three and six plainly displayed next to each other on the door.

Her heart sank. No, there was no mistake. Whether she liked it or not, this must indeed be the villain's abode.

She passed the driver a generous handful of coins,

with the promise of more to come to ensure he would still be waiting once her business inside was concluded. In a quiet, residential neighborhood such as this, finding another hackney cab would be all but impossible. And she hadn't dared take her own private coach, the one with her late husband's family crest prominently emblazoned on the side. No one, absolutely no one of her acquaintance, must ever know she'd been to this place.

Before she had a chance to change her mind and let fear send her scurrying back home like some timid brown mouse, she forced herself to alight from the carriage.

She paused, brushing a nervous hand over the folds of her warm woolen pelisse and the cerise satin day dress underneath. Knowing she couldn't afford to delay further, she forced her feet to action. Climbing the stairs, she lifted the knocker and gave two smart raps.

At length the door opened on a set of silent, well-oiled hinges. Hard black eyes peered down at her out of a long, brutish face. As a woman of diminutive stature, Julianna was well used to craning her neck backward in order to look up at men. But this man, this towering mountain of flesh, was the tallest human being she'd ever seen. He reminded her of a tree. A very large, very dense oak that grew in the deepest, oldest woodlands.

But it was the gruesome, crescent-shaped scar bisecting his left cheek from temple to jaw that made her gasp, saliva drying in her mouth.

"Yeah? What d'ye wants?" he demanded, his bass voice as scary as the rest of him.

Her tongue, usually one of her most nimble allies, lay limp behind her teeth, failing to come to her aid.

The brute scowled harder as she fought for composure.

On a sharp inhale, she made herself begin. "I—I have

come to speak with Mr. Rafe Pendragon. Might you be he, sir?"

Merciful God, she prayed, *let this not be him.*

The Tree scowled harder, thick black brows scrunching like a pair of angry caterpillars on his smooth, bald pate. "Dragon's busy and he don't have no time for no morts today, however tasty they might look. Take it somewhere else, ducky."

Then, in the most appalling display of rudeness she'd ever encountered, he slammed the door in her face.

Shivering from shock, she stood immobile, the cold February air creeping in and around her skirts. She drew her pelisse closer.

What was it that brute had said? Something about tasty morts. What on earth was a *mort*? If it was what she suspected—affront rushed through her, erasing the worst of her chill.

And he'd called her ducky. *Ducky!*

Lips tight, teeth clenched, she raised her gloved hand and knocked again.

The door opened, the Tree reappearing. "What now? Don't yer ears work? Told you already The Dragon ain't interested."

Drawing herself up as tall and straight as her five feet one inch would allow, she raised her chin.

"My good man," she declared, speaking in an aristocratic tone that would have made her late father beam with pride, "you have obviously made some sort of mistake. My name is Lady Julianna Hawthorne and I have a pressing matter of business to discuss with your master. Pray give him this and inform him that I await him directly."

Using her most formal manners, she extended a small white calling card engraved with her name.

Fingers the size of sausages reached out and took the delicate rectangle of paper in their grasp. He barely glanced at it, leaving her to wonder if the oaf could read. Crushing the card inside his hand, he began to close the door. But before he could manage the deed, she raced forward and slipped inside.

"I'll wait here," she stated, taking up a defensive stance in the middle of the attractively tiled foyer. "You may go find Mr. Pendragon."

The huge man raked her with an appraising look, grudging admiration twinkling in his dark eyes. "Yer a pushy bit o' baggage, ain't ye?"

On a booted heel, he turned away and disappeared down the hallway.

Trembling anew at her bold actions, Julianna released a shaky sigh. As a lady born and bred, it wasn't often she had to assert herself in such an overt fashion. Had the circumstances been less dire, she knew she would not have possessed the courage. Had the circumstances been less dire, she would never have come to this house in the first place.

But desperate times, as the saying went, called for desperate measures. Her family's welfare was at stake, and no matter the cost, she meant to save it.

The Tree soon returned, his footsteps amazingly quiet for a man of his enormity.

"He says you can go in." The giant poked a thumb over one brawny shoulder. "Left door, end o' the hall."

A properly trained servant would have escorted her to the room, and announced her to his master as custom dictated. But there was nothing remotely proper about this great lummox, who swung around, opened a hidden panel in a nearby wall, and vanished, presumably belowstairs.

Julianna drew in another lungful of air and braced herself for the confrontation ahead. If the master was anything like his servant, she was in for a truly loathsome ordeal.

The Dragon.

She remembered how her brother Harry's voice had shaken as he'd spoken the name, as he'd drunkenly confessed to her a few nights ago how he'd placed himself in the financier's power.

"I'm sorry, Jules," he'd moaned, brown eyes moist with unshed tears and shame. "I've let you down. I've let us all down. I know I shouldn't have touched the money, but a man's got to keep up appearances."

"What kind of appearances? And what money?" She frowned for a long, thoughtful moment. "Surely you don't mean the loan for improving the home farm? Tell me you didn't risk all that money playing cards?"

He hung his head. "Well no, not all of it, at least not at first. I gambled a bit—all the fellows do—but there were other things as well."

"What other things?"

He hesitated, plainly reluctant to continue. "There was a girl. Prettiest little opera dancer I've ever seen. She . . . um . . . she had a marked partiality for diamond bracelets."

Julianna tightened her lips but somehow remained silent.

"The blunt didn't seem so much at first," Harry continued. "A bit here, a bit there. I thought I could pay it all back once the profits from the fall harvest came through. But the crop didn't fare as well as it should have this year, and I kept waiting for my luck to turn at the tables. Just one more hand, I kept thinking, and I'll win."

"But you didn't."

He shook his head, his face white except for a pair of ruddy streaks across his cheekbones. "The loan came due at the bank and I had to pay. A man has his honor to consider, don't you know."

"So you took out another loan. From this Dragon person I presume."

Harry's shoulders tightened. "At least he's not a cent-per-center. I'm not so far gone in the head as to traffic with one of them. The new loan is fair, even if the interest rate is a bit higher than the bank."

"If this Pendragon person is a fair man, then why not ask for an extension? Surely he can be persuaded to see reason."

"I said the deal was fair, I didn't say Pendragon was. He's as hard and ruthless as they come. There'll be no extensions."

Her brother paused, drawing in a trembling, terrified breath. "If I don't pay up by the end of the month, the estate will be forfeit. I'll have no choice except to sell."

"Oh, Harry," she gasped, raising a horrified hand to her lips.

"And there won't be any money for Maris's come out next month," he admitted. " 'Course it might not matter if we're broke, what with the size of her dowry. Thank God father set it up so I couldn't touch her portion or there's no telling to what depths I might have sunk."

He rubbed a distraught hand over his face. "Plague take me, Jules, what am I to do? Perhaps I ought to put a bullet between my eyes and have done with it."

She grabbed his shoulders and forced him to look at her. "There will be no talk of that. Killing yourself is not the answer and you are never to think of it again, do you hear me? You're our brother and Maris and I love you, no matter if you've made an admittedly dreadful mistake. We'll think of a way out. *I'll* think of a way out. There has to be a reasonable solution."

Since then, Julianna had thought of little else, putting her mind and ingenuity to the test. She'd come up with a plan, an appeal she hoped would satisfy all parties.

Of course, it assumed a bit of forbearance on the financier's part. Harry said the man was remorseless when it came to business, and Pendragon's nickname didn't offer much reassurance otherwise. But surely even the coldest of men had some faint spark of compassion buried deep inside them. Now she had only to see if she could reach it.

Gripping her reticule tightly, she strode forward like a knight prepared to challenge a beast in its lair.

The last door to the left stood open. She didn't knock, just slipped inside. After all, she was expected.

Paneled in dark wood, the room was shadowy but warm, a fire burning hot and red in an immense fireplace built into the center of the wall to the right.

How atmospheric, she thought. *How appropriate for a dragon.*

A log snapped, blazing ash roaring upward into the flue, half-startling her as she proceeded deeper into the room. Shelves heavily laden with books lined the walls, while thick woolen carpets woven with exotic Chinese symbols covered the floor, bathing the space in a cascade of browns and reds.

A branch of lighted candles stood on the corner of a massive mahogany desk at the far end of the room; watery winter sunlight making an ineffectual attempt to shine through the pair of tall, double-hung windows beyond.

A man sat behind the desk, writing something in a thick, leather-bound ledger. As she approached, he set down his pen and looked up. It was only then that she saw him clearly.

Perhaps the notion revealed a measure of prejudice on her part, but she'd been ready to encounter ugliness and severity, picturing him as some sour, cruel-lipped old man, shriveled by age and the callous nature of his profession.

Instead, the sight of him drove the air from her lungs. Rugged and very nearly beautiful, he possessed an aura of pure masculine power. Its impact shot like an energy bolt straight through to her toes. And he was by no means old—far from it. In his early thirties, if she guessed correctly, he was fit and in his prime.

His features were refined, even elegant, with a straight nose and strong, square chin. Long dimples creased the bronzed skin of his angular cheeks, intriguing slashes that framed a firm yet winsome mouth. His hair was brown, but not an ordinary brown—as rich and decadent as the chocolate that arrived each morning on her breakfast tray. He kept it short, trimmed in the current fashion, a few tendrils left to droop invitingly over his high forehead.

Yet for all his beauty, his eyes were what sent a shiver rippling over her skin. Bright and penetrating, they were the same translucent green as cool river water on a new spring day. Eyes of power and insight. Eyes of deep intellect. Eyes that seemed as if they could reach inside a person and pierce clean through to the soul. She wondered if this was how Archangel Gabriel had appeared on the eve of the Fall—dangerous, deadly, and sinfully appealing.

Watching him rise to his feet made her pulse quicken, his lean height complementing the impressive width of his shoulders and the narrowness of his hips. Dressed in a conservative shade of blue, he wore the well-tailored clothing of a gentleman. Everything about his appearance, from pristine cravat to polished Hessians, spoke of tasteful, understated elegance.

He quirked a single dark brow at her bold perusal, his own curiosity about her undisguised. "Lady Hawthorne, I presume?"

His words startled her out of whatever trance she had apparently fallen into, abruptly recalling her to her purpose.

"Yes," she replied. "And I assume you are Mr. Rafe Pendragon, the man who makes loans."

"Among other investments and financial dealings, yes. I see you are a woman who likes to get straight to the point, but first, why don't you allow me to take your cloak?"

Julianna realized she had been so mesmerized by him that she'd forgotten she still wore her pelisse. Now that she recalled it, she also became aware of how warm she had grown, perspiration beginning to dampen her collar. With a nod, she reached up and unfastened the garment's clasp.

Moving behind her, Pendragon lifted the fur-lined cloak from her shoulders. His actions were nothing but polite, his large hands careful not to touch her in any way. Yet he was too close, his physical presence unnerving, overwhelming.

Suddenly breathless, she took a hasty step forward.

"You must forgive Hannibal," he said as he crossed to drape her pelisse neatly over the back of a chair. "He's never been much for the refinements."

Did he mean The Tree? So the brute had a name, did he?

"Then perhaps you ought to consider employing someone else to greet your front-door callers."

An amused gleam shone in the financier's gaze. "No doubt. But he has his uses."

Yes, she thought, *I can well imagine some of the uses to which he might be put. Such as frightening the supper out of imprudent youth like my brother.*

"Would you care for a refreshment?" Pendragon asked. "Tea, perhaps? Or a sherry?"

Every syllable that came from his lips flowed with the warm richness of a fine red wine. He spoke like a gentleman, the cadence and intonation of his words bespeaking a life of culture and education. So what was he doing working for a living? Making loans and investments and trading on the Exchange?

She wondered at his upbringing. He was no ordinary middle-class Cit, that was for certain. If she had met him while shopping on Bond Street, she would have taken him for a gentleman. Might have inclined her head and granted him a polite smile as they passed. Clearly, he had the bearing to move easily among members of her class, even those who prided themselves on their elevated status and the innate superiority of their birth.

So who was he to be nearly a gentleman and yet not one? It was an intriguing mystery indeed.

Her curiosity almost got the better of her, questions stacking up like tiny dominoes on her tongue. Abruptly, she shook off the wild impulse to pry.

This is not a social call, she scolded herself. She'd come to rescue her family from the very brink of disaster—her dear brother and sister, who meant more to her than anything else in this world. She needed to focus on that fact and only that fact.

"No, thank you," she said, refusing his offer of a drink. "I should prefer to discuss the reason for my visit here today."

"Ah, yes, of course." He walked behind his desk, then gestured a hand toward a chair on the opposite side. "Pray be seated and tell me why you have come."

He remained standing while she arranged herself on the seat before he took his own. Silently, he waited for her to begin.

Her heart thumped, a familiar, half-sick rush of anxiety returning to twist uncomfortably in her stomach. She clutched her reticule and drew a breath, wondering how best to start.

"I am Lady Julianna Hawthorne," she stated, her words dwindling to a rapid halt.

"I believe we've established that, my lady."

She swallowed, her throat dry. Suddenly she wished she'd taken him up on that drink. Knowing she would lose her nerve if she didn't get on with it, she compelled herself to speak. "I am told you've had business dealings with my brother, Harry Davies, the Earl of Allerton."

His face remained impassive. "His lordship and I are acquainted, yes."

"I understand he owes you a sum of money, a debt whose repayment is due very shortly."

Pendragon inclined his regal head. "As you say."

"Which is why I have come . . . to discuss the loan on Lord Allerton's behalf."

He raised a sardonic brow, censure darkening his gaze. "I take it he can't pay and has importuned you to plead his case, has he? I had thought your brother possessed a bit more pride and sense than that."

A flush rose in her cheeks, further heating her already warm skin. "His pride is very much intact, as are his faculties. Actually, Harry knows nothing of my visit today. If he did, he would be greatly displeased. But I felt compelled to meet with you nonetheless."

She paused and lowered her voice to a confidential tone. "My brother is over-young, Mr. Pendragon, only twenty, and still learning how best to manage his affairs. Our father died a little more than a year ago, and I fear Harry wasn't yet ready to assume the pressures and responsibilities that come with a noble title. But he is a fine young man, a good boy, who simply needs time to find his feet. I can assure you he has every intention of satisfying his obligations."

"Then he ought to have used his head instead of foolishly squandering his money. What was it, gaming or women?"

Her eyes grew wide.

Pendragon gave a rueful shake of his head. "Both, I

see. Allerton's certainly been a busy boy, has he not? His vices, however, are really none of my affair."

"Actually I should think they are, under the circumstances. I cannot defend Harry's ill-considered behavior, but I can assure you he is extremely sorry for what he has done. I promise you he will do everything in his power to make things right if but given the chance. You seem a reasonable man. Maybe you would be willing to grant him an extension. Another ninety days, perhaps—"

"Your pardon, my lady, but what good would that do? If Allerton doesn't have the funds now, there's little chance he'll have them three months from now. The outcome will be the same."

"But surely everyone deserves a measure of compassion."

"Just so, which is why this good city has any number of fine churches and charitable organizations. I, however, run an investment business and am not in the habit of granting imprudent favors."

Julianna refused to let herself tremble. *Harry is right,* she thought, *this man has no heart.*

The Dragon relaxed back in his chair. "Now if I might be permitted to ask you a question."

"And what, pray tell, is that?"

"I'm curious to know what your husband thinks of you coming to see me in your brother's stead. Or is he also unaware of today's visit?"

She stiffened. "I am a widow, sir. I make all of my own decisions."

"Well, that explains a very great deal."

His remark rankled, but she decided to let it pass.

"If you refuse to grant my brother an extension," she continued, "then I am prepared to offer you an alternate form of payment." Tugging open the drawstrings of her reticule, she reached inside. "Here is a list of several very fine paintings in my possession. Included among them are an original Tintoretto and an extremely beautiful Caravaggio, old master works of great value."

She passed him a sheet of paper, then returned to dig inside her reticule again. "I have also brought several pieces of jewelry. They include a necklace, bracelet, and ear bobs—a matching set given to me by my late husband at the time of our marriage. The sapphires and diamonds are worth at least five thousand pounds. They're completely mine and in no way entailed to my husband's estate."

Opening the velvet pouch, she drew out the jewels and set them on his desk for display. The gemstones winked and sparkled with vivid life in the candlelight.

He leaned forward. "Quite lovely."

Heartened, she pressed on. "I did some calculations and concede these items do not fully repay my brother's loan. But if you would agree to accept these valuables now, I will promise to pay you the remaining thousand pounds in cash come the first of April. My quarterly allowance is placed into my account then, you see."

Pendragon set aside the list of oil paintings. Steepling his fingers, he rested the tips underneath his chin and regarded the woman on the opposite side of his desk.

She really is magnificent, he mused, *lush and lovely and so full of earnest animation and optimistic hope.* What a shame he was going to have to disappoint her yet again.

How dare Allerton, he thought. What had the careless whelp been thinking to endanger his family's welfare and reputation in such a manner? Even if the earl was completely ignorant of his sister's presence here this afternoon, the young lordling deserved nothing less than a sound thrashing for his irresponsible behavior.

A lady of Julianna Hawthorne's obvious sweetness and grace should not be discussing business with a man like him. She shouldn't be discussing business at all. Instead she ought to be home sipping tea with her circle of elegant friends, laughing and trading amusing stories, not be here in a stranger's study doing her level best to barter her finest jewels to him.

His jaw tightened. Striving for a pleasant yet firm tone, he proceeded. "These are very fine items, my lady. However, they are of insufficient value to cover your brother's outstanding obligation."

Her pretty lips fell open. His gaze followed, drawn like a firefly to a flame. Unable to prevent himself, he visually traced their shape, finding them full and pink and every bit as enticing as a dish of ripe June strawberries. And soft. Oh, they looked soft enough to put silk to shame.

Shaking off the sudden rush of desire, he returned to the matter at hand. "The jewelry would need to be appraised," he said. "Assuming the stones are real—"

Her eyes flashed with offense.

"—which I have no doubt they are," he amended. "I imagine the set would fetch a little over two thousand pounds."

"Two thousand, but—"

"Resale, your ladyship. What a person pays for jewelry in a shop is far more than what the pieces are actually worth. As to the paintings, art, even fine art, is a difficult commodity to trade. It could take months to sell the paintings, and then likely for far less than you have estimated."

Her mouth drooped, her lovely brown eyes awash with disappointment.

For a moment he felt sorry for her, an uncharacteristic urge rising inside him to grant her the boon she so desperately sought. But as he'd already told her, a few months more would make no difference, not in the end. Experience had taught him that if a man couldn't pay his shot by the due date, chances were excellent he would never be able to pay it at all. Besides, he reminded himself, a businessman who let his sentiments override his sense soon finds himself playing the fool. And one thing he had never been was a fool.

"Perhaps I have some other belongings that might make up the difference," she continued. "I own a very nice set of silver, and there is my husband's book collection—"

He held up a hand. "Please, do not continue to put yourself through this turmoil. It's of no use. Even if all the items you've mentioned were worth what you imagined them to be, they still wouldn't cover your brother's vowels."

"But I don't understand," she sputtered. "Of course it should satisfy the debt."

"How much do you imagine he owes, then?"

"A little over ten thousand pounds."

He sighed. So the whelp hadn't been honest with her. Delusions, he mused, were a convenient thing.

"His debt is triple that amount."

"Triple?" Her voice quavered.

"Yes. He owes roughly thirty thousand pounds."

The blood drained from her cheeks, leaving them parchment pale. "Good God," she whispered.

"Perhaps you'd care for that sherry now?"

When she said nothing further, he rose to his feet. Soon after, he returned bearing a small glass filled with a translucent amber liquid.

"Here," he coaxed, holding out the drink. "I'd advise you to take a sip or two."

But she made no move to accept. In a sweep of lashes, her gaze lifted to meet his own. "Do you know that Harry will lose his estate if he defaults? That he will have no choice but to sell a home that has been in our family for over a hundred and fifty years?"

Rafe forced aside any inkling of compassion. In his

profession, he'd long ago learned to do without such tender emotions. "Yes, I am familiar with the property. Allerton used it as collateral when he secured the loan. To be frank, your ancestors were remiss not to have entailed the estate. Given that, it seems surprising the property wasn't lost or sold off many years past."

Visibly, she struggled for control, her breath moving rapidly in and out, causing her ample breasts to rise and fall beneath the rich silk of her bodice and the delicate lace fichu tucked above.

He couldn't help but watch.

What a fine example of womanhood she is, he thought. Her lush body seemed perfectly designed to make a man want to tumble her into his lap and play love games. She wasn't pretty in the conventional sense— far too brown for a traditional English beauty—yet she was stunning all the same. Deeply dark, her hair gleamed with a lustrous hue, as fine and satiny as the polished mahogany wood of his desk. Her eyes complemented her, their color an unusual shade of coffee containing tiny flecks that sparkled like gold dust. And her skin . . . ah, her skin, smooth and translucent as a summer peach, and no doubt every inch as tasty. He wondered if she had French blood in her veins, or maybe Italian, her look exotic and nothing short of intoxicating.

A real sigh escaped her lips, the sound shattering his heated thoughts.

Realizing he still held her drink in his hand, he set it down before her with an unintentional snap. Carefully, he worked to erase any hint of his former musings from his expression. Only then did he speak.

"Hard as it may be for you to accept, the financial arrangement between Lord Allerton and myself is binding and will stand as written. Now, my lady, I believe you should go. I shall see you to the door, since I am sure Hannibal is busy somewhere belowstairs."

Reaching for the small black velvet pouch that lay on his desk, he began to slip her jewelry inside, signaling once more that their interview was at an end.

"Wait!" she exclaimed.

He paused, sapphires and diamonds dangling from his fingers. "Yes?"

"I can't leave things like this," she said, her panic plain. "I came to help my brother, to save my family. I cannot go away empty-handed. Surely there must be some other arrangement we could make? Surely there must be something I can offer you, something of mine you want?"

Repressing a sigh, he slid the last of the gemstones into the pouch and tightened the strings. Silently, he set the sack before her.

Over the past several minutes, Rafe thought, he'd done his best to be attentive and polite, striving to help her see that her pleas and exhortations, no matter how prettily done, would not sway him to her cause. He could only admire her for her steadfast tenacity, but now she really did need to admit defeat. Lady Hawthorne, however well meaning, should go home and let her thoughtless puppy of a brother swallow a dose of his own medicine.

Rafe decided then and there to give her a shove in the right direction. He'd tried reasonable persuasion, cool argument, even a splash of cold reality. Perhaps a more fundamental approach was needed, something cruel enough to wound her, appalling enough to send her fleeing out his door.

"Something of yours I want?" he drawled darkly.

Appearing to be in no discernible hurry, he rested his hip against the edge of his desk, his large body looming suddenly above her own tiny frame. Pinning her with a bold look, he gave free rein to all the lustful desire he'd been feeling since the moment she'd strolled into his study. Blood running hot, he let his emotions gleam openly in his eyes.

Beginning with her exquisite face, he raked her with his gaze, roaming slowly, appraisingly, over her neck and onto her breasts. He lingered for a few long, pointed moments before traveling onward to rove across her belly and thighs, and downward all the way to her feet. Then he started the process again, upward this time, returning for a last slow, voracious caress.

Her lips parted, color blazing on her face.

"Madam," he said, his voice a low murmur of danger and sensuality, "I have told you already that your belongings are of no worth to me. There is only one thing from you I want, and that would be to strip you naked and take you to my bed. So unless you're willing to offer yourself to me in exchange for your brother's debt, we have nothing further to discuss."

She gasped, her body visibly shivering. He waited, expecting her to leap up, grab her possessions, and run screaming from his house.

Instead she sat, silent and utterly still, only her cheeks displaying her inner turmoil, her skin flushing alternately pink, then pale, then pink again.

Finally she drew a shaky breath and raised her chin. "If I agree," she murmured, "what would be your terms?"

Chapter Two

ᘓᕱᘗ

RAFE BLINKED AND nearly lost his balance, catching himself a split second before his hip slipped off the desk.

Did she say what I think she said? No, he assured himself after a moment, *I must have imagined it.*

"My terms?" he said slowly, waiting.

Instead of shooting him a horrified glare, she twisted her fingers together and gazed down at her lap.

"Yes," she whispered. "What would you want?" Her cheeks flamed hot as a July sun at her own question. "I mean, I know *what* you'd want, but when would you . . . umm . . . where would you . . . would it be just one time? Heavens, you wouldn't want it now, would you?"

As if she'd laid a hand between his legs, raw need sprang to life, his arousal stiff and strong. His imagination went wild, conjuring all sorts of heated sexual scenarios. For a moment, he pictured himself dragging Julianna from her chair and laying her across the wide, solid expanse of his desk. After kissing her half-senseless, his own thoughts scorched to a sensual haze, he would lift her skirts and . . .

Realizing he'd better find a sturdy seat before he un-manned himself and actually did land ass-first on the floor, he carefully straightened and retreated to the safety of his desk chair.

Sinking back against the comfortable leather, he used the moment to regain his sense of control. To say she had surprised him was an understatement, especially considering he was not a man who often found himself caught off guard.

Is she truly contemplating my audacious suggestion?

When he'd issued it, he'd never expected her to take his proposition seriously. He'd assumed such bold talk would frighten her away, making her hurry home like any ordinary woman would have done.

But then no ordinary woman would have come to his home in the first place, nor sat bravely pleading her brother's case in spite of an almost certain refusal. Julianna Hawthorne was most decidedly out of the common way, yet a lady through and through from the tips of her manicured fingernails to the ends of her dainty toes. And as such, she ought to be tossing his base declaration back in his face, not giving it additional thought.

She ought to be offended. Why wasn't she offended? Why wasn't she telling him he was a loathsome, contemptible swine?

And why wasn't he doing what he knew he ought by climbing to his feet and hustling her out the door? Shifting uneasily in his chair, he knew exactly why.

Narrowing his eyes, he surveyed her. Just how far would she take this? He decided to test the waters.

"No, not today," he stated. "As to the frequency, I hardly think one time would be sufficient." Drawing a breath, he continued, making sure to keep his voice deliberately matter-of-fact. "The best bang in the world isn't worth thirty thousand pounds. No madam, our association would need to be of a much longer duration, should we agree."

Now she will leave, he thought. Now, she will gather up her cloak and her dignity and return to her fancy, in-

sular world, where ladies did not find themselves importuned by baseborn financiers like himself.

Lips firming, she squeezed her fingers together so
tightly it was a wonder she didn't snap one off. "H-How
long then?"

How long? she'd asked. How long indeed, to pay off
a debt of such magnitude? How long to take and keep
her as his mistress while he slaked his desire for her?
How many days, weeks, and months would it take for
him to sate himself with her rare, unusual beauty before
her allure began to pale? Before he grew bored, as he in-
evitably would, and craved her no longer?

What price to place on a lady's virtue?

Lower-class women offered their bodies for sale all
the time, of course, bartering sex in order to earn a few
shillings for food, for shelter, for survival. But this
woman was no common whore; she wouldn't starve or
freeze to death in some alley if she didn't give herself to
him.

Abruptly, the knowledge of what she was contemplating angered him. Was her brother so very important to
her, then? Was keeping the young earl safe from financial and social destruction worth placing herself quite
literally into the hands of a stranger?

"Before I ponder such a detail," he mused aloud, "tell
me why. Why would you do this?"

Her gaze flashed up to his. "I've told you why. I have
to help my family."

"Your brother, yes. And is he truly worth such a
price? Even if I accept you in trade, so to speak, what's
to keep him from frittering away his fortune after this
debt is paid? What's to guarantee your noble gesture
won't be for naught when he tosses away his fortune
again at some future date?"

"Harry's promised me he'll never gamble again, and I
believe him. He's miserable and repentant, enough so

that I'm convinced he's learned his lesson. He's not a bad young man, only a misguided one."

"The debtor's prisons are full of misguided men whom others once thought were good."

"Harry *is* good," she defended. "Besides, he's not the only person who would be harmed. I have a little sister. She's seventeen and ready to make her come out in a few weeks. I won't have her embarrassed, nor will I see her put in the position of having to marry for money. I want her to be able to love and admire the man she marries, not feel as if she must wed in order to replenish the family coffers."

As Julianna herself had once done? he wondered. Had she been forced into a marriage not of her own choosing? She was young to be a widow, younger than his own thirty-five years. Twenty-seven, twenty-eight, he'd guess, a woman still at the height of her bloom with many, many fine seasons yet to come.

Hawthorne.

He vaguely remembered hearing of a property by that name that had passed to a distant relation when the old lord died without leaving a male heir. Was she his widow? If so, her husband had been several decades her senior.

He watched her for another long moment, his body hard and aching for a taste of her. Suddenly he wondered why he was arguing with her. What did he care about her motives or reasons? If this woman wanted to offer herself in exchange for Allerton's debt, who was he to dissuade her?

Still, was a chance to bed her really worth thirty thousand pounds? Years ago, he'd have given a firm, if regretful, no. He'd have *had* to say no. But through force of will and his own stubborn determination to succeed, he was now a wealthy man, a very wealthy man who could easily afford, should he choose, to do precisely as he wished.

So, should he give in to temptation?

God knows he wanted her, his body hungering with a fresh, belly-tightening pull of desire. He couldn't recall ever craving a woman with such instantaneous need. There was something about her that attracted him on a basic, elemental level, igniting a visceral reaction quite at odds with his usual state of calm, calculated restraint.

He imagined how it would feel to hold her in his arms, to kiss those soft, cherry-ripe lips, to settle his naked body against her own and sink himself deep, deep into her moist, heated flesh.

State his terms, she'd told him. State his terms and there was a very good possibility he could do all those things with her and more.

"Six months," he said in a brusque tone.

"*Six?*" Her dark eyes grew round.

"Yes, six. Five thousand pounds per month until the debt is paid. It's an extremely generous offer, I do assure you. Most mistresses don't get a fraction of that."

She lowered her gaze again. "And is that what I'd be," she murmured low, "your mistress?"

"Seems the most appropriate, least offensive term for what we are discussing." Needing a distraction, he drew his thumb along the smooth edge of a silver letter opener. "I'll want you at least three times a week. Under ordinary circumstances, I'd set you up in a house that provided me with access to you whenever I wished. But I assume that won't be an option in this case."

Her head jerked up, a bit of fire returning to her expression. "No. No one of my acquaintance can ever be permitted to know about us. And you will have to promise never to breathe a word to anyone about our arrangement, most especially not to my brother or to any of his peers."

"Wouldn't want it to leak out that you're trafficking with a baseborn commoner like me, hmm?"

A faintly alarmed look came over her face, as if afraid he'd withdraw his offer because of her declaration. "It's not just *my* reputation at stake," she defended. "I have my sister's welfare to consider. She mustn't be tainted by my actions. Even a whisper of scandal could ruin her chances in Society, you see."

Yes, Rafe thought, he did see. The aristocracy, when it chose, could be vicious as snakes, especially to members of its own class. Particularly to its women, when they were perceived to have broken the rules.

"Don't worry," he assured her, "no one will ever know. I've a reputation of my own and am well known for my tact and discretion in all matters. It will be our private business and ours alone."

Julianna let out a shaky sigh of relief and struggled against the shivers that threatened to take hold of her.

For mercy's sake, what am I doing? she kept asking herself. Was she really sitting here across from this chillingly lethal man discussing how best to barter her body to him for payment of Harry's debt? Harry would be livid if he knew and would unquestionably forbid her to proceed. But what else was she to do?

From the time of their mother's death when Julianna was eleven, she'd cared for her two younger siblings, more mother to them in many ways than older sister. They were all the family she had left in the world. She couldn't abandon them now, no matter the sacrifice.

"Very well," she murmured. "That leaves where and when. Even as a widow, I can't come and go at all hours. We would need to meet at times when my absence would go unremarked. Afternoon, perhaps."

She flushed at the thought. *How mortifying!* In all the years of her marriage, she'd never once had relations at any time other than night.

"Afternoon is agreeable. I'll rearrange my schedule. As for where, I have a couple of locations in mind. I'll think on it and let you know. You'll need to give me your direction so I can send 'round a messenger. Discreetly, of course."

Half numb, she repeated her address on Upper Brook Street, realizing as she did the magnitude of her actions. Was she really going through with this shameful plan? With every word spoken, every second that passed, the likelihood increased.

A queasy fist clenched tight in her stomach. Only by sheer force of will did she remain seated, powerfully tempted to hurry out to her waiting hack and race back to the security and comfort of her home. A home where he now knew she lived. She'd come to offer him her possessions. Instead she was offering herself.

"I can think of only one final item that requires discussion," he said in that deep, smooth drawl that made shivers tingle deliciously along her spine. "The likelihood of you getting in a family way."

Her mouth fell open, her shock so profound she couldn't utter a squeak.

He went on. "I'll do what I can to prevent a pregnancy. There are a few methods available, though admittedly none that are foolproof. You should take precautions as well, efficacious herbs and such; that way both of us can increase the odds no unwanted issue shall spring from our liaison. Lord knows the last thing I want is to bring another bastard into the world."

Was he illegitimate? she thought, wondering at his remark. She recalled the earlier statement he'd made when he'd referred to himself as a "baseborn commoner." Well, many men of his class came into this world outside the sanctity of marriage. If he had, it didn't matter to her.

She swallowed a sigh, an old, familiar sadness sweeping through her as she considered the topic at hand. Though in this instance, all she could feel was relief. She no more wanted to find herself pregnant with his child than he did.

"You needn't worry, Mr. Pendragon," she said, rediscovering her voice. "There will be no child."

He frowned. "And why is that?"

"Because I am barren." She gazed toward the window and stared half-seeing at a weak shaft of light reflecting against the pane.

"Are you certain?"

Painfully embarrassed at having to discuss such a delicate, private matter, her head snapped around. "Quite certain. In the five years of my marriage I never conceived. My husband had three daughters from a previous marriage. It doesn't take a genius to figure out which one of us was at fault."

For a moment he had the grace to look chastened. "My regrets."

"Keep them," she tossed back. "Given our impending arrangement, my inability to conceive a child would appear to be a blessing."

He stood and came around his desk again. "So, we are agreed then?"

His cool green eyes regarded her the way a panther might its prey. Large and supremely male, he loomed over her despite the space separating them. She suppressed the need to tremble, aware of him in a way she didn't believe she'd ever before been aware of a man.

Was she truly prepared to place herself within his power? Inwardly she quaked at the thought. How would it be to let him touch her, kiss her, to give him the right to take her body? Her blood beat unsteadily at the notion. Yet it would only be for six months, she reminded herself. For her family, she could endure anything for six months.

"Yes," she murmured softly, "we are agreed."

He leaned even closer. "Shall we seal our bargain with a kiss?"

"No!" she exclaimed, jolting in her chair. "There will be no kissing today."

He laughed, emphasizing the long dimples in his cheeks in a way that made him appear even more fiercely handsome than before. "Then it seems I shall have to console myself with mere fantasies until our next meeting."

Leaning across his desk, he reached for a ledger bound in fine quality leather, then flipped it open. Running a finger down one page, he paused on an entry near the middle. "Lord Allerton is scheduled to pay his obligation a week from Thursday. Would Wednesday next be a suitable date to begin our arrangement?"

So soon? she thought, dismayed. That would leave her only eight days, a little over a week to adjust to the life-altering step she was about to take. And once she set herself onto that path, there would be no turning back.

Yet a week, a month, a year, what difference would it make? No matter how much time she had, it would never be enough. Time would not make this bargain of hers any easier to face.

"Very well," she agreed before she had an opportunity to turn coward. "Next Wednesday it shall be."

He nodded. "What about your brother? What will you tell him?"

Oh, dear. Harry. What would she tell him? Certainly not the truth.

"I'll think of a story," she said. "Something he'll accept without too many questions asked, something he'll believe."

She stood, glad to be on her feet, even if her legs were a bit wobbly. "Well, the hour grows late and I must be going. I'll await your message."

"You shall receive it shortly."

Julianna crossed to retrieve her pelisse. Before she could reach it, Pendragon strode up behind her and grasped the cloak. Silently, he held the garment up for her to don. Hesitating for a long moment, she slowly presented her back to him and waited.

Her throat grew suddenly dry, heart pumping fast as the clean, masculine scents of writing ink, bayberry, and a hint of what must be Rafe Pendragon himself curled enticingly beneath her nose.

He slid the cloak over her, then rested his broad palms on her shoulders. "If you don't arrive by one in the afternoon next Wednesday," he murmured, his mouth very near her ear, "I will assume you have changed your mind about our agreement. If that should prove the case, the original terms of your brother's loan stand, including the due date. Think carefully about the lies you tell him lest they come back to haunt you."

She pulled herself out of his grasp and swung around to face him. "And what of you, sir? I have nothing but your word, and though I should likely make you write down the terms of our agreement, to whom would I show it should you decide to defraud me? How do I know you will uphold your end of the bargain and set my brother free when this . . . arrangement between us is at an end?"

His jaw tightened, eyes lambent beneath hooded lids. "You do not. And though I can't claim to be a gentleman, I am a man of my word. So long as you abide by the terms of our agreement, I will do the same. No tricks. No deceits. Whether or not you trust me is entirely up to you. You have my permission to forget this day ever happened and let your brother settle his own debts. Good day, Lady Hawthorne. I have other business to conduct."

He was angry at her accusation, she realized. Even more, he was insulted. Yet his words rang with truth, his demeanor radiating the kind of offended pride only a man of honor would display. If she chose to go through with this bargain of theirs, she felt reassured he would honor the terms exactly as agreed.

"Until next Wednesday, Mr. Pendragon," she said softly. "Do not bother ringing for your man, I shall see myself out."

Chapter Three

❧ ❧

"WHAT ABOUT THIS one, Jules? Wouldn't it make a stunning riding habit?"

Julianna glanced over at the sample of cloth Maris held out, a luxurious Prussian blue velvet far too bold for an ingénue of seventeen. Julianna raised a ruefully amused eyebrow, well aware of the game she and her sister had been playing ever since they'd arrived at the dressmaker's shop nearly an hour before.

"It would make a lovely riding habit for *me*," Julianna said. "As I think on it, I may ask Madame LaCroix to make it up for my wardrobe. I could do with a new riding outfit."

Maris thrust out her lower lip in an exaggerated pout. "I don't see why I cannot wear any of the pretty colors. Pinks and whites and pale yellows, *ugh!* I shall look like a washed-out fright in all these insipid pastels."

"You won't look a fright," Julianna repeated, doing her best to hide her amusement at her sister's melodramatic declaration. "You'll look beautiful. You know you are radiant in whatever color you wear."

"Well, I don't *feel* radiant. I feel ordinary. Don't you think I would look much better in this?" Maris lifted up a length of emerald green satin. "See?" she urged, displaying the cloth next to her fair skin and dark hair. "Isn't it gorgeous?"

Julianna shook her head. "You are not going to talk me into it, dear. You know debutantes must wear subdued shades. When you are a married lady, you may wear any color you like, but until then . . ." She shrugged, letting her statement drift off.

"How wonderful to be a married woman!" Maris sighed. "Free of all these horrid rules and restrictions."

Not always so wonderful, Julianna thought as she perused the bolts of available fabrics. Contentment in marriage and the amount of freedom a lady had depended largely upon one's spouse. She wanted Maris to take her time and find the right man. She wanted Maris to find someone who would make her happy.

Julianna reached for a sprigged muslin, cream-colored with a sprinkling of tiny purple violets. "How about this? It would make a charming day dress."

"Hmm, I suppose it would." Reaching out a hand, Maris held a length of the material up to the cheery sunlight streaming in through the shop's front windows. "Actually, I quite like it." She paused. "I'm sorry to be so difficult, Jules. I know you are right and only trying to advise me properly. I'm just nervous about my debut. What if I don't take? What if no one likes me? They say blondes are *de rigueur* this year."

"Don't be silly," Julianna shushed. "Everyone will adore you, and once they see that pretty face of yours, brunettes will suddenly be all the rage instead of blondes." She dusted a reassuring kiss over her sister's youthful cheek. "Quit worrying. You are going to have a wonderful Season, and you are forbidden to fret about a thing. Your only task is to have fun. You are a dear, sweet girl. No one will be able to resist you, especially the gentlemen."

Maris gave her a hopeful smile. "You truly think so?"

"I *know* so. Now go try on the pink polonaise Madame set aside for you. Let's see if the style suits."

"Pink, ugh!" Maris gave a mock shudder, rolled her eyes, and stuck out her tongue like the child she still was. Grinning, she strolled dutifully toward the fitting rooms in the rear.

If only my own troubles could be so simple, Julianna mused. *With nothing more to worry about than the color of my next dress, and whether or not I will be popular this Season.*

Over the past week, Julianna had racked her brain, trying to conceive of some way out of her agreement with The Dragon. She understood now why others called him that, the moniker more than a simple play on his unusual surname.

The man truly was a beast. A quick, cunning adversary who could mesmerize a person with his cool green gaze, lull you with his words, then burn you crisp as toast before you understood you'd been neatly snared inside his trap.

As ridiculous as it seemed, she'd clung to the faint hope that Harry would dig himself out, that he would arrive on her doorstep to tell her he'd found the money and had paid off the debt. But a look at him last night, when she'd gone to the family townhouse for dinner, had shattered her illusions.

Dark circles had ringed his worried brown eyes, a sickly pallor adding a faint green undertone to his usually swarthy complexion. Then there'd been his drinking as he tossed back glass after glass of wine, swallowing it the way a thirsty man would guzzle water.

She'd realized then that their salvation would be up to her.

But could she do it?

Did she really have the courage, the conviction to put herself, her body, quite literally in the hands of a man like Rafe Pendragon? Did she have the strength of will to become The Dragon's mistress?

She could always marry, she supposed. Her friends were continually urging her to find a new husband. She was young, they said. Attractive. Look how the men flocked to her. It was a running joke how Lord Summersfield kept proposing to her—a half dozen times at last count. And there were at least two other gentlemen, wealthy men both, who were always tossing her hints. Any one of them would offer her a ring tomorrow, she knew, if she'd only say the word.

But she didn't want to say the word. The plain truth of it was she'd had a husband, and she didn't want another.

Unlike the married women of her acquaintance who had to beg and cajole their husbands for every farthing in their purse, she had her own income. Her stipend wasn't large but it was comfortable, allowing her adequate money for necessities, a few servants, and the occasional luxury or two. And she owned her townhouse on Upper Brook Street, a property that had come solely into her possession after her husband Basil's death.

No, Julianna reasoned, *being a widow isn't so bad.* The status gave her an immense amount of freedom, a rare independence that she cherished and had no desire to give up.

Marriage, of course, would be the respectable way out of her present dilemma, a choice most women in her position would make. But she'd been forced into marriage once, and by God, she would never let herself be forced again.

Many would condemn her if they learned of her bargain with Pendragon, would shun her for consorting with a man not her social equal. But in spite of the risks and the indignity of letting such a man use her body, she would rather spend six months as his mistress than a lifetime trapped in another empty marriage to a man she did not love.

Nerves ate at her stomach at the thought of what she would have to do in only two days' time, together with an odd tingle in her blood that she could only describe as an innate sexual awareness.

Jittery as she might be, there was no denying the fact that Rafe Pendragon was an incredibly handsome man. The mere memory of him—his penetrating green eyes, the sculpted line of his jaw, the dimples that would send a nun into a swoon—made her go all hot and shivery. The idea that she would soon be granting him the right to kiss and touch her, to explore her body in the most carnal of ways, left her throat dry and her pulse alarmingly unsteady. She'd never particularly enjoyed the mating act, but with a man like Pendragon, who knew what might transpire?

Gracious! she thought, feeling warmth spread over her cheeks.

A movement from the far side of the shop interrupted her musings as Maris emerged from the fitting room. Her young sister looked a picture of vibrant youth and beauty, the new dress and its color genuinely flattering despite Maris's poor opinion of the pale shade.

Julianna smiled, more determined than ever to see Maris enjoy all the things she herself had not—a carefree Season filled with innocent joy and fun. And most of all the freedom to choose her own spouse, and to marry for no more important a reason than love.

If Harry went bankrupt, all those dreams would perish. Maris's come out would be forfeit, since there wouldn't be enough money for the clothes and the parties and the balls it took to launch a debutante. And though she wished she could help, her own finances would never come close to covering such an expense.

My path is clear, Julianna realized. And in two days' time, regardless of her private reservations, she would do what she must to keep her family happy and whole.

*   *   *

After the shopping excursion, she and Maris drove back to Allerton House in Grosvenor Square.

Hoping to catch Harry before he dashed out to spend the evening with friends, she agreed to stay and share a quiet dinner with Maris and Henrietta Mayhew, a distant cousin from their mother's side of the family. Widowed with grown children, Henrietta had gratefully accepted the offer to act as Maris's chaperone for the Season. Until last month, Maris had made her home with Julianna, but Julianna had decided her sister would be better off launching her coming out from the far grander family townhouse.

The evening progressed, filled with good food and enjoyable conversation. However, Harry did not appear.

Penning a note to her wayward brother, Julianna left instructions with the butler that Lord Allerton was to be given her message the instant he arrived. Saying her good-nights, she made the short carriage ride home and retired to bed.

She was frowning over a barely touched plate of eggs and toast, tea growing tepid in her cup, when Harry finally strode into her dining room the next morning. She gazed up at him in relief.

Disheveled and bleary-eyed, he looked as if he hadn't slept. "Got your message," he mumbled as he pulled out a chair at the table and sat down across from her. "What's so urgent I had to run over here before I'd even had m'morning coffee? Feel dashed rotten, I do, despite some bloody awful concoction my valet poured down my throat not an hour since."

She motioned to her footman to bring her brother a cup of hot coffee. Once done, the servant bowed and departed the room, shutting the doors behind him.

His eyes closed, Harry sipped his beverage as if for strength. "Devil take this head of mine."

"Out drinking, I see," she observed, trying not to sound as disapproving as she felt.

"Plague take me, yes. What else should a man do when his own ruin's so near at hand? Just trying to forget my problems the best way I know how."

"Well, if you'd come home yesterday I could have saved you a great deal of anguish. I have good news." She pushed her plate away and leaned forward.

Harry reached out and shoved the plate even farther down the table, the scent of food obviously sickening him. "What sort of good news? Don't see how anything can be good, not when The Dragon's breathing down my neck, ready to destroy me day after next. Uncharitable as it might be to say, seems a shame somebody couldn't do us a favor and run him over in the street."

Julianna cleared her throat, an image of Rafe Pendragon lying prostrate in the middle of some London thoroughfare flashing into her mind. Knowing Pendragon, even as little as she did, she suspected he'd live through such an attack, climb to his feet, dust himself off, then methodically set about hunting down the man who'd done it.

"Well, put away your murderous thoughts because they're completely unneeded."

She paused, knowing once she recited the lies she'd prepared there would be no turning back. Taking a deep breath, she plunged ahead. "Harry, the most miraculous thing has happened. I've found the money to pay your debt."

His dark brows shot upward. "What?"

"Yes. After you told me everything last week, I began searching the accounts, trying to find some means of aiding you. And I came across an old box."

"A box?"

"Something of Basil's that I'd put away and quite forgotten. Inside, you wouldn't believe, there were certificates, investment shares for a shipping company. Curious to know their value, I immediately contacted my solicitor and asked him to look into the matter. Well, it turns out the stock is worth a veritable fortune."

"Really? H-How much of a fortune?"

She could see him running calculations in his head, worrying that the found money still wouldn't be enough to cover the true extent of his indebtedness.

"Enough to pay off your loan, your *entire* loan, not just the portion about which you chose to tell me," she admonished in a stern voice.

He tugged at his neckcloth. "What do you mean?"

"I mean that I *know*. I paid a call on Mr. Pendragon and he told me how much you really owe him, all thirty thousand pounds of it."

He scowled darkly. "Jules, what were you thinking to visit such a man? He's not at all the sort with whom a lady should associate."

Shooting up from the table, Harry began to pace. He stopped seconds later, groaning and clutching his head between his fists, no doubt due to last night's overindulgence. "Oh," he moaned, "I knew it was a mistake to have told you any of it."

"It's a good thing you *did* tell me, otherwise you'd be up the River Tick without a paddle. Is your manly pride worth losing your estate over, worth bankrupting the family over?" She huffed out a breath. "Besides, it's already done. The debt is paid."

The pacing stopped. "Paid? You mean the stock certificates were worth that much? Egad, Julianna, did he accept your payment? Is the nightmare really over?"

She lowered her eyes, thinking of the real payment Pendragon had accepted. "Yes, it's over. You are a free man and the estate is safe. At least for the present."

A shaky smile broke over his face. Rushing forward, he grabbed her in a fierce bear hug. "Jules, Jules, how can I ever thank you? How will I ever repay you? Thirty thousand pounds—it's a beastly lot of money, but I'll find a way to return it. I swear I shall."

He released her, clearly jubilant. "You shouldn't have done it, but blister me if I'm not glad you did. Though you ought to have given the money to me so I could have been the one to approach Pendragon. Don't like the thought of you with him." He hugged her again, then gave her a smacking kiss on the cheek. "You're the best sister a man could have, have I told you that?"

She laughed and pulled away. "Yes, well, you're welcome, so long as you promise never to do anything of the sort again. You are to stay away from the gaming tables. And if you take out any more loans for the home farm, you are to use the money for the home farm."

He laid a palm against his chest. "Oh, I will. I'll be a regular gentleman farmer, spouting nothing but talk of new cultivation methods and modern agricultural equipment."

"Well, you needn't go *that* far," she said on a laugh. "I want you to stop risking your security, not turn into a bore. After all, I shan't be there to bail you out if you land in the suds again, since I doubt I'll be discovering another fortune in lost stock hiding in Basil's office."

"Dashed amazing about that. Rather startling, really, since I didn't even know Basil dabbled in stock investments. He was always prattling on to me about the strength of land and gold, and how a man couldn't go wrong with those. Shows you never can tell about a person, I suppose."

Yes, she thought, that's exactly what it showed, relieved Harry had so readily accepted her fairy story about the money and her payment of his debt. Perhaps in his distress he didn't want to question her explanation. Perhaps in his relief, he never would.

Leaning over, he gave her another buss on the cheek. "I can never thank you enough, Jules. You're simply the best. And I will pay you back, I promise, though it may take me some time. Still, I'll find a way to make it right."

"The money's not important so long as you and Maris are safe and well. The two of you are all I truly care about in this world. Just be a good steward of your legacy and lead the family with pride, that's all I ask."

Harry grinned, then returned to collapse onto his chair. Reaching out, he grabbed up her square of cold toast and slathered it with strawberry preserves from a nearby pot.

"Hmm," he said as he bit in and swallowed. "My appetite has returned. Do you think Cook could make me some breakfast?"

"I'm sure she could." Julianna crossed the room to ring for a servant.

"So, where are my vowels?" Harry asked casually.

"Pardon?"

"My vowels. I.O.U.s, don't you know. The Dragon must have returned them when you paid him. It's customary when clearing a financial obligation."

His vowels. Dear Lord, she'd never thought about that!

"Hmm, well, yes," she dithered. "Of course he gave them to me, but I . . . I burned them."

"Burned them!"

"Yes. The debt is paid, and I thought it best to put the whole dreadful affair in the past. You are to think on it no more."

Please, she prayed, *please, think on it no more.*

He frowned for a long moment, then reached for another slice of toast. Gradually, his expression cleared. "I guess you are right. Best to forget it ever happened and start afresh."

"Yes," she murmured dully, her stomach churning to remember that she didn't have such a luxury. For her, the indenture was only just beginning.

Chapter Four

R AFE CLICKED OPEN the engraved cover of his
gold pocket watch and checked the time.

Ten minutes to one.

He snapped the watch closed again and tucked it into
his vest pocket, then settled back on the drawing room
sofa to wait, his long legs stretched out in front of him.

He tossed an idle glance around the room, eyeing the
red brocade draperies with distaste. It's what came, he
supposed, of using acquired properties, such as this
house, for his own purposes. If he were going to keep
the place, he would make some changes to the decor,
such as replacing several of the older, heavier pieces of
furniture with lighter, more modern ones. But for now,
the house was comfortable and well suited to his immediate needs.

Assuming he continued to have such needs, he thought
ruefully.

He'd give Lady Hawthorne to the top of the hour as
agreed, and perhaps ten minutes more. After that, he'd
ride home and begin preparations for collecting the
young earl's debt.

It was growing ever more obvious that Lord Allerton's sister wasn't going to show. And to be perfectly
honest, he hadn't really expected she would. Despite all

her pleas and protestations on behalf of her sibling, she'd obviously had second thoughts concerning the bargain she'd struck.

And justifiably so.

Her scapegrace brother had plunged himself deep into the abyss, and by rights, he ought to be the one forced to claw his way out. A tragedy, though, that the earl would need to put Davies Manor on the auction block.

The estate was a fine property with a grand house, a thriving tenantry, and two hundred acres of prime farmland situated in the heart of the Kent countryside. Perhaps he would bid on it himself, Rafe considered. With a trustworthy manager to tend to the day-to-day details, the estate had the potential to generate a nice, steady income. If that had not been the case, he would never have agreed to extend financing to Allerton in the first place. Truly, Julianna Hawthorne was doing him a favor by reneging on their agreement.

So why do I feel so vastly disappointed?

He sighed, suddenly annoyed by the desire humming in his blood, merely the notion of having Lady Hawthorne in his bed enough to bring him to a state of partial arousal. Normally, he wasn't the sort of man to let lust cloud his mind, but where this particular lady was concerned, there was no fathoming his reactions. The logical, reasonable part of him still marveled that he'd proposed such a bargain with her at all. The animal part of him cheered, howling now at the likely prospect of being denied.

In all probability, he knew he would never see her again. Over the years he'd indulged in a couple of liaisons with aristocratic ladies, each of whom had been eager to add an element of verve and excitement to her otherwise tedious life. As a rule, though, he tended to steer clear of such associations, since they never ended well. As for virtuous widows like Lady Hawthorne . . . well, ladies like her were very selective when taking lovers, and they certainly never chose men from outside their own narrow social circle.

How ironic, then, to know his blood was every bit as blue as her own! But matters like legitimacy made all the difference in the world. He should know. He'd spent his entire life battling the slurs and slights of illegitimacy because his parents had dared to love outside the bounds of marriage.

His father, a viscount from the the Home Counties, had already been a married man when he'd met Charlotte Pendragon, the daughter of a poor clergyman who ministered to a small rural parish. The young viscount, miserable in his arranged marriage, had come north to visit a friend and to do some hunting. He'd been riding home through an icy fall rain when he'd come upon a bedraggled girl struggling to make her way. He'd stopped, lifted her up onto his horse, wrapped her in his warm coat, and taken her home.

Over cups of hot tea, huddled under blankets in front of a roaring fire, the two of them had fallen in love. Though they knew it was wrong, though they tried to fight their feelings, they'd continued to meet, their love too strong to be denied. And when Miss Pendragon—a good girl from a good family—found herself enceinte, the viscount set her up in a house in the neighboring county, vowing to care for her and their child for all the rest of their days.

He was that child, Rafe thought, his father's firstborn son, who could never openly be acknowledged no matter how beloved he might have been. His upbringing, his education, his manners—none of it mattered, only the circumstances of his birth and the side of the blanket on which he'd been born.

He wondered what Lady Hawthorne would think if she knew. Then again, what did it matter, since her opinion of him changed nothing.

He was, and always would be, a bastard. And that's precisely what she must think of him after receiving his disreputable offer the other day.

He checked his watch again: ten minutes past one.

Oh, well, he reasoned with a shrug, *some fantasies are simply not meant to be.*

Seconds later, a knock sounded on the door.

His eyebrows shot skyward, blood jolting through his veins with renewed anticipation. Climbing to his feet, he made his way to the entrance.

Opening the door, he discovered her on the stoop, looking small in her heavy cloak. A plain gray hood was draped over her head in such a way that all he could see were her nose and mouth and chin.

He fought an impulse to reach out, to drag her inside and into his arms. Instead he contented himself with a look.

"I'd nearly given up on you," he murmured, the fragrant scent of her as stirring as a caress.

"I had trouble finding a hack," she replied in a near whisper. "My coachman lingered longer than I'd anticipated."

A raw gust of wind rushed over them, rustling her skirts and fluttering the edges of her hood. Despite the crisp sunshine, it was a cold day.

"It's freezing. Come inside."

She hesitated for the faintest instant, then did as he commanded. He noticed the hack driver watching them and signaled with a hand for the man to depart.

Julianna whirled as Rafe closed the door. "Was that my hack leaving? I told him to wait."

"It's too cold for anyone to wait today. Don't worry,

I'll see you return home safely." He strode closer. "Now, why don't I take your cloak?"

She hadn't lowered her hood, he noticed, as if loath to shed the protection of the garment. As if she still harbored doubts about her presence here with him in this house.

It was brave of her to come, he admitted. Brave and bold. And if he were any sort of gentleman he'd leave her wrapped up in her cloak, go to the coaching house for his carriage, then take her home. But he'd long ago given up any notion of being a true gentleman since it was the one thing he would never be.

Slowly, she reached up and pushed back her hood. Underneath she wore a long-brimmed bonnet with a dark lacy half veil that covered her eyes.

He couldn't help but smile. "I see you took every precaution to conceal your identity."

"I must," she replied, deadly serious. "No one can ever suspect."

"No one will," he assured, equally serious. "This neighborhood is very quiet. There are few residents, and those there are tend to keep to themselves. It's why I chose the place, for its pleasant, somewhat rural location—not easy to find in a bustling metropolis like London."

The house, just south of Queens Square, was perfect. An attractive, two-story brick Georgian, it blended easily into its surroundings. The house and drive were flanked on both sides by rows of mature evergreen boxwoods and towering elm trees, their branches now bared of leaves. A high brick wall ringed the front of the two-acre property, providing a deep sense of privacy and seclusion.

He'd acquired the house only a month ago from the Marquis of Durbenham, who'd used it for exclusive parties, the kind of entertainments about which a man would rather his wife know nothing. But after getting caught en flagrante by said wife, the marquis had put the property up for sale, remarking that the old harridan had tainted the place with her invective and quite ruined his fun. Rafe could well imagine.

"Now," he continued, stepping closer. "Let me assist you with your outer garments."

She moved back. "I-I'll do it, thank you."

Hands visibly trembling, she tugged loose the bow of navy grosgrain ribbon tied beneath her chin, then pulled off her hat. Her hair gleamed, dark and sleek as sable, the clean scent of French-milled soap drifting faintly in the air. He took her bonnet and set it on a nearby marble-topped foyer table.

When he turned back, she was fumbling with the clasp on her mantle and doing a poor job of it. Crossing to her, he covered her small hands with his own much larger ones and gently stilled her movements. "Please, allow me."

After a moment, she relented, her hands falling to her sides, her eyes averted.

Smoothly, efficiently, he unfastened the small, filigreed gold and pearl clasp at her throat but made no move to slide the garment from her shoulders. Drawing a finger over her satiny cheek, he watched her eyelids fall shut and her lips tremble. Was she truly prepared to take this scheme through to its conclusion? Would she be grateful, even relieved, if he offered her one last opportunity to escape?

He sighed. "Are you certain this is what you want? It's not too late to change your mind, you know."

Her eyes sprang open and her jawline firmed. "Please don't toy with me. I've already told my brother the loan is paid. I can't go back to him now and say I've lied. This . . . bargain between us is the only way." She paused, a sudden glimmer of hope dawning in her expression. "Unless you'd be willing to forgive the debt."

Rafe blinked at the suggestion.

Forgive the debt? Impossible.

Even if he was magnanimous enough to contemplate such an action, he wasn't that much of a fool. After all, he hadn't earned the nickname "The Dragon" by letting people cozen him out of money—not even pretty little widows with eyes as rich and dark as fine, melted chocolate, and lips that beckoned with the sweet perfection of a newly blossomed rose. If he were inclined to act the gallant, he supposed he could allow her to walk out the door with no more than a few kisses and a gracious thank-you. But he had a reputation to maintain among his business-minded brethren, and that was one thing he could never afford to lose.

Besides, he wanted her.

Wanted her badly. So no matter what wild impulses might be swirling inside his head, there would be no foolish acts of charity in the offing today.

"No," he said in an implacable tone. "The agreement stands. Six months as my mistress or thirty thousand pounds payable on the morrow. The choice is entirely yours. But if you choose our arrangement, acknowledge you do so willingly. Tell me you come to my bed of your own accord."

A long silent moment passed before she drew a deep inhale and met his gaze. "I come to you of my own accord. You may take my mantle now if you like."

Tension he hadn't known he felt eased from his muscles, quickly replaced by a renewed simmer of desire. Reaching out, he lifted the heavy garment from her shoulders, then turned to hang it inside a closet under the staircase.

When he returned, he stopped directly in front of her,

letting his gaze rove over her body in a leisurely downward sweep. She wore a long-sleeved, dark green ker-
seymere wool dress, conservatively decorated with black
ribbon stitched at the throat and cuffs. A modest garment, he was certain she'd worn it for warmth, not style.
Despite its plainness, the gown did nothing to disguise
her generous curves, nor hide the shape of her breasts
and hips that so overtly declared her femininity. He
couldn't wait to peel her out of the thing and reveal all
the glories he was sure awaited him underneath.

Her chin came up as if she could read his lascivious
thoughts, as if she were waiting for him to pounce on
her right there in the hall.

Tempting idea, he thought wickedly. But he'd leave
that pleasure for later when the foyer wasn't quite so uncomfortably chilly.

Squaring her shoulders, Julianna braced herself for
whatever was to come next. Not an easy task when her
instincts were ringing an alarm, warning her that Rafe
Pendragon was far more man than she could handle.

If she had any sense, she would run. *Now!*

But she couldn't retreat, nor could she rescind her
promise to give him access to her body, to let this
stranger touch her in the most personal of ways. She
only hoped she had the strength of character to see it
through.

Lord above, she whimpered silently, *what have I done?*

Before she had time to panic further, Pendragon reached
out and lifted one of her gloved hands into his. Slowly,
mesmerizingly, he began to remove the glove, tugging it
free one finger at a time. Ever so gradually he slid the
cloth away until her hand lay naked within his own. The
move seemed an astonishingly intimate act somehow,
even more so than a kiss might have been.

Linking his clear green gaze with hers, he raised her

hand upward and pressed it against his cheek and jaw. Warmth spread like fire across her palm, his skin smooth and recently shaven, the plane of his jaw firm, the muscle and bone lying strong beneath.

Captured inside the moment, Julianna waited, her heart hammering, her breath a shallow draught in her lungs. It grew shallower, faster, as he turned his head and slid her hand sideways, positioning her palm so its center pressed against his lips. A gasp escaped her as he opened his mouth and drew a sleek circle on her skin using only the wet tip of his tongue. He kissed the spot, then lowered her hand, curling her fingers into a gentle fist as if to hold his touch in place. She shivered, a surge of electricity rippling over her body, her skin flushing hot, then cold, then hot again.

Mortified, that is what I ought to be, she chastened herself. Mortified and shocked all the way to her core. Not even Basil had ever touched her in such a way, and he'd been her husband. Only she wasn't mortified, she realized, nor was she pulling away.

I can't refuse him, she told herself. That's why she allowed such an embrace. That's why she remained still in his grasp.

Yet it wasn't coercion that kept her quiescent as he repeated the process on her other hand—glove, caress, kiss. At length he moved away to calmly deposit her gloves on the hall table next to her hat.

Her hands throbbed, skin oddly tight and tingly, almost swollen. Crazy pulses beat in her wrists, making themselves known to her in a way she'd never before experienced.

What has he done to me? she marveled. *And what will he do to me next?*

Crossing back, he captured her right hand in his own;

then without speaking a word, he pulled her gently after him.

Up the stairs they went, then along a carpeted hallway toward a tall wooden door at the end. Pausing, Pendragon swung the door wide to reveal a vast room that she surmised must be the master suite.

Decorated in browns and greens, the masculine atmosphere announced itself immediately. Bookshelves carved of dark walnut lined the sitting room walls while in the center sat a broad sofa done in hunter green, flanked by a pair of matching leather armchairs. A cheery blaze crackled within the fireplace, the mantel above cast in gold-and-white marble. Italian, she guessed, noting the tiny sheep and ethereal shepherdess carved on its face.

Beyond, through a set of connecting double doors, lay the bedroom. Peering through, she could see a tall armoire and large dressing table with a gilded mirror, both pieces finely made. Yet it was the huge tester bed that caught and held her attention. High and wide, the bed was carved from the same dark walnut as the bookshelves and other furniture. It dominated the room, eclipsing everything else, its canopy rising to nearly the height of the ten-foot ceiling, hangings and tester sewn from a heavy, pale bronze satin.

Her mouth dry, Julianna forced her eyes past it to the stately casement windows. Bright sunlight poured through the glass, spilling in an arc across the carpeted floors like a pool of liquid gold.

Behind her, Pendragon shut the door, the soft click of the lock sounding loud as a gunshot to her ears. Only then did he relinquish her hand.

"Would you care for a drink?" he asked, nodding toward the heavy sitting room sideboard, and the silver tray on top with its trio of crystal decanters and glasses.

Ordinarily she didn't drink spirits, certainly nothing

stronger than the occasional sherry. Then again, she didn't ordinarily find herself in an unfamiliar house, inside a bedroom suite with a man who shortly expected her to become his mistress.

"Yes," she agreed, deciding a dose of false courage might be exactly what she needed right now.

Crossing to pour the drinks, he returned far too quickly for her comfort. He held out a snifter, an inch of amber-hued brandy inside. Accepting the glass, she cradled it in both hands, afraid she might drop it otherwise. Giving a curious sniff, she let the sweetly pungent aroma curl inside her nostrils.

She'd never had brandy before.

Screwing up her courage, she took a healthy swallow and promptly lost her breath, the inside of her throat burning as if it had been set ablaze. Gasping, she fell into a paroxysm of coughing, wheezing faintly as she strained for air.

"Easy," he counseled, rubbing a palm between her shoulder blades. "Don't take so much at once. Small sips."

She coughed a few more times until the agony in her throat and lungs finally began to subside. When she could speak again, she held out her glass. "Take it, please. I've had enough."

His eyes twinkled, but he made no comment as he accepted her glass. Raising his own snifter to his lips, he downed the contents in a single swallow.

She stared, first in amazement, then in admiration, when he showed no signs of ill effect.

Pendragon moved away, disappearing from sight. A faint click of glass sounded behind her, and she assumed he must be refilling his drink. Moments later, though, his hands settled on her shoulders. She jumped, quivering as he placed his lips against the sensitive skin of her neck.

"Oh!" she gasped. Fighting her reaction, she tried not

to tremble as he skimmed his mouth over her nape, and again when he started dropping delicate touches along her jaw, her cheek, and finally across to her ear.

"You smell delightful," he murmured. "What is it?"

"Oh, it . . . it's just a touch of rose water. I always dab a little on before I get dressed."

Mercy, she cringed, realizing what she'd said and the images her admission must be creating.

"I like it." His words came out low and husky, almost a growl.

Before she had time to fashion a reply, he nuzzled her earlobe, then caught the nub of flesh between his teeth. He bit, just hard enough to sting. Shock and pleasure winged straight to her toes. Then he was kissing her behind her ear, drawing his tongue in a long, wet line along its edge. Opening his mouth, he fanned his breath over the spot in a way that made her skin tingle and flush. Her eyes fell closed, her knees abruptly weak.

Adrift, she didn't at first notice when his hands left her shoulders and began unfastening the column of tiny buttons that ranged down the back of her dress. By the midway point, though, she awakened from her haze, his movements a brazen reminder of his ultimate purpose.

She waited until the buttons were undone, then stepped away, clutching the sagging bodice to her breasts. Turning, she stared at her shoes, unable to meet his gaze.

"I'll make myself ready," she murmured as she backed toward the bedroom.

He quirked a brow as if surprised. "As you wish."

Using one hand to keep her bodice up, she closed the double doors behind her.

The room was warm, another healthy fire burning in the grate. Despite the comfortable temperature, she shivered, nerves churning viciously in her belly. Oddly, it reminded her of the way she'd felt on her wedding night so many years before. Only this time the man on the other side of the bedroom door wasn't her husband, it wasn't night, and she was a great deal more anxious now than she had been then.

Of course, she'd been far too naive on her wedding night to know what was to come next. At least it wouldn't hurt, she reassured herself. Unless he was rough. But Pendragon had been gentle so far, and there was no reason to suspect he would change. Perhaps it wouldn't be so very dreadful. She'd simply lie there like always, and let him do as he wished until it was over.

Basil had never taken more than fifteen minutes at most. Hopefully Rafe Pendragon would be quick about it as well. She'd told her coachman to return for her at four and wait in front of the millinery shop on Bond Street, where she was supposed to be shopping. It was a quarter of two now; she knew she had plenty of time.

Fearing Pendragon must be growing impatient, she hurriedly doffed her dress and hung it neatly inside the armoire. Struggling with the laces of her stays, she tugged and pulled until she loosened them enough to remove her corset, leaving her stripped down to a single silk petticoat and her chemise.

He hadn't provided her with a nightgown, and she refused to go without any sort of clothing at all. She prayed it didn't mean Pendragon expected her to appear naked in front of him. Not even Basil had demanded such an intimacy of her—not once in the entire five years of their marriage.

She left on her stockings to keep her feet warm, her hair pinned into a snug knot that she hoped wouldn't get too terribly mussed since she wouldn't have the assistance of her lady's maid, Daisy, to tidy her up for her journey home.

Finally, knowing she was as ready as she was ever going to be, she folded back the heavy satin coverlet on the bed and climbed beneath the sheets. Tucking the cool linen tight under her chin, she tried not to feel utterly ridiculous lying there during the middle of the day in her unmentionables.

With her heart pounding like a drum in her chest, she called out. "You may come in now."

Half-sick with anxiety, she watched the doorknob turn.

Chapter Five

WHATEVER RAFE HAD been expecting, it wasn't what he found awaiting him on the other side of the door.

For a second he thought she'd disappeared, climbed out a window and dropped down into the snow-covered garden below. Then he noticed her face peeking out from behind the sheet and blanket she'd drawn tight over herself like a shield.

She looked unsettlingly childlike, her dark, melting eyes wide and unsure. If he didn't know better, he would think she was an innocent rather than a widow of mature years. But she *was* a widow, he reminded himself. She understood full well the ramifications of their liaison, knew all the intimate dealings that went on between a man and a woman.

They would have a satisfying affair, he mused, one he would take care to see they both enjoyed. Unlike some men, he wasn't the sort who thought solely of satisfying his own pleasure and nothing more. Sex, he'd discovered, merely improved when the woman took delight in the act, when she experienced as much physical gratification as did her lover. There was nothing better than watching a woman lose herself to pure carnal delight, hearing her throaty sighs and breathless cries of pleasure as she came in his arms.

He planned to hear Julianna Hawthorne sighing and crying for him often. Very often.

Loosening his cravat, he drew the cloth from around his neck and tossed it onto a nearby chair. While he'd been waiting for her out in the sitting room, he'd removed his jacket and waistcoat and kicked off his shoes. For now, he decided, he would leave on the rest of his clothing—shirt, pantaloons, and stockings. If all went well, he hoped to persuade Julianna to assist him in removing the last of his garments.

He stiffened in painful arousal at the idea, his pantaloons suddenly too snug as he imagined her tiny hands roving over his naked flesh, cupping him, caressing him. It had been a while since he'd kept a mistress. As a breed he found such women a nuisance, not worth the trouble and expense required to see to their myriad pleas and demands, at least not after the first few weeks.

But Julianna was unlike any woman he'd ever known. True, she might be selling herself to him, but she was no courtesan. There wasn't a coarse, crude bone in her body; her every movement and gesture was one of gentle grace and elegant refinement.

He didn't understand why, but his hunger for her went bone deep, leaving him glad he would have her in his bed for six months. More than enough time, he decided, to extinguish even the fiercest of flames.

Strolling forward, he watched her track his progress with her dark, velvety gaze. Her eyes snapped closed, though, the moment he reached the bed.

What is she about? he wondered. *Is she really, truly as nervous as she appears? And what, if anything, is she wearing under those sheets?*

Julianna held herself motionless, her body board-stiff as she tried her best not to tremble. But her efforts proved useless, a faint quiver traveling through her the instant his weight depressed the mattress. She swallowed as he scooted close, vitally aware of his long body stretched out at her side.

He was staring. She could feel his eyes—those cool, clear green eyes—moving over her with bold intent. She could feel the warmth of his body as well. Sense his male strength. Smell the light, pleasant scent of the bayberry soap he used, and something more, something earthy and masculine that could only be his own.

Gently, but firmly, he tugged at the sheet and blanket. Julianna bit her lower lip as he pulled the bedclothes slowly from her grasp and folded them back to expose her body.

Her cheeks warmed as she waited. Waited for him to touch her. Waited for him to kiss her, maybe once or twice if she pleased him. Then he would squeeze her breasts, push up her chemise, climb between her legs, and enter her.

Instead he did nothing.

Didn't so much as run a fingertip over her cheek. Didn't even lean close enough to let her hear him breathe.

What is he doing? Is he just lying there, watching me?

Goose bumps broke out over her limbs, nerves rippling just below the surface of her skin. She tried to keep her eyes shut, but finally could stand it no more.

Her lids popped open, her gaze flying immediately to meet his own. Lying on his side with his head propped against one hand, he studied her, an expression of patient curiosity on his chiseled face.

"What are you doing?" she demanded, flummoxed to discover him in such a pose.

Up went one dark brow. "Observing you. I wanted to see exactly how long you'd lie there with your eyes squeezed shut."

She frowned. "Why would you care whether or not my eyes are closed?"

A slow, seductive smile curved his lips. "Because I

want to see you when we make love, see the look in your eyes while I'm giving you pleasure. What's more, I want you to see the look in my eyes while you're giving me pleasure back."

Her lips parted on a silent exhale.

He skimmed a knuckle over her jaw. "You have truly beautiful skin, do you know that? Creamy. Soft. Translucent." With his thumb, he traced her cheek and across her bottom lip in a slow, meandering caress. "Pretty cheeks, pretty lips. Kissable lips."

Her mouth throbbed at his touch.

"I've only now realized I have yet to kiss you. You wouldn't let me before, as I recall."

A small shiver rippled through her. "No," she murmured in soft reply.

"Seems I shall have to rectify that, now that we are here together. Alone."

She waited, forcing her eyes to remain open as he leaned across her, his shoulders seeming wider than ever, his arms long and powerful.

Despite his confident words, she didn't expect anything grand. She'd never much liked kissing, finding the act little more than a lot of wet, clumsy rubbing.

But when they met hers, Rafe's lips were warm and smooth, and only the faintest bit moist. Silky, almost feather-light, they played over her own—skilled, certain, and in no way clumsy. He didn't demand. Didn't press her lips painfully into her teeth. Didn't try to force open her mouth, or jam in his tongue.

With palpable relief, tension began to ease from her shoulders and neck, her thoughts drawn to the sensations he was creating. Delicious sensations, sensations she hadn't imagined she might feel. Her lips parted beneath his, allowing him greater access, greater freedom.

Suddenly she wanted more.

As if sensing her response, he deepened the kiss ever

so slightly, letting his warm, sweet breath fill her mouth. She tasted the brandy they'd drunk earlier, sharp but without the sting now.

His tongue emerged. She waited for it to invade her mouth, to gag her like some wriggling snake. Instead, he licked her, reminiscent of the way he'd licked her palms earlier when they'd stood in the downstairs foyer. Using only the tip of his tongue, he painted her lips with a thin damp line that left them moist and aching.

Suddenly, she couldn't get enough breath, her lungs searching for air. Nerve endings alive, she lay enthralled as he repeated the process, circling her lips from the opposite direction this time.

He groaned, the sound vibrating against her mouth before he angled her head and slanted his lips over hers to take their kiss to the next level. Blood beat at her temples, vision blurring as he kissed her in myriad ways, kissed her as she had never before been kissed. She lost all sense of time, of place, her mind dulling as he drew upon her—his touch that of a master, hungry yet patient, demanding but oh so exquisitely tender.

After a while, he coaxed her mouth wider. And when he stroked his tongue over hers, over her teeth and inner cheeks, what she experienced wasn't a sense of invasion, but invitation. A need to take him inside, to let him have more of her, as much as he desired.

Without thought, she began to kiss him back, pressing her lips harder against his, imitating his actions. Swirling her tongue around his, she nibbled at his lips, kissing him with a sweet suction that shot a rush of longing straight to her center, where it blossomed into a poignant ache. By the time he broke their kiss, her breath was coming in rapid pants, her chest rising and falling in staccato rhythm.

His gaze lowered to her breasts, to the quivering tops revealed by her chemise. Her nipples tightened at his perusal. Faintly embarrassed, she glanced away, hoping he hadn't noticed.

He caught her face in one hand and skimmed his lips over her cheek before dappling kisses along the line of her throat.

"You're very passionate," he murmured, nuzzling a particularly sensitive spot behind her left ear. "I knew you would be."

"Basil said I was frigid." The words were out before they'd scarcely had a chance to form in her mind.

He raised up again on an elbow. "Who is Basil?"

She flushed, ashamed by what she'd revealed. She never talked to anyone about her marriage, not even to her closest friends. Why had she told him?

"He is my late husband. Please forget what I said; I shouldn't have mentioned it."

He drew the tip of one finger over the exposed curve of her breast. "So how long has it been for you?"

She swallowed, a quiver racing through her at his leisurely touch. "How long for what?"

"Since you last made love?" His fingertip took a turn, trailing slowly up the center of her chest before fanning out to trace the shape of her collarbone where it protruded beneath her skin.

She swallowed convulsively. "My husband died five years ago."

"Yes. But how long since your last lover?"

She felt her eyes widen. "I've never had a lover, only my husband."

A spark, intense as gleaming emeralds, flared deep in Rafe's gaze. "Then I suppose I ought to thank him."

"Thank him?"

"Hmm," he whispered, dropping a kiss on the top of each of her breasts. "Your husband was obviously a fool who knew nothing about satisfying a woman. Believe me, sweeting, you are far from frigid. Because of his ineptitude, he's left the joy of enlightening you to me."

"But I don't think—"

"Shh," he hushed, laying a finger over her lips. "You don't need to think; all you need to do is feel." Reaching for the ribbon holding her chemise closed, he slid the slender pink bow free of its knot. "Let's see how you feel about this."

He began to fold back one side of her chemise to expose her bare breast. She stopped him with a hand. "Don't."

He raised his head and questioningly met her gaze. "Why not?"

Her eyelashes fanned downward. "B-Because it's daylight and you'll see. Couldn't we both slip under the covers and you could just . . . touch me there?"

"No. I want to see you. Seeing is one of the very best parts."

He reached again for her chemise.

"Oh, but—"

He paused. "But what?"

A blush crept over her skin like a sunrise as she forced herself to continue. "I'm big," she whispered. "Too big."

He arched a brow. "From what I've observed, you're shaped like a goddess. But I see, for your own piece of mind, that I shall have to make a closer study of the subject."

Her blush heated further. Knowing there was nothing she could do to stop him, she shut her eyes and prepared to endure.

A delicate shiver went through her as he peeled back the soft white silk of her chemise, exposing her naked breasts to his view. She felt him watching her again in that intent, solemn way of his, but refused to open her eyes, even to peek.

A slow humiliation slid through her at his prolonged silence, making her long to curl in upon herself and hide. Before she could act, he covered one of her breasts with his palm and held her, cradling her flesh as if testing its shape and weight.

"You're so beautiful, Julianna." Low and throaty, his voice sounded like warm honey dripped over rough bark. "Open your eyes," he commanded, "and see how exquisitely God has fashioned you. You've nothing of which to be ashamed, dear lady, nothing at all."

Despite her reluctance, she obeyed, startled yet strangely mesmerized at the sight of her breast filling his broad palm, her skin so very pale against the darker bronze of his own.

"See how you fit?" he said, caressing her slightly. "You are perfect. Absolutely perfect."

A sharp gasp of pleasure fell from her parted lips as he brushed his thumb across her nipple, followed seconds later by a tiny moan. Round and around he went, drawing lazy, utterly wicked circles over her areola.

"Do you like that?" he inquired, continuing to rub her in leisurely, tantalizing, delectable strokes.

Unable to speak, she answered with a nod, her body suddenly restless against the sheets.

"What about this? You must let me know if it's not to your liking."

Before she knew what he intended, he bent and took her breast into his mouth. Her head rolled against the pillow as he drew upon her, suckling deeply, his tongue teasing and tormenting her in ways she'd never imagined possible.

Squeezing her hands into fists at her sides, she fought to stem the tide of whimpers that rose into her throat. But that became a complete impossibility when he captured her nipple between his teeth and bit down ever so gently.

A raw cry tore from her lips.

He smiled against her sensitized flesh, then gave her a few more licks before moving on to lavish her other breast with the same kind of devastating attention. Threading her fingers into the thick silk of his hair, she pressed him closer, urging him to seek out exactly the right spots.

Wet heat pooled between her legs when he did, a hungry, empty ache throbbing in her core that cried out to be filled. She couldn't recall ever wishing to be filled so intimately before, but Rafe did things to her—magical things—that made her burn with longing.

As if he knew her thoughts, her desires, he reached down and grasped the hem of her petticoat, inching it upward over her thighs.

Instinctively she tensed, glimmers of old memories returning. But he soothed her, quickly making her forget everything else as he blew a light stream of air across her engorged nipples, a sensation that set her atremble. Kissing her quivering belly, he trailed his hand along the inside of her thigh and began to play.

She could barely think as his touches and kisses continued, her sense of place and time ceasing to function. He dipped his tongue into her belly button and sent a flash of heat through her middle. Growling against her flesh, he murmured soft, sensuous words of praise. Then the stroking hand between her thighs went higher and before she knew what he meant to do, he slid a long, very male finger deep inside her.

A fresh rush of wetness gathered low, her body embarrassing her with its uninhibited response. But Rafe didn't seem to mind as his hand moved, finger stroking in and out, and in and out, and in and out again. When he added a second finger, she nearly forgot her name, enraptured by the sensation of him working within her and the escalating need she didn't fully understand even now.

Led by her own powerful yearning, she spread her legs wider and let him do as he wished, her breath sighing between her lips in harsh, gasping pants.

"That's it," he murmured, increasing the rhythm of his hand. "Let it go. Let yourself go. Feel it, Julianna. Simply feel it."

Tossing an arm over her face, she obeyed, giving herself over to the pleasure.

And merciful heaven, what pleasure it is! she thought.

Suddenly, a pressure rose within her. She bit her lip to hold back the moan, but he wouldn't let her keep in the sound, urging her to cry out, to scream if she needed.

And then, just when she thought she couldn't bear even one more second, when her body was awash with flame and fire and mind-numbing need, he curved his hand, flicked his thumb and sent her winging over the edge.

Her back arched, her spine rising off the mattress. Blinding delight took her in its grasp and shook her in a merciless grip, leaving her weak and whimpering.

Long moments passed before her mind settled and she could catch enough breath to speak. "Oh, dear God."

He laughed and shot her a smoldering look. "I don't know that God had anything to do with it, but you're very welcome all the same."

She stared, then smiled, a giddy rush of pleasure still glowing inside her. "And you are very wicked."

"So I have been informed. Shall I be wicked again?"

Before she could agree or disagree, his fingers started moving inside her once more, stretching her, filling her, making her crave again in ways she was helpless to resist. He held her completely in his thrall, dependent on his every touch, needful as she'd never been needful in her life. She wouldn't have thought it possible, but in seconds, he reawakened her desire, her senses swamped by a passionate longing she could do naught to control or deny.

Without slowing his rhythm, he slipped an arm behind her back and drew her upright. Then he was feeding again at her breasts, suckling intently as if she were a feast and he could not get enough of her delectable flavor.

Shuddering, she gave herself over, her entire focus narrowing down to Rafe.

Rafe's hands.

Rafe's mouth.

His body cradled her close as he drove her toward a pleasure so intense she wasn't sure she could bear it. Then, as before, he sent her soaring, cries of completion wringing from her throat as she quaked in his arms.

Raising his head, he claimed her lips, suddenly savage in his purpose and demand. No longer afraid, she met him kiss for kiss, touch for touch, drinking from his open mouth with the same ferocity with which he drank from hers. He kissed her in a way that called for her total surrender, and she gave it.

His breath echoed harshly from his parted lips when he broke away, his eyes hot and glassy with passion. "Let's get you out of the last of your pretty things before I'm tempted to rip them off your body."

She gasped at his blatant remark but did nothing to deter him. Reaching out, he loosened the petticoat ties at her waist, then peeled her thin skirt and silken shift up over her head and arms.

His gaze intensified as he swept his eyes over her exposed body, naked now except for her sheer stockings and beribboned garters. She crossed her arms over her breasts, her sense of vulnerability returning together with an all-over blush.

But Rafe would have none of it, leaning forward to gently pry her arms loose and lower them to her sides.

"No hiding," he admonished in a stern yet tender voice. "You have nothing that needs the least conceal-ment, my dear."

She swallowed and met his gaze. Reading the honest admiration and undisguised passion glittering in his beautiful green eyes, her anxiety slowly eased.

Maybe he truly does like what he sees, she realized, a faint smile playing at the corners of her mouth.

He smiled back, deep grooves appearing in his cheeks that quite literally made her toes curl and a swooping sensation clench inside her belly.

Her nipples tightened.

He captured one between playful fingers as he leaned upward to give her a slow, wet, open-mouthed kiss. She sighed and sank deeper into his embrace. Long moments later, he thrust his fingers into her hair, little silver pins popping in every direction.

"Oh!" she exclaimed as her long tresses tumbled like a dusky waterfall across her shoulders. Wrapping a hand-ful of her hair around one wrist, he buried his face in it and inhaled, his eyelids falling closed with obvious delight.

At length, he raised his head, his voice pitched to a grave whisper. "Help me off with my clothes."

Her breath caught in her lungs at his request.

Did I hear him correctly? she questioned.

From the intent, smoldering expression on his face, she knew she had. Her heart stuttered in her chest, ex-citement clashing with trepidation. She quivered, vitally aware that she'd never before performed such a service for a man.

Dare I do so now?

Rafe forced himself to relax, waiting to see if she would do as he asked. In the past hour, he'd brought her a long way. Challenged her assumptions and sensibilities about herself, and about her own capacity for passion.

Her husband had obviously been an arrogant, self-important ass who hadn't cared for anyone but himself. Clearly, he'd treated Julianna with callous disregard, taking her with no thought for her feelings or her needs. All the man must have cared about was using her for breeding stock. How disappointed he must have been when she couldn't be brought to foal!

Well, all of that was in her past now, and she would find no such mistreatment here in his bed.

He studied her as she lay naked before him, her clean, shiny hair hanging dark as the veil of night over her shoulders, reaching nearly to her waist. Her gorgeous breasts peeped from beneath that hair, round and ripe and pert—a perfect fit inside his hands. Below them, her waist was hourglass tiny, her hips flaring out in a generous feminine curve, her legs long, soft, and supple.

When she made no move toward him, he decided his request must indeed be too much for her. He should not be surprised given her shyness, he thought in resignation. There would be time enough in the coming weeks to persuade her.

But before he could act, she reached out and laid an elegant hand upon one of his shirtsleeves. His erection jumped as if she'd touched him there instead. Slowly she went to work on his cuff buttons, slipping them free one fastening at a time. Once she was done with that, she reached upward to work loose another trio of buttons at his neck.

His hunger raged. He swallowed against it as her cool fingers brushed along the hot skin of his throat.

One. Two. Three.

It seemed as if an eternity passed while she opened his collar, the edges of his shirt hanging open to mid-chest.

Done, her gaze lowered, a tiny line forming between her lovely brows.

He held his breath as her little hands hovered. *Will she continue? Does she have the courage?*

He sent up a silent prayer of thanks when she gave her answer by grasping his shirt and yanking loose the tails. In a rush of movement, she pulled the linen up over his arms and head, then away. Clutching the shirt, she shook out the garment before leaning sideways to drape it neatly at the foot of the bed. Her breasts jiggled, sweet and lush.

A wild moan leapt into his throat. Rafe tightened his fists at his sides and fought the urge to tumble her back across the bed and be done with this torture. He could have his pantaloons freed in a thrice and be settled between her thighs, kissing her and taking her as his body was urging him to do. But he didn't wish to alarm her, nor ruin the gradual trust building between them. Biting the edge of his lip, he fought for patience, knowing his satisfaction would be sweet in the end.

She shifted back, her gaze falling upon his naked chest. He could see her curiosity, along with a kind of rapt fascination. Holding himself still, he let her inspect him—his broad shoulders, his long arms, and his firm chest with its thatch of dark curling hair.

He hoped she liked what she saw. Women usually cooed when he stripped off his shirt, wanting to run their hands over his muscles and naked skin.

But she said nothing, just swallowed and leaned down to his feet to roll off his stockings. He hid a smile, her avoidance of his pantaloons painfully obvious. She set the stockings atop his discarded shirt.

Leaning back on his elbows, he waited, watching as she considered his last item of clothing and the prominent bulge straining against the fabric. Rafe was beginning to think he was going to have to remove the garment himself, after all, when she gathered her courage on a swift inhale and reached out to pluck at the gold buttons of his falls.

He hadn't thought he could get any harder, but amazingly he did, his flesh aching powerfully at the sight and sensation of her hands so near the part of him he most wanted her to touch. Near his breaking point, he clasped her arms and pulled her atop his chest. Tunneling his fingers into her hair, he crushed his lips to hers, growling all his pent-up need into her mouth.

She made a small, mewling sound of surprise, then yielded, curling against him as she stroked a tentative palm along the side of his chest.

"Yes," he muttered. "Touch me. God yes, touch me."

At his urging, her hands began to explore, drifting over his shoulders and arms, across his chest and back, before trailing down as far as his stomach.

And while she touched him, he was touching her. Sliding his palms over her silken skin, caressing every ripe, succulent inch of her figure, trailing his fingertips far and wide.

Then he knew he could wait no longer.

Julianna strained to catch a full breath, panting as her pulse raced. Her blood churned in her veins and thumped forcefully behind her temples, her heart thundering as if she were caught inside the eye of a storm. And perhaps she was, a wild, fearsome maelstrom where heat and hungry aching need were the only laws, and Rafe Pendragon her one salvation.

He commanded her, ruled her every move, making her crave and yearn and yield in ways she would have blushed to consider only a short while ago. Writhing against him, she let him press her back into the mattress and position himself between her thighs.

She ought to have been afraid, she knew. Ought to be flinching instead of welcoming what was to come next.

But for the first time in her life she truly wanted to couple with a man.

Pleasure caught her in a hot rush as he thrust inside—deep, then deeper still, her senses spinning outward on a dark, silken thread of euphoria. She gasped, submerged beneath an avalanche of sensation.

I didn't know, she thought. Hadn't realized how glorious making love could be, nor how wonderful he would feel buried thick and strong inside her. Kissing him, she reveled in the taste and scent and sounds of their mating, her body singing in a kind of glorious joy she would never have dreamed possible.

She called out his name as her inner muscles strained to accommodate him, adjusting to his impressive size. He was big, filling her as she'd never been filled before, stretching her nearly to the edge of her limits. But she wanted this, wanted him, hanging on while the sensations intensified to a sharp knife-edge of bliss.

She moaned as he set a pace within her, moving in deep, penetrating strokes that he wickedly alternated with tantalizingly shallow ones. Body burning, her thoughts scattered to the four winds, her senses were utterly consumed by the demands raging inside her.

And all she could do was hang on for the ride. Hold him with her arms and then her legs when he shifted against her, urging her to lock her ankles against his back. She heard keening, a high feminine wail that vibrated in her ears and inside her head. *Is that me?* she wondered, barely recognizing the sound as her own.

Rafe was relentless, driving her on and up until she thought she quite literally might die. And even when she knew she could take no more, he pressed her further and further until there came an instant of stillness, then a jolt as if she'd been struck by lightning. Shuddering, the rapture caught her and exploded, rocking her body in great shimmering waves that wiped everything else clean.

Above her, Rafe gripped her hips in his hands and drove himself furiously in and out. Long moments later, he shouted and stiffened, a delicious warmth filling her as he, too, found his release.

And there in the aftermath, as she lay spent against him, she began to cry.

Not with sorrow, but in joy.

Chapter Six

JULIANNA MISSED AFTERNOON tea.

As she walked into her townhouse, she thanked her lucky stars that none of her family or friends had been expecting her to join them.

Her body still tingling from her encounter with Rafe Pendragon, she made her way upstairs to her bedroom and ordered her maid to draw her a bath. If she didn't have a good, hot soak now, she feared she'd barely be able to move come morning. She'd used muscles this afternoon that she suspected she'd never used before in her life.

A tremor of remembered pleasure coursed through her.

What a difference a few hours can make, she mused. When she'd left her house earlier today to keep the scheduled rendezvous with Pendragon, she'd steeled herself to bear the indignity to come. Her path was a noble one, she'd convinced herself. Even heroic, an honorable sacrifice she was making for those she loved.

But what she'd done today hadn't felt like a sacrifice, not once Rafe had begun to touch her, and kiss her, and show her the glory lying dormant within herself. Instead of degradation, she'd experienced bliss. Instead of powerlessness, she'd found freedom, an awakening of senses and emotions she hadn't even realized she possessed.

How noble, then, to take such pleasure? she considered with irony. How heroic to tremble even now in anticipation of her next encounter with him?

Daisy bustled in from drawing Julianna's bath and began to assist her off with her clothes. Julianna hoped her maid didn't notice anything amiss, didn't catch the faint scent of bayberry on her clothing, or notice the lingering glow of recent sex on her skin.

She waited as well to see if Daisy would say anything about her hair. To her relief, Rafe had proven an able lady's maid, brushing out her tresses in long, efficient, yet seductive strokes. Skillfully, he had wound her heavy locks into a becoming style atop her head before securing them with the pins the pair of them had laughingly gathered from the sheets and off the floor.

But dear Daisy said nothing, merely assisted Julianna into her robe, then let herself quietly from the room to let her mistress bath in private.

Drawing off her robe and chemise so she could step into the tub, Julianna gazed down at herself and was glad she'd refused to let Daisy strip her to the skin. Decorating the curve of her inner thigh were a pair of pale blue bruises. She rubbed a finger over the spots and remembered Rafe kissing her there, drawing upon her flesh with an intensity that had left his mark.

Indeed, I have been marked, she thought as she sank into the steaming water.

Branded to the bone by Rafe Pendragon.

Rafe.

She sighed his name in her mind, as she leaned her head against the rim of the copper tub and closed her eyes.

Her thoughts drifted, recalling how boneless she'd felt earlier that afternoon when he'd finished arranging her hair. Setting down the brush, he'd bent close and whispered into her ear.

"Come earlier next time," he murmured in a mellifluous baritone. "Come at noon so we won't be rushed. Today only whetted my appetite, sweeting. I've so much more to show you. A couple of hours together simply will not do."

Her belly had quivered as he dusted his lips across her cheek and down her throat, his hands coming around her from behind to cup her breasts and caress them. Swallowing hard, all she'd been able to do was nod her agreement and let the delight of his touch radiate through her.

But he isn't here now, she scolded herself as she struggled to force him from her thoughts. Rafe Pendragon was an obligation to be kept, not a true part of her life—not her real life—and she would do well to keep her time with him neatly segregated, even in the privacy of her own mind.

Tonight she was promised for an evening out, dinner and a play with Maris and cousin Henrietta. Harry, celebrating his last-minute escape from ruin, had sent round a note this morning saying that he and a trio of his cronies were leaving Town to attend a rousing boxing mill in the south. So it would be just the ladies tonight, and although Maris wasn't yet officially out, Julianna could see no harm in the theater.

Part of her wished she could cancel and spend a quiet night at home, alone, to regain her newly shaken equilibrium. But Maris had been pleading for weeks to see Mrs. Siddons play Lady Macbeth, and Julianna didn't have the heart to disappoint her.

With a sigh, she reached for the soap.

"Are you enjoying the performance?" Maris asked as the house lights brightened for the interval.

Julianna roused herself from her musings and focused on her sister's expectant face. "Of course. Why?"

"You seem distracted tonight."

Julianna fought down a blush, very much aware of how distracted she'd been. Despite her earlier vow to think no more of him, memories of her afternoon with Rafe kept assailing her thoughts and teasing her body. Wrapped inside a tantalizing, daydreamy haze that made her blood secretly hum, she'd barely heard a word of the entire first act.

"Just a bit tired," she defended. "Perhaps a turn about the theater will refresh me, so I'll be sharp for the next act."

"Oh, let's." Maris sprang up from her chair. "Maybe they're selling punch or lemonade. I could do with a cool drink; it's so warm in here."

With Cousin Henrietta's agreement, the three of them strolled out into the corridor. Cologne and burning tallow hung heavily in the air as they made their way toward the staircase that would take them down to the refreshment tables. Before they reached it, a tall, sandy-haired gentleman rounded the corner.

Stopping, he bowed, his blue eyes alive with genial welcome. "Ladies, how do you do? What a delightful surprise to find you here tonight! I'd thought myself one of the few in attendance this evening, Society being rather thin and all at the moment."

She recognized him. Everyone in Society knew Burton St. George, Viscount Middleton, even though Julianna's association with him had never moved beyond that of simple acquaintances.

"Yes," she said, "most families have yet to leave their country homes for Town, since the Season is still a few weeks away."

He nodded his agreement. "Just so. Will you do me the pleasure of making me known to your friends, Lady Hawthorne?"

"But of course."

After she made the introductions, he bowed grandly over Henrietta's hand, then transferred his attentions to Maris, whose cheeks flushed pink as a summer peony.

"Lady Maris, may I speak for all gentlemen by saying how glad we shall be to have such beauty in our midst. Perhaps I should lend my sword to you now so you will have some means of defending yourself from the inevitable male onslaught."

Maris's eyes widened at his compliment, her cheeks growing even rosier. "I'm not yet out, my lord. I have not been presented to the queen."

"An occasion for which to be fervently hoped. Pray tell the queen to hurry and make your acquaintance."

"Enough of that now, my lord," Julianna scolded lightly, not sure if she approved of his flirtation. "If you continue, my sister's head shall be as swollen as the hot air balloons we viewed during last year's exhibition."

"Middleton," Henrietta interrupted. "Are you by any chance related to the late David St. George?"

Politely, the viscount turned toward the older woman. "Why yes, ma'am, I am. David St. George was my father, God rest his soul."

"Oh, well, fancy that. I knew your father when I was but a green girl no older than our Maris. So handsome he was, too, your father. Now, he was a man who knew how to cut a swath with the ladies."

"As you say, Mrs. Mayhew, my father was a fine man who found favor among both sexes. Now, where were you ladies headed when I happened upon you? Back to your box?"

"Actually, we were in search of refreshments."

"Pray permit me to fetch them for you. You never know what sort of rabble you may find on the lower levels. By no means the sort gently bred females should be near."

Julianna frowned, thinking once again of Rafe. Did he keep a box at the theater? she wondered. Surely she would have noticed him before if he did. Then again, despite his wealth and sophistication, she knew he didn't travel in the same social circles as she and her family. Many, in fact, would lump him in with the "rabble" to which Middleton referred, based solely on his lack of a title and the circumstances of his birth. Disturbed by the notion, she said nothing.

Cousin Henrietta meanwhile accepted the viscount's offer to procure their drinks. With a bow and a smile, he turned away.

"My, what a handsome rogue!" Henrietta observed once he'd gone. "Though he must take after his mother, since he doesn't resemble his father at all." The older woman turned a teasing gaze on Maris. "And what did you think of his lordship, young miss? He showed a marked preference for you, I thought."

Maris fanned herself as the three of them started back to their box. "He was very elegant and dashing. Quite gentlemanly."

And so Middleton was, Julianna thought. The epitome of the perfect aristocrat. Strange, then, that she always experienced the oddest sense of misgiving whenever he was around.

I am just being foolish, she told herself. The man is gracious and amiable, exactly as a gentleman ought to be. Still, whatever his nature, one thing was clear: he was far too mature for Maris.

Deciding the conversation needed an immediate change of subject, Julianna launched into the one topic sure to divert her companions—fashion.

Moments later, Viscount Middleton had been supplanted by talk of ribbons, sleeve lengths, and the best colors to dye hat feathers.

* * *

Burton St. George jogged down the theater staircase, roughly elbowing his way past a pair of middle-class men when they didn't immediately give way at his passing. He ignored their exclamations, dismissing them instantly.

Silly old biddy, he thought as he strode forward. It had been all he could do to keep the smile on his face as he'd listened to Henrietta Mayhew prattle on about his father like some starry-eyed girl. He doubted his father had even known she existed. Addlepated old women like her ought to know their place. Even more, they ought to know how to keep their mouths shut unless spoken to directly.

It's what came of letting females run about without proper male guidance. Allerton really ought to take them in hand, he thought, but the boy was too weak and self-indulgent to do his familial duty. Far more apt to let his older sister lead him around by the apron strings than take a stand against her.

Julianna Hawthorne, now there was an attractive armful. A plump little partridge just waiting to be flushed from her nest. Long ago he might have made some overtures in her direction, but had decided she wasn't worth the trouble. Thoughtful and reserved, she had too much stubborn willfulness in her, too much bold independence. She was the sort of woman who would put up a struggle, if required.

No doubt the reason she was still a widow.

Submissive women made far better wives, in his opinion. Women who knew to bow their heads and be thankful for the rule of a superior male. His own wife had been obedient. At least she had been once he'd taught her how to obey, how to bend to his needs and serve his will. Before her death, she'd become rather like a trained poodle, quivering and fearful yet always subtly begging for his attention and praise.

Too bad she'd outlived her usefulness.

He'd almost felt sorry when he'd had to put her down. He could still remember the sound of her neck snapping against the railing when he'd pushed her down the staircase, the way her gray eyes had stared upward, body broken like a doll's.

Alas, her money was nearly gone now as well.

He gave his order to the waiter at the refreshment table, three lemonades and a port for himself. Tapping his fingers, he waited impatiently as the man moved away to fill the glasses.

Burton sighed. He supposed it was time he looked for a new wife—a rich one, of course, a match that would help replenish his dwindling resources. He'd drained the profits dry on his estate, raised tenant rents until they couldn't be raised any more. Marriage, it would seem, was his only recourse.

The Davies chit was a comely little thing, sweet and pleasingly shy. Likely she would be biddable as well. He could easily imagine himself bedding her.

The waiter appeared, brimming glasses arranged on a tray. Burton bade the man to follow as he led him up to Lady Hawthorne's box.

Yes, Burton decided, he would have to make discreet inquiries about Lady Maris's finances. If her dowry was temptingly large, he just might make the effort to have her. After all, why bother marrying a plain heiress when you could wed a pretty one instead?

"So, did Challoner take the bait?"

Rafe poured draughts of Scotch whisky into a pair of heavy cut glass tumblers. Picking up the stopper, he fit it into the crystal decanter with a faint clink, then returned the container to its place inside the liquor cabinet. Crossing his study, he stopped to hand one of the glasses to the room's other occupant.

Ethan Andarton, Marquis of Vessey, accepted the drink with a nod of his golden, leonine head. Rafe watched as his friend settled back in his chair and stretched out his Hessian-clad feet, his long, lean frame completely at his ease.

He and Ethan went back many years, meeting first as boys during a brawl when the two of them were students at Harrow. As Rafe recalled, he had been defending himself against the vicious slurs and fists of five other boys when Ethan rushed to aid him. Despite being outnumbered, the pair of them fought like demons, emerging bruised and victorious, and most of all, friends. A short time later, they added a third member to their small circle—Anthony "Tony" Black, already the Duke of Wyvern at only ten years of age. Despite their differences, or perhaps because of them, Ethan, Tony, and he had formed an unlikely and unbreakable association.

Since those days, life had taken them in separate, and not always pleasant, directions, but they had never completely lost touch, their loyalty and liking for one another remaining strong and vital to this day. He even forgave them for being aristocrats, a breed for which Rafe generally had little tolerance. But Ethan and Tony were rare exceptions—proud men who stood on their own merit. Men who could be trusted to keep a secret, or even agree to assist a friend in his quest to seek justice and revenge.

Rafe thought of Challoner and how good it was going to feel after years of waiting to see the blackguard pay for his sins.

"Oh, he took the bait all right," Ethan confirmed, his amber eyes twinkling wryly in answer to Rafe's initial question. "Snapped up the information like a hungry trout after an angler's worm."

Taking a seat in his wide leather desk chair, Rafe leaned back to absorb the news. Tipping his glass to one side, he gently swirled the spirits. At length, he drank a swallow, the alcohol strong and smooth against his tongue. "And Challoner wasn't suspicious?"

"Not a bit. He eavesdropped on Tony and me in the gaming room at Brooks's Club, just like you said he would. You should have seen the greed gleaming in his eyes. Our little stock tip quite put the winnings on the card tables to shame. And well it should have done after he listened to the pair of us speculate about the quick profits to be made." Ethan paused to take a drink. "After all, as I made sure to ask Tony in a voice just loud enough for Challoner's ears alone, how often does a man come across an opportunity to make a fortune from rare Indian silks, ivory, and trunks full of gold bullion?"

"Never, thankfully, in Challoner's case." Rafe said. "If only he knew those merchant ships and their precious cargo never made it into English waters, he'd be running the other way. But then, he doesn't have the contacts to have heard that all four merchantmen were seized by the French near Gibraltar four days ago, the goods taken and the ships scuttled."

"I doubt even the Foreign Office has that information yet," Ethan quipped. "You know, you really must tell me one of these days how it is you're privy to such timely and confidential information. Do you have access to a network of smugglers, or is it spies?"

Rafe smiled and said nothing as he opened a carved satinwood box on his desk to offer the other man a cigar. Then he asked, "You're certain he bought shares this morning? Once word gets out of the loss, Kratcher and Sons Shipping will be in ruins."

Ethan leaned forward and selected a cheroot. Using a silver cutter, he trimmed off one end. "I'm sure. Saw him purchase shares worth seventy-five thousand pounds. He was rubbing his hands when he came out of the Exchange, chuckling about what he was going to buy for himself first—a team of matched grays and a new carriage, or a hunting box in Scotland—since to quote him, he'll soon be 'richer than Prinny.' "

"The irony is, he would be if those ships had a chance of arriving in port. When they don't, he's going to find himself bankrupt and at the mercy of his creditors. And when he can't pay his shot, he'll be tossed in the gaol to enjoy Fleet's less-than-fine accommodations."

"Considering the man's real crimes, it doesn't seem right that he'll only be going to debtor's prison. Blighter ought to be swinging from a hangman's noose as he deserves. And he might be, had you let Tony and me speak to a few influential members of the Lords."

Rafe shook his head and clipped the end off his own cigar with a savage snip. "Even had they believed you—long after the fact, I might add, since you were both on the Continent at the time—the courts would never have taken my word against his, nor against any of the others. No, as much as I appreciate your and Tony's recent efforts on my behalf, the actions of those four were done against me and mine, and I shall be the one to see that each of them receives his just rewards. At least those that may be granted on this earth. Their ultimate punishments will be meted out by the devil himself, since all of them will assuredly go to hell."

And who will decree my own fate? Rafe wondered. Would he join them there to burn inside the inferno? Not for sins committed, he thought, but for ones he had not been able to prevent. Even now, guilt and sorrow tormented him over what had been done to Pamela. Poor, sweet, beautiful Pamela, who had become an unwitting pawn and senseless victim in another man's twisted game.

Tossing back the last of his whisky, Rafe let the drink

numb a bit of his misery. Rising, he crossed to pour himself another.

"Will you go after Middleton next?" Ethan inquired.

Rafe's fists tightened at mention of the man's name. *Burton St. George,* the worst villain of them all.

"No. I'm saving him for last. When I take that bastard down, I want to make sure he knows exactly who's responsible for his ruination. I've been patient for a long time. I can be patient a while more. Underhill has already met his fate, and now Challoner will as well. Hurst is the next target, then finally . . . Middleton."

He spat out the last name, barely able to stand having the fiend's name on his tongue. Old hatred swirled inside him black as a cancer. Rafe fought against it as he poured another large splash of whisky into his glass.

"Best be careful with that," Ethan said, levering himself out of his chair to cross to the fireplace. Drawing one of the slender reeds from a jasperware jar kept on the mantel for just such a purpose, he stuck it in the fire, then used the kindling to light his cigar. He inhaled, the cheroot's tip glowing red hot. Discarding the reed in the fireplace, he tilted back his head and blew out a thin stream of smoke.

"And there's no point glaring at me," Ethan remarked. "You know I'm right, and if you drink the rest of that bottle, you'll only be angry with yourself when you wake up with a sore head come the morrow."

"It's my head. I'll do with it as I please."

But after one last defiant swallow, Rafe set down the glass on a nearby tray, leaving most of the whisky untouched.

Ethan strolled back and dropped down into his chair. "Besides, from what I hear you have an assignation tomorrow with a very tempting widow. I should imagine you'll want to be at your best."

This time Rafe really did glare. "I thought Hannibal

had learned to keep his mouth closed by now. I see he and I will have to have another talk."

"Don't worry. He barely mentioned her and refused to give a name." Ethan took another slow draw on his cigar. "You wouldn't care to enlighten me as to her identity, would you?"

Rafe met the teasing amusement in his friend's eyes and relaxed, knowing his and Julianna's secret was safe and would go no farther than this room.

"No, I most certainly would not. And I'll thank you to forget all about the lady."

Vessey raised a golden brow. "My, she must be special for you to be so protective."

Special? Yes, Julianna Hawthorne was that and so much more. Rafe's body tightened at the thought of seeing her again, imagining how it would be to have her moving beneath him, her intoxicating scent a heady drug inside his brain, her taste warm and delicious as honey on his tongue.

Realizing where his musings were leading him, he stopped and forcibly shook off the fantasy. More than enough had been said about Julianna Hawthorne, for today and the future.

"So," Rafe remarked, crossing to the fireplace to light his own cigar. "Tony has gone back to the country. Some difficulty at his estate, you said. How long will he be gone?"

Chapter Seven

RAFE WAS WAITING for her when she came through the door of the Queens Square house, greeting her with a kiss so devastating it sent her pulse skipping like a pebble across a placid lake.

Slowly, lingeringly, he eased away.

"Let's get you out of that cloak and bonnet," he murmured in a deep, silvery tone.

Without waiting for her agreement, he unfastened her mantle and swept it from her shoulders. Crossing, he draped the garment over the banister, obviously too impatient to bother hanging her cloak inside the closet this time. Next, he slid her hat free of her head, then set the velvet confection atop the carved newel-post finial, the headgear's pretty emerald-hued ribbons dangling downward like streamers. She removed her gloves and passed them to him. Setting them aside, he enfolded her hand inside his own and led her forward.

Julianna shivered as she followed in his wake.

How similar everything seems today, and yet how vastly different, she mused.

On her first visit to this house, she'd been so afraid, convinced she would take no pleasure in an act she had always considered a duty, intrusive and rather demeaning by its very nature. Her stomach had churned then with anxiety, her devotion to her family the only thing that had held her to her pledge.

But today there was no fear and no thought of having to worry about promises, excitement the only sensation trembling inside her stomach, tingly as a hundred tiny butterfly wings. There was anticipation, too, jigging in her bloodstream like a lively hornpipe as her and Rafe's shoes tapped out a duel rhythm against the wooden stairs before whispering across the thick wool of the Turkey carpet hall runners. Together they entered the sitting room, fragrant spice and earthy sweetness drifting on the air.

She inhaled, then smiled. *Hot mulled wine.*

Apparently Rafe had been busy, she thought, noticing a small copper pitcher that rested on the fireplace hearth so its contents would stay warm. A pair of delicate, engraved silver cups sat nearby, waiting to be filled. Darting a glance toward the bedroom, she saw he had made preparations there as well: a fire burning in cozy contentment, the bed's counterpane and sheets turned back, pillows plumped in silent invitation.

The butterfly wings in her stomach fluttered anew, a thousand strong this time. Laying a hand against her middle, she considered what it meant.

Dear heavens, I want him. For the first time in her life she was looking forward to sleeping with a man, genuinely craving all the intimate things he would do to her, what they would do to each other, this afternoon in that bed.

She grew a little dizzy at the thought.

"So how was your morning?" he asked in polite inquiry as he released her hand.

My morning? Why was he asking about such mundane topics when he could be hurrying her into the bedroom and tumbling her down onto the mattress? Perhaps he thought to set her at her ease again. After all, this was only their second time together. A real gentleman would never rush a lady, and Rafe Pendragon, as she was coming to realize, had manners as refined as those of the best peers of the realm.

He crossed to the hearth.

"My morning was fine," she said, watching as he poured out a cup of wine. "I kept to my usual schedule."

"And of what, precisely, does that entail?"

"Oh, nothing special. Breakfast and my morning ablutions. Today, a meeting with my housekeeper to review the week's menus and any staff concerns. A few minutes of sewing."

He offered her the wine.

"Embroidery, I assume."

"Yes. I'm stitching handkerchiefs at present." She accepted the cup, the metal's gentle warmth radiating pleasurably against fingers she only now realized were chilled. Raising the drink to her mouth, she sipped, enjoying the contrast of flavors, sweet but tart, robust yet mellow.

When she was finished, he took the cup from her.

"I thought we'd share." With their gazes locked, Rafe turned the cup so he could place his lips where hers had just been.

A quiver ran down her spine as she watched him drink, his strong throat working as he swallowed. Moisture glistened on his mouth when he was finished. He licked it away.

Turning, he walked to one of the wide wing chairs and sank down. He patted his knee.

"Come here."

Breath hitched in her lungs. *Does he really want me to sit on his lap?* she wondered.

He gave her his answer by beckoning again, holding out a hand for her to take. For a long moment, she stared, tracing the shape of that hand—the strong, masculine palm and long, elegant fingers that were capable of giving so much exquisite pleasure.

With her knees on the verge of buckling, she hastened forward and let him tug her down onto his lap. His arms tightened around her hips to pull her close.

"Hmm, even better than I imagined," he murmured low.

So he's thought about holding me like this before? she mused. Her nipples peaked beneath the material of her bodice at the idea, finding herself liking it. She liked as well the unmistakable evidence of his arousal thrusting against her thigh with a boldness that didn't seem to discompose Rafe in the slightest.

He stroked a palm over her back, the caress evoking a shivery kind of lassitude.

"So, what's on these handkerchiefs of yours?" he inquired.

"What?"

"Are there flowers, mayhap? Something light and feminine for you to tuck into your reticule?"

She blinked. *Is he really talking to me about handkerchiefs?* Inhaling deeply, she tried to clear her brain enough to respond.

"They're . . . um . . . they're not for me. I'm embroidering monograms actually, for my brother. His birthday isn't too far distant. A man can always use handkerchiefs, I thought."

"Very true. A most considerate gift, especially since you are making them with your own hands." Rafe bent forward and pressed his mouth to her throat, his fingers gliding upward from behind to unfasten the first of the buttons that ran along the back of her gown.

Her eyelids fell to half-staff.

"What color did you choose?" He popped another button loose from its mooring. "You know, for the thread?"

Thread? Mercy, how can he think about thread?

"Hmm, it's blue," she sighed. "Dark blue on white silk squares."

He caressed the skin at her nape, then dusted a line of kisses over her jaw to her ear. Taking the fleshy lobe between his teeth, he gave it a little nip.

Fire shot along her nerve endings, flashing from her ear all the way down to her toes. She arched in his lap, his erection swelling thicker against her in response.

"And what color do you prefer?" he asked. "What's your favorite?"

"My favorite color?" Her bodice sagged, full-length velveteen sleeves gathering around her elbows.

"Mmm-hmm."

"I . . . oh . . . p-purple. It's purple."

"A regal and passionate color. I approve. You'll have to wear a purple frock for me one of these days. You would look radiant in that shade."

His fingers moved with an easy dexterity against the laces of her stays. "And your favorite food? What's the one victual you simply cannot resist?"

Her head buzzed, trying to keep hold of the conversation when her body was awash with urges of the most elemental kind.

"Oh, I . . . I'm not sure. I like many things."

"Pick one."

Stay laces slid free, her corset growing looser by the instant. Desperately she searched her mind. "Chocolate. I love chocolate."

"In bonbons, or do you like it best grated into milk?"

"Hmm, it's lovely in milk. I often have h-hot . . . chocolate for breakfast."

He dotted her collarbone with a seductive line of kisses. "I should have known."

"Known what?"

"That you'd like it hot. Hot and steamy and thick."

Something deep inside her convulsed.

With the last of her laces undone, he eased off her corset, then cast the whalebone and linen to the floor. Her breasts pressed against her chemise, nipples taut and faintly visible beneath the sheer silk. She trembled, knowing that all that lay between her bare flesh and his bare hands was the pull of a single slender white ribbon.

She waited, her breath shallow, her senses afire.

"What about books?"

"Pardon me?"

"Books? What authors do you enjoy reading, or are you like most ladies and prefer paging through copies of *La Belle Assemble*?"

Her brows furrowed. *I can barely think, and he wants to know about authors and books?*

Shifting against his muscled thighs in restless frustration, she fought to stay sane.

"I . . . like books and the . . . um . . . fashion pages too. But why? Why do you want to know?"

He paused and met her gaze, his green eyes blazing with intensity and a wild passion she realized he was forcing himself to hold at bay. "Because I want to know you."

"But why? Our arrangement is temporary. Why do you care who I am, when you can have me regardless?"

And that was the plain truth. Given their agreement and her undeniable desire for him, he needn't have spoken so much as a word to her. He had only to lay her down and have his way.

"Because, temporary or not, we're lovers," he told her. "For right now you're mine, and I want to know the woman in my bed. I want to know *you*. Who Julianna Hawthorne is. What she likes. What she thinks and desires and dreams."

Her heart squeezed out a quick double beat beneath her breasts, Rafe's words touching her down to her soul. In a single moment, he'd shown more interest in her, and respect for her, than her husband had granted her in all the years of their marriage.

The knowledge proved a powerful aphrodisiac, her core turning molten, her limbs pliable as warmed wax.

"Jane Austen," she blurted out.

"Hmm?" he murmured, as if he'd forgotten his own query.

"You . . . asked who I like to read. Jane Austen. I liked her book *S-Sense and Sensibility*."

He smiled, long, devilishly appealing dimples appearing in his cheeks. "And here I thought you'd name a poet. Lord Byron, perhaps."

She shook her head, rubbing her cheek against his as he bent to nuzzle her throat again.

"Lord Byron is far too t-tragic a figure."

Rafe moved lower, brushing his lips over the tops of her exposed cleavage.

"F-Far too enamored of himself and his talents . . . myriad though they may be. I much prefer . . . Miss Austen."

"And I much prefer you," he stated on a purring growl.

Straightening, he clasped a hand against the back of her head, then crushed her mouth to his. All of Rafe's questions ceased as he demanded nothing less than her full participation, urging her to respond without restraint or hesitation, his arms strong and steady and reassuring around her.

Julianna capitulated on a joyful sigh, giving herself over to the rivulets of pleasure coursing through her veins like lava. Pleasure that only increased when he finally tugged on her chemise ribbon to bare her breasts.

Sweeping the straps down her arms, he cupped an eager globe, thumbing one already taut nipple to an even tighter, aching peak. She moaned into his mouth, his tongue taking advantage to forage between her open lips.

He tasted delicious—of wine and warmth and man, a combination she found both potent and inviting. Kissing him back, she tangled her tongue with his, then surprised herself by conducting her own exploration. Over hard teeth and smooth inner cheeks she roamed, lapping and licking at all the sleek wet heat she found, losing herself to the sensations.

This time his groan filled her mouth. She smiled against the vibrations.

Wanting more, she tried to lift her arms, hungry to run her hands over him, needing to hold him closer. But she couldn't escape, discovering that her elbows were trapped within the cloth of her gown and chemise.

She twisted, but to no avail.

Apparently realizing her dilemma, Rafe smoothed his hands along her upper arms. Yet when he might have freed her, he hesitated, holding her in place instead.

In a kind of divine torture, he arched her back to give himself more room, then lowered his head, fastening his mouth to her flesh with the voraciousness of a gourmand indulging in a magnificent feast. Suckling deeply, he widened his lips over one breast, circling his tongue around her nipple in a devastating sweep before pressing the nub against his teeth.

She shook in his grasp, feeling every nibble and pull all the way to her feminine core. Alternating, he drew upon one breast then the other until she thought she might shatter apart.

Then, as abruptly as his torment had started, he stopped. Releasing her, he yanked the sleeves and chemise straps off her arms, leaving her clothing bunched at her waist.

Fitting his hand to her hips, he lifted her off his lap and stood her before him.

Now, she thought, *now he'll take me to the bedroom.*

She only hoped she could manage the trip, her legs so weak she feared she might fall along the way. Maybe Rafe would carry her.

Stripping off her dress, he tossed it onto the nearby sofa.

She expected him to stand, but he reached down a hand to unbutton his falls instead. Her eyes drank in the brazen sight of him, long and thick, rigid with arousal.

Reaching out, he turned her so she faced away.

She was still adjusting to his actions when he caught the hem of her petticoat and raised it to her waist, caressing her naked thighs and over her buttocks in sweeping strokes that made her tremble and ache. Wet heat gathered in a heavy rush between her thighs, her legs quivering.

"Rafe, please," she moaned, certain she might fall.

But she needn't have worried, held safe within his powerful grasp.

"I've got you, sweeting," he said. "Come and have a seat. I promise you'll like it."

A seat?

Before she had a chance to wrap her mind around his comment, he walked her back, moving her so that her feet and legs were splayed on either side of his own. Pressing his knees outward, he spread her wider, then wider still, leaving her open and completely exposed.

Even then, she didn't fully understand his intent until he tugged her downward and fit her straight onto his shaft.

Then she understood everything.

"Oh!" she cried. "Oh, God."

"Oh, God, is right."

Taking her hands, he set them on the chair arms and wrapped her fingers around the wood. Pumping his hips, he burrowed himself deeper.

"Hook your feet around my ankles and lean forward," he commanded, his breath soughing against her neck in a warm, panting gust.

Forward? How could she?

But she saw the way when he looped an arm across her chest and stomach, using the corded strength of his forearm to cradle her. Arching, she leaned out, enough to let him slide fully into her aching depths.

Head hanging, she struggled to catch her breath, her entire body on fire as if she'd been dipped in liquid flame. She felt Rafe everywhere. Inside her and around her. His will suddenly her will, as if they shared a connection of more than the corporeal.

He kissed her neck and cheek, then set his hips in motion, thrusting first hard, then soft. Shallow, then deep.

Eyes closed, she let him take her, allowing each sensation to arc and zing through her, dazzling as a fireworks display. But her body had its own ideas and without even realizing, she began to press back, grinding down even as he shifted up.

Rafe groaned and pumped harder, making her cry out with each and every heated stroke. Her fingernails dug into the chair arms, her fists clutched in a death grip around the carved wood. Gasping and clawing for air, she wondered how much more she could take, already dizzy on a surfeit of pleasure.

As if sensing how close she teetered to the edge, Rafe kissed her neck again, then spread her thighs even wider with his knees. One solid thrust buried him impossibly deep, so deep her inner muscles instantly began to spasm around his hard, hot length.

And she was lost, bliss roaring through her, harsh and earth-shattering as the most fearsome storm. Dimly, she heard herself scream, limbs shaking, her whole body awash in unimaginable ecstasy.

On an oath, Rafe shifted his hold upon her, bending

her back against his chest as he reached down to grasp her hips inside his splayed hands. Controlling her movements, he drove himself into her in a wild rhythm, over and over, the power of his thrusts igniting her own need once again.

Rafe gave a rough shout, claiming his release only seconds before her own. Quivering and spent, they slumped together back into the chair, her legs dangling next to his own.

At length, he angled her head onto his shoulder and claimed her mouth, their kiss slow and sweet and drowsy.

"Let's go to bed," he murmured. She nodded, but neither of them moved.

Shifting, she curled against him to stroke a palm over his chest, his skin damp from their exertions.

"So, tell me," she murmured. "What is *your* favorite color?"

His eyes widened, a smile spreading across his mouth. Tossing back his head, Rafe began to laugh.

Chapter Eight

JULIANNA DRANK A sip of punch, wrinkled her nose, and set her cup aside.

Ghastly, she thought, wishing there was something else available to wash away the cloying aftertaste. But alas, this sad excuse for a beverage was the best Almacks could provide. Or *would* provide, since the Patronesses—leaders of Society all—certainly had the means to offer better had they wished.

If not for Maris and the official start of the Season, Julianna would have been enjoying her evening elsewhere. But gaining vouchers and attending the weekly dance held at the assembly rooms was essential to her sister's success in the Ton.

So here Julianna stood, grimacing over bad punch while she watched Maris dance the quadrille. At least her sibling appeared to be having a good time.

I wish I were. Julianna sighed.

If only Rafe was here to keep me entertained, she mused with an inner smile. Although the ways he usually found to bring her pleasure weren't at all the sort of thing fit for a public ballroom. Her skin warmed at the memory of their last encounter, her mouth growing dry in anticipation of their next, now only a day away.

In the month since their affair began, she found herself becoming obsessed with the man. When she was with Rafe, he commanded her focus entirely. When they were apart, he was never completely out of her thoughts.

Just yesterday she'd ruined the list of household accounts on which she'd been working, rousing from thrilling daydreams of Rafe to find her fingers stained black with ink, her earlier handwriting obliterated by drips from the pen forgotten in her hand.

He even invaded her dreams, leaving her skin damp, her body awash with desire as she tossed against her bedsheets. Most frustrating of all, she would awaken and long to find him beside her, wishing he were holding her, his arms offering strength and comfort.

And does he comfort me? she asked herself. Not entirely comfortable with the answer, Julianna forced herself to shake off her musings.

She was glad she had when she saw the dance end and Maris's partner lead her sister toward her, as propriety demanded. After exchanging pleasantries with the gentleman with whom Maris had been dancing, he bowed and moved away.

"Thank heavens he is required to mingle," Maris whispered as soon as the young man moved out of hearing range. "I feared he was about to start drooling on me like one of Squire Newington's mastiff dogs. During the dance, he would not stop staring at my bodice."

Julianna frowned. "Well then, I am glad he did not linger. The next time he asks you to dance, find an excuse to refuse."

"Oh, do not worry. I shall."

"Other than the Leerer, are you having a good time?"

Maris's dark eyes came alive with pleasure. "Oh, yes. With but a few exceptions, the evening has been wonderful. The only thing better was my come out ball last week. I'm still pinching myself over how well everything went."

The ball had gone well, Julianna thought. Splendidly,

in fact, with the cream of Society in attendance, including the Prince of Wales, who rarely put in appearances at such events. And the gentlemen were already calling at Allerton House, sending sweetly scented bouquets and begging Maris to go walking or driving with them.

When the time came, Julianna knew her sister would not suffer from a lack of marriage proposals. She only prayed the right man for Maris would be among the group of hopefuls.

She wondered what Rafe would think of tonight's festivities, imagining he would likely consider everyone here a dreadful snob. And he would be right, she realized, disgraceful as it was to admit.

Sophisticated and suave, Rafe Pendragon could easily hold his own among any of the Ton's peers. And yet, because of his birth, he was excluded. In the past, she'd never been one to rail against class inequities and social injustices, but then she had never before known anyone like Rafe.

A shiver raced along her spine, wishing again that he were beside her. How magnificent he would appear on the dance floor, holding her scandalously close as he whirled her to the strains of a waltz! Every other woman in the room would watch them, envy and longing in their eyes. And later, during the carriage ride home, he would plunder her mouth with wild kisses, rousing her hunger to a fevered pitch until neither one of them could form a single, coherent thought.

"Jules, are you warm? Would you like some punch?"

Her sister's question brought her back to the present, real heat spreading upward into her cheeks.

"N-No, I'm fine," she said, striving to regain her composure. "And the punch is dreadful, by the way."

Opening her fan, she waved it in front of her face, hoping Maris and anyone else looking would attribute her heightened color to the room's warmth.

Dear heavens, what is the matter with me? she scolded. *I have no business, no business at all, standing at a dance—next to my innocent young sister—fantasizing about Rafe Pendragon! Obviously, he is turning me wanton.*

Before she had time to castigate herself further, a new gentleman made his way toward her and Maris—Burton St. George, looking elegant and urbane in a formal black coat and knee breeches, his white shirt and cravat impeccable.

"How do you do this evening?" the viscount greeted, executing a smart bow.

This was the first time she and Maris had encountered him since that night at the theater. She shivered, telling herself the reaction must be a bit of residual embarrassment from her recent musings.

"My lord," Julianna said, compelling a smile.

The three of them exchanged the usual round of polite small talk before Middleton directed his attention toward Maris. "Miss Davies, might I request the pleasure of the next dance?"

Maris appeared surprised. "Oh, I'd be honored, my lord, but it sounds like the musicians are preparing for a waltz, and I haven't yet been given permission to engage in that particular dance. Perhaps my sister would enjoy a turn about the floor."

"Maris," Julianna replied, "do not be foolish. I am fine right where I am. You know I rarely dance."

The viscount smiled, appearing not at all disappointed by the proposed change of partners. "Then let this be one of those occasions, madam. I should be delighted to share the next dance with you." He held out his arm.

"Oh, do go on, Jules," Maris encouraged.

"But what about you?"

"I see Sandra Conniver across the room. I shall visit with her for a while."

Trapped with no polite way out, Julianna agreed. Laying her fingers on the viscount's sleeve, she let him lead her onto the dance floor.

The musicians soon struck up an energetic tune, setting all the couples in motion.

Tipping back her head in order to see his face, she couldn't help but notice the viscount's height. Without question, he was taller than most men, but not as tall as Rafe, nor as broad in the shoulder. And although his movements were smooth and coordinated, she suspected his ability came from practice rather than natural grace. Such would not be true of Rafe, she mused. A confident, physical man like Rafe Pendragon would always know the exact spot to place his feet without having to first consider his steps.

Realizing she needed to redirect her thoughts away from Rafe once again, Julianna searched for a conversational opening. "I must tell you, my lord, you surprise me."

"Oh? In what way?"

"I would not have thought to see you here this evening. Almacks has never struck me as the sort of entertainment gentlemen of your tastes generally prefer."

He raised a sandy-colored brow. "Gentlemen of my tastes, Lady Hawthorne? And what exactly would those tastes be to which you refer?"

"Something a bit more lively than tame country dances, bland punch, and the chance to play penny-a-point whist."

He gave a short laugh. "You have caught me out, my lady, and are quite correct. Almacks, despite its illustrious reputation and elegant company, isn't one of my usual haunts."

"Your appearance here this evening has quite set the rumor mill ablaze with speculation, I must tell you."

"Has it, indeed? A good thing, then, that I've never

been one to shy away from attention." After a pause, his face sobered. "I have been a widower for some while now. Four years and three months nearly to the day since I lost my own dear Eleanor. Having lost a spouse yourself, you must know the kind of sorrow I've endured."

"Yes," she murmured, a twinge of guilt pinching at her.

Her marriage to Basil had in no way been a love match. Her father had wanted her to marry him, and being a naïve eighteen-year-old and a very dutiful daughter, she'd done as he had asked. But sorrow? No, she had felt no real sorrow at Basil's passing, only regret and relief.

She considered the viscount's words. She'd had no idea he had harbored such deep feelings for his wife. He must have loved her a great deal to still mourn her so keenly after all this time. Over the years, she'd heard a few murmured asides about his supposed profligate ways, despite the fact that he was a respected member of the nobility. Perhaps he was one of those men who hid his grief in work and occasional bouts of wild living.

"Thus my appearance here tonight," he continued. "I have decided, somewhat reluctantly, to surround myself with eligible ladies to see if I might by chance cross paths with a girl who can engage my affections. Single life grows lonely after a time, I'm afraid. And a man in my position has need of a family. My dear Eleanor and I were not fortunate enough to be blessed with children before her untimely demise."

More sympathy rose inside her, since she knew first-hand the pain of being childless.

"An accident, was it not?" she murmured. "Her death?"

A quick flash of pain shone in his blue eyes. "Yes, a tragic accident. She was afflicted with sleepwalking, and—" He broke off, involuntarily squeezing her hand as they continued to dance. Swallowing, he collected himself. "She stumbled on the stairs . . . I'm sorry, I don't like to speak of it."

"Of course not. I should not have inquired."

"No, no, it's quite all right. But perhaps we should talk of more cheerful subjects."

"Yes, I quite agree."

He paused for a moment as if to collect his thoughts and emotions before continuing the conversation.

"The Season seems to be off to a fine start," he said. "Already London is brimming with elegant Society, and your sister appears to be enjoying herself. From what I understand, she's already making a bit of a splash among the Ton, if it's not too forward of me to say."

"Yes, she is taking very well." Julianna smiled. "But then I knew she would. Maris is a sweet girl and cannot help but be liked. Even the queen commented on her delightful, unaffected manner."

"Look, there is your sister now," Middleton observed.

Julianna turned her head, locating Maris among the crowd that lined the sides of the assembly room. Her sister appeared to be having an animated discussion with Major William Waring, a handsome, forthright young man who'd returned from fighting in Spain only a few weeks ago.

So sad about the loss of his arm, Julianna thought, noticing the one pinned-up coat sleeve. She had heard that due to his disability, he'd been compelled to sell his commission as a cavalry officer and retire from active battlefield service. Despite being the son of the Earl of Grassingham, he had two older brothers, a circumstance that must surely leave him few career options and little money. She supposed he might accept a position in the Home Office, or even in Parliament should he ever wish to run for a seat.

She watched Maris place her hand over the Major's good arm and begin to stroll the perimeter. Her sister's cheeks were flushed pink as June roses, her pale cream gown an attractive foil beside her escort's dark attire.

"A remarkably pretty girl, your sister," Middleton commented in an admiring tone.

"Yes, but young yet."

"Not too young to be out in Society, though, or to take a husband."

She stiffened, not quite liking the viscount's obvious interest in her sister. "Maris has plenty of time to make her choice."

He gave her a quizzical look. "You aren't warning me off by any chance, are you?"

Part of her wanted to say yes, wanted to tell him he was too mature and too sophisticated for her innocent sister. But young or not, Maris had a good head on her shoulders, and would be capable of making the right decision about her own future.

Wouldn't she?

If Rafe were there, Julianna would have sought his advice.

But he isn't here and never will be, she admonished, abruptly recalling the social chasm between them. Besides, family matters such as these were up to her to decide. What was she doing considering asking Rafe, anyway?

He is my lover, not my husband, after all.

No, she told herself, if Middleton courted her sister and Maris genuinely came to love him, then she would not stand in her way. After all, Julianna had promised herself not to interfere. So long as Maris was safe and happy, she would be content.

"Of course not," Julianna said, swallowing her misgivings. "It's just that I would ask any gentleman with an interest to have a care. Society is new to Maris. It's possible she could be swayed by a charming manner or a handsome face."

"Well, I suppose I should take that as a compliment, you considering me both charming and handsome. But not to worry, my lady, my intentions toward your sister are strictly honorable."

"Thank you, my lord, I am sure they are."

So why do I still feel uneasy? she questioned.

"I have your permission to pay my addresses then?"

She hesitated for one last second. "Unless my sister has some objection, yes, you are most welcome to call upon her."

"So you'll come again on Monday?" Rafe murmured the following afternoon as he tied the laces on one of her kidskin half-boots, her ankle propped on his knee as he knelt at her side.

"As early in the day as I can manage," she promised. As she now understood, to deny him was to deny herself.

From her seat on the padded dressing-table stool, she gazed at his bent head. Without knowing she meant to do it, she sifted her fingers through his hair, then along the curve of his ear and jaw. A new growth of whiskers scratched faintly against her skin, the dark shadow giving him the look of a rake or a renegade.

He certainly ravished me, she thought with a secret smile.

Yet even in the deepest throes of passion, Rafe was careful, always seeing to her pleasure, even if it meant delaying or denying his own. His consideration never failed to warm her heart or wring a smile from her lips. The more she knew him, the more she liked, his thoughtfulness but one of the qualities that had turned what might have been bondage into nothing less than bliss.

Despite being well satisfied from their energetic lovemaking, she still craved the connection of touching him, the satisfaction of maintaining the simplest of joinings. Moving her hand to his neck, she caressed the skin just under his cravat.

Finished tying the lace of her boot into a neat, snug bow, Rafe gave her stocking-clad calf a gentle pat. Easing her foot onto the floor, he lowered her skirts into place. Rising to his full height, he offered a hand to assist her to her feet. "Ready?"

She nodded, stifling a sigh at knowing she must leave. Preceding him, she moved to the door.

"Wait," he called. "What's this?"

Crossing back to the bed, he bent down and retrieved something from the carpet. As he turned, she saw the slender length of gold and seed pearls that dangled in his hand. "Your bracelet, my lady. It must have slipped to the floor after I removed it earlier."

"Oh, heavens! I don't know how I could have been so careless. I would be most distressed if this went missing."

He quirked a brow. "A gift, then? From someone special?"

"My mother. She gave this to me for my birthday the year before she died."

His face grew solemn. "Then I am glad it has come to no harm."

Taking her hand, he looped the jewelry around her wrist and fastened the clasp. With the bracelet secure, he raised her palm and pressed a kiss onto its center.

"I know I shouldn't wear it," she said, "since I would be crushed if it were to get lost or broken someday."

"But where is the joy in keeping precious things locked up out of sight? Your mother would want you to enjoy her gift rather than let it molder away in a dark box somewhere."

She smiled, his words echoing what she herself had always thought, and what so many others failed to appreciate. "Exactly so. Thank you."

"For what?"

"For understanding, that's all."

Dimples popped to life in his cheeks as his lips turned up.

Watching them, and him, her heart turned over.

Bending, he took her mouth in a last passionate joining. Closing her eyes, she hummed out her pleasure and kissed him back.

Two evenings later, Burton St. George paid a visit of an entirely different sort.

Seated in a chair he'd been compelled to brush off beforehand with a handkerchief, Burton watched his old friend Sir Stephen Hurst pour himself a fresh whisky.

Hurst's hands shook as he drank the glass's contents in a few gulping swallows. A thin line of alcohol escaped his thick lips to slide over his chin, a single droplet collecting on the full underside. The drop waggled there for a long moment before falling off to stain his cravat. Hurst wiped his lips dry on his shirt cuff, then reached again for the whisky decanter to pour himself another glass.

Unable to stand seeing a repetition of the other man's repellent display, Burton looked away to survey the shabby interior of Hurst's drawing room. Years ago, the room had been lovely, pristine and fresh, styled with fine furnishings and elegant silken appointments done in warm shades of blue and gold. But that had been in the day when Hurst's parents had been alive, before he had come into the title and been allowed to run unrestrained through the family fortune.

The whole townhouse needed a good airing and a thorough scouring, since the rooms now smelled of alcohol, stale cigar smoke, and dust. A plate of half-eaten cheese sat moldering on one of the Chippendale end tables.

Disgusting really, how low the man has allowed himself to sink, Burton decided. Anyone else would have maidservants to keep things tidy. But Hurst had trouble retaining the girls he hired, since he insisted on bedding them all, even the ugly ones. Of those who hadn't run away, Burton knew of at least six Hurst had gotten pregnant before turning them out into the streets.

There was such a thing as prudent discretion, after all. A gentleman, Burton believed, should never let himself devolve into mindless animal behavior. Nor fall so deeply beneath the power of his own urges that he forgot things like cleanliness and comfort.

There truly was no excuse for such stupid, excessive debauchery. He didn't know why he continued to tolerate Hurst. Loyalty to a boyhood friend, he supposed. Loyalty, however, had its limits.

"So what's this all about, Hurst?" Burton demanded with unconcealed impatience. "What's so urgent I needed to cut short my evening to come over here and listen to your whining?"

"I don't whine," Hurst whined, wiping damp fingers through his disheveled brown hair. "And I take exception to your tone."

Burton got to his feet. "Then I'll take myself off. I have far more interesting things to do than sit here watching you drink yourself into a stupor."

"N-No, Middleton, don't go. I'm sorry. P-Please, please sit. I . . . I need your help."

"My help with what?"

Hurst's eyes widened in a rather bovine bulge as he leaned closer. "Pendragon. The bloody bastard's after us. All of us. He's hunting us down one by one, and you and I are next."

Burton shot out a laugh. "Don't be ridiculous. I have

told you before, Pendragon's not a threat. The whoreson may have his fingers in half the business dealings in the country, but he isn't after any of us. He knows we can't be touched. After all, who would believe him or his slanderous accusations?"

"No one needs to believe them. He's finding ways to destroy us behind the scenes. Haven't you heard about Challoner?"

Intrigued, Burton resumed his seat. "What about Challoner?"

"He's in debtor's prison. They came and clapped him in irons yesterday morning and dragged him off to Fleet. He mortgaged his estate for a huge sum and now it's gone, all of it, when he couldn't pay."

"Did Pendragon hold the note?"

Hurst shook his head. "There was no note. Challoner invested heavily in a shipping company that went bankrupt. When its four best vessels sank, Challoner's fortune went down with them."

The slight tension in Burton's shoulders faded. "Man's a fool to have tossed his money away on a speculative investment. If he landed himself in the River Tick, then it is no more than he deserves. As for Pendragon, he may be an admittedly cunning bastard, but I fail to see the connection."

"I don't know, it's just a feeling I have, especially after hearing the truth about what happened to Frank Underhill."

Burton thought about Underhill.

Brash, bombastic, swaggering Frank, who had always been primed for a prank or a dare. Years ago, in their salad days, the four of them had been inseparable: Underhill, Hurst, Challoner, and himself. They'd wenched and caroused and gambled from one end of the English Isles to the other. But times changed, men matured. Friends, even close ones, drifted apart.

Three years ago, Underhill had gone missing during a trip to Southampton. At the time, no one knew for certain what had happened to him, but the authorities surmised he'd been kidnapped by a press-gang. Inquiries had immediately been put out seeking his recovery, but no trace of him had ever been found.

Then, two months ago, his family received a letter from the Royal Navy. The notice informed them of Underhill's status as a common seaman and his death by execution for deserting his post in His Majesty's navy. They went on to offer their posthumous apologies for not ascertaining his true identity until after his trial and execution.

The shock of it had sent his loved ones into the deepest of mourning. The puzzlement of it had given others, friends and enemies alike, much speculative grist. Had he simply been the unlucky victim of happenstance? Or had someone deliberately lured him to his unhappy, and ultimately fatal, plight?

"Sent chills down my spine when I heard the news," Hurst muttered, swilling more whisky. "Been watching my back ever since."

Paranoid sot, Burton thought, *seeing shadows everywhere he goes.* Hurst really was beginning to unravel.

"It's doubtful that you will be impressed after all this time, Hurst," Burton said derisively, "especially here in the heart of London. Underhill's kidnapping was unfortunate, but he ought not to have frequented taverns in dangerous parts of seaport towns. No doubt he was looking for a drink and a likely whore when he was set upon."

"Yes, but what was he doing there in Southampton? Not a place Underhill seemed likely to go."

"Who knows what he was up to by then. If it will put your mind at ease, I did a bit of investigating at the time of his disappearance and found nothing suspicious. The press-gangs were very active that year. I think the poor blighter was simply in the wrong place at the wrong time."

Hurst frowned and poured another drink. "Still, what about Challoner? Two of the four of us, seems suspicious to me."

"Coincidence. Challoner is an idiot when it comes to money; you know that as well as I. I'm not surprised he has ended up in the gaoler's grasp. Which may be your next home, if you aren't more careful."

Burton surveyed the room with revulsion before pinning a condemning eye on Hurst. "Straighten yourself up, man. You've turned into a disgrace, letting drink and dissipation addle your mind."

"But what about Pendragon?" Hurst whined.

"What about him? You give him far more credit than he deserves. He is an insignificant worm I crushed years ago, and you worry far too much about matters that are best left in the past where they belong. He's *not* some avenging angel sent down to punish us, you know."

"More like the devil, that's what he is."

"You may fear him, but I do not. I lose no sleep worrying over Mr. Rafe-bloody-Pendragon," Burton spat with dismissive vehemence.

God, I hate the very sound of the bastard's name, Burton thought, his hands curling into fists at his sides. Pendragon had been a plague upon his life for as long as he could remember. Even as a young child, he had known the name and despised it.

But he had put Pendragon in his place once, and if the lowborn jackanapes had the temerity to strike at him again, he would find himself sorry.

Very sorry indeed.

Pendragon might have a reputation for ruthlessness, but there was no man alive more genuinely ruthless than Burton St. George.

Burton rose from his chair. "Put away the bottle, Hurst, and get someone to clean up this pigsty you call a house. And while you are at it, take a bath." He wrinkled his nose. "You smell."

Hurst sputtered out an objection.

Burton waved it aside. "And don't bother me again with any more of your ridiculous rantings. If I get another summons from you like the one tonight, I'll take pains to make sure you regret disturbing me. Do I make myself clear?"

Hurst nodded furiously, his hands shaking like leaves in a storm. To stop their movement, he curled them into balls on his lap. "Yes, Middleton," he murmured obsequiously.

"I bid you good evening, then," Burton said, donning his hat and picking up his cane. "Do call when you are feeling better. Perhaps we can take in a boxing mill or a horse race. Nothing better than a good bit of sport, eh?"

Chapter Nine

"WHAT'S THIS?" JULIANNA asked as she crossed into the Queens Square sitting room.

Resembling a bright patch of ocean, a wide blue cotton blanket lay on the floor before the fireplace, the wood in the grate burning with a contented crackle. Off to one side stood a wicker hamper, the top closed so its contents remained a mystery.

"This," Rafe declared as he followed her into the room, "is a nuncheon. I thought you might enjoy a light repast. After that welcome at the door, you must have worked up an appetite. I know I have."

A sizzle streaked over her skin, her body even now alive with the memory of his passionate greeting. During the weeks she had been meeting him here, Rafe hadn't once let her come upstairs without stopping her beforehand to give her a most thorough and enthusiastic embrace.

One time, in fact, he'd been so impatient for her that he'd lifted her into his arms and taken her right there against the front door, the two of them setting the door knocker a-tapping as he brought them both to an extraordinarily satisfying climax.

Of all the things she admired about Rafe—and there were many—it was his ability to constantly captivate and surprise her that she enjoyed the most. Generous and ever inventive, he never failed to delight her with his creativity, both in bed and out.

For example, today's impromptu nuncheon. What other man of her acquaintance would think to pleasure a woman with such simple, yet thoughtful, arrangements?

She smiled and strolled toward the blanket, intending to take a seat. Before she could, he stopped her with a touch.

"Don't sit down. Not yet. First, take off your clothes," he commanded on a velvety rumble.

There it was again—surprise. "But I thought we were going to eat."

"Oh, we are."

Unbuttoning his coat and shirt, he tossed the garments onto the nearby sofa. "I thought we'd dine alfresco. Not out-of-doors, but *out-of-our-clothes*."

Her mouth fell open. "A naked picnic?"

He laughed wickedly and arched a single eyebrow. "What better?"

"But it's chilly out. We'll take our death," she protested weakly.

"Don't worry, the fire will keep us warm. And if it doesn't, I shall find a way to heat things up."

Faintly scandalized, yet aroused all the same, Julianna unpinned the lace fichu covering her bosom. As she laid the delicate garment across a chair, Rafe shucked off his shoes and stockings, then reached to remove his pantaloons and drawers.

Saliva pooled in her mouth as he drew off the clothing, the sight of his sculpted, hair-roughened thighs and muscular calves sending her pulse speeding. Half naked, with his shirt and starched cravat still in place, she found him somehow more provocative than if he were completely nude.

What might he look like, she wondered, if he moved to the bedroom doorway and stretched his long, powerful arms overhead to grip the frame? A hard quiver traveled through her at the idea.

Staring with undisguised hunger, she licked her lips.

He padded toward her. "And what are you thinking? You look like a vixen who's found a tasty morsel." Gently, he turned her so he could help her out of her dress.

"Oh, I was only noticing that you haven't taken off your neckcloth yet."

"Hmm." He leaned down and brushed his mouth over her nape in a spot she particularly liked. "I'll get around to removing it eventually. One never knows when a nice length of cloth will come in handy."

Sense-memory tingled through her, recalling last week and the way he'd bound her wrists together above her head as they'd made love, Rafe bringing her to a peak so stunning she recalled the power of it even now.

Catching a small, escaped tendril of her hair between his fingertips, he gave the lock a teasing tug. "Springs back like a little cork," he murmured. "It'll go well with our wine."

An answering smile moved over her mouth as he unfastened her dress. Laying the garment neatly aside, he set to work on her stays. With the dexterity of a skilled dresser, he soon had her stripped bare.

Quickly, competently, he plucked the pins from her hair, then finger-combed her tresses so they fell in a dark wave down her back. Rafe crossed to place the pins in a little pile on a side table. Turning, he raked his gaze over her exposed body with a sweeping perusal that turned his cool, green eyes dark with heat.

Unhurried, he unwound his cravat and flung it atop his pile of clothes, then, with a devilish grin that emphasized the dimpled grooves in his cheeks, he unfastened his shirt one slow button at a time. Only breaking eye contact for a moment, he drew his shirt over his head, then stood motionless to let her look her fill.

And look her fill, she did.

Over his broad shoulders and across his firm chest with its growth of curling dark hair that begged to be explored. Onward to the flat plain of his stomach and narrow all-male hips—lean musculature that dipped and flowed downward into sleek, sturdy thighs, firm calves, and long, beautifully shaped feet. And finally between his legs, where the well-defined proof of his virility had grown unashamedly stiff and impressively long beneath her inquiring gaze.

She suppressed an appreciative sigh, aware how brazen she had become since he'd drawn her into his spell. *If all men looked like him,* she mused lasciviously, *wearing clothes would surely have been declared a crime.*

Feeling a bit like Eve to his Adam, she let him take her hand and lead her to the blanket. They stretched out opposite one another, bare hip to bare hip.

The fire burned contentedly in the grate, radiating enough heat to keep her comfortably warm. Realizing she was actually hungry for more than Rafe, she watched with interest as he opened the basket.

Out of the hamper he produced a whole roasted chicken, a small wedge of soft buttery cheese, biscuits, and a little jar of honey. One last container he left inside the hamper.

"For later," he told her, as he popped the cork on a bottle of champagne. With the wine frothing, he poured out two glasses, the liquid sparkling and golden. Handing one across to her, their gazes locked as they drank, the alcohol cool and sharp on her tongue.

"Hmm, delicious." Reaching out, he traced the edge of a finger along her cheek. "But do you know what's even better?"

Her skin tingled where he'd stroked it, and she shook her head. "No."

"Drinking it with you."

A warm glow spread through her, together with an ir-repressible smile. Lowering her lashes, she took another drink of champagne. Her nose twitched seconds later and she gave a small, delicate sneeze.

"Bless you," he said.

"The bubbles are tickling my nose."

"Lucky bubbles." He grinned.

Feeling silly as a schoolgirl, she giggled.

No, lucky me, she mused, *being here with Rafe.*

Utterly relaxed, he set his wine aside to feed her small bites of succulent chicken and tender pieces of biscuit smeared with the tangy cheese that melted like heaven in her mouth. Without much urging, he coaxed her to do the same for him, careful to lick her fingers clean in between bites, nibbling playfully at her palms before nuzzling the delicate skin along the inside of her wrists.

She laughed and pulled his head down, his lips brush-ing hers with the finesse of a gentle summer breeze. Opening her mouth, she circled her tongue around his to sample his unique flavor, adding and comparing it to all the other flavors lingering sumptuously on her palate.

Time passed in a leisurely haze, her wineglass emptied and filled and emptied again. Her head buzzed, her senses reeling. Yet she knew she could not truly blame the alcohol for her level of intoxication. She had Rafe to reproach for that—the man like an addictive drug that had seeped into her bloodstream, leaving her needy and never entirely satisfied. The more of him she had, she discovered, the more of him she wanted.

When she had agreed to their bargain, the parameters had appeared simple. An exchange of flesh for money and nothing more. But from the first moment he'd touched her, their union had been incendiary, like lamp oil tossed onto a roaring fire.

Never in a thousand years would she have thought she'd be taking a lover when she had granted him access to her body. But that is precisely what Rafe Pendragon had become.

And it wasn't only the sex. How much easier everything would be if her reaction to him were purely physical, if her emotions were not entwined the way dye bonded to cloth—once combined, the color impossible to leach free.

She did her best not to dwell upon her feelings, shying away from truly exploring such dangerous and forbidden territory. Perhaps it was wrong of her to desire a man who held such power over her. Yet the price he asked of her seemed small now in proportion to the myriad pleasures he lavished upon her in return.

Who, she wondered, *is really using whom?*

Her nerve endings hummed as she saw him open the jar of honey and dip in his index finger. Her breath caught on a ragged gasp when he reached out and began stroking it over and around her lips. They throbbed, sticky and warm from his touch.

Then he kissed her.

And licked her, literally eating from her mouth.

With a boldness she hadn't known she possessed, she repeated his gesture, dipping her finger into the honey pot to paint his mouth and cheeks with a pair of long, sticky stripes. On a moan, he closed his eyes as she bathed him with her tongue, savoring the sweet taste of the honey and the even sweeter taste of his skin.

Harsh yearning beat in her blood, in her body, urging her closer as she enfolded him in her arms. Suddenly he was touching her everywhere, slanting his mouth over hers in a series of a raw, penetrating kisses.

Breathless, he broke away. "I nearly forgot."

"Hmm?" she murmured, half-lost in a sensual daze.

"Dessert."

"You want dessert? Now?"

"Yes," he told her, dropping another kiss on her swollen lips. "And you will, too, once you see what it is."

Curious despite her desire, she released him and let him scoot over to lift a small cloth-covered dish from the hamper. Setting down the china container, he pulled away the material to reveal a mass of plump, red, newly picked berries.

"Raspberries," she sighed in amazement. "Where on earth did you get raspberries at this time of the year? It's impossible."

He gave a careless shrug. "Not impossible. One just has to know the right people. You did say they are your favorite fruit."

Another item in the long list of favorites she had shared during their many trysts.

She nodded. "But I never dreamed. Oh, my, and don't they look delectable."

Her fingers itched to take one.

"Go on," he encouraged. "That's what I brought them for. To eat and enjoy."

She grinned, giddy as a child at Christmas. Reaching for a berry, she popped one into her mouth and savored the exquisite combination of tart and sweet. In heaven, she plucked up two more berries, stuffed them into her mouth and chewed. Next, she took a small handful, laughing guiltily as she filled her mouth, a drop of juice sliding from one corner to trickle down her chin.

"Allow me," he offered. Eyes deep and green as a dense forest, he leaned over and caught the drop on the end of his tongue.

She shuddered with pleasure.

"Tasty," he murmured.

She swallowed. "What a wonderful treat! Thank you, Rafe."

"You're welcome." He stroked a finger along the

curve of her cheek. "I like hearing you say my name. It's not often you call me Rafe."

She sobered. "Do I not? I certainly think of you that way."

He lifted a strand of her hair and toyed with it. "And *do* you think of me, Julianna? When we're not here—together, that is?"

She knew she ought to say no. Ought to lie and tell him he left her thoughts the instant she left him. That when she returned home to her life, he vanished like a figment, distant and forgotten.

But she could not.

"Yes," she whispered. "I think of you. I think of you often."

An intense yet enigmatic look came into his eyes before he glanced away.

"Good," he said, shifting upward to sit on his knees. "Roll over onto your back."

She raised an eyebrow. "Why?"

"Never mind why, just do it." He smiled, slow and full of wicked promise. "You know you won't be sorry."

No, she thought on a belly-clenching quiver, *I am certain I shall feel many things, but none of them will have anything to do with regret.*

Letting her hesitation float away, she stretched out exactly as he wished. While she waited and watched him, anticipation ran through her with the speed of a live current.

Picking up the honey jar again, he dipped his fingers inside, using two this time.

"More honey?" she questioned, relaxing.

"Yes. More honey."

But it wasn't her lips upon which he lavished the sweet, his hand moving in a direction she had not expected him to go.

Her breath caught on a sharp inhale as he spread

honey over her nipples, taking his time to massage the sticky substance into her flesh. Only when he was satisfied did he stop, careful to leave a large, glistening bead shivering on each hardened tip, her flesh peaked and aching from his touch.

From there he moved lower, choosing an unused spoon as an aid. Dipping the handle into the pot, he extended the utensil and began drawing a thin, sticky circle around her belly button. Ladling out more of the honey, he dribbled the nectar into her navel, her stomach muscles contracting involuntarily as he filled the small indentation to the rim.

Her body in torment, she restlessly shifted her legs.

"*Shh,* don't move," he cautioned. "Lie utterly still and wait until I'm done."

Swallowing, she nodded and did her best to obey, her heart threatening to hammer out of her chest as she waited to see where he would next put the golden sweet.

Her answer came quickly, and astonishingly, as he painted another circle even lower, at the base of her belly, and then again on the last bit of skin that lay just above her triangle of dark, tight curls. She quaked as he spread the honey, biting the corner of her lip against the hot, wet need burning inside her. She felt her eyes widen when he reached for the dish of fruit, speechless as he positioned a single ripe, red raspberry on top of each sticky circle.

When he was finished, he gazed at her in obvious satisfaction, like a chef admiring a culinary masterpiece.

"And now, my dear," he said on a dark rumble, "it's my turn to enjoy dessert."

Cupping one of her trembling breasts in his hand, he opened his mouth and began to feast, using teeth and lips and tongue to utmost effect. Helpless, she let him suckle, every pull and lap and nip driving her mad.

Palming her other breast, he held her and feasted again, his fingers and mouth sensitizing her flesh to a virtual flashpoint.

She whimpered when he finally abandoned her breasts and started kissing his way toward her belly. Moments later, she cried out in delight, moaning as he dipped his tongue into her belly button. Working the spot with gentle concentration, he teased and licked, drinking from her the way a hummingbird might sip nectar from a flower.

Her mind spun, faint red pinpricks of light dancing beneath her closed lids as he bathed her in a kind of erotic magic. Twisting beneath him, she reached out blindly, needing to touch him as he dappled her flesh with kisses and caresses, tiny bites and soothing, loving strokes.

Sliding lower, he trailed his hand across her quivering thighs, pausing to pluck away the final raspberry with his tongue. Grinning, he raised his head and swallowed the fruit with an appreciative growl. Then he dove back, leisurely bathing away the last of the honey.

Wet heat pooled between her legs, her pulse thumping at a frantic pace. She expected him to conclude his delicious torture, rise, and take her lips in a fiery kiss before taking her body as she yearned for him to do.

Instead, he knelt between her legs, spread her open, and buried his face where she'd never imagined she would ever be kissed.

Dizzy with shock and mortification, she reached down to push him away. But even as she touched his head to make him stop, her will weakened, her shaking fingers threading into his hair to instinctively pull him closer. She moaned, the pleasure all but overwhelming.

Licking her the way he would some delectably irresistible confection, he pressed on, ardent and relentless.

A wail rose into her throat, singing uncontrollably from her lips.

More, she thought, her eyes rolling back in her head. *Oh yes, please, more.*

Divine. Exquisite.

Those were the only words to describe what he was doing to her, her body held in the grip of a rapture so intense its power melted away every inhibition she'd ever had. Writhing beneath his embrace, she gave herself free rein.

Her peak hit in a great, dark wave that slammed through her with stunning violence. Drifting, she rode the storm to shore. But she had no time to recover as Rafe began to drive her upward again, firing her passion to a ragged, feverish, frenzied pitch. Helpless, she could do nothing but give herself to him, letting him take her wherever he willed.

Slipping his hands beneath her bottom, he spread her legs wider and continued his sensual onslaught. She came twice more, the last time with a scream as he gave her a small bite that hurtled her brutally over the edge.

Panting, she fought to recover her breath, and her faculties, bliss still riding her hard.

With her inner muscles still pinging and twitching, Rafe sat up on his haunches, draped her legs over his thighs, and thrust himself into her as far as he would go.

His facial muscles tightened as he pumped inside her, his jaw drawn, teeth clenched, his hunger for her naked and exposed. And though she wouldn't have thought herself capable of climaxing again, his movements soon had her craving another. She matched him stroke for stroke, claiming her release only moments before he shuddered out his own.

Visibly exhausted, he crawled up next to her and collapsed, pulling her close inside his arms to share a kiss. Entwined and satiated, they drifted together into sleep.

*   *   *

A long while later, Rafe leaned up on an elbow and reached for the pocket watch he'd left on the nightstand. Opening the gold cover, he checked the time.

Behind him in the bed, Julianna roused, stretching catlike against the sheets. "Do I need to get up?"

He snapped the watch closed and set it aside. "No, we have time yet. Go back to sleep if you're tired."

He knew he'd worn her out with their vigorous love-making. He'd worn himself out as well, as wild to have her this afternoon as he'd been their very first time. Yet with Julianna he could never seem to get enough—of her or their coupling, every encounter with her better than the last.

Frankly, by now he'd expected that first intense, all-consuming flash of lust that comes with any new affair to have passed, or at least waned a little. But the more often he took Julianna, the more he wanted her, coming to depend upon these assignations in a way that might have made a more prudent man reconsider the arrangement altogether. After all, it wouldn't do for him to develop feelings for her.

Not that I am in any real danger of doing so, he assured himself.

He liked Julianna; that was all. She was a kind, passionate woman with a warm sense of humor and a keen mind. In her company, he never felt bored, enjoying the conversations they shared to an extent that surprised him. With his previous mistresses, he'd never found much intellectual common ground, their out-of-bed talk generally centering around her jewelry preferences, her most recent shopping excursion, and which play she most wanted to see next.

When he and Julianna were not making love, they liked to talk of art and music, literature, sailing—a sport both of them loved but in which they rarely had the opportunity to engage—and the occasional smattering of philosophy. When she wanted, the woman could argue with the conviction of Sophocles and the wisdom of Aristotle. He felt certain she would have impressed both ancients had they somehow defied the laws of time and physics and been able to meet her.

In all ways, Julianna was a lady, without a single avaricious bone in her body. She would no more think to ask him for a trinket than she would stand on a street corner with a tambourine and sing, her palm outstretched. Such cupidity was simply not in her nature.

Nor did she indiscriminately take lovers, as many women of her class did. As only the second man ever to share her bed, he was proof of that. Although now that he had taught her the pleasures of the flesh, perhaps she would seek out a new lover once the two of them parted ways.

With their bargain concluded, would she long for intimacy? Would she seek out a lord, perhaps, a good man of good lineage who could openly share her company instead of sneaking around in furtive secrecy the way he and Julianna were forced to do?

His hand curled into a fist next to his hip, a knot forming in his stomach at the thought of Julianna making love with another man.

"Where did you get this scar?" she asked, her lilting voice speaking from very near his ear.

Shaking off his thoughts, he relaxed and turned, his skin tingling beneath her fingertips as she trailed them over a spot high on the back of his neck.

With his hair trimmed only two days prior, the mark was more visible than usual. Most of the time, he scarcely remembered the crisscrossed patch, having long since ceased to give it more than an occasional passing consideration.

Faces close, he met her gaze, reading the lazy curiosity

in her melting chocolate eyes. "Oh, that. *That* is the result of a rather nasty collision between my head and an iron crowbar."

Her eyes rounded. "Mercy sakes, do you mean to say someone hit you?"

He nodded. "It hurt like a fury of harpies set to dance on my skull." Even now, he could still recall the blast of pain and the way blood had dribbled down his neck to seep into his frayed cambric collar.

"That's awful. Were you very badly injured?" She stroked a hand over his bare shoulder in an obvious need to comfort.

One corner of his mouth turned up in a wry smile. "Not as badly as the fellow who did it. When I failed to pass out from the cosh to my head, he soon found himself on the punishing end of my fists. Believe me, it was the last time that scoundrel ever tried to steal from a fellow dockman."

Her brows rose. "*Fellow* dockman? What do you mean?"

His jaw tightened, wondering what she would think if he told her the truth. That once, years ago, he'd fallen on hard times, very hard times, and been compelled to take any job he could find, no matter how rough or low. That there'd been months of his life when he'd gone hungry, so broke he'd been grateful to earn enough to buy a single potato or a day-old loaf of bread.

Yet no matter how desperate he'd been, he'd never stooped to begging. Nor had he ever once felt ashamed of having to work with his hands, his labor simple but honest.

"I mean," he said, "that I once worked on the London docks."

"You owned a shipping company."

"I do now. I hold investment majorities in several firms, including a couple of shipping concerns. However, during the time period we are discussing, I was a dockman, and not even a permanent employee at that, working day to day for nearly a year."

"But I don't understand. You are educated and literate and, quite frankly, richer than most of the dukes I know. How could you have ever been a common day laborer?"

Sliding back against the sheets, he plumped his pillow and folded an arm beneath his head. "I said I was a laborer; I never said anything about being common."

Moving to lie beside him, she leaned her forearms on his chest. "No, you are markedly *uncommon*. So tell me, how did a man like you end up working on the London docks?"

"It's a long story." One he had no intention of sharing with her. "Suffice it to say, my brush with poverty was not of my own choosing, nor was it pleasant. But the experience was quite enlightening. I learned more about survival and cunning and good business practices than any gentleman's education could ever have taught me. In a few short years, I acquired all the skills I needed in order to prosper, quite beyond my wildest dreams it would seem, since I am indeed richer than most dukes."

In obvious contemplation of his statement, Julianna traced a meandering circle across his chest. When her fingertips rubbed across one flat male nipple, he reached out and caught her hand. "You'd best stop that unless you're ready for another tumble."

Her gaze flashed upward. "I will be. In a little while. First I want to know more."

"More what?"

"About you. Where did you grow up? In London?"

"No. West Riding."

At least that's where he'd passed his early years, then later his summers and vacations when he wasn't away studying at Harrow at his father's insistence. Nevertheless, West Riding and his mother had always meant home, a retreat from a world that never let him forget his illegitimate origins.

He supposed, in retrospect, he should thank his father for sending him off to school instead of letting him be educated by a tutor, as his mother had wanted. Those brutal years away had taught him to be tough, taught him to survive by using his fists, and more important, his wits. Another set of skills that had served him well, quite literally saving his life during those early days in London.

"So far north," she murmured. "What made you move to the city? Or were you the restless sort and longed to leave the country behind?"

Reaching out, he caught a strand of her silky, dark hair and stroked it between his fingers. "It wasn't a matter of *wishing* to leave. I still love that land, the windswept hills and dales, the sturdy houses and long, stone walls. But ultimately there was nothing for me there. I'm no farmer content to raise sheep, and I hadn't the choice of living the life of an aristocrat."

"So you left home intending to be a financier?"

His lips curved in a pensive smile. "Actually, I intended to study the law."

"Really?"

"You needn't look so astonished. Is it so impossible to believe I once thought to become a barrister?"

"No," she admitted after a considered pause. "You have the intelligence for it, and the clever tongue. But somehow the idea of you in robes and a powdered wig, standing obeisant before a judge—well, it just doesn't suit you."

"I suppose I'm not really the obeisant type, am I?" he conceded.

She shook her head. "You're far too independent for such constraints. The law would have suffocated the life out of you."

He hid his surprise at her perceptive answer, knowing she was exactly right. He loved what he did. Loved the art and, yes, the risk, of wielding vast sums of money, positioning and leveraging his funds in order to out-smart the market and turn investment into profit.

After earning his first million pounds, his business had turned into a game—a very real, very serious game, but a form of entertainment nonetheless. There was nothing quite like seeking out the next miracle deal to get his blood flowing, to raise his excitement level to an almost fevered pitch.

Except for Julianna, of course. She got his blood flowing and his excitement level near peak with no more than a glimpse or a whisper.

Cupping her cheek, he drew her forward for a kiss, fresh arousal turning him aching and hard.

She kissed him back, then leaned away. "So why didn't you pursue it?"

"Pursue what?"

"The law?"

On a sigh, he decided he could indulge her curiosity for a little while longer.

"The simplest reason of all, my dear. I ran out of money."

"But was there no one to help you? What of your parents?"

"My parents were dead." As for the cause, he didn't want to dwell on that, especially not in his mother's case.

"And you were left with nothing?"

A muscle twitched near his eye. "No, nothing."

When he saw her expression, he moved to correct her misassumptions. "But don't think harshly of them, since it was not a situation of their own making. My father's estate was heavily entailed."

"He was a peer?"

"A lord, yes."

"What of your mother?"

"A clergyman's daughter who had a bad fall from grace, though in my estimation she was never anything but an angel."

A dozen questions shone in Julianna's expressive gaze. "And afterward you went to work on the docks?"

"Since I lacked the proper references, there was little other employment to be had."

She caught the edge of her lower lip between her teeth, obviously longing to press for further details.

Before she could, he circumvented her. "To make a long story brief, I worked as a laborer until it came to the notice of the foreman that I was making extra money reading and writing letters for the men. Once the boss found out that I could not only read and write but do ciphers as quickly as any man he'd ever seen, he took me on as a clerk. From that moment forward, I set myself to learning everything about business that I could."

"What about the company? Is it still in business?"

"Yes, though it's under new management now. I bought out my old employer's shares years ago, then sold them again for a tidy profit." Reaching out, he enfolded her in his arms. "Now I have a question for you."

"For me?"

"Hmm. I want to know whether you would rather be on top"—holding her close, he rolled her over—"or on the bottom?"

Growling playfully, he crushed his lips to hers. Laughing, she kissed him back while she gave her response.

Chapter Ten

JULIANNA PLUCKED A copy of Lord Byron's *English Bards and Scotch Reviewers* off the bookstore shelf and leafed through a few pages before pausing to read a stanza or two. She smiled and thought of Rafe, wondering what he would make of her selection. Likely he would scold and tease her, then take her in his arms and befuddle her with kisses until she had forgotten all about Byron and his poems.

Returning the volume to its shelf, she moved on. After all, she mused, Baron Byron could be a bit too controversial at times for her tastes. Robert Burns might suit her mood better, mellow and dreamy. Thinking of Rafe seemed to make her that way no matter how she fought against it.

Selecting another book at random, she forced her mind to the task at hand.

Pernicious Vices and the Road to Eternal Damnation: A Treatise on Sin in Our Times by Reverend Goodsbody. Julianna jumped slightly in astonishment as she read the title. *Pernicious vices, indeed!* Hastily she shoved the book back onto the shelf and walked onward.

Where is soothing Robbie Burns when a lady needs him? she wondered. And why, after seeing the reverend's hellfire-and-brimstone tome, had she started thinking again of Rafe?

Was what she and Rafe did together a sin?

No, she assured herself, *despite the admittedly unusual origin of our liaison, it is not wrong. Whatever anyone else might think, I have no need for guilt.*

Do I?

Refusing to dwell further on the subject, Julianna strolled out into the main room, glad to find Maris safely occupied in front of a long wall of books.

As they did upon occasion, she and Maris had stopped today at Hatchard's book shop to peruse the latest inventory. Cousin Henrietta was absent, having decided instead to visit a friend in Kew. Laughingly, Henrietta had remarked that she'd been so busy of late she scarcely had time to think, what with all of Maris's callers and social engagements. An afternoon of quiet, she had said, was exactly what her old bones required.

Cousin Henrietta was right about Maris, Julianna thought. Her sister was in great demand these days with a regular circle of friends and several attentive gentleman callers, including Viscount Middleton. Lord Doughton, a young man with a love of art and music, frequently stopped by the Allerton House drawing room, as did the handsome, stalwart Major Waring.

Julianna wasn't certain, but she wondered if her sister might be developing a special affection for the major. Maris's eyes seemed to sparkle more brightly and she laughed more often whenever he paid a call. And she was always pleased to accompany him on a stroll or for a ride in the park, returning in a sunny, exuberant humor.

But her young sister was having far too much fun flitting from ball to rout to soiree to worry about anything more serious than what to wear on her next outing and which gentleman she would choose to escort her into supper at midnight. Let her be busy, Julianna decided, and enjoy the rest of the Season.

Yet Maris wasn't the only one with an abundance of obligations these days. Julianna's own schedule was inordinately full—though for completely different reasons than her sister's. Juggled into the mix of parties and teas and balls were her afternoon assignations with Rafe.

With the Season in full swing, meeting him had become more complicated, and she'd taken to having to switch the occasional day. She'd even met him a couple of times in the morning, getting only a few hours' sleep before sneaking over to the house in Queens Square while most of her acquaintance were still fast asleep.

Luckily, Rafe didn't seem to mind the adjustments, or if he did, he refrained from saying. She knew he understood that her time was no longer completely her own. She had a duty to her sister and needed, more than ever before, to be careful when and where she went, and by whom she was seen.

Neither of them ever discussed their initial bargain, nor mentioned the debt still owed to him. Four months from now and her obligation would be met. She would be free to walk away and never see Rafe again, if that is what she wished.

But do I wish it? she pondered.

Footfalls intruded upon her thoughts. Glancing up, she watched the Earl of Summersfield stride toward her, his patrician face alive with pleasure.

"Lady Hawthorne, well met! I did not expect to find you here today. What a happy occasion this is!"

Executing an elegant bow, he straightened, displaying a set of straight, white teeth in an irresistibly cheerful smile.

She smiled back, finding it quite impossible to do otherwise. Not that she had any reason to resist—Lord Summersfield was a very amiable man. He was also a very persistent man, never seeming to fatigue in his quest to convince her to accept his hand in marriage. He had asked so often, and she had refused so frequently, that the ritual had by now taken on the semblance of a game.

She worried about hurting him, but he assured her each and every time she refused his suit that he was in no way wounded, content to be her friend until she decided to let him become more.

Secretly, she suspected he was not truly serious, wondering whether he would be more alarmed than thrilled if she ever did decide to accept. But therein lay the perfection of the game, since she assumed both of them knew he was safe from any real risk. As much as she liked and respected him, she felt no more than mild affection for him and would never consent to be his wife.

"My lord, always a pleasure, though I would have expected to find you out-of-doors on such a gloriously sunny day as this."

"When radiance such as yours can be discovered inside, why would any man venture out?"

"Please, my lord, what have I told you about such unnecessary flattery? You must stop this instant." She softened her command with a smile.

He laid a gloved hand across the breast of his finely tailored Clarence blue coat. "But that would be censorship of the grossest kind, and to that I must object. When beauty appears in my path, I must stop and sing out its praises. And you, dear lady, are very definitely worth the effort of a song. An entire chorus, in fact, you are looking so markedly lovely. I assure you, my feelings cannot be contained."

She chuckled and shook her head. "Enough. You will make my head swell to three times its normal size and then explode. Only think of the dreadful mess that would make."

The earl barked out a laugh, drawing the attention of several nearby patrons.

"See, you are getting us in trouble," Julianna said.

"Would that I could convince you to let me get you into more. Care to run away? Gretna is only a coach ride distant."

"What I care to do is choose a book. Now tell me, my lord, which authors have you come here seeking?"

At the shout of a man's laugh, Rafe turned his head, the book he held suddenly forgotten in his hand.

Julianna.

There she stood, only a few feet across the room, luminous in a day dress the color of young green apples. Lush and dark as sable, her beautiful hair was neatly tucked beneath a very fetching hat, a pert white feather bobbing as she nodded her head.

His heart gave a single hard thump, blood quickening the way it always did when the two of them were in the same room. So powerfully attuned to her, Rafe didn't know how he could have walked into the shop and not known instantly that she was there as well.

Smiling merrily, she laughed at some remark made by the man at her side.

Who is he?

Rafe clenched his teeth as he watched. Obviously the man was known to her, their demeanor speaking of long acquaintance and an intimacy he did not like.

No, he didn't like it one jot.

Barely watching what he did, Rafe shoved the book he held back onto a shelf. He'd taken two steps forward before he stopped, remembering where he was and why he could not approach her. Here in this bookstore, he and Julianna were not supposed to have met. In public, he had promised her they would always behave as strangers. Fists tight at his sides, he swallowed a growl and fought the need to stride forward and whisk her away.

The other man wanted her, of that he had no doubt. Did Julianna realize it? Did she know she was the object of her companion's desire, all the leather-bound tomes surrounding them nothing more than a convenient distraction?

The aristocrat extended his arm. A muscle twitched near Rafe's eye as Julianna laughed again and set her hand on his sleeve.

Rafe must have made a noise, he realized, because just then she turned and looked straight at him. Her pretty eyes widened, an expression of surprise and, if he was not mistaken, undisguised pleasure warming her velvety gaze. In the next instant, though, the expression faded, replaced by clear concern.

Raising a single eyebrow, he gave her a nearly imperceptible nod.

From across the room, Julianna stared, awareness sizzling inside her.

Rafe is here, she thought. *Oh my!*

Her lips curved slightly at the corners before she dipped her chin and let her lashes fan downward to shield her gaze.

If they had been alone, she knew Rafe would have wrapped her in his arms and crushed his lips to hers in some remote corner of the store. With her heart threatening to jump out of her chest, she inhaled and strove for calm, astonishment rushing like quicksilver through her veins.

Looking as powerfully resplendent as any lord, Rafe stood tall and impressive in a form-fitting bottle-green coat that displayed the breadth of his shoulders and enhanced the color of his eyes, his irises gleaming like shards of pale green glass. Impeccable cravat, tan waistcoat, buff trousers, and polished Hessians completed his

attire, together with a fine beaver top hat perched at a
rakish angle atop his head.

She shivered, feeling his presence as strongly as if he
were touching her. Perversely she was also aware, almost painfully so, of the social distance between them.
More than the illicit nature of their affair, the yawning
chasm of class distinctions rose between them, solid and
unscalable as a brick wall.

Had she been alone in the shop, she might have ignored prudence and crossed the room to greet him.
Heaven knows she longed to do so. But with Lord Summersfield looking on, as well as her sister nearby, Julianna felt compelled to maintain her place and her
silence. To all outward appearances, Rafe must remain a
stranger in her eyes. Catching her lower lip between her
teeth, she forced herself not to gaze in his direction
again.

"I may be mistaken, but I think that is Rafe Pendragon," Summersfield remarked in a low voice. "They
say he's giving Rothschild real competition in financial
circles these days, and is very nearly as wealthy. I understand Pendragon recently brokered some loans on behalf of Wellington in order to help finance the continued
push into Spain."

Really? she thought. She knew Rafe was a rich, influential financier, but she hadn't realized he was assisting
in the war effort. Her heart warmed at the information,
even as her guilt increased for her decision to ignore
him.

"Curious," Summersfield continued, "but he seems to
be looking at you."

Her gaze flashed upward again, dismayed to see that
the earl was correct.

What does Rafe think he's doing?

"Well, if he is looking my way, I cannot imagine
why," she dissembled.

Summersfield smiled. "I assume the man is smitten with your beauty."

"Yes, well, he should know better than to stare."

Dear God, Rafe, quit staring!

"Good day, my lord," Maris chimed, approaching quite unexpectedly from behind them. "Whatever is it the two of you are discussing so hush-hush? Ooh, who is that? He is quite the handsomest man I have ever seen."

Summersfield quirked a brow in mock offense. "I may be in error, but was I just insulted?"

Maris giggled, quite at her ease. "Oh, never fear Lord Summersfield. You are quite handsome too."

He exchanged a smile. "My thanks, Lady Maris, for the reassurance to my poor deflated pride."

"Oh my, is he coming over?" Maris exclaimed. "Do you think he means to speak to us?"

In dread, Julianna watched Rafe saunter forward, his gaze sweeping over her.

Surely, he doesn't mean to speak to me.

She knew she wasn't a good enough actress to pretend to make his acquaintance, scandalous as such a meeting would be. One word, a single look from her, and everyone would realize the truth. The whole world would know he was her lover.

Panic threatened as he walked closer, each step bringing him dangerously near. Then, only a few feet distant, he made an abrupt left turn and disappeared into the stacks as if books had been his intent all along.

She exhaled, only then realizing she had been holding her breath, leaving her mildly dizzy.

"What a shame," Maris declared. "I was hoping for an introduction to find out if he sounds as wonderful as he looks."

Better, Julianna thought silently, *he sounds even better.*

Instead, she steadied herself, then turned to her sister. "An introduction would have been quite improper, as well you know. Now if you are done perusing the shelves, I believe it is time we departed."

Maris shot her a puzzled look. "I am sorry, Jules. I did not mean to upset you. You look a bit pale. Are you all right?"

Summersfield nodded. "Yes, Lady Hawthorne, you do appear peaked of a sudden."

"A touch of the headache, that is all. It shall pass away soon enough, I expect."

"I know just the cure." Summersfield smiled and rubbed her gloved hand where it still rested on his arm. "Cakes and ices at Gunter's. Why don't you ladies allow me to escort you for a restorative repast? We'll order a large pot of tea as well. That and a sweet will put everything to rights again."

Julianna wanted to refuse. After her encounter, or rather her near encounter with Rafe, she would much rather have retreated to the safety of home. But she could tell by the expression on her sister's face that Maris was excited by the thought of the outing.

"Yes, thank you, my lord. That would be most delightful."

Pausing at the counter first to pay for Maris's selection, they soon made their way outside. It was only as she was climbing into Summersfield's carriage that she saw Rafe again, coming out of the shop.

Their gazes collided, a glower on his saturnine face. Turning on his heel, he strode away.

Oh dear, she thought.

Moments later the carriage moved forward.

The following day when she walked into the house on Queens Square, she didn't quite know what to expect. Relief washed through her when Rafe greeted her as usual, then pressed a pair of hot, hungry kisses upon her lips.

Smiling and relaxed, she hurried up the staircase, taking the lead and leaving Rafe to follow. Inside the sitting room, she crossed to the sofa and sank down upon the cushions, while Rafe went to the sideboard to prepare drinks.

The tranquil scents of beeswax and lemon drifted on the air, the house as clean and tidy as ever. She'd asked him once about the servants, since she and Rafe were always utterly alone on their days together. A trio of charwomen came to dust and wash and polish on the days he and Julianna did not meet, he'd told her. And Hannibal—the huge man who had scared her so thoroughly that long-ago day when she'd boldly gone knocking on Rafe's door in Bloomsbury—stopped by once a week to stock a few provisions in the larder and leave various other necessities.

Glassware clinked, followed by the liquid sound of wine being poured, its color as bold and red as blood. Lifting a glass in each hand, he strode toward her.

She was just taking her first swallow when Rafe spoke.

"Who is he, then?"

Her gaze flew upward, the wine going down a second too fast. She coughed once. "What?"

His eyebrows furrowed. "In Hatchard's bookstore. Who was the man?"

"Oh. Lord Summersfield, do you mean?"

"If that's his name, then yes. How well do you know him?"

Although his words were issued in their usual silky, deep-throated cadence, she thought she detected an underlying edge, just the faintest note of challenge.

She stifled a sigh. *So,* she mused, *we are going to talk*

about yesterday after all. And here she'd been hoping they could put the whole encounter behind them.

"I know him well enough, I suppose," she said. "His lordship and I are acquaintances."

Rafe quaffed some wine. "The pair of you looked a great deal friendlier than mere acquaintances. Do you always laugh like that with virtual strangers?"

"I didn't say he was a stranger. We are friends of a sort and acknowledge each other when in company."

"What else do the two of you do together? *In company,* of course."

"We dance and converse and have been known to share the occasional midnight supper. Does that satisfy your curiosity?"

He sank down beside her and negligently stretched an arm along the top of the sofa. His new position made him seem larger somehow, more intimidating, like a big, sleek cat who'd found an interesting bit of prey with which to entertain himself.

Reaching out, he slid a pin from her coiffure, then a second, letting a long tress of hair tumble free. With a leisurely touch, he twined the loose strand around the tip of one finger. "He wants you, you know."

A quiver rippled over her skin at Rafe's touch. "Well, he can't have me, as I have told him on more than one occasion."

A sharp emerald glint flashed in Rafe's eyes. "So he's open about his desire for you, is he?"

"Yes, assuming it's really genuine. Summersfield loves women and he enjoys flirting at every possible opportunity. I am but one of many."

Rafe's fingers stilled for a second before he continued stroking her hair, absently twining and untwining the strand. "Believe me, his interest is real."

"Maybe so, since he asks me to marry him nearly every time we meet."

"He's proposed, has he?" Pausing, he raised his glass and took a slow drink before setting the beverage aside. "And what have you answered, pray tell?"

"I've answered no, of course," she said, aware once again of the hard, barely perceptible edge to his tone. "There's no need for you to be jealous."

His dark brows lowered into a scowl. "I am *not* jealous."

Noting the expression on his face, she decided to hold her tongue. Nonetheless, he must have read the retort in her eyes.

Leaning forward, he cupped her cheek in his hand. "I just don't like sharing what is mine, that's all."

Her pulse fluttered as he captured her mouth, his kiss possessive and demanding, rich and warm with the flavor of the wine, and of Rafe himself. Closing her eyes, she kissed him back.

After a minute, he drew his lips across her cheek to her ear. "Nor do I like being forced to stand idly by and watch another man seduce you under my very nose." Gently, he nipped her earlobe, then kissed her cheek.

"Hmm? Oh yes, the bookstore. He was not seducing me." She caught his look and rephrased her reply. "I wasn't *letting* him seduce me. And I'm sorry about yesterday, but I couldn't acknowledge you, not openly. You understand, do you not?"

She waited, nerves tensing suddenly.

"I understand how it would have looked, even if I can't say I enjoy kowtowing to Society's rigid dictates and blatant inequities."

"If not for Maris . . ."

"*Shh*, don't worry. I saw your sister and know you couldn't introduce me to her. It's all right."

In silent consolation, she laid a hand against his clean-shaven cheek.

"The two of you share a marked resemblance," he observed.

"So we are often told. Maris thought you were very handsome, by the way."

His lips curved. "Is that so? You aren't trying to turn me sweet now, are you?"

Using the manicured edge of her fingernail, she skimmed it teasingly across his lower lip. "If I am, is it working?"

He laughed. "Very nearly. But first, I want to make my original point."

"About what?"

"You know what." Playfully, he nipped at her finger, then pulled away. "About this lord of yours."

"He's not *my* lord; I've already told you that."

"Good. Then you will have no difficulty severing ties with him."

Her eyebrows drew inward. "Severing ties . . . oh, I don't see how I can do that."

"Why not? Simply tell him you do not wish to see him anymore."

She released a half-exasperated breath. "I don't *see* him now, not the way you are implying. And it's not so easy. He and I travel in the same social circles. It would be extremely awkward if I attempted to ignore him. Cutting him is out of the question. Doing so would cause talk, when there is no need for talk."

His jaw firmed. "So you refuse to stop associating with him?"

"I refuse to be less than polite to him in a public setting, and he does not call at my townhouse, if that is your concern. Do you imagine there is more going on? Surely you do not think I am sharing my bed with him as well as you?"

"Of course not, I know you would never do such a thing."

"Then do not be concerned."

He really is jealous, she realized. How extraordinary that a man like Rafe Pendragon could work himself into such a passion—over her. Was his outburst a case of simple male possessiveness, a dog with a toy he didn't want any other dog to have, even if he might eventually grow tired of it? Or could Rafe's reaction mean more? And did she want it to?

"But what of these marriage proposals of his?" he challenged.

"What of them? I do not want to wed Russell Summersfield, nor any man for that matter."

"How can you be so sure? What if you change your mind? One day, you might be tempted to say yes."

She shook her head. "I've been married, remember? I do not want to say yes, not ever again."

Compassion eased some of the fierceness from his expression. "Not all men are like your husband. A few of us aren't selfish brutes."

"I know. But in my widowhood, I have come to appreciate my independence, you might say."

"What of companionship? Do you never fear you might be lonely?"

"I would rather risk an occasional bout of loneliness than shackle myself inside another unhappy union. I am content to remain just as I am."

Am I, though? she wondered. If it was Rafe who loved her, would her answer be the same? If Rafe fell to his knees and proposed marriage and asked her to share his life, would she so easily refuse him as she had every other man who had asked?

But thinking such thoughts was ridiculous. Even if they wished it, there could never be anything permanent between her and Rafe.

Nor do I want there to be. Do I?

Enjoy the moment, she told herself. *Be glad for these days and want nothing more.*

With that in mind, she smiled and leaned forward to wrap her arms around his neck. Slowly, she joined their mouths for a long, languorous kiss. At length, she drew back a few inches. "If I promise to in no way encourage Lord Summersfield, will that satisfy you?"

"No flirting?"

"Not by so much as an eyelash."

"No laughing?"

She steadied her expression. "I will be as severe as a parish vicar."

"No more midnight suppers?"

"I will refuse to sup with him even at the risk of passing out from hunger."

His lips curved into a grudging smile. "You need not go that far. Eat a large dinner first before you arrive at the ball."

She laughed.

"Very well," he agreed. "But I expect strict compliance."

"My word of honor."

Her tresses fell in a wave across her shoulders as he plucked the rest of the pins free.

She returned the gesture by tunneling her fingers into his hair to pull his head closer. "Now, will you do something for me?"

He raised a brow. "What?"

"Quit talking and take me to bed."

Crushing her mouth to his, he kissed her with an unrestrained need that left her breathless. Moments later, he stood and swept her off her feet.

"Your wish, my lady, is my command."

Chapter Eleven

RAFE SURVEYED THE shadowed interior of the gaming hell, tobacco smoke and the pungent scent of burning tallow curling together to create an almost suffocating blue haze. Commoners and gentlemen alike were packed into the house, their voices loud, their actions boisterous as they crowded close around the various baize-covered tables.

In the main salon, players tried their luck at hazard and faro. Alternating choruses of cheers and groans rang out as bets were placed, die cast, cards drawn, and money won and lost. For those who preferred skilled card playing at a quieter, more relaxed pace, games of piquet, whist, and vingt-et-un were arranged in several of the side rooms. It was into one of these chambers that Rafe wandered, having failed to locate his quarry in the more populated areas.

A waiter approached and offered him a beverage. Rafe refused with a shake of his head, wanting to keep his wits sharp. After all, he wasn't here for his own entertainment, and he had no intention of remaining a minute longer than his mission required.

As he knew, gambling was an extremely popular pastime, one that was nearly like a religion for some. But he'd seen too many lives destroyed by an addiction to betting and the heady rush it could bring. He was no prude, no puritan. A man, in his estimation, possessed free will and had every right to destroy his life if he so desired. But did that same man have the right to drag his family down with him?

Rafe had come here to convince one particular young man that he did not.

Spying the imprudent whelp at last, he strode forward, stopping a few feet to the right of his quarry's shoulder. Silently, he watched the play.

Vingt-et-un was a game of odds and calculations, requiring a keen mind and a knack for knowing which cards had already been played, and which were likely to turn up. The dealer had fourteen showing, a queen and a four. The young man had a five and a two displayed, with a third card turned facedown.

Rafe watched Allerton flip the edge of his concealed card up, then down. A long moment of quiet followed as he clearly tried to decide his best move.

"Stay," the young earl declared.

"Dealer takes a card. Four of spades. Dealer has eighteen."

In a practiced gesture, the dealer reached out and turned over Allerton's cards. "Player has seventeen. The house takes the hand."

Coins and cards were swept clear of the table.

"You ought to have taken the hit, Allerton," Rafe advised as he stepped closer. "Odds were fair you'd have come out ahead."

Julianna's brother turned his head, dark eyes flashing at the interruption. They lost some of their fierceness when he saw who had spoken to him. "Pendragon. How do you do?"

Rafe dipped his chin in reply.

"Must say I'm surprised to see you," Harry said. "Didn't know you frequented places like this."

"I don't. But I understand you've been making a habit of it again lately. Are you here alone?"

The young lord shook his head. "No, I came with a pair of my cronies, but they preferred the hazard tables, so I left them to it. Fool's game, hazard. All luck with no need for skill."

"I've found that most games of chance cater to the fool in a man." Before Harry had a chance to think about the statement and ruffle up, Rafe continued. "Why don't we adjourn to a more private location. There are matters that require discussing."

Harry's lips thinned as if he was going to object; then he shrugged. Pocketing the few coins left to him on the gaming table, he rose from his chair.

They found a small, unoccupied table in a corner of the room and settled in across from each other. Harry signaled for a drink—a brandy, which was promptly brought across to him.

Rafe waited while the younger man took a swallow, an action he assumed stemmed more from an attempt to look mature than a genuine desire for the liquor itself. He wondered if that might be the main allure of this rather seedy gambling establishment as well—the need many young men had for showing off and trying to prove their worth to their friends.

"So what's this all about?" Harry asked, swirling the alcohol in his glass as if he were completely at his ease. "I thought our business was finished. The loan is paid off in full. My sister told me she had taken care of the matter some weeks ago."

"Yes, indeed, Lady Hawthorne came to me and settled your accounts. But that matter is not why I've sought you out tonight."

A puzzled frown settled on the young lord's brow. "What, then?"

"It is your current behavior about which I've come to

talk, my lord. I've heard several unsettling reports concerning your renewed interest in the gaming tables. Sadly, I understand you are in a fair way to becoming as deeply sunk in the hole as you were when you came to me to bail you out."

"It's not so bad as that," Harry protested. "I'm only a few hundred down." He caught Rafe's gaze, then glanced away. "A couple thousand, then, but all fellows face a few ups and downs; it's part of living the life of a gentleman-about-town. My luck will turn in a thrice. It's bound to do so."

"And if it does not? Luck is a fickle mistress. And if I am not mistaken, it was your presumption that your luck would turn for the good that led you into dun territory in the first place."

Allerton spun his glass in a stationary circle. "And so, you what? Want to give me another loan?"

"Quite the contrary. I want you to stop gambling."

Harry stared for a long incredulous moment, then barked out a laugh. "You what!"

"I believe you heard me just fine, my lord. Your behavior is foolhardy in the extreme. If you do not bring yourself under control, you will soon find yourself at ruin's doorstep with no hope of recovery."

Harry drained the last of the spirits and set his glass down with a mild thump. "I shall be fine."

Rafe leaned forward, his words low. "Were it up to me, I'd let you stew in your own rash misfortunes, but you have others who depend upon you, tenants and servants who count on you for their livelihoods and welfare. Even if you care nothing for them or for your legacy, you must surely have a care for your family, your sisters. Lady Hawthorne did not beggar herself on your behalf only to see you fall back into your old ways. For reasons I cannot fathom, she loves you and trusts you. Do not abuse her faith. Your sister is a good woman and she deserves better than to be disgraced by your reckless excesses."

A long moment followed as Harry gawped at him. Red washed into the younger man's face like an incoming tide, his shoulders turning stiff with ill-concealed defensiveness.

Rafe watched as Allerton tried to gather his composure.

"You may be my elder, sir," the earl finally sputtered, "but I do not believe my private affairs are any of your concern. Nor do I think it proper for you to discuss my sister in such a familiar manner. I d-demand that you apologize at once."

A few gamesters turned their heads at his outburst, then glanced just as quickly away when they encountered Rafe's steely glare.

"Be quiet, boy," Rafe ordered with soft menace. "We don't need the whole room listening."

Harry scowled, but lowered his voice. "You do not have the right to lecture me. You aren't my father, after all."

"No, but if I were, I would have seen to it you were reined in long ago. Since your father is dead and you have no proper male to guide you, I have reluctantly decided to act in that capacity. From this moment forth, you are banned from the gaming tables. You are also banned from participating in any other form of betting, including cockfights, bear baiting, horse racing, boxing, and the like."

Harry crossed his arms over his chest. "And if I refuse?"

"There will consequences."

"What sort of consequences? You've a reputation, Pendragon, but I don't see how even you can stop me. Nor do I see why you should care to do so."

If not for your sister, I wouldn't lift so much as my pinky finger to aid you, Rafe wanted to say. But Julianna

would be devastated if she found out what her scapegrace brother was doing. If Harry could be made to see
reason before any lasting harm was done, Julianna need
never know anything of her brother's brief return to disgrace.

"I have my reasons," Rafe stated. "As far as stopping
you, I will have no need. I shall simply put out the word
that you are no longer to be welcomed in establishments
such as this one and that your credit is not good. You
will also discover that no one will loan you the funds to
cover your vowels should you be foolish enough to seek
out their services."

Harry's hands trembled. "I can't believe you control
all the moneymen in the city."

"Quite correct, I do not. I've only influence with the
reputable ones. Should you venture into the clutches of
the cent-per-centers, I believe you'll find those chaps far
less understanding than I when you come to them begging for more time."

"You weren't understanding. You would have taken
my estate."

"Yes, but they'll take your life. Oh, they'll start small,
a broken thumb, maybe a crushed hand or foot . . ."

Harry gulped, his Adam's apple bobbing like a fishing
buoy.

". . . And if they don't get results after the hand and
perhaps a shattered kneecap, they might decide to beat
you severely enough to rupture an organ or two. If you
don't succumb from that, there are other ways to prove
their point."

"W-What point? What d'you mean?"

Rafe leaned casually back in his chair. "I mean that
men, even those of good family, occasionally wash up in
the Thames. Or come spilling out of a wharf barrel,
where their dismembered bodies have rotted into something that rather resembles soap." He pinned Harry

with a gimlet eye. "I wouldn't ever want to hear that had happened to you."

A green cast to his complexion, Harry looked as if his brandy might decide to make a reappearance.

"So tell me, my lord," Rafe continued. "Can I count upon you to take my suggestion and stop gambling?"

Eyes wide, Harry nodded.

"I didn't hear that, my lord. What did you say?"

"Y-Yes. I said yes. I'll stop tonight. I promise."

"A wise choice." Rafe glanced up as a pair of young lords stumbled into the room, both of them obviously well into their cups. "I would also advise a change of friends. Find a few fellows who don't depend upon a bottle or a deck of cards to be entertained."

Harry frowned, then gave another nod.

Rafe pushed back his chair. "I'm glad we had this chance to talk. Now, I really must be leaving. It grows late and I've business to attend to early in the morning. Good night, my lord." Rafe climbed to feet.

"Good night," Harry mumbled, eyes cast downward.

Rafe began to walk past, then paused and bent toward Harry's ear. "Oh, one other thing, in case you find yourself having second thoughts about your decision to reform. My associate is just across the way."

Rafe watched Harry glance past his shoulder, saw his eyes widen to an alarming size as he located Hannibal waiting near the salon doors, big arms crossed like hams over his massive chest.

"I've shared the particulars of your little situation with him and he says he'd like to have a brief word as well. I'll just leave the two of you to get better acquainted."

"Acquainted?" Harry squeaked.

"Hmm. He thought you might enjoy a tour of the wharf district. It's quite illuminating at night."

Rafe nodded and turned on his heel.

Hannibal would scare the stuffing out of the boy, but he'd make sure he came to no harm. Rafe just hoped this lesson would finally do the trick.

Julianna stepped into the Allerton House drawing room and crossed to take a seat in a chair near the fireplace. Alone, she found she didn't mind the solitude, knowing it would be of a brief duration. Once Maris and Henrietta finished changing into their evening attire they would join her for a quiet family dinner. Afterward, the three of them planned to attend the Farisbrooks' rout, which from all reports promised to be a mad crush with more than three hundred of London's finest in attendance.

Lord Middleton had agreed to act as their escort.

Julianna didn't know if she approved, nor could she say she was pleased by the amount of time the viscount seemed to be spending with her sister of late. She had rather imagined Major Waring to be Maris's favorite but apparently no longer. Once a frequent visitor at Allerton House, the major had stopped calling some two weeks before.

Had he and Maris had some sort of falling-out? Julianna had tried to discuss his absence once, but Maris hadn't wished to talk, so Julianna had said nothing more. In the meanwhile, Maris and the viscount had grown closer, her sister accompanying him riding and driving and dancing.

Now, he was bringing his carriage around to take them to tonight's ball. Handsome and charming, Middleton seemed an excellent catch—Society certainly thought so. Perhaps she was worrying for nothing, Julianna decided. Maybe the viscount's affection for her sister was genuine.

Julianna sighed. *If only Rafe were escorting us this evening.*

She paused at the thought, a little startled to realize how much she wished it could be true. Her lips curved, imagining how magnificent he would look in a black tailcoat and satin evening breeches. And how divine she would feel strolling into the ball on his arm.

But what a pea goose she was to even consider such fancies. Rafe would never be welcomed at such an exclusive Ton party. The Lady Farisbrooks of the world did not invite men like him to their homes, regardless of his wealth or the excellence of his manners.

At least she would see him tomorrow. Lately, though, she found herself wishing they could meet more often than their agreement prescribed. A few stolen hours no longer seemed enough.

A footfall sounded at the entrance. Turning her head, she expected to see her sister or cousin. Instead, Harry strode into the room, handsome in formal black evening clothing, his crisp white neckcloth tied in a perfect mathematical.

Julianna raised a brow, surprised to see him so elegantly attired and wearing breeches, no less. Harry rarely wore breeches.

"Well, don't you look dapper tonight!" she said, offering him a smile. "Going to a ball?"

Subtly tugging at one of his sleeve cuffs, he crossed the room and took up a position near the fireplace mantel. "Yes, the Farisbrooks'. I thought I might accompany you ladies this evening, if you have no objection."

Now she really was surprised. "Well, of course not. We'd all be delighted to have you come with us."

He gave a nod. "Thought I'd stay in for dinner as well. Been too long since I remained at home for an evening meal."

Good gracious, what is amiss? she wondered. As a young man still earning a few additional coats of Town bronze, Harry never wished to stay in. Being with his friends seemed to always come first these days.

"Yes, you are right," she said, "it has been a while since the four of us sat down to a family meal. Since before the start of the Season, I suspect."

He nodded again, then glanced down, scuffing the bottom of his evening shoe against the marble fireplace surround.

"Is anything wrong, Harry?"

His head jerked up, his brown gaze colliding briefly with hers before turning away. "No, not a thing."

A long moment passed. Releasing an audible breath, he crossed the space and lowered himself into a chair next to hers. Raising his chin, he met her gaze. "Jules, I owe you an apology."

"Why, whatever for?"

"Neglecting my duty, for one. I should be more considerate of you and Maris, be more available to escort you places and see to it you are both well looked after."

She gave him a puzzled smile. "We are fine; you need not worry. Cousin Henrietta and I are old hands at maneuvering in Society, and we find proper male escorts when needed. For instance, Lord Middleton is arriving later with his carriage to take us to the rout."

Harry's eyebrows drew together. "Well, his aid won't be required in the future. I'll take you where you need to go—you have only to say the word."

"That's very good of you, but what of your friends?"

He shrugged. "I've been spending too much time of late with my friends. A certain distance from a few of them won't hurt. Besides, before long the Season will be over and all of us on our way back to the country. I have duties at Davies Manor that need my attention as well. I'll be glad to be back in Kent. It's peaceful in the country, easy and uncomplicated."

My goodness, Julianna thought, *from whence has this*

epiphany come? Well, whatever or whomever had inspired it, she could only be grateful. Seeing Harry willingly assume the responsibilities of his title settled her mind and reassured her heart. He had a great deal of growing up still to do, and would surely make a few mistakes along the way, but for the first time she truly believed he was on the right path.

"And I'm done with gambling," he continued, looking very earnest, though a bit uncomfortable, as if his cravat were tied too tight. "I . . . um . . . I believe I've finally come to my senses on that score. A man can come to a bad end if he isn't careful. A very bad end."

His skin blanched faintly for a moment before his natural color returned. Reaching out, he took one of her hands and gave it a lingering squeeze before letting go. "And I wanted to thank you again for bailing me out as you did. I do not deserve having a sister as wonderful as you. I don't want you to worry ever again. I swear I won't give you cause for disappointment."

"I know, dear. And you're welcome. For everything."

Yes, everything, she thought.

Harry would be appalled if he knew the truth, that even now she was paying his debt by being Rafe Pendragon's mistress. Yet even if she could turn back the clock, she knew she would not. How could she want such a thing when it would mean she would never have met Rafe? Never lain in his arms? Never shared secret moments and intimate thoughts with him, divulging things about herself that no one else knew?

And he did know her, more deeply than her closest friends. Her heart clenched at the realization.

Seconds later, female voices sounded in the hallway.

Harry gave her a smile before standing to greet Maris and Henrietta. Glad of the interruption, Julianna stood as well.

*   *   *

Warm May sunshine streamed through the bedroom windows, flowing in a gilded wash across the carpet, and over the coverlet that had been kicked into a heap at the foot of the bed. Draped in nothing but a sheet, Julianna snuggled against Rafe, her head pillowed comfortably on his shoulder.

". . . So it turns out the salt had been switched for the sugar," she said, continuing the story she was telling. "Never in my life have I witnessed a more miserable group of diners. And poor Lady Milton, I thought she was going to have some kind of seizure after she and her one hundred guests, including the Prince, all tried her prized dessert of cream puffs."

"Salt puffs, don't you mean?" Rafe chuckled. "That must have been a sight."

"Oh, it was. Every fork at the table went down in unison and every single person reached for their wineglass at the same time. What a flurry of coughing and choking there was! For a moment, the dining room sounded like a plague house full of consumptives."

He laughed again. "I wish I'd been there."

"I wish you had been too. It's not fair I'm the only one of us to still have that miserable taste in my mouth. *Bah!*"

Grinning, he angled his head and captured her lips. Eyelids fluttering closed, she let him take her deep.

"Mmm, I think you taste wonderful," he murmured against her mouth. "Sweet as candy."

She smiled and slid her fingers into his hair. "And you taste like sin. I believe, sir, that I will have some more."

Barking out another laugh, he wrapped her close and did his best to comply.

A long while later, Julianna stretched, her body lazy and relaxed and very satisfied. "Oh lord, I don't ever want to get up."

"Then don't." He stroked a languid palm over her bare back. "Stay exactly where you are."

How lovely that would be, she thought. *How glorious if both of us could just laze the rest of the day away, and the rest of the night as well.*

Instead, she heaved out a sigh. "I can't. I promised Maris I would accompany her to the theater tonight. Sheridan's *The School for Scandal* is playing at Drury Lane."

"Good play." He shifted against the sheets and bent to dust his lips across her forehead. "Perhaps I'll buy a seat in the gallery and entertain myself by gazing up at you in your box."

"Don't you dare," she admonished, giving him a light tap. "I'd spend the entire evening trying not to look back at you and get caught in the process. Please do not tempt me."

He gave a playful growl. "I like tempting you. It's so much fun."

She buried her fingers in his thick, wavy hair and welcomed his kiss, ripe and warm and delicious. When she knew she'd reached her safety limit, Julianna broke away on a regretful groan. "Oh, we must stop, or I never will have the strength to leave. What time is it, do you imagine?"

"I have no idea. Shall I check my watch?"

"No, I'll do it. Stay there." Pressing a palm against his sturdy chest, she levered herself into a sitting position and crawled out of the bed.

Not bothering to cover her nakedness, she crossed the room and reached to retrieve his waistcoat from the back of a chair, where he'd discarded it earlier. Drawing the timepiece from its silken hiding place, she nestled the smooth golden case inside her palm, finding it faintly warm to the touch. Clicking open the cover, she checked the position of the hands.

Three seventeen. Not as late as she'd thought, but definitely time to begin dressing and start for home.

She was about to snap the watch cover closed when her gaze fell upon the inscription engraved on its inner face. Curious, she read the words.

> *Time passes, but love lasts forever.*
> *Yours Eternally, Pamela.*

Her heart gave a sharp, hard squeeze.

Flicking a quick glance toward Rafe to make sure he wasn't watching, she turned her back and read the words again.

Who is Pamela? she thought.

Clearly not a sister or his mother. He'd never mentioned having siblings, and she knew for a fact that his mother was dead. Besides, a watch wasn't the kind of gift a female relation would normally give a man. And the inscription—well, it was far too personal, too intimate to be mistaken for anything other than a love token.

A buzzing pulse raced down her spine. *Does he have another lover? Worse yet, does he have a wife?*

Her stomach clenched, a faint rush of bile rising into her throat. Dear God, in all the time they'd been together, she had never thought to ask him if he was married!

The idea was so terrible, so devastating, she swung around to confront him, anxiety sharpening her words. "Who is Pamela?"

"Hmm?" He rolled his head and gazed sleepily at her from beneath hooded lids. "Did you find out the time?"

"Never mind about the time." She strode forward, the watch extended in her hand. "Who is Pamela?"

Rafe stared for a long moment, his drowsiness vanishing in an instant as his gaze fell upon the timepiece she held. Sitting upright, he tossed back the sheet and stood, crossing to reach for his pantaloons. He said nothing as he dressed, needing the extra few moments to deal with his uncertain emotions.

"Well?" she repeated. "Are you going to tell me or not?"

Not, Rafe wanted to answer. *Plague take it,* he swore to himself, *what is wrong with me, letting Julianna look at my watch?* Usually, he was more vigilant about that sort of thing, since Pamela was the last person he wished to discuss with anyone, even Julianna.

Especially Julianna.

Cursing himself, he fastened the buttons on his falls. How could he have been so careless? Comfort, he supposed. He was comfortable with her, relaxed and at his ease in a way he was with no one else. Familiarity had made him sloppy and forgetful.

He yanked his shirt over his head. "She's no one, all right?"

Her pretty brows drew together. "Since when does *no one* go to the trouble of inscribing a love poem inside your pocket watch? Who is she, Rafe?" She paused, vulnerability shadowing her expression. "Is she your wife?"

Surprised, he glanced up. "Is that what you think?"

"I don't know what to think, especially given your reaction."

He stared at the watch in her hand—his blessing and his curse. He should have disposed of the piece long ago, he knew. Sold it to a jeweler. Had the case melted down and recast. Stood at the bank of the Thames one morning and tossed the whole damned thing into the river where it could sink into a cold, watery grave.

But he couldn't. The watch had been Pamela's gift to him. Destroying it would be like destroying her, defiling her memory and all she had meant to those who had loved her. Perhaps the timepiece and the words inside served as cruel reminders, but such was the penance he felt honor bound to bear.

He remembered the day she'd given him the watch, how her cornflower blue eyes had danced with nerves and happy anticipation, her pert blond curls bouncing around her rosy cheeks. She'd been so pretty and so young. Too bloody young, only two months into her seventeenth year.

Her father had been a watchmaker and she'd talked him into letting her have the piece, a fine new design with a sweep hand that could monitor the time down to the second. A pampered only daughter, Rafe knew she'd had her parents twisted around her little finger. But there hadn't been a mean bone in her body. A kinder, more generous spirit had never been born. Everyone loved her; the neighborhood men tipping their hats to her in admiring respect when she passed, the women smiling as they remarked what a darling, good-natured girl she was, what a blessing to her family.

She had known a bit about watchmaking, having spent time in her father's shop over the years. Wanting no one else but her and Rafe to read her words, she'd told him how she'd engraved the message herself. Her heart had outpaced her skill, though, her unsteady hand forming a slight wobble on the word *forever*. But to him, the minor flaw only made the piece more precious.

He'd loved it on sight, the way he'd loved her.

He met Julianna's dark, velvety gaze and realized he had to tell her something. She deserved that much, and probably more.

"You can put aside your affront. She is not my wife," he said.

Her shoulders lowered, tension draining visibly from her body. "Still, she is someone important to you."

"She *was* important." He shrugged into his waistcoat, fastening the golden buttons with impatient fingers.

"Pamela was an artisan's daughter from Cheapside, where I lived many years ago. We were engaged to be married."

"Engaged? What happened?"

"She died, that is what happened. Now, if you don't mind, I would prefer not to discuss the details. Hopefully I've managed to allay your fears."

"My fears, yes, but not my curiosity." She held out the watch, letting him lift it from her palm and return it to his waistcoat pocket. "Rafe, I am sorry."

"Do not be. She died many years ago. There is no need for pity."

She walked to him and laid her palms against his cheeks, her touch like warm satin against the faint roughness of his skin. "What of comfort, then?" she murmured. "Would you accept a measure of that?"

Drawing his head downward, she settled her lips against his own. Feather light, she kissed him. Softly, slowly, she wrapped him inside her embrace, one that was as gentle as a whisper, as tempting as the apple offered by Eve.

For a moment he tried to resist, but such attempts were purely senseless. Surrendering, he hauled her naked body close and plastered her against him as he ravished her mouth.

Accepting, she let him use her, let him focus upon her all the raw emotion boiling up inside him. Hunger raked him like a claw, demanding release, demanding the relief and oblivion he knew Julianna could provide.

Before he was able to sweep her up in his arms, though, and carry her back to the bed, her fingers went to work on his pantaloons. With an amazing deftness, she opened the front flap and slid her hand inside.

His belly muscles clenched as she wrapped her small, cool fingers around the hot length of his tumescence, his shaft hardening and thickening as if it truly did have a mind of its own. Stroking him, she made him moan, made his brain empty of everything but her and the exquisite sensation of her touch.

Playing with the sacs between his legs for long seconds, she explored their shape, their size, before gliding out along his throbbing erection. Reaching the tip, she rubbed it briefly, then flicked her fingernail ever so lightly across. He shook and nearly came, barely holding on to the last of his withering control.

Suddenly desperate, he urged her toward the bed, needing to plant himself between her thighs in the worst way. But she refused to lie down, coaxing him into a reclining position against the sheets. She often liked to be astride and he waited, expecting her to throw a leg over his hips and mount him, take him into her silky warmth from above.

But she surprised him again by kneeling at his side and taking him into her mouth. Eyes glazed, he raised his head to watch, noting the way her long, dark hair fanned over his thighs while her lips and tongue moved like wet silk upon him.

The sight and sensations brought him to the very brink of completion. Yet again, he somehow held back, wanting, needing to come inside her.

Roughly, he drew her up and over him, positioning her so he could plunge fully into her velvety depths. She cried out as he pumped inside her, leaning up to suckle her breasts, her nipples tight little nubs against his tongue. He bit her lightly and rotated her hips in a wild, circular grind, going deep, then deeper still. Gripping him like a fiery glove, her inner muscles clenched tight, spasming as she began to go over.

He thrust a few times more, fierce and penetrating. Then he was coming too, coming so furiously it felt as if his vitals were being shot straight from his body. Overwhelming and devastating, he knew he'd never experienced such magnificent pleasure, nor found such profound release.

Cradling her to him, he held her, both of them exhausted and supremely replete.

Gradually, awareness returned, along with a realization that the room was now bathed in a heavy twilight of shadows.

She sat up, their bodies still connected. "Blast it, I've missed tea."

He chuckled and skimmed a hand down one of her arms. "You were too busy feasting on other things."

She cuffed him on the shoulder. "Behave, sir, or I shall never make the mistake of doing so again. Now, help me dress and let's be quick. I've got to be going or I shall be missed."

"As you wish, my dear Julianna." He drew her close for one last kiss. "And thank you."

Surprise lit her eyes. "For what?"

"For making it better, sweeting. And for giving me exactly what I needed."

In answer, she smiled and bent down, making herself another five minutes late.

Chapter Twelve

COACH WHEELS HIT a rut, making the landau rock on its springs. Julianna caught her breath and reached for the inside strap, clutching the leather for a long moment until the ride became smooth once more.

Ensconced on the matching silk upholstered seat opposite, Maris held on as well, the disturbance briefly interrupting her observation of the verdant English countryside passing by outside the windows.

Catching each other's gaze, Julianna and Maris exchanged smiles, then Julianna returned to her book. She wished Maris had brought her own novel to keep her mind occupied during the journey to this weekend's country house party. But Maris had said that reading in the coach gave her a headache and she preferred a few hours of boredom to the possibility of pain.

Maris sighed and fell to staring out the window once more.

Turning a page, Julianna tried to concentrate on the printed words, but she'd scarcely finished a single sentence before her thoughts drifted away, settling—as they far too frequently did—upon Rafe.

What is he doing? she wondered. *How is he doing? Has he returned to London yet?*

She nearly expelled a sigh of her own, recalling the long, disquieting two weeks that had passed since he'd been called away on unexpected business at his estate in West Riding. She hadn't even realized he owned an estate, and certainly not in the north country where he had grown up. But apparently he did, as she'd discovered the last time they met.

"I am sorry, my dear," Rafe had said, drawing her down next to him on the sofa in the first floor drawing room soon after her arrival, "but I cannot stay today. An emergency has cropped up at one of my estates that I see no reasonable way of avoiding."

"What has happened?" she asked, turning toward him in concern.

"There was a powerful thunderstorm apparently, with a great deal of wind and lightning. A few of the cottagers' homes lost roofs and barns, leaving people in need of temporary shelter. As for my own house, a tree, of all things, blew in through one of the library windows and caused a fair amount of damage. My steward wrote to tell me about the trouble and asked me to come as soon as may be."

"Certainly you must go. How long will you be away?"

"I don't know for certain. A week, perhaps two." Raising her hand, he brushed his lips across her knuckles. "I would have left this morning, but I couldn't go away, not without seeing you first."

Meeting his river-green gaze, she smiled softly. "I'm glad you did not."

His mouth had crushed hers then, joining their lips and tongues in a passionate kiss that she knew would have to last them both until his return.

A short while later, he'd driven her toward Mayfair, then stopped to procure a hackney cab that would take her to Bond Street, where she could walk to her own waiting carriage.

And then he'd been gone.

Since that day, she had not heard from him—they had

agreed that exchanging letters was unwise. Now, though, she wished she'd urged him to write, each day more interminable than the last.

Does he miss me? she wondered. For as foolish and ridiculous as it might be, she had felt his absence with a fierceness that alarmed her, and with a strength she knew was dangerous to feel.

So when Viscount Middleton invited her and Maris to join him and a dozen others for a house party at Middlebrooke Park, his estate in Essex, she had agreed. Henrietta had been included in the invitation, but had bowed out because of her dislike of road travel. And Harry, who was to have accompanied them, stayed home, confined to his bed with a dreadful spring cold.

Before leaving the city this morning, though, Julianna had broken her agreement not to contact Rafe, penning him a note to let him know that she was away and would return at first week. Assuming, of course, he reached London again before she did.

The landau's wheels rumbled over a bit of rough earth, the perfume of wild lilacs wafting briefly into the coach's interior. Sweet and luxurious, the scent, together with another one of Maris's poignant sighs, proved powerful enough to disturb Julianna's musings.

Glancing across at her sister, Julianna couldn't help but notice the downward turn to Maris's lips, nor miss the sheen of melancholy haunting her usually lively gaze. For a girl traveling into the countryside for a weekend of relaxed entertainment, she did not look happy or excited.

Julianna gave up all pretense of reading and closed her book, setting it next to her on her seat. "Is everything all right?"

Maris glanced over, sadness visible in her gaze. Her expression cleared seconds later and she smiled. Or rather she forced herself to smile, Julianna realized.

"Of course things are fine," Maris declared in a cheery voice. "Why would they not be?"

Now I know something is amiss, Julianna thought. Maris was generally cheerful, but never *that* cheerful.

"Are you sure?" Julianna pressed.

Maris stared for a long moment, emotions racing like a dark river in her eyes. Still, she remained silent.

"Are you concerned about the weekend perhaps?" Julianna queried. "I know you may have certain expectations, which are only natural given the circumstances. Viscount Middleton has been extremely attentive over the past few weeks, making a point of singling you out. And now this invitation to his home. Any woman would be wondering if an offer of marriage is imminent."

Maris frowned and stared down at her clasped hands. "Yes, that is what Cousin Henrietta said. She is sure he will come up to scratch during our visit."

"Are you worried she is wrong and that he may not?"

When her sister said nothing again, a new speculation dawned.

"Or are you worried that he will?"

Up flashed Maris's eyes, a hint of guilt in their depths. "He is very charming and handsome. I should be ecstatic at the prospect of being his bride."

"But you are not?"

"I do not know," she said, pleating her skirt with her fingers. "I like him, but he is so much older and I . . . I just am not sure."

Julianna had told herself she wouldn't meddle, but how could she not when Maris was so clearly in need of guidance? "If you are not sure, then you are not ready. If he asks, you must refuse."

Maris's lips trembled. "But how can I? Especially after agreeing to come here for the weekend. No matter how I may feel, I have given him every reason to think I would be agreeable to his suit. If he asks for my hand, I will have to say yes."

"You most certainly do not have to say yes. Haven't I told you that you are to marry for love and nothing less?"

"Yes, but what if I never find the right man? I must marry sometime, so why should it not be the viscount?"

"Because he is not the one for you, and more than anything you deserve to be happy."

As Julianna watched her sister, a fresh suspicion emerged.

"Unless you have already found that special someone. Major Waring, perhaps?"

Heat leapt into her sister's cheeks, turning her fair skin the color of a ripe strawberry. "The major is not in the least special. Besides, he has stopped calling and has no particular regard for me."

Lips drooping again, Maris lowered her eyelashes, her misery plain.

"I always thought he seemed to have a great deal of regard for you," Julianna observed in a gentle voice. "Why did he stop coming around? Did you quarrel?"

"No, I . . . well, in a way, I suppose. Oh, Jules, I thought he truly liked me . . . even loved me perhaps, especially after he kissed me at the Chiltons' garden party—" Maris clapped a hand over her mouth, eyes rounding like saucers. "Oh, gracious, I shouldn't have told you that, should I?"

How innocent she can still be, and how glad I am of it, Julianna mused. "So long as it was no more than a kiss, there is little harm done."

Maris shook her head. "It was only the one and nothing else. He stopped calling on me soon afterward and I . . . haven't known what to think. I can only conclude that he took me in disgust. Maybe he simply did not like me . . . that way."

"Hmm, or perhaps he liked you that way too much."

"What do you mean?"

"He is a younger son and has few prospects. Perhaps his feelings for you were genuine, but he did not believe he could approach Harry to ask for your hand. To continue to court you under those circumstances would not have been honorable, and so he withdrew."

"If that is true, then he ought to have told me. How utterly foolish to walk away when my dowry is more than sufficient to support both of us."

"Perhaps he worried of being called a fortune hunter. Men have their pride, you know, some more than others. And I think the major may have lost more than just his arm over there on that bloody field in Spain."

"Mayhap. Poor William has suffered much, it's true. But that is no reason to have made me miserable as well, assuming you are correct about him. I still believe he simply does not care. If he loved me, he would never have let me go, no matter the state of his finances."

Weaving her slender fingers together in her lap, Maris hung her head. "No, what was between him and me is dead and I must move on. I had convinced myself to do so with Viscount Middleton. But now that the moment is nearly at hand . . ." Her head lifted and she met Julianna's gaze. "Oh, Jules, what am I to do?"

"What I told you to do ten minutes ago. Do not accept."

"But he will be hurt. Or worse, angry."

Maris might be right, Julianna decided. For all the viscount's outwardly affable behavior, she wasn't sure he would take a rejection, especially one given in his own home, with equanimity. And at the very least, the party atmosphere would be in ruins, forcing her and Maris to race back to London with gossip trailing not far behind.

Hmm, she considered, *what to do?*

"Do not refuse him outright. Simply tell him you need a few days to consider the matter. Explain that you are young and still in your first Season and do not wish to hurry into matrimony without making sure you are ready. He may well be annoyed by your hesitation, but he'll accept it nonetheless. Can you do it, Maris? Can you put him off?"

"Yes," Maris agreed. "I believe I can manage."

"And maybe you will find you have worried for naught and he will not propose. Either way, there are a dozen other invited guests, ladies and gentlemen both, so relax and make merry. When we return to London, we will tell Harry you do not wish to accept Middleton and he can do the refusing."

Relief swept across Maris's face. "Would Harry do that, do you think?"

"I am sure he will. He is your brother and guardian, after all. It is no less than Papa would do if he were still alive."

A long moment passed, the sound of the coach wheels rumbling over the Essex county roads.

Maris smiled, her expression genuine this time. "Thank you, Jules. I feel much relieved."

Bending forward, Julianna reached across and covered one of her sister's hands. "You may always come to me, you know. So next time, do not keep everything bottled up inside. Talk to me, please!"

"I will," Maris said with a laugh. "I promise."

"And now if you would all follow me, we will visit the portrait gallery."

With that statement ringing on the air, Mrs. Thompson, Viscount Middleton's plump, apple-cheeked housekeeper, led the way out of the ornate gold ballroom and down a long second-floor hallway.

Julianna exchanged smiles with Maris, then strolled

forward with the rest of their small group, mostly ladies, who had decided to stay and tour Middlebrooke Park. The other house-party guests had left with Lord Middleton shortly after breakfast to survey the extensive grounds of the estate by way of horseback.

Plainly, the viscount had been hoping Maris would make herself one of his party—he'd even picked out a gentle mare for her to ride. But she had declined, pleading weariness after her long journey the day before. Smiling politely, Maris had told him she would see him during nuncheon at midday. Having no choice but to accede to her wishes, he had bowed and moved away.

Although Maris appeared lighthearted and smiling, as if she were having a delightful visit, Julianna knew her sister's nerves were on edge. Busy with his duties as host, Middleton had made no attempt to speak privately with Maris—so far. Yet with nearly two days of the visit ahead, plenty of time remained for him to make Maris an offer should that be his wish.

" . . . The portraits you see displayed here date back to the reign of Her Majesty, Queen Elizabeth," Mrs. Thompson explained as their group walked into the long portrait gallery, shoes rapping softly against the polished oak floorboards.

"For his brave and loyal service to the crown," the housekeeper continued, "Her Majesty bestowed this land and the title upon the first Viscount Middleton, Lord Gregory St. George. As I mentioned previously, Lord Gregory is responsible for building the central portion of Middlebrooke Park. Here is his portrait, and alongside it the likenesses of his wife and their three sons. The entire St. George family is represented in this hall, forty-two paintings in total."

As they moved slowly along the gallery, Julianna watched history unfold before her eyes, generation by generation, as fashion and hairstyles changed in intriguing, and sometimes amusing, ways. Van Dykes and ruffled collars gave way to towering pompadours, panniered skirts, frock coats, and beribboned high heels—shoes even the men wore—before finally evolving into the more modern styles of the past few decades.

The housekeeper drew the group to a halt. "And this is my master's father, the late David St. George. What a kind man he was, and generous to a fault. I remember him quite fondly from my youth, for he used to give all of us children peppermint sticks whenever he'd return from one of his many trips away."

Several people chuckled at the enthusiasm in Mrs. Thompson's voice for her childhood remembrance. Julianna smiled and gazed upward at the painting.

Her heart leapt in a crazy beat, blood thundering suddenly in her ears as she stared into the face of her lover.

Dark hair. Cool river-green eyes. Strong, square chin and cheeks with long, enchantingly male dimples.

Rafe's cheeks.

Rafe's eyes.

Rafe's face!

The room whirled strangely around her, blood rushing through her veins with the speed of a raging river, while saliva dried uncomfortably against her tongue.

Barely aware, she gave a strangled whimper.

Maris turned, her look curious. "Jules, is anything the matter?"

"Fine. I'm fine," she squeaked, doing her best to ignore the buzzing in her brain.

In confused disbelief, she gazed at the painting again, stunned to her toes by the unmistakable resemblance between the man in the portrait and Rafe Pendragon.

The gentleman in the painting wore an old-fashioned, elegantly embroidered knee-length coat and lace-cuffed shirt. Silk knee breeches, stockings, and wide-buckle shoes completed his ensemble, his long, unpowdered raven hair pulled back and tied with a black silk ribbon.

Looking at him was like looking at Rafe had he been born decades earlier.

Yet as she peered closer, she could make out a few subtle differences. A slightly narrower shape of the mouth. A thicker, less refined sweep of the brows. And an unmistakable gleam of aristocratic arrogance that had never shone in Rafe's brilliant gaze.

How can it be? she wondered. How can Rafe Pendragon—financier—and Lord David St. George— nobleman—be virtual mirror images of each other?

Only one way that I can think of, Julianna realized.

The group broke up to explore the gallery. Encouraging Maris to wander through the room on her own, Julianna waited until the housekeeper stood alone. Catching the woman's eyes, she strolled forward.

"Excuse me," Julianna said in a quiet voice. "Do I understand correctly that this is a portrait of Lord Middleton's father?"

Mrs. Thompson nodded, her pudgy hands clasped at her waist. "Yes, indeed. 'Twas painted a few years after Lord David came into the title, when Lord Burton was still a tiny lad."

Rafe must belong to this family, she thought. A cousin, she rationalized, shying away from any other conclusion.

"And Lord David," Julianna encouraged. "Did he have any brothers or sisters, by chance?"

"No, he was an only child."

"What about other children, then?" She hesitated, then blurted out what was on her mind. "Did Lord David have any other sons?"

A peculiar, faintly alarmed expression crossed over the housekeeper's face, then vanished just as quickly as it appeared. "No, my lady. Only Lord Burton and his sisters, Miss Phyllis and Miss Vanessa. Now, I think we should be moving along. The hour grows late, and there is so much more to be seen."

She strode away, beckoning everyone to gather into a group again. Heels clicking, the older woman led the way from the room.

Julianna lagged behind, turning her head to catch another glimpse of the portrait. Her heart thumped again as she stared, confronted by the all-too-familiar features of her lover.

And yet not her lover, not Rafe Pendragon, but another man.

David St. George, *his father*.

The rest of the weekend passed by in a strange, slow haze. Julianna could think of little else but the portrait and all of its startling implications.

If it was true and Rafe was the illegitimate son of David St. George, that meant Viscount Middleton was his brother.

Half brother, she amended.

How extraordinary.

She'd realized Rafe's father was a nobleman, but she had never thought she might actually be acquainted with his family. Certainly, Rafe had never given her a clue about the connection, or so much as hinted he had siblings, even half siblings.

Although why would he have, she reasoned, given that the topic of Viscount Middleton had never come up between them? Nor had she ever asked him directly if he had brothers or sisters. Foolish of her not to have thought about the possibility. When Rafe had told her he was his mother's only child, she should not have assumed that situation applied to his father as well.

If the late Viscount Middleton was indeed Rafe's father. But he must be, she thought. What other reason could explain the marked resemblance between the two men?

Questions fluttered around inside her mind like little moths circling a flame, so many she could scarcely contain them all. Tossing and turning, she barely slept that night, wondering when she might next see Rafe and what she would say to him.

On Sunday, her thoughts were pulled in a different direction entirely when Middleton proposed to Maris.

As she and Maris had discussed, her sister did not refuse the viscount outright but instead begged his indulgence by asking him for a few more days to consider her answer. Once they were back in London, where there would be no interested observers to overhear, Maris would kindly but firmly tell him she could not agree to be his wife.

As she later related to Julianna, Maris had been surprised how well the viscount had handled her request for delay, outwardly affable despite any feelings of disappointment or frustration he may have been suffering. And his pleasantness continued the remainder of the day and into the evening as he resumed his duties as host, treating Maris with as much gracious attention as ever.

After a delicious dinner, whose highlight was roast squab with brandied currant sauce and an utterly decadent cheese soufflé, all the guests repaired to the music room.

The beautiful, but unfortunately penniless, Miss Dalrymple stood up to sing, accompanied on the pianoforte by an eager gentleman. While the lilting music filled the room, Julianna let her mind and her gaze wander around the room.

Everyone was watching the performance, she noticed. Everyone, that is, but herself and Viscount Middleton.

Clearly believing himself to be unobserved, he stared at Maris, an expression in his gaze that Julianna had never before seen. Unmistakable temper shone from his eyes, together with a petulant glint that reminded Julianna of a spoiled child who'd been denied a favorite toy.

Her fingers trembled faintly against the handle of her teacup, rattling the china in its saucer. Leaning forward, she set the cup onto the safety of a nearby side table. When she glanced upward again, her gaze collided with Middleton's.

She nearly gasped as he smiled, nothing but genial pleasure showing in his bright blue eyes. It was as though his earlier expression had never existed. But she knew she had no more imagined his look of rage than she had imagined Rafe's resemblance to the painting hanging in the Middlebrooke gallery.

Both were very real, and very disconcerting.

Focusing her gaze upon Miss Dalrymple, she pretended to listen.

Thank heaven Maris and I are returning to London tomorrow, she thought. *I only hope Rafe has returned. We have much to discuss, including whatever he knows about his brother.*

It's good to be back in Town, Rafe thought as he crossed his study and dropped down into his large desk chair, the leather squeaking faintly as he settled his weight. Loosening his cravat, he reached up to unfasten the top two buttons on his waistcoat while he flipped through the stack of correspondence that had collected during his absence.

At least the crisis at his estate was resolved, repairs under way on all of his tenants' cottages and outbuildings. As for his own home, the storm debris and dirt had been cleared from the library and wooden boards nailed over the broken windows while new glass panes were shipped north for installation.

The most tragic loss had been to his book collection—nearly a hundred volumes damaged, almost fifty of those so waterlogged they'd been deemed unsalvageable and tossed onto the rubbish heap. He would have to make a visit to Hatchard's bookstore to see about replacing them. He only hoped he could.

But first, there were far more important and pleasurable visits to make, he mused with a smile, his body tightening at the idea of having Julianna back in his arms. How wonderful it would be to feel her lips on his, to know once more the delight of her lush, pliant body moving eagerly beneath his own.

But it wasn't just the sex he'd missed; he'd missed Julianna as well. The gentle, vibrant, intelligent woman whose beauty and grace could bring a room to life by the simple act of her walking into it.

Since his departure, not a day had passed that he hadn't thought of her. So frequently, in fact, he probably ought to have been concerned by his need for her. And yet he had no regrets, savoring every moment in her company and glad for it.

What I wouldn't give, he thought, *to call for my mount and ride over to her townhouse right now.*

Of course he could not, since he'd given his word that they would meet only in secret, and only at the house in Queens Square.

With a sigh, he shifted in his chair. He'd waited the past two weeks, so he supposed he could wait another day or two, however much he chafed at the delay. Besides, she had probably accompanied her young sister to a ball tonight and was even now dancing with some arrogant lord. He could only hope that man and all of Julianna's other partners were homely with deadly dull personalities, and nothing to tempt her. Especially that Summersfield chap. She'd sworn to stay away from the

earl, and he trusted her. It was Summersfield he didn't
trust!

Shaking his head in derision at his own foolish jealousy, Rafe resumed his review of the mail. His hand
stilled when he came upon a small square of heavy,
cream-colored vellum, his name and direction inscribed
on the front in a delicate, flowing hand.

Obviously the missive had arrived by private messenger, since the letter bore a wax seal but no frank or
postage. He'd only seen her handwriting a few times,
but he knew the letter was from Julianna.

When had she sent this, and why? he wondered, particularly since she had insisted there be no correspondence between them until he wrote to her of his return.
Reaching for his silver letter opener, he split the seal.

> *Dear Rafe,*
>   *I know I said we should not write . . .*

Rafe smiled, then continued reading.

> *. . . but I did not wish you to return to Town and find
> me away. Maris and I have been invited to a house
> party for the weekend. There are to be a dozen other
> guests, not including ourselves and our host. My sister
> and I plan to make our return journey to London on
> Monday. Should you have made the trip home by then
> as well, pray send me word and we will meet. My di-
> rection, should you require it, will be Middlebrooke
> Park, Essex, the estate of Burton St. George, Viscount
> Middleton.*

For a long moment Rafe could not move, the name on
the page coming at him like an unexpected fistful of
knuckles. Acid pitched inside his stomach, leaving a sick
ache deep in his belly and a vile taste on his tongue.

Dear God, it couldn't be true, he thought. *Surely Julianna had not gone to that villain's lair, had not placed herself and her sister in the power of that corrupt and evil man?*

Yet how could Julianna have known not to make the visit? She would have no reason to be aware of Middleton's crimes. He should have warned her, Rafe realized. He should have known she and Middleton might meet, as part of the same social circle. But an invitation to the blackguard's estate—he'd never thought such a possibility would exist.

Scanning the note a second time, he read again that she was to return on Monday, which happened to be today.

Was she home already, tucked secure and innocent inside her townhouse? Or had something dreadful befallen her or her sister?

Of course with other guests attending the party, chances were unlikely that Middleton had done anything more dreadful than play host. Still, given what Rafe knew of the man, he would not underestimate him, since Middleton was capable of almost anything, no matter how immoral.

Rafe knew he wouldn't be able to rest until he assured himself that Julianna was safe. Tossing down the letter, he rose to his feet.

Chapter Thirteen

❧ ⁂ ☙

JULIANNA DREW A brush through her hair and thought of Rafe.

She'd had a long day, beginning with numerous hours confined inside the landau as the coach bowled across the English countryside toward home. Once in London, she and Maris drove straight to Allerton House, where they received hugs from Henrietta and a happy greeting from Harry, who had emerged from his sickbed, thankfully over the worst of his cold.

Despite being dressed in her traveling clothes, Julianna agreed to stay for dinner, too weary to go to her townhouse, change gowns, then come back. Over the meal, she and Maris regaled the others with news of the weekend's events, including the proposal from the viscount and Maris's decision not to accept him.

Of course, Julianna said nothing about the portrait of Rafe's father—or at least the man she now thought of as his father. Despite her near bursting curiosity, she knew she could tell no one. Her discovery of the painting was yet another secret she must keep to herself—until she saw Rafe again, that is.

After arriving at her townhouse, she went upstairs to her bedchamber. Once there, Daisy helped her bathe and change into her favorite pale lavender silk peignoir. See-

ing her maid's tiredness, she bid the girl a good night
and sent her off to seek her own rest.

Nearly midnight now, Julianna sat on the padded
stool in front of her dressing table and drew the boar
bristles of her brush through her long hair. The act was
engrained from childhood, a ritual she still found relaxing.

I wonder if Rafe has returned to Town? Her pulse
sped faster at the idea of seeing him again, her lips curving upward as her thoughts turned dreamy, her eyelids
half-closed.

A second later a quick, sharp rap sounded against the
glass of her bedroom window. Her eyes opened wide,
her brush flying from her hand and bouncing across the
floor when she saw a dark, shadowed face peering inside. Her heart slammed in her chest, a harsh scream
curling into her throat, ready to be unleashed at a volume sure to bring the rest of the sleeping house awake
and running to her aid.

But just as she was about to let loose, an instinctive
sense of recognition clicked inside her mind. Clasping a
hand over her mouth, she managed to turn the loud,
shrill scream into a well-muffled shout. Trembling, she
gripped the padded stool beneath her and stared at Rafe
as he eased her window upward.

"Sweet Lord, Rafe, you scared me nearly to death!"
she chided, laying a hand over her chest, her heart hammering at three times its normal speed.

He threw a leg over the sill and ducked his head down
to climb inside. "Sorry, sweeting, I didn't mean to frighten
you."

"Well, you did. How did you get up here, anyway?"

"Trellis." Standing fully inside the room, he picked a
small, mangled strand of ivy off one trouser leg and
tossed it outside. "You really ought to lock your windows, you know."

"Before tonight, I've never had cause," she retorted, still smarting from her scare.

Gathering her weakened legs beneath her, she rose and strode across to the window. Reaching out, she drew the peach-colored velvet curtains closed with a snap. "What if someone saw you?" she said, turning to face him.

"No one except but the flowers in your garden." Pausing, he spread his arms open. "So, is that all the greeting I'm to get after two weeks away? Nothing but a scold?"

At his words, the starch came out of her like a wrung-out linen shirt. "Of course not."

Hurrying forward on bare toes, she flung her arms around his neck and urged his head down to hers. Setting his hands on her hips, he lifted her up and claimed her mouth, his arms strong as oak limbs against her back.

Humming low in her throat, she matched his kiss, pouring all her longing and frustration at their recent parting into her response. Opening her lips, she slid her tongue against his, loving his taste, adoring the fire of his questing hands and seductive mouth. Her thoughts grew dim as he led her down a dark path where nothing existed but Rafe and the pleasure he wrought inside her body, and even deeper, in her soul.

At length, as if sensing her need for air, he broke their kiss. Surfacing, she was happy to notice that he was laboring for breath as well.

"Hmm," he murmured, "now that's a much better hello."

She rubbed her forehead against his cheek. "Not that I am in any way complaining, but *what are you doing here*? I thought you were going to send me a note. I would have come to the house tomorrow. You had only to say the word."

At Julianna's mention of notes, Rafe felt his shoulders

stiffen, the memory of his earlier fears, as well as the news that had sent him racing across the city, once again sharp in his mind.

He tightened his hold upon her, cradling her close. "I wanted to make certain you were all right."

Leaning back slightly, she tipped her head to one side. "Why wouldn't I be all right? You had my letter, did you not, telling you I would be away?"

"Yes, I received your missive when I arrived home this evening."

Her brows drew close. "Then I don't understand. Why were you worried?"

"Because of where you went, and in whose house it was you stayed. Thank God, you are well and safe. I know you do not realize it, Julianna, but Viscount Middleton is not a man to be trusted."

"I am beginning to think you may be right. But are you telling me this because he is truly dangerous, or because you would rather I not know that he is your brother?"

His arms loosened, and she slid abruptly down to her feet. "What did you say?"

"I am sorry to startle you, but I *know*, Rafe. While I was at Middlebrooke Park, I saw the painting of the late viscount in the portrait gallery. The painting of your father."

"And what makes you suppose that man was my father?" he said in a guarded tone.

"How could I not? You look the very image of him, down to the color of your eyes and the shape of your jaw. Do you mean to deny it? Are you going to tell me David St. George is not your father?"

Hell and blast, he swore silently, *what was the chance of her seeing that particular painting and guessing the truth!*

He'd seen the portrait only once himself and scarcely

even recalled its existence. In his entire thirty-five years he'd visited Middlebrooke Park only once, and that on the whim of his father. He still recalled the day, during a ride home at the end of school term, when he'd been fourteen. In a moment of impulsiveness, his father had decided to take Rafe to see the estate while his wife and other children were away on summer holiday. At least they were supposed to be away—and were, all except for Burton.

He and his younger sibling had met quite by accident in one of the gardens. The encounter had been disastrous—a case of hatred at first sight, at least on Burton's part. Obviously well aware of Rafe's existence and having built up a grudge against his older half brother, thirteen-year-old Burton had taken one look at him and had known exactly who he was.

Burton tossed out several insults and then threw a punch. Rafe had deftly countered. The pair of them had been pummeling each other when their father arrived and pulled them apart.

Before that day, Rafe hadn't really thought much about the marked resemblance he shared with his father. And later, after his father's death, he'd ceased giving it much consideration. Lord knows he'd never dreamed Julianna would have occasion to visit Middlebrooke Park and see the portrait.

The idea of Julianna being in Middleton's house and within easy reach of his half brother made Rafe's blood run cold all over again.

"Well, Rafe?" she asked. "Is it true?"

"Yes, it's true, but since you already knew I was the illegitimate son of a nobleman, why should you be so amazed?"

"It's not that. It's simply that I wasn't expecting to discover such a connection. I had no notion that Burton St. George is your brother."

He released her and stepped away. "We may share a common bloodline, but I assure you, St. George is *no* brother of mine." Pacing a few steps, he swung back. "Now, I have a question for you. What in the blue blazes were you doing attending a house party at his estate?"

Her spine stiffened, making him regret that his words had come out carrying an edge of accusation he had not meant. Still, he didn't for an instant regret the question.

She drew the edges of her negligée closed and crossed her arms. "The viscount has been calling upon Maris these past weeks, and asked us to his home. There was nothing improper about the visit, if that is what you are implying."

A scowl lined his forehead. "By *calling upon,* I hope you don't mean to say Middleton has been courting your sister?"

"Yes. In fact, he proposed to her this weekend . . ."

His stomach twisted, and for a moment he could barely focus on her next words.

" . . . but Maris has decided to say no," she finished.

He raked his fingers through his hair and paced a few steps. "Thank God for that! He's a vile blackguard and under no circumstances are you to permit your young sister to marry the man. She shouldn't even go near him, and that applies to you as well." Stepping forward, he caught her by the shoulders. "Promise me you will stay away from him, Julianna. Swear to me now that you will sever all connection."

Her dark eyes grew wide. "Well yes, I will try if you truly believe I should. But I do not understand. What is it he has done?"

Done? If she only knew the truth, he thought, *she would recoil in horror.*

Even now, after all this time, he could barely stand to think about it himself. The sounds, the sights, even the smells—terrible memories that haunted his dreams, plaguing him with a guilt whose stain he knew he would never be able to fully erase.

"I must confess there are times when I am not entirely comfortable in the viscount's company," Julianna continued, "but he is well accepted in Society, and well liked in most circles."

"They say the devil is invited to all the best parties too."

"What are you saying? Did he cheat you or lie to you? What?"

Worse, he thought. *Far, far worse.*

Closing his eyes for a moment, he gathered himself to speak. "I told you about Pamela."

"Yes. The girl you were going to marry. The one who died."

He swallowed, his throat tight. "What you don't know is that nine years ago Middleton and three of his cronies kidnapped, raped, and tortured her in revenge against me."

Julianna inhaled audibly, lifting a hand to cover her mouth.

Rafe barely heard her reaction as the night came back to him, as clear and vivid in his mind as if it were all happening again . . .

The grandfather clock in the hallway rang once, the house hushed and still, dark in the early-morning hours. Rafe yawned, replaced the stopper in his bottle of ink, then set down his pen. *Time to catch a few hours' sleep,* he decided, putting away his work for the morrow.

He'd been so rushed lately, what with the wedding less than a month away, and the distraction of the improvements he was having done to his new house here on Gracechurch Street. He wanted everything to be perfect for Pamela when she took up residence as his wife.

He was also busy rearranging his business dealings.

The last few years had been lucrative, so much so he knew he would never again need to worry about a life spent laboring for a pauper's wage. Yet he wasn't satisfied; he wanted more, and knew with his skills that he could take himself farther than most people even dreamed.

Pamela would be by his side, loved and pampered. He would keep her dressed in silks and satins, and make sure her every need was met. And once they had a family, all of them would retreat to the countryside for part of the year. Already, he had begun renovations to the house in West Riding where they would reside.

And he had finally received his rightful inheritance from his father, long denied him while the St. George family had tried unsuccessfully to contest the will. He'd already invested the twenty thousand pounds he'd received, a sum that would provide further avenues upon which he could build his financial empire. Even more important, the money had come as a well-earned vindication, one that just might allow him to put the past where it belonged.

Yawning, he stood and began snuffing out the candles.

Outside, a clatter of horse hooves rang noisily in the street, coach wheels rumbling fast against the pavers. Instead of continuing past, though, the vehicle stopped, a man's voice issuing a muffled command.

Moments later, a fierce pounding came at the door.

Who can that be at this hour? he wondered. He certainly wasn't expecting any visitors.

Knowing the servants were already abed, he strode out into the entry hall. Cautiously, he eased opened the door.

His jaw knotted when he saw who waited on the other side.

Standing near the open door of his black barouche,

Burton St. George loitered on the sidewalk. Flanking him opposite stood one of St. George's friends, Lord Underhill. Two more men sat inside the vehicle, their faces shadowy beneath the weak glow of the streetlights.

"What do you want, St. George?" Rafe demanded, irritation clear in his voice.

"Would you listen to that?" the viscount announced to his companions. "Do you hear the lack of respect in his voice? The disdain he shows for his betters?" He threw up an arm, his elegant black evening cloak tumbling back over one shoulder. "And here I am come to give you a gift, Pendragon."

Rafe scowled, uneasiness creeping over him like the crawl of a clammy hand. What was St. George talking about? The two of them despised each other. His brother would never bring him a gift.

"Come, come gentlemen," the viscount ordered in a sly tone, "bring out our little surprise."

One man sprang from the coach, the other maneuvering inside to help him lift out a large bundle. Together they carried their burden, dropping it onto the sidewalk at the base of the stairs—an unidentifiable heap wrapped in an old brown woolen blanket.

Rafe's heart pounded as he stared, imagining all kinds of dreadful possibilities. A dead dog, perhaps? Or a large rotted fish they'd procured from the refuse along the wharfs? Yet he detected no odor of decay, nothing but the faint, metallic sweetness of blood. If it was an animal, he reasoned, why the elaborate show? Why not simply fling the poor creature onto his doorstep and be gone, a loathsome prank well done?

"Are you not even going to take a peek?" the viscount taunted. "I know you'll want to see what's inside." When Rafe made no move, St. George approached. "Perhaps you need some encouragement."

Using the toe of his boot, the viscount gave the bundle a hard nudge.

A moan of agony rose up out of the blanket.

Dear Lord, is it human?

No longer hesitant, Rafe hurried down the brick stairs and dropped to his knees beside the huddled form. Drawing back the blanket, he gasped at what he saw.

A woman lay virtually naked, her bloodied, shredded undergarments all that remained of her clothing. Bruises in vicious shades of purple and blue and red stained her pale skin. Her eyes, lips, and cheeks were so swollen she was all but unrecognizable, her long, golden hair matted with sweat and dried blood.

Golden hair.

He swallowed down the bile that rose in his throat, hands trembling as he reached toward her. She whimpered at his lightest touch, shrinking away. As she shifted, her movements revealed a slender chain encircling her neck. Metal winked in the dull lamplight. A locket with its delicate sweep of forget-me-knots engraved on the front, identical to the one he'd given Pamela when they'd first been courting.

No! his mind screamed in denial. *No, no, no, it can't be her!*

Tears scalded his eyes, clouding his vision as they streamed down his cheeks without his awareness. Then the voice of Satan whispered in his ear, silky and despicably self-satisfied.

"When we heard you were going to be married, Underhill, Challoner, Hurst, and I all wanted to give you something extra special. We decided that breaking in the bride would be just the thing. I must say she wasn't terribly cooperative at first, but after a while she did plenty of moaning. A real randy little bitch, your fiancée. I'm sure you'll enjoy having her warm your bed, unless you're picky about using other men's leavings."

The viscount chuckled as if he'd made a very fine joke.

Rage, chilling and black, washed over Rafe. But instead of leaping to his feet and tearing into St. George, he knelt nearly paralyzed, his body quaking, a silent scream trapped in his throat.

"I warned you not to cross me, Pendragon," St. George said. "Don't ever make the mistake of doing it again."

Footsteps moved away. Still frozen, Rafe forced up his head in time to watch the coach and its occupants race away, the sound of male laughter echoing obscenely into the night . . .

Rafe shuddered and returned to the present.

"That bloody bastard hurt her to hurt me," he murmured. "And he succeeded."

"Dear God," Julianna whispered in horrified understanding, her eyes damp with sorrow.

His own eyes remained dry, his tears long ago burned away in the heat of his hatred and in his consuming need for revenge.

Julianna reached out and caught one of his hands, then led him to her bed. Drawing him down beside her, she slid her arms around him and hugged him tight. Leaning up, she kissed his cheek, then his temple.

"Tell me," she murmured, stroking a consoling palm across his chest.

For a long moment he resisted, the memories too raw, too deep. But her quiet, simple entreaty called to some hidden need inside him. Without consciously realizing it, he began to speak.

"After they tossed her on my doorstep, battered and brutalized, I rushed her inside and called for the physician. She'd lost so much blood, we all feared she would die that night, but by some miracle she held on. Gradually, she began to recover, physically at least. She ate and slept. She went through all the motions of living. But the girl I knew was gone. She used to laugh all the time and smile. Pamela was one of those rare souls who never saw the bad in people. But those bastards stole that from her, snuffed out the light in her eyes."

He paused, a leaden lump in his chest. "She couldn't bear to look at me after that and cringed at my slightest touch. Not because it was me, but because I was a man, and it was men who had hurt her. There was nothing I could do or say to make it better. Hell, I couldn't even give her the consolation of knowing her assailants were being punished."

He pulled away and strode across to stand in front of the fireplace. Picking up a poker, he jabbed it at the unlighted logs in the grate.

"But surely you reported the attack to the authorities?"

He laughed, the sound hollow and bitter. "Yes, her father and I went to the so-called authorities and told them what those monsters did to her. They just stared at us and smirked, then asked what she'd done to tempt them. St. George and his friends were all respectable gentleman, wealthy, powerful men of privilege and importance. Who would believe the claims of a Cheapside watchmaker and a businessman of dubious parentage when pitted against the testimony of four wealthy aristocrats?"

"But you saw them! Middleton admitted to you what he'd done. What they had all done."

"And all they had to do was deny it, assuming the constables had even bothered to ask. They didn't, of course. Instead, they tossed me into a cell for making false accusations. They would have locked up Pamela's father as well, but I convinced them to let me serve out his term along with my own. Two weeks in the London gaol."

"Rafe, no!" She leaned forward, her expression one of shock and outrage.

That was the day he'd lost all respect for the law. The day he came to understand that a man had to take care of his own, and seek justice by whatever means he possessed.

"St. George and his fellow rapists continued their lives as if nothing had happened," he continued in a chill voice. "They went on living with no apparent remorse, as if they had never violated a poor, sweet girl whose only crime was the mistake of loving me."

Mercy, how I longed to kill them! he thought, remembering those times. At first he'd ached to hunt them down, one man at a time, and put a bullet between their eyes. But he'd decided that was too easy, choosing instead to give each of them a taste of his own particular kind of misery. Years may have passed, but his revenge was starting to come to fruition.

Underhill and Challoner had met their fates, while the other two would soon face their own day of reckoning. A drunkard bent on his own kind of ruin, Hurst was nearly destroyed, while St. George was beginning to feel the squeeze on his finances, squirming as one investment after another mysteriously turned sour.

Seeing them all brought down would be sweet vengeance indeed.

"What about Pamela?" Julianna ventured softly. "You told me she died."

"Yes. Those villains murdered her, just as surely as if they had come to the house and slipped the rope around her neck with their own hands."

He turned and met her anguished gaze. "She hanged herself, three months after the attack. She'd . . . found out she was pregnant. There was a note saying she was sorry but that she could not bear the idea of having such disgrace growing inside her. She'd been a virgin before that night. She couldn't expect me to marry her, to raise an abomination as our child. She told me she could not be my wife. Could never be anyone's wife, since she knew she would not be able to bear the touch of a man ever again."

Taking a deep breath, he went on. "Pamela wrote that she loved me. She even begged me to forgive her. How could she not understand she wasn't the one in need of forgiveness? It was me. It still is me."

"You're wrong. You must not blame yourself."

"Mustn't I?" he challenged bitterly. "The fault was mine. If not for me, he would never have come after her. If not for the house, he would not have had a reason."

"The house? What house?"

He paused before answering. "My mother's house in the Yorkshire countryside, the home where I was raised."

Julianna waited, her hands clasped tightly in her lap, as she watched emotions shift like passing clouds across his chiseled features.

Her heart ached for him, for all he'd lost and been forced to endure. She wanted to offer him comfort, but she knew right now he would not accept her consolation, would see it as pity instead of compassion. So she kept her seat, held her silence, and waited for him to tell her more in his own time and in his own way.

He prodded the logs again with the fire poker. Long moments passed before he set the brass tool back into its holder and turned her way.

"Despite the circumstances of my birth," he began, "I had a good childhood. No matter the taunts and the fights other boys were forever picking with me, I knew my parents loved me, that they loved each other. My father spent as much time with us as he could, and he saw to it I had an education when the time came. He made certain my mother had a comfortable home with enough money for a few servants and as many fine gowns as she desired. But all she really wanted was him. I remember the way her face would glow whenever he came for a visit. And how she would lock herself in her room and cry after he left."

Rafe thrust his hands into his trouser pockets. "I knew my father had another family. Another son and two daughters, my brother and sisters, whom I was never to mention or admit to having knowledge of. I thought of them occasionally and wondered what it might have been like had I been born the legitimate son and St. George the baseborn one. But by and large it didn't trouble me. I loved my mother and our home. No matter what, I would never have traded either for all the world."

He strolled toward her dressing table and perused the contents. As if needing to distract himself, he uncorked her bottle of rose water and raised it to his nose, closing his eyes for a pleasurable instant. With a careful hand, he stoppered the container and returned it to its place.

Drawing an audible breath, Rafe continued. "I knew St. George bore a resentment toward me, but until the time of my father's death, I didn't realize just how deep it ran. Papa died very suddenly, without any warning at all, the year I turned twenty. I was away at university and happened across the notice in the *Times*."

His face tightened in obvious affront at the memory and the insult of not being notified of his own father's death. "I learned that my mother was given the news in a far more brutal way. Only days after my father died, a pair of riders appeared. It was late January and freezing cold, with inches of snow blanketing the ground. The riders banged on the door, told my mother the viscount was dead, and ordered her to get out—and by out they meant right that minute. She wasn't even allowed to pack a suitcase, nor take so much as a single belonging or memento. The house and all its contents belonged to the new viscount, she was told, Burton St. George."

Julianna's chest squeezed tight. Only by sheer force of will did she keep from going to him.

"St. George sent them to claim the property and toss his father's *whore,* as they called her, out into the street. They followed his orders to the letter, leaving her with nothing but the clothes on her back. They even denied her the comfort of taking shelter with one of her neighbors. The blackguards posted a notice in the nearby village warning that anyone giving her aid or assistance would be evicted from their home. Luckily, the innkeeper defied the order and gave her a place to stay in his stables until a message could be sent to me. I came as soon as I could. By the time I arrived, she was ill, a pleurisy brought on by chills and shock."

His face looked drawn, his sorrow acute even now. "Somehow she rallied enough to be moved. Having nowhere else to go, I took her to London. I didn't know what else to do. I used the last of my allowance to find us a room, buy her some clothes and food, then fuel for the grate. For a few weeks she seemed better; then her illness returned. I called a physician but there was nothing he could do. She died soon after."

A single tear slid down Julianna's cheek, remembering the pain she'd suffered at the time of her own mother's death so long ago. She wiped the back of her hand over her damp cheek. "Tell me the rest."

Rafe collected himself and gave a suddenly weary sigh. "I went out into the world and made my way as best I could. For a long time I blamed my father for not making provision for my mother. Then Tony, a titled friend of mine, managed to get his hands on a copy of the will. In it, we discovered my father had indeed left money for both my mother and myself, money the St. George family did its best to keep out of my hands.

"It's my firm belief as well that my father left my mother the house. She'd mentioned several times over the years that he'd put the deed in her name. I think St. George altered it, changed the deed so the property would come to him."

One of his hands curled into a hard fist. "St. George *stole* that house from my mother and threw her out into the street like yesterday's rubbish. So when the opportunity presented itself, I arranged things so my 'little brother' would have no choice but to hand the property over to me."

A shiver of trepidation ran through her. "What did you do?"

"I quietly bought up his debt, including several promissory notes whose repayment was fully enforceable in a court of law. When it came time to pay his creditors, he discovered it was me he owed. Rather than risk dragging his name and his lack of funds out in public, I proposed a deal, the West Riding house and grounds in exchange for his outstanding notes. He had little choice but to accept. It made him angry. My mistake was in not realizing how angry. I got the house but lost Pamela. A devil's bargain to be sure."

He raised his gaze, sharp as green glass and filled with self-loathing. "So you see, sweeting, I had as much of a hand in her death as he did."

"His actions were not of your making," she stated with a shake of her head. "What he did to her was unspeakable. No matter the history between him and you, that did not give him the right to attack an innocent girl, to hurt and destroy her like some insect he could squash. He's a monster with no morals. Considering everything you've told me of him, he ought to be hanged for his crimes. He is the one responsible, not you."

Climbing to her feet, she crossed to Rafe. "You are not at fault and you must stop torturing yourself with the idea that you are. Pamela would not want that. I read the inscription in the watch she gave you. No woman who loved you like that could ever wish to see you anything but happy."

Then, before he had a chance to refuse, she wrapped her arms around him and held on tight. Rafe stood stiff and unyielding, as if he were going to pull away. Then suddenly he crushed her to him, burying his face in her hair as his arms locked at her back.

They held each other for a long minute, drawing strength and succor from their embrace, their bodies pressed together warm and vital and alive, so very much alive. Instinct urged an even closer bond, his lips seeking and finding hers, his kiss soft and slow and tender. She responded, opening her mouth and urging him to take his fill.

Her senses spun in a dizzying whirl, boundless pleasure taking her in its grasp. She met his every move, teasing his tongue and nibbling at his lips, playing a tantalizing game that made her head hazy with yearning.

Passion billowed through her blood like steam heat, setting her nerves afire. Burrowing closer, she urged him to deepen their kiss, to raise the level of intensity between them in ways that should probably have frightened her, but didn't.

Craving more, she ran her hands across his chest and over his shoulders, clutching him tight as she put everything she had into her kiss. He responded, trailing his thumbs along the sensitive length of her spine.

With a sigh of almost feline satisfaction, she arched her back. Seconds later, she literally purred when he gave her bottom a caressing squeeze, then lifted her off her feet for a second time that evening.

All restraint fell away, her kisses turning as wild as his. Two weeks apart had been too long, leaving both of them eager to make up for lost time.

Rafe took a few steps forward, then stopped, obviously recalling that they were not in the Queens Square house, but instead inside Julianna's bedroom in Mayfair. She felt a shiver of repressed need go through him as he reluctantly broke their kiss. "I should probably go." He caught her lower lip between his teeth for a quick second before pressing another pair of kisses on her throbbing mouth.

"Hmm, probably," she sighed as she strung a line of kisses across his jaw and over the faint roughness of his cheek. When she reached his ear, she traced the edge of her tongue along the rim, then blew out a light stream of air.

He shuddered.

"You could stay." She tunneled her fingers into his thick hair.

He nuzzled her neck, then lifted and angled her hips so her femininity brushed against the hard tip of his erection, only the barrier of their clothing separating them.

This time she was the one to shudder.

"We might get caught," he whispered, taking a few more steps toward the bed.

"We might," she agreed, curling her legs around his hips. "Oh, heavens, please do not stop."

In that moment, she wanted him so much that no amount of risk could have kept her from him.

With a low growl, he carried her the rest of the way to the bed. After he laid her down upon the mattress, she expected him to strip off her nightgown, then hurriedly work to remove his own garments, leaving both of them naked.

She watched as he shrugged out of his jacket, then unwound the cravat from his neck, tossing both to the floor. After unfastening the short placket of buttons on his shirt, he toed off his shoes. But instead of continuing, he set a knee onto the bed and eased down so he lay full-length at her side.

Reaching out, he stroked a slow palm along the length of her hair, fanning her tresses out across the cool expanse of her pillow. Her pulse jittered, his simple touch sending her senses aloft. She began to reach for him, but he captured her hands and bore them back down.

"Let me," he whispered, dusting a kiss across her cheek. "Let me pleasure you. We have 'til dawn. Why not indulge our desires? There's no need to rush, is there?"

With a shake of her head, she agreed. Relaxing her muscles, she willed herself to do as he wished, knowing he would bring her delight, certain he would take her all the places she most longed to go.

Leisurely and lazily, he began to play, starting with light caresses and kisses, dappling her skin with a stroke here, a nibble there. Without removing a single scrap of cloth, he roused her need, making her ache as damp heat burned between her thighs. With restless need, she shifted her limbs beneath the skirt of her peignoir, wishing he would take it off and touch her bare flesh.

Instead he stroked her through the thin silk, the cloth growing wet when he fastened his mouth to one of her breasts and began to draw upon her with the most exquisite suction. Moaning, she bit the edge of her lip and closed her eyes, her brain buzzing, knowing her bliss was just out of reach. But he held her there on a wire-thin edge of need, stretching out each moment in a torment of glorious delight.

She cried out in relief when he finally drew off her nightgown, leaving her completely naked. "God, Rafe, take me," she urged, her control breaking as she reached for him.

But he slipped out of her grasp, sitting up to peel his shirt over his head and slip out of his trousers. "Be patient," he whispered as he turned back. "I haven't pleasured you enough yet."

She wanted to disagree, but couldn't seem to form the words, especially not when he set his wide palms upon her and began moving them in a long, gradual sweeping glide across her exposed flesh.

Capturing her mouth in another series of hot, wet kisses, he buried his face against her neck. A groan escaped her lips as he caught her nape between his teeth and gave her a gentle bite, adding a soothing lick and a kiss at the end.

Time took on a dreamlike quality as he repeated the process—bite, lick, kiss—working his way over her body, leaving no inch of skin untouched.

She whimpered, nearly feverish with need, when he reached the last spot, spreading her legs for the most intimate caress of all. Before he did, he pressed one of her hands across her lips. She didn't understand until a moment later when the barest brush of his lips and teeth sent her flying, her scream of release muffled against her skin. With a control that amazed her, he brought her to another peak before levering his body up and over her.

With a trio of sweet thrusts, he sheathed himself deep inside her. Clinging, she locked her legs high around his waist and kissed him, urging him to take his own climax as quickly as he wished.

But again, he didn't rush, drawing out the pleasure, pacing himself so he could reignite her hunger and take her with him over the brink one more time. Enthralled, she held on, her body, perhaps her very soul, his to control.

Opening his mouth over her own, he caught her cries of ecstasy along with his own rough shout, his body shaking hard in her arms as he claimed his own powerful release.

Long minutes passed as she drifted back to herself. Curling into him, she snuggled, nearly on the verge of sleep.

How I love having him here, she thought, her eyelids growing heavy. *How I love him.*

Her eyes blinked open and she stared.

Shifting her head to watch him slumber, her heart melted, and she knew it was true. Despite all the difficulties and improbabilities, in spite of everything that made their being together impossible, her heart knew what it wanted.

Quite without knowing how, she had tumbled headlong in love with Rafe Pendragon.

Chapter Fourteen

RAFE AWAKENED JUST before dawn.

For a long moment, he stared into the darkness, Julianna curled beside him. Breathing in the sweet warmth of her skin, he wished he could stay, wished he could kiss her awake and make love to her again.

But he knew if he remained, chances were good they would be caught. For him discovery mattered little, but Julianna did not feel the same. To protect her and guard the secret nature of their relationship, he knew he must go, and go now.

Careful not to wake her, he eased from the bed. Crossing the room, he tugged open the curtains to let in the last waning bits of moonlight, the room's heavy shadows tempered just enough to allow him to find his clothes.

In silence, he dressed.

Outside in the trees, birds began to chatter, warning of the impending break of dawn. Fastening a final button on his coat, he turned for one last look at Julianna.

Slumbering as deeply as a child, her features held an angelic cast, sooty lashes fanned over sleep-warmed cheeks, her cherry-hued lips parted as though she were an enchanted princess awaiting the kiss of her lover.

His body let him know just how much he'd like to

give in to temptation and slide back between the sheets with her, but he forced himself to resist.

There would be time enough later, when they next met.

After awakening to make love a second time, she'd promised to meet him at the Queens Square house in two days—tomorrow now. He would have preferred seeing her again this very afternoon but he knew she couldn't manage to slip away, having only just returned to Town last night.

Thinking about last night, he couldn't quite believe all the things he had revealed to her. Only his closest friends knew of the tragedy of Pamela, understood the circumstances and the reasons for his hatred of St. George.

But Julianna now knew more. With only a few soft words and the tenderness of her touch, he had found himself telling her things he'd never told anyone, sharing emotions he'd kept locked tightly away inside. Perhaps he should regret having said so much, but surprisingly he did not, knowing all his confidences were safe in her keeping.

Unable to resist, he bent down and pressed his lips to her temple, his touch as light as a whisper against her petal-soft skin.

Julianna stirred slightly, her lips curving into a dreamy smile.

With one last lingering glance, Rafe turned and strode to the window to climb out the way he had come.

How dare she!

The familiar phrase repeated in Burton's head as it had a hundred times before, the week just past doing nothing to dull his fury or salve his slighted pride.

Maris Davies was supposed to have been mine! How dare she refuse my offer of marriage!

Outwardly calm, he relaxed into a chair in the front room of his carriage-maker's, a clerk sent scurrying to inform his master that Lord Middleton awaited his immediate attention. Bathed in a stream of morning sunlight, Burton tapped his gold-topped cane against the dull wooden floor, his thoughts preoccupied by his recent misfortune. His careful planning, his skillful pursuit, his diligent investment of time and money and energy, had all come to naught.

Maris had been his for the taking. He'd known it, sensed it; she was a sweet, rosy apple just waiting to be plucked from the tree. She'd been on the verge of accepting him. After all, isn't that why he'd gone to the bother of hosting that dreary weekend party at his estate? So she would be flattered by his attention? So his interest in her would be made clear beyond any doubt?

Then something had occurred to change her mind, to put her off of him. He'd noticed a difference in her not long after she'd arrived at his home, a new reticence that set an invisible barrier between them.

He'd been quite justifiably annoyed when she'd begged for a few extra days to consider his proposal. He'd been absolutely livid when he'd called upon her in London and she had refused to see him.

Who does she think she is to send her brother to deliver her rejection? She ought to have had the courage to tell him herself.

But women were cowards, vain, idiotic creatures good for only one thing. Well, perhaps two, he corrected, if he considered the rich purses girls like Maris Davies could bring.

Whatever the reason for her change of heart, it scarcely mattered. She would be his whether she came to him of her own free will or not. He'd devoted far too much time and expense to let her flee now.

Stupid baggage, he fumed, *leading me on the way she*

did, causing me to waste the entire Season on her when I might have been pursuing another suitable heiress!

And now it was too late. Lady Maris really gave him no choice. He must have money, and she was his prime candidate. Once he compromised her, her family would have little option but to see them wed. And after they married and her fat dowry was tucked safely in his accounts, he would make certain she learned a few lessons at his hand. When he was done with her, she would be careful never to displease him again.

"My lord, my sincere apologies for making you wait." Higgins, the carriage-maker, hurried through the door separating his shop from the front room. He stopped and bowed low, then straightened. "How may I be of assistance?"

Burton rose from his chair, accepting the older man's groveling as his due. "I have come to order a new phaeton. A black one this time, I believe."

A long silence followed. Higgins, not a tall man, drew himself up to the full extent of his height, setting his eyes on a level with Burton's cravat. Swallowing audibly, the carriage-maker squared his shoulders as if readying himself for battle.

"Ahem, my lord," he began, refusing to meet Burton's gaze. "I would be delighted to fashion you a new vehicle . . . um . . . however . . . that is . . . well, there is the matter of your account."

Burton scowled. "What about my account?"

Higgins coughed, ruddy veins popping out across his fair cheeks. "Well, my lord, there is an outstanding balance remaining from your last, um, two purchases. I have been carrying your debt on my books for some time now and I . . . well . . . Unhappily," he continued in rapid staccato, "I feel I must ask you to bring your account current before I undertake any new jobs of work on your lordship's behalf."

Burton's hand curled over the head of his cane, the skin around his knuckles turning white.

Did I hear correctly? he thought. *Did this insolent little worm actually say what I think he said?*

In his imagination, Burton reached out and grabbed the older man by the throat. Maintaining his hold, he lifted him off the ground, then increased the pressure of his grip, smiling as Higgins's feet kicked wildly, his eyes bulging as he clawed and scraped and gasped for his life.

Burton's fingers twitched at the notion, and he very nearly gave in to temptation. But he was a man of control. A man of reason and forethought, who maintained governance over his emotions and his actions at all times.

His anger, he decided, would be wasted on someone as insignificant as this lowly shopkeeper. Dismissing him would be as simple as flicking a speck of lint off his coat.

Still . . .

"You shall receive payment in full at my earliest convenience," Burton said, fully aware his "earliest convenience" would most likely be never.

The tradesman—ungrateful wretch that he was— smiled, then bowed. "Why thank you, my lord. And about the new phaeton—"

Burton cut him off. "Don't trouble yourself. I believe my business, *all* my business, with you is concluded. I shall be taking my trade elsewhere from now on. Good day." Giving his cane a hard tap on the floor, he strode toward the door.

"But my lord—" the carriage-maker sputtered, hurrying after him.

Burton ignored the man and stalked out of the shop. The inside of his belly burned as he strode ahead, leaving his tiger to take the reins of his carriage and follow at a discreet distance behind.

Humiliation ate at his nerves like tiny nibbling fish.

To be spoken to in such a manner, he raged, *to be dunned in person for money! It was insupportable.* Worse, it was galling, particularly since he didn't have the funds to pay, a pair of his investments having recently gone bad.

Of course, all would be well if a certain female had done as she was supposed to and had agreed to marry him. Every tradesman in Town—pesky insects that they were—would have known he had a rich bride on the string, and would have been willing to extend him even more credit.

But now he was left with nothing but aggravation.

Higgins was the third merchant in as many days who'd come whining to him, demanding to be paid. It was a trend that must not be allowed to continue. It wouldn't do for Society to become aware of his financial difficulties, to suspect he was anything but the wealthy man they imagined him to be.

When he considered the matter, he could place a large measure of his woes at Maris Davies's doorstep.

Striding onward, he let his feet take him where they would, his impromptu journey bringing him long minutes later to the edges of Hyde Park. He was about to return to his carriage and drive home when he caught sight of a familiar dark-haired female.

His blood pumped faster, his simmering anger heating to a fresh boil as he watched Lady Maris amble along one of the paths. *How pretty she looks,* he mused, perfect as a hothouse rose in a morning gown of pale yellow muslin, a little feathered bonnet perched at a jaunty angle atop her head.

Is she alone? he marveled, searching for sight of an escort. But as far as he could tell, her only companion was a maid, the girl following at a respectful distance behind.

How imprudent of her brother to let little Maris out on her own. How serendipitous for him.

A smile turned up the corners of his mouth.

Should I? Could I? he wondered, casting his eyes around to see who else might be nearby. But the two of them appeared to be alone, as if fate were granting him a boon, one that was far too tempting to pass up.

Without another moment's hesitation, he turned to his tiger and told the young man to wait. Then he strode purposefully into the park.

Attired in an Alice-blue day dress with a pretty pair of matching shoes on her feet, Julianna glided down the staircase of her townhouse. Under her breath she hummed a merry tune, her senses alive with the knowledge that she would soon be with Rafe.

She was drawing on her gloves in the foyer, her butler holding open the front door in anticipation of her departure, when the beat of horse hooves rang out against the street pavers. Moments later, the horse came to a halt just behind her waiting carriage.

Up flew her eyebrows as she glanced out to discover that the horse had two riders: Major Waring and, seated inside the cradle of his good arm, her sister Maris.

What in heavens? she wondered, moving to the front step to watch as the major made an agile descent from his horse, then reached up to help Maris down.

As soon as Maris's feet touched the sidewalk, she rushed forward. "Oh Jules, it was dreadful. He tried to abduct me!"

Breath squeezed inside Julianna's lungs. "Who tried to abduct you?"

"Lord Middleton. But William . . . I mean, Major Waring saved me." Turning her head, Maris sent the major a dazzling smile as he came up beside her.

At the mention of Middleton's name, an icy chill raced along Julianna's spine.

"Why don't you go inside and tell your sister what happened," Waring suggested, setting a gentle hand at Maris's elbow to urge her up the stairs. "If I have any chance of tracking him down, I need to leave now."

"Oh William, please be careful."

"Never fear. I am well skilled at stalking an enemy." Lifting Maris's hand, he brought it to his lips and pressed a tender kiss upon it. With a bow, he mounted his horse and raced away.

Wrapping an arm around Maris's shoulder, Julianna ferried her inside and up the stairs to the drawing room. After gathering her sister into her arms for a reassuring hug, she led them both to the sofa.

"Now," Julianna declared, "tell me everything."

Rafe paced the length of the Queens Square drawing room.

Where is Julianna? he thought, a heavy scowl furrowing his brow.

She was supposed to have arrived over an hour before.

Has she mistaken the day, he mused, *and believes we are to meet tomorrow? Or is it something else? Has something untoward befallen her?*

His stomach clenched at the idea. Shoving his hands into his pockets, he paced another few steps, then forced himself to stop.

She is fine and I am worried for naught, he told himself.

Or am I?

Five minutes later he was seriously contemplating paying another visit to her townhouse, this time not so secretly, when he heard the front door open and close.

Moments later, Julianna stood in the drawing room

doorway, her cheeks stained a dusky rose, an escaped wisp of brunette hair pasted in a damp curl against one temple.

"Forgive me for being so late," she said, hurrying forward. "I would have sent you a note but there simply wasn't time."

"Where have you been?"

"With Maris." She stopped and clutched a fisted hand against her breast. "He tried to take her, Rafe. He tried to abduct her right out of the park in broad daylight."

Striding forward, he caught her inside his arms. "Who? Surely you don't mean St. George?"

But of course she does, he realized. *I can see the truth in her eyes.*

Leaning against him, she nodded. "Maris went walking in Hyde Park with her maid this morning. She said everything was fine, then suddenly Lord Middleton appeared on the path in front of her. He was quite pleasant at first and suggested he drive her home, but Maris refused. That's when he grabbed her and tried to force her into his carriage. He told her she was going to marry him whether she wished or not, and if compromising her and taking her to Gretna was the only way, then so be it."

A sick lump collected deep in his chest. "Did he hurt her?"

"Thank God, no. As providence would have it, Major Waring was riding past and saw her struggle. He came straight to her aid. Apparently words were exchanged and the two men nearly came to blows. With them standing in so public a location, the viscount was finally forced to retreat."

St. George must be feeling truly desperate, Rafe thought, to have tried something like this with a girl of good family. Kidnapping, especially of an innocent young lady, was a serious offense, one even Society would not tolerate. Of course, if the blackguard had succeeded in his plan to force her to wed him, the Ton would likely have forgiven him, since he would have done the "right" thing by her in the end.

Thank heavens, poor young Maris had escaped with no lasting harm done. Rafe couldn't have borne knowing he'd had a hand—even a peripheral one—in her ruin.

His heart squeezed out an extra beat, seeing the sheen of tears glistening in Julianna's dark, velvety eyes.

"Oh Rafe," she cried, "what if he'd taken her? What if he'd done something unspeakable? After she told me everything, I scolded her for going out into that park with only her maid. But I never thought to forbid her. Even knowing what he is, I never imagined he would attempt something like this."

"*Shh,*" he hushed in a soft voice, brushing his lips across her cheek. "You could not have anticipated his actions and I don't want to hear any more of such talk. Now, you told me yourself that she is safe and well. You will know to guard her in the future."

She nodded and burrowed closer against his chest. "From now on, Harry and I have sworn not to let her out of our sight. And Major Waring will keep her safe. He went to challenge Middleton, by the way. I hope he puts a bullet through the monster."

Rafe's jaw tightened. "It's unlikely a duel will ever take place. I strongly suspect St. George will go to ground. He may even leave Town. Dueling gains him nothing, and he has no use for the risk. His so-called honor is already besmirched by today's attempt. No, if I don't miss my guess, he'll simply disappear."

She sighed. "I suppose it is just as well. Maris would be devastated if the major came to harm."

Setting her hands flat against his chest, Julianna shook off the worst of her distress and flashed her first smile since entering the room. "I did not tell you. Maris and Major Waring are to be married."

"That seems rather sudden."

Julianna shook her head and laughed. "Quite the contrary. Maris loves him and has been pining over him for weeks. Apparently after rescuing her, the shock drove the major to confess how much he loves her too. Misplaced pride over his lack of fortune made him withdraw his suit, as I suspected. Apparently Maris convinced him to change his mind. I believe she also pointed out that Middleton would no longer be interested in abducting her if she were already wed to another."

"So she will be very amply protected."

"Amply," she agreed. "They're already planning a short engagement. Once Maris is Mrs. William Waring, she will have nothing further to fear from the viscount." Pausing, she frowned. "I only worry that he will attempt such an act with some other young girl."

Bending his head, he gave her a kiss of reassurance. "Word will get around and parents will keep their daughters from him. He'll have a much more difficult time than before, I assure you."

And when my plan succeeds, St. George will find himself with far greater problems than running from scandal. Never fear, he thought. *I will see to it he pays.*

"You've had a shock today," he said. "Would you rather I drive you home?"

Julianna shook her head and slid her arms around his neck. "Not unless you want me to go?"

He tightened his embrace. "What I want is to take you upstairs."

"Then take me. We've already wasted half the day. Pray let us not squander the rest."

With a playful growl, he swept her off her feet and into his arms.

*   *   *

Over the next couple of days, Rafe's suspicions about Burton St. George proved correct. Vanishing like a wraith, the viscount fled the city, leaving a mountain of unpaid debts and a host of disgruntled creditors howling in his wake.

As for the major, Julianna told Rafe of Waring's unsuccessful attempts to find the viscount and see honor satisfied. Apparently the major had called first at St. George's townhouse. When he'd been informed the viscount was not at home, he'd forced his way inside to search, but to his disappointment discovered the servants had been telling him the truth—St. George was nowhere to be found.

Deciding to widen his search, the major next tried St. George's haunts—his club, a few gaming hells, the theater, even the residence of the viscount's latest mistress—but all to no avail. The following morning Waring returned once more to the viscount's townhouse, only to discover the door knocker removed and the house closed up, the furniture looking ghostly, concealed beneath a multitude of white dust sheets.

Earlier today when Julianna arrived for their rendezvous, she had told Rafe she was relieved by St. George's departure.

"With him gone," she said, "he'll be of no further threat to Maris. And once she weds, we can stop worrying. He will thankfully be out of our lives forever."

Rafe had held his silence, knowing nothing involving St. George was ever that simple.

Now, with Julianna dozing in his arms, Rafe skimmed his gaze over her lovely features and wondered what he should do.

I've put her in danger, he realized. Without question, St. George bore a grudge against Maris Davies and her family, Julianna included. If he should ever chance to discover her involvement with Rafe . . .

A shudder ran through him at the thought.

So far he and Julianna had managed to keep their affair secret, but one small slip, one tiny mistake, and everything could unravel in dangerous ways. Already, the two of them were growing careless. Despite having a sound reason, he'd broken the rules by going to Julianna's home and spending the night in her bed. Without much convincing, he knew he could be coaxed into doing it again.

His blood quickened at the idea of having her next to him at night, all night. Every night.

I've let her get too close, he realized.

If he were prudent, he would cut his ties now, before he fell irrevocably under her spell. Besides, their parting was inevitable, was it not?

London was already turning steamy and oppressive with the heat of summer—only a little more than a month remained of their original agreement. Once the Season came to an end, she would do as the rest of the Ton and retreat into the country. He, on the other hand, would remain in London, going about his days much as he had always done, his affair with Julianna Hawthorne nothing more than an enjoyable memory.

So why did he want more of her instead of less? Why wasn't he ready to let her go despite all his arguments to the contrary?

If not for St. George, he knew he would keep seeing Julianna. He might even have considered asking her to continue their affair once the six months were through. But so long as he and Julianna were together, the chance existed that St. George might find out about them, no matter how unlikely that chance might be.

It was a possibility he could not ignore.

In Pamela's case, he'd had no way of knowing how vicious St. George could be. This time he was under no such delusions. If the viscount thought for an instant that he could harm him through Julianna, the black-guard would not hesitate to use her in any heinous manner he chose.

Closing his eyes, he rubbed a hand over his jaw. For Julianna's sake, he knew he must put an end to their liaison.

Although he'd broken off relationships with women in the past, this time would be different, because Julianna was different. Of all the women he'd known, she was unique.

Special.

The kind of woman who would be impossible to ever forget.

And as peculiar as it might seem considering the calculated nature of their original agreement, they now shared a bond.

Which left him with a dilemma.

Judging by the undiluted strength of her passion for him, he did not believe she was any more inclined to end their affair than he. Which meant that being honest with her about his concerns over St. George would not be enough to convince her they must sever their connection. Knowing Julianna, she would argue and try to persuade him that he was being too extreme.

"Middleton has left Town," she would say. "He won't find out about us. But if it will ease your worries, we will both be more careful. I promise I will take every precaution and make doubly sure I am not followed."

But she couldn't guarantee her own safety, and neither could he. Of paramount importance was keeping Julianna safe. If he had to tell her a lie to force her to go, then lie he would.

But Christ, he realized, *cutting her out of my life is going to be hard, one of the hardest things I've ever had to do.*

To protect her, though, he would do what must be done.

Beside him she stirred, making a throaty little purr of contentment that never failed to rouse his desire. Her lashes fluttered open, her beautiful dark eyes lifting to meet his own. Slow and lazy, her lips curved into a smile.

He tried to smile back but failed.

Tipping her head to one side, she arched a brow. "What is it? You look troubled."

Scolding himself for letting his emotions show so plainly, he made a second attempt, managing the smile this time. "Just thinking, sweeting. Nothing over which you need be concerned."

Leaning up, she rested her forearms on his chest, causing the tips of her bare breasts to brush against his skin. He hardened instantly at her touch, his body throbbing with desire.

So little time, he thought, *so damned little time.*

Clamping a hand around the back of her head, he pulled her over him and plundered her mouth with a kiss that knew no bounds. She let out a muffled murmur of surprise, then began to kiss him back, matching his ardor with an eagerness of her own.

Racing his hands over her lush flesh, he traced each curve, memorized every sensation, storing them away as if to keep something warm for all the nights to come. Then he could no longer wait, could not bear to be separate from her a moment more.

Without preamble he positioned himself and thrust inside her, clasping her hips tightly as he drove himself as high and deep as he could go. When his penetration still wasn't enough, when his senses screamed out for more, he rolled her onto her back and plunged deeper, harder.

Her pleasured moans played like music in his ears, her

hands delicate as the finest silk as they stroked over his heated, sensitized flesh. Soon, he felt the familiar contraction of her inner muscles squeezing around him as her body crested to release. And though his body urged him to take his pleasure as well, he held back, prolonging the moment, determined to make each sensation last as long as it possibly could.

He brought her to climax twice more, leaving her weak and overwhelmed as she drifted on a sea of bliss. Finally he could wait no longer. Letting his body override his mind, he claimed his own satisfaction, her name a prayer on his lips.

Lying above her, her sweet scent all around him, he wondered how he was ever going to bear her loss.

Chapter Fifteen

THE NEXT FEW days passed by in a flurry of activity. Maris was giddy in love and delirious over plans for her wedding, every third word out of her mouth William-this or William-that. And it was obvious Major Waring felt the same about Maris, now that his reservations had been overcome. Every time he gazed at her, love shone from his eyes bright as stars.

Julianna heartily approved the match despite the major's lack of fortune, and Harry had taken an instant liking to Waring, soliciting advice from him on a number of business and estate matters. The major might be a third son, but he came from a family of great landholders and knew far more on the subject of estate management than many titled lords.

Waring's parents sent a lovely note and a gift welcoming Maris to the family, together with an invitation to join them for a visit at their estate in Berkshire as soon as the Season was done. And more surprising, the major's maternal uncle wrote, telling them he planned to give William and Maris a fine house in Wiltshire upon their marriage, along with a sum of ten thousand pounds.

The wedding would be in September, forcing them all into a rush of preparations. But Julianna was glad, for once Maris was wed and off to begin her new life, Julianna would have more time to spend with Rafe. *At least that is my hope,* she thought as the hackney carriage drove her toward the house in Queens Square.

Since realizing that she loved Rafe, she felt every bit as euphoric and fanciful as her sister. Often she would find herself daydreaming about something Rafe had said or done, or fantasizing about the last time they had made love. And she would long to be in his arms, repining about the fact that they must confine their time together to a few brief hours a week, hours that were no longer enough.

Although he had made no specific mention of wishing to continue their affair past the original six months of their agreement, she didn't think it would be too difficult to persuade him otherwise. If the ferocity of his lovemaking were any indication, she had nothing to worry about at all.

She would perforce have to leave for a few weeks to assist Maris with the wedding, but afterward, she could return to London. With Society gone from the city, meeting Rafe would be much easier. Perhaps they might even go away somewhere to spend long, sultry nights and even entire days or weekends together. Richmond, she'd heard it whispered, provided a lovely rural setting where lovers could meet in discreet privacy. Considering Rafe's vast holdings, he might even own a house there, another cozy property they could turn into a lovers' nest.

Beyond that she didn't know. She loved Rafe and wanted to be with him, but anything permanent seemed impossible. Despite his fortune, he was not a suitable parti. To marry him would be to give up her place in Society. She would face social censure, and no doubt lose most of her friends and connections. Harry would likely disapprove of the match, and Maris . . . well, her little sister might be sympathetic, since nothing, not even Society's strictures, would have kept her from William.

But I am being ridiculous, Julianna thought as the

hack drew to a halt. *Rafe is not likely to make me an offer of marriage anytime soon, and I am not even sure I want him to do so.*

The idea of turning her entire life over to a man again was a frightening notion. She liked her independence and did not wish to be married. Although if Rafe truly loved her, she strongly suspected she would consent to almost anything he asked.

Paying the driver, she approached the house, her shoes crunching quietly against the gravel drive. A familiar sense of excited pleasure trickled through her, a smile playing upon her lips.

He would already be in the drawing room, she expected, his cravat loosened, his long legs stretched out in a relaxed sprawl as he read one of the books taken from the room's expansive shelves.

The moment she arrived, he would toss the volume aside, then draw her down beside him for a welcoming kiss, followed by a few minutes of desultory conversation. Lately some of those conversations had been growing longer and more involved, but she adored every minute of them. And he never failed to please her afterward, upstairs in bed . . . unless they didn't make it to the bed. One thing upon which she could always count was the passionate inventiveness of Rafe's touch.

Letting herself into the house, she closed the door and started forward. She stopped abruptly when she saw him looming large and commanding in the drawing room doorway.

She laid a hand on her chest. "Oh, you startled me."

"My apologies. I heard you come in and I . . . well, I am sorry."

Something is wrong, she thought.

"What is it?" she asked, noting the serious, almost dour expression lining his handsome features. "Has something happened?"

"Come in and we'll talk," he said, making no attempt to refute her statement. Stepping back into the room, he left her to follow.

Her earlier cheerfulness faded, her stomach squeezing with nerves.

Whatever this is, she thought, *it cannot be good.*

Ignoring her sudden reluctance, she walked ahead and entered the room.

Rafe stood near the window gazing out, a glass filled with what appeared to be whisky in his hand. Swirling the liquor, he tossed back a long swallow.

"Would you care for a drink?" he inquired, glancing toward her. "A sherry perhaps?"

She shook her head. "No, nothing, thank you."

On a nod, he downed the last of the alcohol, then set the glass onto a nearby table.

"Why don't you have a seat?" He gestured a hand toward the sofa.

Swallowing past the tightness in her throat, she moved forward. Only as she sank down against the silk covered cushions did she realized he hadn't kissed her.

Rafe always kissed her. She couldn't remember a time in all the months they had been together when he hadn't immediately swept her into his arms and made her blood hum from one of his passionate kisses.

But not today.

"What is this, Rafe? What has happened? Have I done something wrong? Are you angry?"

Clear surprise shone in his gaze. "No, I am not angry, not in the least. And why would you think you have done anything wrong?"

She shrugged. "I don't know, but you don't seem quite yourself. I must say you are setting me to worry."

"That is not my intention. I am handling this badly, my apologies." He thrust his hands into his pockets for a moment, then just as quickly took them out again.

"We've had a good time together these past months, have we not?"

"Yes, of course we have."

"Considering how things began between us, our liaison has turned out to be very enjoyable. More than enjoyable . . . wonderful really."

Her head began to buzz.

"There are still a few weeks remaining of our six months, but some . . . out-of-town business has come up—"

Business? Oh, he has business.

She let out a breath, relief sweeping through her. *He is only going to tell me he has to be away for a while. For a moment I thought he was going to . . .*

"—which is why I think it would be best if we simply end things now."

Her gaze flew to his. "Y-You want to end things? You mean not see each other for a while?"

A shadow passed through his eyes, turning them dark as a forest. "No, I mean not see each other *at all.* Julianna, I am breaking things off with you."

His words hit her like an icy slap, her extremities turning cold. For a long moment she couldn't seem to catch her breath.

"But why?" she said. "I don't understand."

"If it is the unpaid portion of the debt that concerns you, rest assured I consider it paid in full."

Opening his coat, he reached into an inner pocket and pulled forth a sheaf of papers. Crossing to her, he held them out. When she made no move to take them, he set the papers onto the sofa next to her.

"Your brother's note," he explained. "I have marked it as satisfied."

"But it isn't the debt. How could you think that? How could you even mention our bargain? I thought . . ."

"What did you think?" he asked, his tone quiet.

"That you wanted me. Desired me. Only three days ago you couldn't keep your hands off me."

"You are a beautiful woman and you were in my bed. Of course I desired you."

"Then there is no reason to break things off," she said with forced optimism. "Go ahead with your business. I will be here when you return."

His hands clenched at his sides. "But I shall not. Don't make this harder than it needs to be."

"But you care for me," she argued, a sudden burst of defiance burning like fire in her belly. "I know you do. Why else would you have come to my house and climbed into my window, fearful I might be in danger? Why else would you worry about me and confide in me, telling me things I know you did not share easily? You and I have something special, Rafe. Never have I felt such gentleness from a man, such caring, so don't tell me I do not matter to you."

His hands curled into fists at his sides and he turned his head to gaze out the window. For a second she thought she saw an expression of pain flicker over his face. But when he looked at her again, his gaze held no such emotion, only a kind of indifferent calm.

"I never said you didn't. You have been a good lover, Julianna. A good mistress. I would care about any woman who shares my bed, but not in the way I believe you mean." He glanced toward the floor, momentarily silent. "I wasn't going to say anything, but the truth is I've grown a little bored lately."

"*Bored?*" She felt the blood drain from her cheeks.

"Hmm," he drawled. "It's been coming on gradually for a while now. One of the perennial signs that an affair has run its course. When this . . . um . . . business of mine came up, I realized it was as good a time as any to say good-bye."

He crossed his arms over his chest. "I can see now

that you've become too involved, too emotional, spinning a whole romantic fantasy around what we have together. But it's an illusion. Where did you think all this was going to lead, anyway? Did you imagine we would go on forever just as we are? Meeting as lovers year after year until we turned old and gray?"

With unseeing eyes, Julianna stared down at her lap. She wouldn't tell him what she had thought, cringing inside at all her stupid, naïve dreams.

I am such a fool, she thought, tears stinging her eyes. She blinked hard to keep them from falling.

"Oh, I very nearly forgot," he said, reaching inside his coat again. Out came a black velvet jeweler's box. Opening it, he revealed a stunning bracelet fashioned from rubies and diamonds, the gemstones vivid as tiny suns.

"A small token for our time together." Gently, he placed the box in her hand.

A crushing weight settled upon her chest, as if all the air had been swept from the room. His "gift" said everything. There were no words, no possible way he could have found to better express the true nature of his feelings for her.

Or rather his lack of feelings for me, she thought, devastated.

Before she even knew what she meant to do, her fingers curled around the gemstones. Snatching the bracelet out of the box, she hurled it at him, then hurled the box after. "Take your whore's gift and get out. *Get out!*"

The bracelet and box bounced harmlessly off his chest, tumbling forgotten to the floor.

He stretched out a hand. "Julianna, I didn't mean—"

She brushed his touch aside and leapt to her feet. "Then I'll get out. I'll go."

Unable to bear looking at him for another instant, or witness the pity she knew must be in his gaze, she hurried forward. Tears streamed like raindrops over her cheeks, blurring her vision. When she reached the doorway, a harsh sob caught in her throat, threatening to choke her.

"Sit down," Rafe said, catching her by her elbow. When she flinched at his touch, he released her but did not withdraw.

"There is no need for you to go now," he said. "I shall procure a hack for you, since I am sure you would rather I not be the one to drive you home today. I'll ask him to wait for you out front. Stay here however long you like."

She wanted to toss his offer back in his face and tell him she would find her own way home. But she knew he was right. In her current state, she would not get far.

Without a word, she moved away and sat in a chair.

He strode back to the threshold, then stopped. Reaching out, he gripped the doorknob, his knuckles turning white. "Julianna, I wish . . . well, never mind. Good-bye, Lady Hawthorne."

She winced to hear him use her title, so formal, already so remote.

And he wished? He wished what? She nearly asked, but could not seem to make her tongue form the words.

Moments later, he moved away, the sound of his boots ringing against the floor tiles. Next came the opening and closing of the front door, and then Rafe was gone.

Oh God, he is really gone!

The realization struck her like a blow. Not only was their affair over, but she would likely never see him again. Bursting into a flood of tears, she buried her face in her hands and wept.

Rafe parked his carriage on the opposite side of the street, well back from the Queens Square house while he waited for Julianna to emerge. The hackney sat in the front drive, where the man had patiently kept his horses standing for the past twenty minutes. Rafe had paid the driver well to ensure he stayed. So far he'd obeyed Rafe's directive to the letter.

At length, Julianna appeared, looking pretty as an apple blossom in a gown of cream and pale green. Head down, she hurried out of the house. Even from a distance, he could see the ruddy stain of color across her cheeks, the swollen cast to her lovely, exotic features.

He hated himself for making her cry, for having put that glazed look of betrayal and pain in her eyes. She'd taken his rejection harder than he'd thought she would.

Hell, I took it harder, he thought, *the deed far, far worse than even my worst expectations.*

Right after he'd first told her, when he saw her shock and unhappiness, he'd felt himself hesitate. For a moment his resolve had wavered and he'd found himself on the verge of taking her in his arms and confessing the truth, telling her that everything he'd just said was a lie.

But then he'd remembered his reasons, remembered St. George and the potential danger he represented. Regardless of his wishes or hers, Julianna must remain safe and unharmed. That single fact held precedence over all else. And so he'd continued, forcing himself to say the words, making himself end what neither of them wished to end. When it was over, he felt as if he'd taken that last bit of her innocence and ground it under his boot heel.

For a moment, he'd felt like a monster, worse even than St. George.

Yet when it came to the bracelet, he had not meant what she thought. It had been an idiotic idea, he realized now. When he'd purchased the gemstones, he'd taken great care in his selection, wanting to find something beautiful and lasting that she could keep as a memento of their union. Instead, he'd made a complete hash of things, and hurt her even more deeply. He'd tried to apologize but had stopped, realizing the futility of the attempt. After all, what could he say?

He'd meant to drive her away, and he had succeeded admirably. So why did knowing he'd done it for all the right reasons feel like such cold comfort now?

Taking one final glimpse, he watched her climb into the hack. With a flick of the reins, the driver set the carriage in motion. Far too quickly, the vehicle and its occupant disappeared into the distance.

A long time passed before he drove himself home.

Burton St. George shoved his plate aside in disgust.

"Couldn't you do better than that slattern you've hired in the kitchens, Hurst? I've seen more palatable fare tossed out for pigs and rats. Why, I bet even your dogs won't eat this slop."

He stabbed a fork into the half-burnt, half-raw piece of chicken on his plate and flung it onto the floor, where Hurst's three hounds lay before the hearth. Two of them rose in interest, but after a few inquiring sniffs, the dogs returned to their earlier spots, the inedible fowl abandoned.

"See?" Burton declared. "What did I tell you?"

Stephen Hurst poured himself another glass of ruby-red Bordeaux, drank down half, then swiped a palm across his mouth. "Sorry, old man, but I didn't have many options, what with the rush to leave Town and all. Had to take what servants I could find."

Which leaves slim pickings, considering the wages Hurst is willing to pay, Burton thought. Given the current emptiness of his own pockets, however, he supposed he had little right to complain.

Grinding his teeth at the realization, he leaned forward and plucked a peach out of the silver epergne in the center of the table.

Even Hurst's sluttish cook can't ruin this, he mused. Opening his penknife, he began to peel the fruit.

"Thought we might take in some fishing tomorrow," Hurst suggested. "The trout run thick in the lakes this time of year."

Idiot drunk, Burton thought as he chewed a slice of peach. *Listen to him prattle on as if the two of us really did come up here on holiday.*

If he'd had any other choice, he'd never have set foot in the Lancashire countryside. But with his recent financial setbacks and his lamentable failure to spirit off Lady Maris as his bride, he'd decided it prudent to remove himself from Town for a while.

When he returned in a few months' time, should rumors of her attempted abduction still be on the wind, he would declare his innocence and feign ignorance of the entire matter. After a while, enough people would believe his lies so that the scandal would fade away into nothing more than a nine-day wonder.

He understood that crippled do-gooder, Waring, had come looking for him, wanting to demand satisfaction. *The fool should be glad I didn't stay to take up his challenge,* he thought. *As a skilled marksman, I would have enjoyed putting a bullet between the good major's eyes.*

A smile turned up the corners of his mouth at the notion, but his pleasure quickly evaporated as he recalled the other news he'd heard, that the inestimable Lady Maris was now engaged to the major. *Hadn't taken Waring long to cast aside his lily-white honor and cash in on Maris's fat dowry,* he mused.

He thrust his knife deep into the fleshy peach, juice running like blood over his fingertips.

Hurst emptied the last of a wine bottle into his glass. "Demmed glad we came up here. A man can relax instead of having to watch his back all the time."

Burton stifled a sigh. Was Hurst singing that tired old tune again?

"He has spies everywhere, you know," Hurst continued.

"I assume by *he* that you mean Pendragon?"

"Who else? Had to dismiss one of my footmen after I caught the weasel reporting on me."

Burton's interest increased marginally. He selected another peach from the epergne. "Caught him how?"

"Followed him one night, down to a tavern. Bloody snoop sat there having a drink for near an hour. I was beginning to think my suspicions about him were wrong when who walks in but Pendragon's giant, Hannibal. The two of them sat whispering thick as thieves, little traitor telling him God knows what about me."

The story gave Burton pause. Perhaps Hurst wasn't as shatter-brained as he'd thought. "What did you do? Did you confront your man?"

"No. Just sacked him a few days later. I didn't want word getting back to Pendragon that I was on to him."

"Why didn't you mention this to me earlier?"

Hurst's hand shook slightly as he drained his glass. "Well, you'd told me not to bother you about such matters."

Burton ignored the reminder as he set down the fruit and dried his hands on a napkin. "Anything else you've noticed?"

Hurst perked up at the query. "I feel as if I'm being watched wherever I go. He's trying to rattle me, that's what I think, rattle me and put me off my nerve. And now that I know about that rat in my house, I suspect he may have riffled through some of my personal papers and belongings. Maybe the run of bad luck I've been having these past few years isn't happenstance, after all." He made a sweeping gesture with his glass, causing a dollop of red wine to splash onto the white tablecloth.

"I tell you, Middleton, he's after us. He's taken down Underhill and Challoner and now he's coming for the pair of us."

Burton considered the matter anew.

Before, when Hurst had carried on about the topic, he'd dismissed it as nonsense. Now he wasn't so sure. Hurst was a drunk and a paranoid, but perhaps a few of his ravings had merit. Not even Hurst could have imagined the meeting between his footman and Pendragon's man at the tavern.

Then there was Burton's own unfortunate streak of bad luck lately. Lucrative investments unexpectedly gone sour. Creditors suddenly unwilling to extend additional lines of credit.

"For all you know, Pendragon sabotaged your plans for that Davies girl," Hurst said. "A few words whispered in the right ears might have been enough to scare her and her family away."

Burton scowled.

"You'd do better to look for a rich Cit's daughter next time," Hurst suggested, his slurred words showing how deeply he was into his cups. "Shameful lineage and all that, but for enough money anything can be overlooked, eh? And if you get tired of her, you can always send her on a quick trip down the stairs."

Burton grew still. "What did you say?"

"Said you can always do her in like you did your first wife."

Hurst froze and clapped a hand over his mouth, eyes widening. "Oh, didn't mean to mention it," he said in a loud, overly apologetic whisper. "Never would say a peep to anyone, Middleton, you know that. Your secrets are *my* secrets. After all, haven't I kept quiet all these years about what we did to that girl? That little blondie who was supposed to marry Pendragon." He rubbed a hand over his dissipated face. "Shouldn't have done it, you know, raped that girl. It was fun and all at the time, but look where it's got us. That's what set him against us, why he's sworn to do us in. You should have killed him years ago when you had the chance. But I guess it's hard to kill kin even when they're some bastard half brother you hate."

Cold fury flowed through Burton. How dare Hurst call that wretched piece of scum his father had sired his *brother!* He had *no* brothers, as his mother had pointed out from the time he'd been a young boy. She'd told him about his father's "other family," refusing to shield him from the degrading truth, as she'd called it.

When his father went away on one of his many trips, Burton had known it was because he'd rather spend time with his doxy and her unholy brat than share it with his real family. He remembered the tears his mother had shed, the pain in her eyes whenever she spoke of his father. He remembered her anguish, her humiliation, and had vowed years ago to assuage it.

He'd done what he could to ease her suffering while she'd been alive. How he'd relished the chance, when it finally came, to toss his father's whore quite literally out into the cold and strip his father's bastard of everything he held dear.

Ah, those had been sweet moments indeed. But he saw now it had not been enough.

No, with Pendragon it was *never* enough.

Deadly calm, Burton finished eating his peach.

"You seem to know a great deal about me, Hurst," he remarked as he patted his lips clean against his napkin. "More, I must say, than I had realized."

"I've got a good eye for detail, even if I'm foxed half the time. Write some of it down, too, don't you know."

Burton's fingers tightened against the napkin. "Really? And where do you do this writing, pray tell?"

"Oh, I keep a journal. Have for years. Helps me sometimes when I can't sleep."

"And what do you say in this journal?"

"Oh, most anything that comes to mind, just random thoughts. Latest conquests, a good bit of liquor I drank, latest mills and routs and such."

"And am I included in any of these musings?"

Hurst scuttled his brow. "You must be mentioned a time or two, but don't worry, I know how to keep mum." He tapped a finger against the side of his nose.

Yes, Burton thought, *I am beginning to realize just how well Hurst keeps secrets. The cabbage-head has probably detailed all of our dealings together over the years, from the rape to my wife's murder. I must get my hands on that journal and see for myself what it contains.*

"So do you have it with you?" Burton asked, striving to sound casual.

"Have what?"

"The journal."

"No, in the hurry to leave, I forgot it back in my townhouse. I'll have to make a trip into the village to get a fresh one."

"Yes, you must do that. Perhaps we'll go tomorrow if we aren't fishing."

Chapter Sixteen

❧❦❧

JULIANNA HURRIED INTO her townhouse and up
the stairs to her bedchamber, desperate to be alone.
Somehow, during the ride home, she'd managed to hold
back most of her tears, but a floodgate threatened again.

Daisy entered the room scant moments after, stopping
to exclaim over the sight of Julianna's swollen, tear-
ravaged face.

"My lady, whatever has occurred? Are you unwell?"

Unwell?

Yes, Julianna thought, *I am most unwell. My heart is
shattered.*

She pressed the heel of one hand against her eyes and
struggled to control her emotions. *The affair is done,* she
cautioned herself, *and I will think of him no more. From
this moment forth, Rafe Pendragon does not exist.*

A hysterical laugh bubbled up in her throat at the pre-
posterous idea. *As if I could ever forget Rafe.*

A pair of hot tears escaped, racing over her cheeks.
"I'm not quite myself today, Daisy. My head . . ." She
heard her voice quaver, high-pitched and trembling, and
knew she might give way if she said so much as another
word.

"Poor ma'am, you must be coming down ill. Perhaps
it's a summer cold. Let me get you out of your things

and into bed. I'll bring you a nice lavender compress for your head, and something soothing to help you rest."

She wished Daisy could bring her something to take away her pain, but she supposed her heart would have to heal on its own. If it ever did. She very much feared even time would fail to repair the rent Rafe Pendragon had torn in her soul.

As she let Daisy tend to her, she realized she hadn't lied—she really did feel unwell. Her head throbbed as if a knife were lodged between her temples, and when she swallowed, her throat burned, raw and strained from the strength of her earlier sobs.

Quick and efficient, her maid helped her out of her dress and into a soft lawn nightgown, freeing Julianna's hair from its pins before giving her tresses a few light strokes with a brush.

On a grateful sigh, Julianna slid between the sheets. Tucking her in with the care she would have used for a child, Daisy closed the drapes to darken the room.

Only when her maid was gone did Julianna give herself permission to break down, bitter tears scalding her eyes, wracking cries muffled by the pillow she held to her mouth. *How could I have so mistaken matters?* she berated herself. *Why did I think he wanted me, when what he actually wanted was to be rid of me?*

His words repeated in an endless loop inside her head, taunting her, tormenting her for having been such a simpleton.

When Daisy returned, she let the other woman think she'd been crying because of her headache. After blowing her stuffy nose, Julianna drank the offered sleeping draught, then lay back with the compress on her forehead. The scent of lavender drifted soothingly around her, but did nothing to ease her misery.

At length, she drifted off to sleep.

But sleep offered little comfort, her dreams filled with

Rafe, changing from images of him as the tender, passionate lover she'd known to nightmares of him at their last meeting, his cool eyes filled with rejection and pity.

She spent the next three days in bed, refusing to get up, refusing company. She even sent Maris and Harry away when they called, the pair of them justifiably concerned about her health.

Daisy fussed despite Julianna's orders to leave her be. As the days progressed, her maid finally threatened to call the doctor. Julianna prevented her, using the excuse that her "illness" was just a passing malaise brought on by exhaustion from her hectic social schedule. She would be better soon, she assured her.

The following morning she awoke to the knowledge that she couldn't continue to hide away from the world forever. Whether or not she wished, she was going to have to climb out of bed and get on with her life.

All was not a loss. She had achieved the goal she'd originally set out to accomplish. Harry and the estate were secure. Maris had enjoyed her Season and found herself a wonderful man to love and marry as well. Those were the things that mattered. The fact that Julianna had traded her body and lost her heart in the process were of scant regard.

For a brief while, she tried to hate Rafe, attempted to revile him for using and manipulating her for his own selfish purposes.

But she could not. She had come to him freely, and he had in no way deceived her.

Six months as his mistress. Six months' use of her body in repayment of her brother's debt. And in the end he had released her early, even going so far as to waive the last of her obligation when he'd decided he no longer wished for her company.

Another man might have demanded the money still owed. A blackguard would have enjoyed her body, then tossed her aside and still foreclosed on her brother's estate.

But not Rafe. He was in all ways an honorable man.

It wasn't his fault she'd wanted more. It wasn't Rafe's fault she had fallen in love, while he had not.

Well, she would repine no more. Her life had been a happy one before, and it would be again.

At least that is what I will tell myself, she vowed, as she reached out and rang for Daisy.

Not long after, her maid tapped on the door and came inside. "Yes, my lady?"

Julianna swung her legs out of bed. "Good morning, Daisy. Would you draw a bath for me please, then set out my apricot walking dress? I've decided to call on my sister and see if she would like to go shopping today. There is much to be done for her wedding."

A relieved smile lighted the younger woman's face. She curtseyed. "Yes, my lady. Right away, my lady."

Julianna stood and took her first steps back into her life.

Seven weeks later, Rafe sat at his desk and reviewed a recent list of acquisitions, including a stud farm that contained one Derby winner and several other prime blooded stallions. He'd already decided to put all but two of the thoroughbreds up for sale at Tattersalls next week, where he knew he would turn a handsome profit on his investment.

A quick knock came at his office door. Without waiting for permission to enter, Hannibal stepped inside.

"We've found him. He's in Lancashire."

Rafe set down his pen. "Lancashire? I wouldn't have thought St. George would decide to go to ground there. He hates the countryside."

Soon after St. George left the city, Rafe had sent Hannibal and a couple of other men off in search of the viscount. For a time their hunt had proven unsuccessful, as if St. George had quite literally vanished. Meanwhile, they had also set out in search of Hurst, his departure suspicious since it conveniently coincided with the viscount's, both men having left London on the same day.

"You were right about Hurst," Hannibal said as he lumbered further into the room. "The two of them are holed up in his hunting box. Seems nobody knew he had it. Won the house off a rich merchant at the gaming tables about six months afore. He finally contacted his man here in the city in need of 'civilized' provisions. Seems he's to gather up a number of items at the house and shops, and ship them north."

"A fresh supply of liquor, most likely. I doubt the local vintages are to Hurst's liking, or St. George's either. Good thing Hurst's man is our man as well."

Hannibal nodded in agreement and settled his large frame into a chair. "After we lost Rogers, it were tricky going fer a time. But Appleby's safe. That mutton-brained willy, Hurst, don't suspect him a bit."

"Not so mutton-brained he wasn't able to spot you and Rogers together in that pub," Rafe reminded him. "He may be a drunkard and a lout, but don't underestimate Hurst. He has the kind of cunning that keeps rats like him alive. He knows when to run and when to fight back, and he's fully capable of using whatever tactic does him the most good."

"Yer right, Dragon, we got sloppy. Won't happen again."

Rafe knew Hannibal well enough to be assured it would not.

"So what do you want us to do now?" Hannibal inquired.

Rafe leaned back in his chair. "Just keep an eye on them. I want to know if St. George or Hurst leaves Lancashire. If either of them decides to come back to the city."

He didn't think St. George would make any further attempts against Julianna's sister now that she was engaged to be married. But with St. George, you could never be too sure.

A surge of bittersweet longing swept through him at the thought of Julianna. Only this morning he'd congratulated himself on going an entire hour without having a single thought about her. Of course, once he'd reminded himself of the fact, he'd done nothing else *but* think of her, entirely undoing any progress he'd made.

Really, he didn't know what was wrong with him. By now he should have been able to put Julianna Hawthorne firmly in his past. Yet she haunted him—by day, and most especially by night. In the dark, quiet hours, he would often awaken from dreams of her, his body hard and aching, his need for her acute.

But more than that, he missed her. The melodic cadence of her voice, the effervescent sunshine of her smile, the graceful, animated way she moved and gestured. He missed their conversations and even their silences, the moments when the world slowed and it felt as if they were the only two people on the planet.

On impulse one afternoon, he'd bought a bouquet of roses from a passing flower girl. Lifting them to his nose, he'd found himself hoping to catch a hint of Julianna's scent. But sweet as the roses were, they were only flowers and smelled nothing like her at all. Disgusted with himself, he'd tossed the bouquet in the rubbish and walked on, calling himself ten times a fool.

Still, try as he might, he couldn't help but wonder about her.

How is she?
What is she doing?
And worst of all—who is she doing it with?

His fingers brushed across the silver letter opener on his desk, the coolness of the metal enough to snap him out of his musings. Glancing up, he discovered Hannibal watching him, a knowing expression in his black eyes.

Ignoring the look, Rafe continued their discussion. "What else did you find out?"

"Our man Appleby says that since Hurst's been gone, he's had more of a chance to poke around his townhouse. Says he found some journals he thinks you'll want to take a look at."

"Journals? I most definitely want to see them. You never know what delicious details Hurst might have decided to jot down."

"I'll get them from him next time we meet."

Rafe nodded.

Their conversation moved on to other matters for a few more minutes before Hannibal stood and walked from the room, his footsteps amazingly silent.

Rafe returned to his work, or at least made the attempt to do so. After five minutes, though, he gave up, reaching for his copy of the *Morning Post* in hopes the newspaper would take his mind off a certain distracting female.

Starting with word of the latest fighting on the Peninsula, he read an account of the British victory at Salamanca, which had occurred a couple of weeks ago, at the end of July. The battle had given Wellington and his forces a tremendous boost over the French, and yet success had come at a price, the lives of thousands of soldiers lost on both sides.

Next, he moved on to the financial pages, checking the latest prices for gold and silver currency before perusing a discussion of the British government's latest efforts to finance the war. Most of those mentioned, as he well knew, barely scraped the surface of England's real dealings. He was currently in negotiations to offer additional bonds to the government himself.

Flipping at random, he was about to set the paper aside when he caught sight of several familiar names in the Society column. Folding back the page, he scanned the article . . .

> *This Tuesday past, an elegant dinner party was held for the family and friends of the Earl and Countess of Grassingham and their son, retired Major William Waring, in honor of his engagement to Lady Maris Davies, sister of the Earl of Allerton and Julianna, Lady Hawthorne. The assembled company dined on roast squab and fillet of sole, finishing with chocolate pot de crème and coffee. At the conclusion of dinner, many of the guests moved into the ballroom, including the lovely bride-to-be—*

Rafe broke off and skimmed downward through the copy.

> *Lady H, stunning in a gown of ruby satin with an overskirt of Valencia lace, danced several times during the evening, including twice with the very eligible Lord S. Might there be more to his lordship's unusual decision to remain in Town well past the end of the Season than mere business? Perhaps Lady M won't be the only one who'll soon be sporting a ring!*

Rafe's stomach lurched, his hand crushing the paper. *Summersfield.* Who else could Lord S possibly be?
Is Julianna seeing Summersfield?
Certainly he knew Julianna and the earl received invi-

tations to the same balls, so their dancing together might mean nothing. Then again . . .

Surely she wasn't actually considering marrying the man? He couldn't believe it, not so soon after their affair. And not when she'd sworn she had no interest in marriage, including to Summersfield.

Still, women were well known for changing their minds.

Has Julianna?

Rafe's gut burned, a vein throbbing in his temple. Smoothing out the paper, he read on.

> *Both families plan to leave shortly for the country. The wedding between Major Waring and Lady Maris is scheduled to take place in early September at Davies Manor in Kent. A honeymoon trip to Scotland is planned for the happy couple.*

So Julianna would be leaving for the country soon, he thought. He'd known she would go eventually. Still, up to now he'd enjoyed an odd sense of comfort knowing she was still just across Town in Mayfair. With her departure, that would end.

Perhaps her leaving London was for the best, though. Maybe with her gone, he would at last be able to forget. Despite her tears that last day in Queens Square, maybe she had recovered and chased thoughts of him from her mind, bounced back so well she was even now considering marriage.

Ripping the page out of the paper, he squeezed the article into a ball.

And if she were planning to marry Summersfield, what was he going to do about it?

Nothing, he realized as he let the wadded paper roll onto his desk. *Absolutely nothing at all.*

* 　 * 　 *

"I now pronounce you husband and wife."

Striving for quiet, Julianna blew her nose into her silk handkerchief, then blotted the tears from her eyes.

I never cry at weddings, she bemoaned, feeling ridiculous at having wept her way through all but the first two minutes of the ceremony. Another tear leaked out as Maris and Major Waring—*William,* she corrected herself, now that he was her brother-in-law—exchanged their first kiss as a married couple.

Julianna wiped fresh moisture from her face as congratulatory clapping erupted from the assembled guests—several of William's military cronies, highly visible in their scarlet dress uniforms, shouting out enthusiastic huzzahs.

Arm in arm, Maris and William started back down the aisle of the parish church, friends and family already assembling outside to wish them on their way. At the entrance, more of William's army friends had gathered, sabers drawn and raised into an arch of honor for the newlyweds to pass beneath.

Laughing, Maris and William ran under the swords and out to the waiting carriage, the vehicle decorated with streaming white ribbons, sprays of fresh yellow hollyhocks, and puffy white hydrangea blossoms. The couple would ride to Davies Manor, where the reception was to take place, everyone else left to follow.

Julianna blew her nose one more time as she exited the church, relieved to have finally stopped crying. She didn't know why but she'd been feeling rather emotional lately, and weary as well.

All the work, she supposed.

The past two months had been a constant whirlwind of activity, the wedding preparations taking up every spare minute of the day. And over the last three days there'd been a convergence of family and friends upon the estate as everyone arrived for the wedding. The manor's twenty-five bedrooms were all in use, a few guests—friends of the major—thankfully agreeing to lodge at an inn in the nearby village.

Smothering a yawn, she located Harry and made her way to their coach. Settling back against the seat, she fought off a wave of tiredness, wishing when they arrived home that she might sneak upstairs for a nap. But as a member of the wedding party, she was required to be in the receiving line. Once that duty was finished, though, she decided, she just might excuse herself for half an hour.

Surely I will not be missed for so short a time? she mused.

Lately she'd been doing that a lot. Stealing off in the middle of the day to rest, so exhausted sometimes she could barely keep her eyes open even though she'd gotten a full night's sleep the evening before.

Yesterday, in fact, she'd embarrassed herself by drifting off for a few minutes during tea while Maris and Maris's new mother-in-law discussed plans for redecorating the newlyweds' new house in Wiltshire. Cousin Henrietta had touched Julianna kindly on the shoulder, startling her awake before the rest of the assembled guests could take note of her lapse.

Once everyone left tomorrow, she knew the house would calm down, and she would be able to relax and start feeling like herself again. *All I have to do,* she assured herself, *is get through the remainder of the day.*

The receiving line went well. Then came the reception breakfast, where she picked at her food, slightly nauseated by the scents and sounds of too many people crowded together. Light perspiration dampened her skin, the late summer day far warmer than anyone had anticipated it would be. In response, she ordered the servants to open a few windows to let in a cooling breeze, but the additional air seemed to make little difference.

Flushed and overwarm, she fanned herself while a series of toasts were given. Maris and William laughed at the good-natured ribbing they received from friends and family, the newlyweds' faces both wreathed in smiles at the bounty of warm wishes they received for their future health and happiness together.

Then the time arrived to cut the cake and toss the bouquet.

Afterward, Maris excused herself to change into a traveling dress for her wedding trip. Julianna came into the room to share a few last words and a warm hug, overjoyed to see how profoundly happy her little sister was. She started crying again, then Maris followed suit, making both of them laugh.

Far too soon, Maris was ready to leave.

In that moment, Julianna felt like a mother bird sending her fledgling chick out into the world. She knew Maris would be fine. She knew she would fly. But she would miss her nonetheless.

Of course she never managed to slip away for the nap she'd promised herself. Bone weary, she made her way downstairs and outside to wave the happy couple off on their journey north. The landau pulled away, wheels crunching on the drive, horse harnesses jingling.

As soon as the coach moved out of sight, she swung around to return to the house. A buzzing hummed in her ears like a thousand bees, and suddenly the world began to whirl. Swaying on her feet, she reached out and tried to catch hold of Harry's coat sleeve, but he was too far away.

Then she was falling, crumpling toward the ground amid a flurry of exclamations from several guests.

Her mind went black.

A sharp, stinging whiff of ammonia brought her

awake, the foul concoction making her cough and setting her eyes to water. Turning her head, she blinked against her distress, recognizing as she did the familiar flocked wallpaper of her bedroom.

As full awareness returned, she realized she was lying in her own bed with her gown loosened and her maid hovering anxiously. At the foot of the bed stood her brother, his brows drawn tight with concern.

"She's coming around now, my lord," Daisy murmured. "The doctor will be here soon."

"Doctor?" Julianna protested.

Everyone in the family knew how she despised doctors and had done since she'd been a child. She avoided them at all costs, even when she was ill.

"Yes, doctor," Harry said in a gruff tone. "And I will not have you refusing to see him."

"I am fine," she groaned. "Just tired."

"You fainted. You're more than just tried. Perhaps you're coming down with a relapse of the illness that kept you in bed a couple of months ago. Remember when you were sick in London?"

Of course she remembered; she wasn't likely to forget. Not a day went by that she didn't think of Rafe, didn't miss him with an empty, wrenching ache. But a broken heart had not made her faint.

Something had, though.

Too weak and miserable to argue further, she closed her eyes and waited for the dreaded physician to arrive.

Thankfully, Harry had the grace to depart soon after the doctor entered the room.

To her vast relief, she saw he was not the same old man who used to come to the house when she was a child. The grizzled quack who had drained half her mother's blood into a basin, then stood around shaking his head in hopelessness as she grew weaker and weaker. Julianna would never forget the horror and pain of that day, nor the grief she'd experienced as her mother, and the infant her mother had labored to bring into the world, died only hours apart.

The new man introduced himself as Dr. Coles, his pale blue eyes kind as he opened his bag and took out a few instruments.

She relaxed slightly when she saw none of the familiar tools used for bleeding or hot cupping. For a moment, a refusal hovered on her tongue as he moved near to begin, but she swallowed her protest as another wave of exhaustion swept through her.

He conducted his examination with gentle consideration, his hands as well as his words calm and friendly. Finishing a few minutes later, he began to repack his medical bag.

"Well, what do you think?" she inquired, sitting up against the pillows. "What's wrong with me?"

"Nothing is wrong with you," he replied with a smile. "At least nothing that is not fully to be expected in your condition."

"My condition? What do you mean?"

"I mean felicitations are in order, Lady Hawthorne. You are with child."

Chapter Seventeen

❧❧❧❧

JULIANNA STARED AT the doctor for a long moment, certain she must have misunderstood him.

"P-Pardon me, but did you say *with child*?"

"Yes. Around three months along, I'd estimate from what you told me concerning your last menses."

Breath rushed from her body, a twinge of her earlier dizziness returning, making her glad she was already lying down.

When he'd asked her about her menstrual cycles she'd never thought, never imagined, that anything other than stress and emotional fatigue could account for the ones she had missed. She'd hardly noticed when she'd skipped the first time. And as for the next, well, she'd been too busy, too exhausted, and too unhappy to worry over a little upset to her body's natural rhythms.

Blood rushed into her cheeks, then drained out again just as quickly. "But it's impossible!"

He raised a brow. "Not according to my examination. Have you and your husband been trying for a long time?"

She flushed again. Quite understandably, he assumed she was married. As a new member of the local community, he obviously didn't realize Lord Allerton's older sister was a widow.

Her heart gave an odd little squeeze. "I thought I was barren."

"Well, you are not. The good Lord has finally granted you a child."

"But I haven't been at all sick to my stomach."

He finished packing his bag, then fastening the leather strap. "Not all women are. You're obviously one of the lucky ones. The tiredness you've been experiencing should pass shortly since you're entering your second trimester. My recommendation is to get lots of rest, eat regular meals, and not push yourself too hard. Take an occasional walk so long as you aren't feeling dizzy like you did today. Have a companion accompany you to make sure all is well. My guess is you fainted from being overly excited from today's wedding festivities."

A funny sensation settled in her chest, her fingers tingling with what she could only assume to be shock and excitement.

Dear heavens, she thought, *I am going to have a baby. A baby!*

Long ago, she'd given up the dream of a family and put aside hopes of ever holding her own child in her arms. She'd wept to think she could not conceive, a failure for which her husband had often upbraided her. But since she was pregnant, it could mean only one thing— the fault had been Basil's. All these years of imagining herself to be barren when she hadn't been at all.

Before she could stop herself, before she had time to let the distressing realities set in, she gave herself permission to be happy.

A baby. At long last, I am going to be a mother.

"Thank you, doctor," she murmured, a tremulous smile breaking over her lips.

"You are very welcome. Now get some rest, my lady."

"I will, and gladly."

He gathered up his medical bag and started for the door.

"Oh, and doctor," Julianna called out softly.

He paused and turned back.

"If you would, I'd prefer you didn't mention this to anyone. I'd . . . um . . . I'd like to break the news myself."

He nodded, smiling in obvious understanding. "Of course. What goes on between doctor and patient is completely private. I'll leave the telling entirely up to you."

Settling back against the pillows, she relaxed, her mind awhirl. Closing her eyes, she let her thoughts wander, sure she was far too restive for sleep. But not long after, she proved herself wrong and drifted off.

She slept for hours, missing the reception, which continued downstairs in merry abandon. Lost in deep dreams, she didn't hear the music nor the occasional bursts of uproarious laughter that wound their way up the stairs.

Near dusk she finally roused.

Harry stopped in to check on her a short time later, along with Cousin Henrietta, who fluffed Julianna's pillows and straightened her covers, all the while tsking and clucking in concern over her earlier dramatic collapse.

After a few minutes of desultory conversation, Harry and her cousin departed, both of them insisting she remain abed and take a light, fortifying dinner in her room. They would see to the overnight guests, they reassured her.

Julianna didn't think she could sleep anymore, but after her meal and a warm bath, the weariness returned. Curling gratefully beneath the sheets, she let the world slip away.

She awakened early the next morning feeling more re-freshed and energetic than she had in weeks.

What bizarre dreams I had, she mused, stretching her arms over her head. First, she'd fainted and the doctor had come to the house, and then he'd told her she was with child.

Slowly she lowered her arms, knowing none of it had been a dream.

Oh sweet lord, I am pregnant!

Sliding her hands beneath her nightgown, she laid her palms over her naked belly.

I don't feel different, she thought, unable to detect any additional fullness in her shape. But when she tried to suck in her stomach, her belly refused to flatten, re-taining a faint rounded curve that definitely had not been there before.

Lying still, she let the full weight of the truth settle upon her.

I am carrying a baby. Rafe's baby.

Oh heavens, Rafe!

What was she going to tell him? Assuming she de-cided to tell him anything, that is. Under the circum-stances she wasn't terribly sure he would even want to know he was going to be a father.

His words from their very first meeting rang in her ears. "Lord knows the last thing I want is to bring an-other bastard into the world," he'd said in a hard voice.

She shivered. Understandably, he would be surprised. He might even be angry, she knew, especially after she had assured him there was no possibility of her ever con-ceiving a child. And after the determined manner in which he'd ended things between them, she had serious doubts he would want her and her child in his life.

So what to do?

Not only about Rafe, but about the baby as well? As a widow, she could not openly have the child. Society might forgive many things, but an out-of-wedlock birth was not one of them. She would have to keep her pregnancy a secret. And once the baby was born? What then?

Rubbing a hand over her abdomen, she fought back the sudden tears that filled her eyes. At least now she understood all the wild emotional swings with which she'd been dealing recently—her bouts of weepiness, her unpredictable moods, her overwhelming tiredness.

At the moment, she had no real idea what she was going to do, but upon one point she had no doubts.

I am going to keep this baby, she vowed.

Many women in her situation would have been thinking about giving the baby away, using the next few months to find a trustworthy couple who would agree to take the child to raise as their own—for a price, of course.

But she could not do that. She'd waited too long for a baby. She wasn't giving it up now.

As for how she was going to find a socially acceptable explanation for the sudden appearance of an infant in her life, she had no notion. Still, she had a bit of time before her pregnancy would start to show. Surely by then she would be able to figure out a solution.

At least she hoped so.

Once again her thoughts turned to Rafe, a familiar ache squeezing inside her chest. Try as she might, she could not seem to stop loving him, though God knows she wished otherwise. Now with the baby, Rafe would be in her mind even more.

A part of her wished she could simply lay her problems at his feet, but she would not beg, not even for the baby. Besides, she had sufficient income and no need of his financial assistance. As for her other admitted difficulties, well, she had already decided she would work those out on her own.

She frowned as her earlier quandary returned.

Should I tell him about the baby?

Moments later she gave a firm, negative shake of her head.

Rafe had made his feelings clear, painfully so. He most assuredly did not want her, and she very much doubted he would want her child, either. Even if he did agree to accept responsibility, she knew he would do so out of duty and obligation. Well, she wanted none of that.

No, she thought, *this baby is mine. I, and I alone, will see to its care.*

A twinge of guilt tingled inside her over her peremptory decision, but she ignored the sensation, brushing it aside.

Seconds later, her stomach gave an empty rumble.

Goodness, I am famished, she thought. Her lips curved, realizing increased hunger would probably be a frequent occurrence now that she was eating for two.

Deciding she would go downstairs for breakfast, she tossed back the covers, then padded barefoot across the room to ring for Daisy.

"I've laid out your lilac traveling dress, my lady," Daisy said, pausing as she finished packing the last of Julianna's belongings into a pair of heavy trunks. "I hope that is agreeable?"

"Quite agreeable. Thank you, Daisy," Julianna said, casting a brief glance up from the letter she was writing to Maris.

After nearly a week, she was leaving Davies Manor and returning home to London.

Just this afternoon the last of the wedding guests had departed, relatives old and new, promising to see her in a few months for the holidays. She'd nodded her agreement but knew she would not be seeing any of them, since by then she would be as round and plump as the goose that would be served for Christmas dinner.

Harry would be accompanying her back to Town, but Cousin Henrietta would not. With Maris now safely wed, the older woman had decided to visit her eldest daughter, who was expecting her second child in November. Henrietta said that perhaps she'd stay on after the birth, buy a small cottage, and act the doting granny. Yesterday afternoon, she and Julianna had kissed and hugged and shared promises to write often; then Henrietta had been on her way.

Upstairs now in her bedchamber, Julianna finished penning her note to Maris, which she planned to leave with today's outgoing post. Dusting the letter with sand, she folded the missive and sealed it with wax. Flipping the paper over, she wrote her sister's new address on the outside in a neat hand.

Knowing Harry must be growing anxious to depart, she set her pen aside, then sprang to her feet. Dizziness hit her like a crashing wave, her thoughts blurring as she swayed unsteadily on her feet. Reaching out, she gripped her chair, then quite abruptly sat back down.

Daisy paused in her packing. "Are you all right, my lady?"

"What? Oh, I'm fine. Fine." Julianna sat trembling, fighting to regain her balance.

Bother it! she cursed. She'd hoped her days of dizziness and fainting spells were over, but apparently her body had other ideas.

When she wavered again, Daisy hurried across the room to her. Setting a cool hand to the back of Julianna's neck, her maid urged her to bend forward and place her head between her knees.

"Go on, my lady. Lean down. It's what always helped my mother when she was expecting. Take slow breaths. You'll be fine in a few moments."

Daisy rubbed her other palm in comforting circles across Julianna's back, holding her steady until her vertigo finally receded. Only after she began to feel herself again did Julianna consider her maid's words.

Slowly she raised herself into an upright position. "What did you say?" she asked in a faint voice.

Daisy met her gaze, the girl's hazel eyes wide with knowledge. "You mean about you being in the family way? Perhaps I shouldn't have said anything, but there's no need to hide the obvious."

Obvious! Julianna's stomach lurched. *How obvious is it?*

Julianna lowered her voice. "What do you mean? How can you tell?" *Could other people tell? Could Henrietta? Or Harry? Oh, my!*

Obviously reading Julianna's distress, Daisy rushed to reassure her. "I'm sure I'm the only one who knows, besides the doctor, that is. I've suspected for a few weeks now, my lady. After all, I do tend to your personal needs, and when you missed your monthly twice in a row, well, I had to wonder. After you fainted, that's when I knew for sure. The doctor did say you're with child, didn't he?"

She straightened her spine. "Yes. Apparently I am the only one of the three of us who didn't have a clue."

"Well, that's not surprising being this is your first babe."

Staring at the younger woman, she crossed her arms. "And how is it that you come to know so much about such matters, seeing as you have no children of your own? Unless I am mistaken about that?"

The maid had the grace to flush. "Mercy no, I've no little ones of my own. But I know a lot about pregnant women and babies. I am the oldest of twelve and helped me mum whenever she was carrying. Saw to the young ones, too, at least until I left to come into service."

Julianna had known Daisy had a great many siblings, but she'd never realized that she'd helped raise half of them.

"It's a good thing that I know," her maid continued. "You'll be needing someone to look after you in the months to come."

Perhaps Daisy was right, Julianna judged. She would need someone to look after her as her pregnancy progressed. And what a relief to have someone in whom to confide, someone else who knew the truth. Only a few days had passed since she'd discovered her condition, but already she was chafing under the weight of the secret. Maybe it was a providential thing that she knew.

"You mustn't breathe a word of this to anyone," Julianna admonished quietly.

A look of hurt flashed over the servant's face. "I would never betray your confidence, my lady. I like to pride myself on my loyalty. I should hope you would know that by now."

Julianna reached out and patted Daisy's hand in apology. "Of course, I'm sorry, and you're right. I know I can count upon your discretion." She paused and drew in a deep, steadying breath. "Are you horribly shocked?" *Disapproving? Scandalized?*

"About the babe? I was a little startled at first, but not really surprised, no."

Julianna raised a brow. "Why ever not?"

Daisy ducked her head. "Well, I've known you were seeing a gentleman for the last while, my lady."

Oh, good gracious! Is there anything she doesn't know?

"And how, pray tell, did you discover that?"

"Well, sometimes when you'd return home, your clothes would smell ever so faintly of bayberry. And then there was your hair."

"What about my hair?" Julianna lifted a self-conscious hand and touched her tresses.

"It were neatly done and all, prettily styled, but not the way I do it. The strands were twisted differently, the pins moved round and such."

And here she and Rafe had thought themselves so clever, so careful, when all along her maid had known about them because of her hairstyle.

"I suppose you know his identity as well?"

The girl shook her head. "No, my lady. I'm no snoop to be prying into such matters as aren't my business."

Julianna released a breath.

"I know he hurt you, though, and I don't like him for it. I don't like him at all."

"Thank you, Daisy, but do not be too severe upon him. He cannot help his feelings any more than I can my own, I suppose. Now let us speak of him no more."

"Of course, ma'am. I'm sorry if I've unsettled you, and you in a family way and all."

Suddenly the door thumped open.

Turning her head, Julianna met her brother's astonished, wide-eyed gaze.

She groaned, feeling a little ill.

Had Harry heard? Of course he had; all I have to do is look at his face to know.

Pushing the door wider, Harry strode inside, pinning Julianna with a condemning glance. "Is it true?"

"What were you doing eavesdropping outside my door?" she said, hoping the question would buy her a few extra moments in which to brace herself for the confrontation to come.

"I wasn't eavesdropping . . . at least not intentionally. I came to ask when you might be ready to depart, and what do I hear but . . . my God, are you really . . . enceinte?" he finished on an appalled whisper.

Drawing a deep breath, she linked her trembling fingers in her lap. "Daisy, if you would be so good, please leave us."

The maid shot her a sympathetic glance, then curtseyed and hurried from the room.

The click of the latch echoed loudly. A long minute passed.

"*Well?*" Harry demanded. "Have you nothing to say?"

She gave a small sigh. "What would you like me to say?"

"To begin, you might tell me when I can expect an invitation to the wedding."

"What wedding?"

"*Your* wedding!" he exploded.

Closing his eyes for a moment, he visibly attempted to calm himself. "You *are* getting married, I presume. The man who got you," he paused, circling a hand toward her stomach, "in your present condition, is going to do the right thing and marry you, is he not?"

She wiped her suddenly perspiring palms on her skirt, then answered as plainly and as bluntly as she could. "No, he is not."

Her words reverberated between them like a thunderclap.

"And why the devil not?"

"I will thank you not to yell or curse in my presence."

Her brother had the grace to look chastened. "My apologies. I did not mean to yell at you."

After a moment, he continued. "So, why aren't you marrying him?"

Glancing away from his probing gaze, she studied the design on the Turkey carpet. "Because I am not, and that is all I have to say about the matter."

Mercy, could this day get any worse? she asked herself.

Why hadn't she thought to lock her bedroom door before having such a personal, private, secret conversation with her maid? Because she hadn't expected to have a personal, private, secret conversation with her maid at all.

Pregnancy is obviously turning me into a muttonhead.

"Well, it isn't all *I* have to say. What sort of cad is he to get you with child, then refuse to take responsibility?"

"He hasn't refused. He doesn't even know I am expecting. And no, I am not going to tell him," she added, intuiting his next question before the words had time to leave his mouth.

"Why not? You need a husband, and he seems the most logical choice." His eyebrows suddenly winged upward. "Unless he's married. Is that the trouble? The blackguard is married?"

She sighed. "No, he isn't married."

"Well, then, I see no impediment to your union. As soon as we arrive back in London, the two of you can tie the knot. I'm sure the archbishop will be more than happy to provide you with a special license."

"The archbishop won't be providing anything because I am not getting married." She huffed out an exasperated breath. "Now, enough. I am done being interrogated."

He glowered.

"This is my business, Harry. Leave it alone."

"You are my sister and I care about you. How can I leave it alone?" He raked a hand through his hair. "Dear God, Jules, what were you thinking? How could you have let this happen?"

"Actually I didn't think it could, if you must know," she told him in a taut voice.

He cleared his throat, looking suddenly uncomfortable. "Oh well, yes, I see your point. But I still don't understand why you aren't telling him about your . . . about the child. Did the bounder toss you aside or something?"

Misery crashed through her at his unintentionally cruel statement.

"I can see by your expression that he did," Harry continued, his voice softening in sudden compassion. "Who is this rogue with whom you've gotten yourself entangled? He's obviously a rake to take advantage of a lady. Tell me his name so I can go beat him to a bloody pulp."

A sad smile covered her lips. "I don't want him beaten. As for his name, it's not important. This is my problem, Harry, and I will deal with it on my own."

Harry scowled and crossed his arms over his chest. "Frankly, I don't see how you can deal with it. You're pregnant, Jules. Unmarried widows don't get pregnant, not if they wish to remain in Society. You'll never be able to keep this child."

Suppressing a shiver, she raised her chin. "I'll find a way."

"What way? Your only option is to marry this man or else have the baby in secret and give it up."

Unconsciously, she placed a hand over her stomach as if to protect the unborn life growing inside her. "I am not giving up my baby."

"Then let me help you. Tell me the name of your . . ." he hesitated, obviously having to force himself to continue, "lover. Let me find a way to force him to marry you."

She shook her head, despair squeezing like a knot beneath her ribs. "It's no use, Harry. You don't understand."

"Then explain it to me, so I will."

He only wanted to help, she knew, but she couldn't afford to confide in him. Doing so would only make an already untenable situation that much worse. So she held her tongue and remained silent.

"This isn't finished, Julianna," he cautioned once he realized she wasn't going to reply. "By whatever means necessary, I will find out the identity of this rogue who has besmirched your honor, and I will see matters put right."

His use of her full name warned her of the seriousness of his statement. He rarely called her Julianna, and only when he was angry or upset.

"Oh, Harry don't, I beg you—"

"Finish packing. We leave within the hour."

Turning on his heel, he strode from the room.

Abruptly exhausted, she closed her eyes and heaved a weary sigh. Her difficulties, she very much feared, had only just begun.

Chapter Eighteen

CHEERFUL MORNING SUNLIGHT flooded in through the French doors at the rear of Rafe's townhouse, the doors opened to let a refreshing breeze waft into the comfortable dining alcove that overlooked the garden beyond. Late-blooming gillyflowers and snapdragons added a last burst of color to the view, the scent of jasmine honey-sweet in the air.

Rafe paid little heed to the idyllic atmosphere as he read his newspaper and ate a breakfast of ham, toast, and eggs. After refilling his cup with hot black coffee, he turned a page of the *Morning Post*'s financial section.

He was engrossed in an article about the burgeoning timber trade in America, and was already considering the investment opportunities, when a set of footsteps rang out against the flagstone floor. Glancing up, he raised an inquiring brow as Hannibal approached.

"Sorry to interrupt, Dragon," the big man stated, "but that young whelp Allerton's at the door. Tried to send him packing, but he ain't having none of it."

Rafe frowned in surprise. "What does he want?"

"Won't say. Most likely he's come to beg for more blunt. Guess my little tour of the Thames wharfs weren't enough of a deterrent to keep him on the straight and narrow. He's got balls o' brass to come 'round here again, I'll say that for him."

"Yes, well, show him in."

Rafe pushed his plate aside but left the newspaper open.

Why the deuce is Allerton here? he pondered.

He hoped Hannibal was mistaken about his intent and that the impudent pup had not come seeking money. If he had, he obviously needed his ears cleaned out, since Rafe had made it patently clear there would be no more funds forthcoming from him or any of London's other financiers. Perhaps he thought Rafe's threats were nothing but bluster. Well, the young lord would soon discover he was mistaken.

He downed a swallow of coffee and allowed his thoughts to touch upon Julianna for a fleeting instant. As always, he wondered how she was faring. He knew she had returned to the city last week after her sister's wedding, and was once again living in her townhouse in Upper Brook Street. Beyond that, her life was now a mystery to him, the two of them little more than strangers.

Shaking his head, he pushed her from his mind.

After all, he thought, *Allerton isn't here to talk about his sister, and I had best remember that fact.*

Not surprisingly, the earl arrived without Hannibal to announce him. Hannibal never announced anyone, and Rafe had long ago given up any expectation that he would.

Attired in fashionable buckskins, brown morning coat, and Hessians, his beaver top hat tucked beneath one arm, Harry Davies marched into Rafe's breakfast room.

At his ease, Rafe leaned casually back in his chair, making no effort to stand in the nobleman's presence. Negligently, he flipped a page of his paper and sipped his coffee. Only when he settled his cup back into its saucer did he deign to look up.

"My lord Allerton, to what do I owe this visit so early

in the day? I must say your presence was not anticipated."

"If it was not, it only shows how shortsighted you
are. You, sir, are an unprincipled blackguard." Striding
quickly forward, Allerton lashed out with the pair of
leather gloves he held in his fist, using them to smack
Rafe across the face.

A swath of fire burned Rafe's cheek where he'd been
struck. Holding himself still, he ignored the pain, as well
as his astonishment, as he turned a fearsome glare upon
the younger man.

Lord Allerton had enough sense to pale beneath
Rafe's menacing look, but squared his shoulders and
held his own.

"I have come," the earl announced grandly, "to demand satisfaction. Choose your seconds, sir."

Rafe quirked a brow, half startled, half amused.

Choose his seconds? What the deuce?

"A thousand pardons, my lord, but have you taken
complete leave of your senses?"

A measure of the starch came out of Allerton's sails at
Rafe's riposte. "Of course not. I have come here to see
honor met."

"Met for what?"

"As if you didn't know. My sister's name and reputation have been sullied and you, sir, are responsible. I
have come here to see that justice is done."

Rafe froze, careful to in no way betray the sudden
leap of his pulses. *Does Allerton know about Julianna
and me? And if he does, how in the devil did he find out?*

Seemingly indifferent, Rafe reached for the silver coffee urn, pouring the last of the beverage into his cup. Ignoring the nearly scalding heat, he drank it down in a
few quick swallows.

"I am sorry, but I have no idea to what you refer."

"Of course you do," Allerton hissed. "I know all about it. How you lured her into your web. How you used and degraded her."

Rafe's gaze flashed up. "Did she say that?"

"She didn't have to. She's too much of a lady to have discussed the details, even with me. But with a bit of digging, I found out what I needed to know. Servants will talk with the right persuasion."

Ah, so he'd bribed or coerced her servants, had he? One of the footmen who'd carried their occasional notes was the most likely culprit. Obviously, Julianna needed new staff.

"If your lady sister doesn't care to share the details of her private life with you, then I see no cause to do so either."

Color crept up Allerton's neck. "You will discuss it, by damn, and take responsibility as well. Though I can see why she doesn't want to marry you. Such a union is utterly beneath her. She'll be cast from Society because of you."

Rafe stiffened. "And why is marriage under debate?"

"Because you got her with child, you knave!"

Rafe's hand struck the coffee cup, toppling it over onto the table. A few remaining drops leaked out to stain the white cloth underneath.

Pregnant? No, she can't be.

"You must be mistaken," he said, his words sounding as if they came from a very great distance.

"I am not mistaken," Allerton asserted. "She admitted it to me herself. I only found out because she's been sick and dizzy. We had to call the doctor for her when she fainted."

Rafe's gaze flew to meet the other man's. "Is she all right?"

"As well as any woman who finds herself in a delicate condition." Allerton tightened his fist. "You have ruined her, you disreputable bastard, and now you must be made to pay."

Julianna with child.

She'd told him she was barren. He could still remember the sadness, the loss in her eyes when she'd explained her inability to conceive. And he knew she'd believed what she said. No one could have faked that kind of reaction and under the circumstances, she would have had no reason to do so. She had thought herself safe from pregnancy. Apparently mother nature had proven her wrong.

He gulped down a ragged breath.

My God, I'm going to be a father!

"Choose your weapon," Allerton declared. "Swords or pistols. We shall meet on the field of honor tomorrow at dawn."

Rafe pulled himself away from his musings and turned a gimlet eye upon Julianna's little brother. "Do not be absurd."

"Beg pardon?"

"There is no need to pardon either of us. There will be no duel."

Allerton sputtered. "But, of course there will. You have wronged me and my family and you must atone."

"If I have wronged anyone it is your sister. This matter is for her and me to resolve."

The earl's cheeks flushed a light crimson. "I protest. I must be allowed to have satisfaction."

Rafe shrugged. "Protest all you like, but it shall make no difference."

Needing something with which to busy his hands, Rafe grasped the newspaper and folded it into neat halves. When Allerton made no move to leave, he sighed. "I will not fight you, my lord."

"Then you are a coward, sir."

Rafe drilled him with a menacing glare. "If you think

that, boy, you are far less intelligent than is generally credited." He leaned casually back in his chair. "Killing you tomorrow would be a waste of my time and your life. Your sister would clearly disapprove."

Allerton puffed out his chest. "And what makes you believe I wouldn't kill *you*?"

Rafe gave a dismissive snort, his contempt at the idea plain. Even Allerton must know he excelled at both shooting and swordplay. He was quite handy with his fists as well.

"A gentleman would meet me," the earl stated.

"Too true. But then you forget I am not a gentleman. Only gentlemen and greentops are foolish enough to advertise their personal difficulties in public. If I met you tomorrow as you propose, your sister's reputation would indeed be damaged beyond all repair. I do not think she would thank you for it. As it is, if you can manage to keep your mouth shut, there may yet be some way of remedying the situation."

"And that would be?"

"That is for Lady Hawthorne and me to decide."

Rafe climbed to his feet, topping the younger man by a few inches and a lifetime of experience. "If you love your sister, as I believe you do, stay out of this. I will see to her welfare."

"As you saw to it before? What did you do to her to lure her into your bed? What tricks and deceits did you employ to steal her virtue and leave her in such straits?"

"I believe, my lord," Rafe continued, "that it is time you were going. I said I will do right by your sister and I shall."

Allerton thrust out a warning finger. "You've hurt her enough, Pendragon. If you do so again, I promise I will kill you, and it won't be on the field of honor."

"Duly noted, my lord."

Hands fisted in impotent rage, Allerton glowered at

him for another long minute, then turned on his heel and stalked from the room. The front door slammed moments later.

Lord Allerton had obviously let himself out.

Knees abruptly weak, Rafe sat down heavily in his chair.

Julianna is carrying my child.

Steepling his fingers, he contemplated his future—and hers.

Julianna threaded a fresh length of rose-tinted silk into her needle, then applied it to the linen cloth tautly secured inside her sewing frame. She was working on a floral design of her own creation, the stitches she took both graceful and skilled.

She liked to sew. Embroidery had been one of her favorite pastimes ever since childhood, when her mother had thrust a sampler and needle into her hands at age four. As a woman grown, she found the activity pleasurable and highly soothing, especially now when she needed to keep her mind occupied and her worries at bay. But even as she concentrated upon forming the intricate pattern of twining leaves and flowers, her mind began to wander into troubling territory.

She wouldn't be able to stay in Town for too much longer, she judged. A month, maybe two, if she was lucky. After that, her pregnancy would start to show. She could attempt to conceal it, of course, but she ran too great a risk that way.

No, I must leave London and retreat to the country, she decided. And it must be unfamiliar country, where she was sure she would not encounter anyone of her acquaintance.

But where? She could travel to Scotland, she supposed. The rugged environs of the north would certainly be remote enough for her purposes. But the thought of spending the winter in such a cold, damp clime brought on a shiver, as if she were already surrounded by chill winds and snow.

The Continent would be far more pleasant, a warm, relaxing place in which to deliver her baby. France was out of the question, of course, because of the war. But maybe Italy or Greece, assuming she could find a ship to take her safely there. And assuming she felt healthy enough to make the voyage.

Two very, very big assumptions.

Tying off the thread, then giving the stray end a quick snip, she reached into her basket for more silk—leaf green this time. Seconds after, a gentle tapping came upon the sitting room door.

She gazed up as her butler, Martin, walked inside.

"My lady," he announced in well-modulated tones. "A caller has arrived. I informed the gentleman that you are not receiving at present but he insists upon seeing you." Martin's nose wrinkled slightly, revealing his annoyance. "He refuses to leave until I have consulted with you directly."

"Did he give you his name?" she inquired, drawing a fresh strand of thread into the needle's eye.

"Yes. Pendragon, my lady. He said his name is Rafe Pendragon."

She flinched and accidentally jabbed the sharp point of her needle into her skin. Grimacing in pain, she watched a bright red drop of blood rise on the wounded tip. Flustered, she reached for her handkerchief and pressed the silk against her hand.

"Shall I tell the gentleman you cannot be disturbed?" Martin asked, obviously aware of her unsettled reaction.

Too late for that, she thought.

"No, no. I will see him," she said. "Please ask him to come in."

The butler bowed. "Very good, my lady."

Her pulse thudded, nervous dread clamoring in her belly.

Rafe is here and there can be only one reason.

Blast Harry for his meddling, and for his insistence in playing the gallant knight. She ought to be furious—and she was—but deep down she knew her brother meant well, even if he had no right to interfere. Had he gone to challenge Rafe? Stars above, surely the two men weren't going to fight! Or had they already met this morning at dawn, and Rafe was here to offer his apologies for having killed her brother!

Don't be a ninnyhammer, she scolded herself. *Of course Harry isn't dead.*

She had no more time for wild speculation as Martin returned, followed into the room by the large, imposing man whose familiar form made her senses swim. Just the sight of him turned her dizzy in ways that had nothing to do with her pregnancy. Curling her fingernails into the seat cushion beneath her, she fought to remain calm.

Dark and beautiful as a warrior of ancient myth, Rafe dominated the room, resplendent in buff pantaloons and a blue cutaway coat that enhanced the luxurious green of his eyes. For an instant, she let herself savor the sight of him, lapping him up the way a cat would a dish of cream.

"Mr. Rafe Pendragon, my lady," Martin announced.

Working to regulate her features, she strove not to allow so much as a single emotion to show. She couldn't afford to let Rafe know she still harbored feelings for him, and that in spite of everything, including his cutting rejection, love lingered even now in her heart.

Securing her embroidery needle in a pin cushion, she moved her sewing frame to one side, retaining her seat in a wing chair beneath a bright side window.

"Shall I bring refreshments, my lady?" the butler inquired.

"No, thank you, Martin," she said in an implacable tone. "Mr. Pendragon will not be staying long. You may leave us now."

The servant bowed and exited the room, quietly closing the door behind him.

Rafe raised a brow at her inhospitable statement, but decided not to take offense. Clearly, she was less than overjoyed to see him, and he couldn't entirely blame her. After all, he'd cast her aside the last time they'd met, even if his motives had been noble ones.

Striding farther into the room, he couldn't help but be struck by Julianna's beauty, lush and vibrant as an exotic hothouse flower in full bloom. If it were possible, she was even more ravishingly exquisite than before.

His pulse quickened, his blood warming as he let his gaze sweep over her. Was his awareness of her stunning looks simply a reaction to his having been parted from her these past few months? Or was she truly that much more beautiful? The result of impending motherhood perhaps. Some women glowed when they were expecting, and apparently, Julianna was one of them.

Without thinking, his gaze lowered to her waist, searching for evidence of a pregnancy. But her figure appeared as always, with no discernible changes.

What a picture she made, he thought, seated within a circle of warm afternoon sunlight—an elegant woman in an equally elegant setting. Refined and airy, the room suited her, the walls painted in delicate feminine shades of pink and cream. A pair of caryatids flanked the white marble fireplace, the toga-draped ladies giving the illusion of holding the mantel aloft. Sleek-legged Chippendale furniture upholstered in green and beige stripes was arranged in comfortable groupings, with several soft Aubusson carpets spread over the polished wood floors.

When his eyes met hers, her chin came up.

"Well, Mr. Pendragon," she said, "are you going to do nothing but stare at me, or have you something to say? You really ought not be here, you know. I thought we had agreed you would not visit this house."

His lips tightened. *So we're back to formalities, are we?* "My pardon, *Lady Hawthorne,* but I did not think a note appropriate under the circumstances, and I rather doubted you would appreciate me crawling through your bedroom window in the dark of night. Or do I mistake the matter?"

A rosy flush burnished her cheeks. "You most certainly do not."

Glancing away, she curled a hand against the material of her skirt. A pretty shade, he mused, the color not so different from the one she had worn on their very first meeting all those long months ago.

He linked his hands loosely at his back. "Your brother came to see me yesterday."

Her shoulders stiffened. "Did he?"

"He challenged me to a duel in defense of your honor."

Her gaze flew to his. "Where is Harry now? Is he all right?"

"I have no idea where your brother might be, and he was extremely well the last time I saw him, although a bit out of temper." He paused. "You don't really imagine I accepted his challenge, do you? Please credit me with having more sense than to fight a young man barely out of leading strings."

"Yes, of course. It is just that Harry can be rather impetuous in his actions at times and, well, he should not have involved you. He had no cause."

"No cause? From what he told me, he had every cause. Were his assertions untrue? He says, madam, that you are increasing. Was he in error? Are you carrying my child or not?"

A panorama of emotions flickered across her features, as if she were debating whether or not to answer him. Finally, she nodded. "Yes, it would appear that I am."

Her confirmation knocked aside the tenuous hold he'd been keeping upon himself. Crossing to the chair directly across from her, he sat down hard, his knees suddenly unsteady despite the fact that she had said nothing he did not already know. Still, her confirmation scattered any last fleeting possibility that Allerton had been wrong after all.

Julianna toyed with a piece of ribbon on her dress. "I realize the news must have come as a great shock. It certainly knocked the wind out of me, and I'm the one who's enceinte." She paused, something fierce suddenly flashing in her eyes. "But if you imagine for so much as a minute that I lied to you about believing I was barren, then I—"

He cut her off with a hand. "I do not. I know you honestly thought yourself to be at the time. What possible reason could you have had to do otherwise? No, madam, if anyone was tricked it was you. Apparently your late husband was a considerably less potent lover than either of us imagined. Obviously far less potent than I."

Julianna flushed at his indelicate remark, but seemed to unbend a bit realizing he was not going to blame her for the pregnancy.

"How far along are you, by the way?"

"Roughly three months. I'm not certain precisely when I conceived, though I assume it must have happened during one of our last times together."

Perhaps our very last time, he thought after a quick calculation.

Clasping her hands in her lap, she twisted her fingers

together. "I am sorry Harry brought you into this. He did so expressly against my wishes."

"Which means, I assume, that you were not going to tell me about the baby," he murmured, sudden anger rising inside him. "Didn't you think I had a right to know? I am the father after all."

She looked him squarely in the eye. "I didn't think you would *want* to know; many men would not. And you made your feelings toward me quite plain at our last meeting. I hardly expected you to be overjoyed by the news that I'm increasing. I assumed it would be the last thing you would wish to hear considering your feelings about bringing unwanted, illegitimate children into the world."

A pronounced silence settled between them.

"You are right," he said. "I do not like the idea of bringing an illegitimate child into the world, which is why I have come here today." Shifting forward, he reached out and took her hand. "Julianna, will you marry me?"

Breath caught in her chest, the strength of his touch warm as a brand against her skin. For a long moment, she couldn't decide which she found more startling—the delightful sensation of his hand clasp, or his unexpected question.

Marry me, he'd asked?

Once, she would surely have leapt at the offer in spite of all the impediments that stood in the way of their union. For the promise of his love, she knew she would have been willing to turn her back on the life she had always known in order to forge a new one with him—Society and its rules be damned.

But Rafe did not love her, she reminded herself, and as honorable as his proposal might be, it came from a sense of duty and pride. For all the real sentiment involved, he might as well have been arranging one of his many business dealings. There would likely have been more genuine pleasure at the anticipated outcome.

Her hand grew cold inside his own.

"I realize marriage was not in either of our plans," he continued, "but then neither was the idea of having a child. Circumstances have changed now, however, and so must our priorities. I am sure you agree."

A shiver rose beneath her skin, making her wish she had her shawl.

"There is still time for a church wedding if that is what you would prefer, but I think it would be wisest not to wait. As it is there will speculation, what with the baby already three months along. I think a special license is our best option."

A wry laugh nearly escaped her lips. He hadn't even waited to hear her answer, the conclusion apparently foregone in his mind. After all, what woman would refuse to marry the father of her baby in order to give the child a name?

Well, my baby can have my name, she decided in a sudden stubborn burst of defiance.

With a tug, she freed her hand from Rafe's. "I thank you for the honor of your proposal, but I am afraid I must decline."

He stared at her, puzzled disbelief on his face. "Excuse me? What did you say?"

Squaring her shoulders, she met his gaze. "I said that I will not marry you."

His dark brows twisted into a scowl. "Don't be absurd. You have to marry me. You're having my child."

"You have done as duty requires and offered to accept responsibility for the baby. I do not wish to wed you, however, so I hereby free you of your obligation. You may leave now, your conscience absolved of any guilt. I will see to the baby."

He sprang to his feet, an expression as black and fearsome as a thundercloud descending over his features. She trembled, reading the anger that snapped like a pair of whips in his eyes.

"See to it how?" he demanded. "I can tell you've done a measure of thinking on the subject, so what are your plans?" Suddenly he paled. "Good God, you're not intending to give the baby away, are you?"

She flinched as if he had struck her. "No, I would never do that."

"Then what?" he asked, towering over her. "Surely you cannot think to openly have the child. Even as a respected widow, Society would never condone such an act."

"I am well aware how Society would greet such news." Turning her head, she glanced toward the window. "I am considering a trip abroad."

"*Abroad?* Where abroad?"

"Italy perhaps."

"Italy!" he blustered. "Out of the question. In case you haven't heard, there's a war going on. What if your ship was attacked? What if it sank? No, you are *not* going to Italy."

"Scotland, then. What harm could come to me there?"

"None, except you'll have to live among the Scots. As a rule, they don't have a great love for the English aristocracy, and since you won't be staying with some rich lord, you might not find it to your liking. Especially since you'll be pregnant, with no husband in sight."

"I'll tell them I'm a widow, which is no lie since that's exactly what I am. I just won't mention that my husband's been dead these past five years."

"Or that you're carrying your lover's baby."

"You're not my lover anymore," she shot back.

"True enough. But that baby you're carrying is as much mine as yours, and I have a say in its upbringing."

"You have *no* say."

A muscle rippled in his jaw. "I will once I am your husband." His eyes narrowed. "Or are you trying to arrange matters so you won't have to go abroad at all and you can still keep the child?"

"What do you mean?"

"I'm talking about you and another man. I understand you've been very cozy with Lord Summersfield again. Is that your hope, that you'll be able to marry him instead of me?"

Her mouth dropped open. "Lord Summersfield! Where on earth did you get such a notion?"

His eyes sparked deep green with a glare she might have mistaken for jealousy had she not known better. "Never mind how I came by the information," he said. "Is it true? Are you going to marry Summersfield and somehow convince him that my child is his own? Is that why you've been seeing him, because you're pregnant and in need of a husband?"

"*How dare you!* I have not been seeing him or any other man. I don't know where you would get such an insulting idea."

"The newspapers have it all wrong then about him dancing attendance upon you again. Or did he ever stop?"

A raw shiver of despair ran along her spine. "Get out."

"Not until we have this settled."

Leaning down, he set his hands onto the arms of her chair, boxing her in between. "Whatever other ideas you may have, you are going to marry me, Julianna. Summersfield and Italy and Scotland, those are fancies that are never going to happen. This baby is mine and will be raised as my child. My legitimate child. Your only task is to decide when and where we will be wed."

"I am not marrying you."

"Fine. I will make all the arrangements for our nuptials, then. You can busy yourself by selecting a gown and having your personal items packed for the move to my house."

Her heart beat painfully beneath her breast. "You cannot force me to marry you."

"That is true, I cannot. But I can inform everyone of your acquaintance that you are with child. *My* child. An ad in the *Times* should do the trick very nicely."

His threat drove the breath from her lungs. "You wouldn't dare."

"I would dare anything for the sake of my son or daughter."

"But you would be ruining more than my reputation. You would ruin my family as well."

"Regretful but necessary. Of course, you can prevent it. You have only to say the word. So I ask you again, Julianna. *Will you marry me?*"

In that moment, she knew why he was called The Dragon. She'd heard he could be ruthless, even cruel, but until this moment, she hadn't realized the depths to which he would go to have his way. She had never known he could be so heartless.

She wanted to tell him to leave, wanted to toss his ultimatum in his face and dare him to actually follow through on it. But what if he did exactly as he promised and broadcast their affair and her pregnancy before the entire world? Rafe didn't strike her as the sort to make idle threats. When he pledged something, she suspected he did not back down.

If there were only herself to consider, she would have cast caution aside and told him to take himself and his marriage proposal and jump into the Thames. But she did not live in a vacuum, and her actions would affect others, most particularly those she loved, like Harry and Maris.

Even more, she had her child to consider. If the truth

was universally known, her baby would forever be labeled a bastard, shunned and ridiculed, condemned to walk through life with a burden she had forced upon him as surely as if she had fastened the chains herself.

How could she do that to her child? How could she ruin his life simply because marriage to his father would surely break her heart?

Her shoulders sank in defeat. "All right, Rafe, I will marry you."

With a satisfied nod, he straightened to his full height.

"But know this," she continued in a low voice as he began to move away. "I will never be your wife."

He stopped. "What?"

She forced herself to meet his gaze. "You may force me to the altar but you cannot force me to pretend happiness inside this sham of a marriage."

"Julianna—"

"If you do this, know that I will hate you."

She saw a flicker of regret move across his face, or at least imagined she did. An instant later, the look was gone, an impenetrable mask in its place.

"That is, of course, your choice, madam." Stepping back, he bowed. "I will apprise you of the wedding details shortly. Good day, my lady."

Refusing to return his farewell, she watched as he made his way from the room. Only after she heard him leave the house, followed by the sound of his carriage wheels moving away, did she let loose the torrent of emotion bottled up inside.

Burying her face in her hands, she began to sob.

Chapter Nineteen

❧

"M R. RAFE PENDRAGON to see you, Your Grace," announced the Duke of Wyvern's very proper butler from the doorway of the duke's palatial study.

Of course, everything about the duke's ancestral home was palatial, from the main entrance, whose drive was flanked by four hundred giant oak trees, planted in the eleventh century by the first duke himself, to the sprawling expanse of the more than 250 rooms that made up the regal home known as Rosemeade.

Rafe watched as his friend, Anthony Black, glanced up from the stack of letters before him, a smile breaking across the duke's dark-haired, saturnine countenance. After tossing his ink pen onto the surface of his desk, a massive hunk of polished wood that was said to have been carved from a lightning-felled great oak nearly three hundred years before, Tony rose to his full six-foot-three and came around to greet him.

"What an excellent surprise!" he declared, reaching out to clasp Rafe's hand for a hearty shake. "I was starting to go mad from the plague of correspondence my secretary has heaped upon me. You are just the excuse I need in order to take a break."

A smile curved over Rafe's mouth. "Glad I could provide a welcome interruption."

Tony glanced across to his butler. "That will be all for now, thank you, Crump."

"Yes, Your Grace."

With a bow, the servant withdrew, leaving the two men alone.

"So, what brings you out of the city in the middle of the week?" Tony asked, his footsteps silent on the plush blue-and-gold Turkey carpet. "You don't generally have time for a visit, even if Rosemeade is little more than a three-hour journey from London, give or take a bit of traffic."

"There's something I need to discuss."

"Ah. Port or whisky first?" the duke offered, opening the glass doors to a tall satinwood liquor cabinet that stood along one wall.

"Whisky." Accepting the drink a minute later, Rafe dropped down into a chair.

Returning with a snifter of dark-hued port in hand, Wyvern resumed his seat behind the desk. "Tell me, then, what is on your mind?"

"Titles."

Tony drank a swallow of the liquor, curiosity gleaming in his intense, midnight-blue gaze. "Really? Whose title in particular?"

"Mine. I have decided to acquire one."

"For yourself?"

"Yes, for myself. Did I not just say? Though, of course, I realize one doesn't actually *buy* a title, but instead performs a service for the monarch. I thought a more-than-generous donation to the war effort would be an effective persuasion."

The duke took another large swallow of port, then set down his glass with a quiet click. "I'm sure it will be. Forgive me for being astonished, though. How many years is it now that I have been trying to convince you to take a title?"

Rafe gave a wry smile. "Several, if I recall correctly. I believe your 'suggestions' began when you realized I had enough money to actually manage the trick."

"I *suggested* it because unlike most of the wealthy Cits who try to muscle their way into the peerage, you actually have the manners and education to comport yourself once you arrive. God knows you're as blue-blooded as most of the lords I know, and quite a bit more than some."

"I thank you for the vote of confidence; however, I doubt I will be so warmly received by most of your brethren in the Ton."

Tony frowned. "A great many of them are terrible snobs, I agree, but if you want this, I know you can make it work. And I will gladly see that you are received. Vessey will as well, I am certain."

"Yes, you and Ethan are loyal friends. You always have been, and I thank you."

The duke waved off Rafe's statement with a hand.

"So why? Why now, when you have never wanted this before?"

And still don't want it, if truth be known, Rafe thought.

But his life was about to change in the next few days. He would have a wife and child, and for them, he wanted more.

If he had a title, his son would inherit not only a solid financial legacy but an aristocratic name as well. The boy would not have to suffer the indignities Rafe had faced growing up. Oh, there might be the occasional sneer about his father's lack of proper lineage, but the world would never be able to find fault on his mother's side. And if he and Julianna should be blessed with a daughter instead, the girl would benefit as well. When the time came, her chances of making a good marriage would be virtually assured.

But more than the child, there was Julianna herself.

Even now, anger smoldered hot as ash inside him to think she had decided not to tell him about the baby. If her brother hadn't interfered, Rafe might never have known. For that alone, he supposed he owed Allerton his thanks.

As for Julianna, he had to admit her refusal had stung. After the way she'd pleaded with him not to end their affair, he'd hoped she might be glad of his proposal. At the very least, he'd assumed she would be relieved that he was willing to take responsibility for their child. But then, as he had to remind himself, she hadn't wanted him to know about the baby, obviously determined to keep him out of her life forever.

Apparently her tears that last day in Queens Square had meant nothing, her emotions based solely on passion. Perhaps her rejection shouldn't have surprised him, but considering her choices—marriage to him or bearing an out-of-wedlock baby that she would never have been able to pass off as anything else—her acceptance had seemed certain.

Unless she'd lied and had been planning to marry Summersfield, after all.

Whatever the case, she'd left him no choice. Though he hadn't enjoyed it, he'd been compelled to force her hand. When she'd said he wanted no bastard children, she was right. Their baby must have a name, and that name would be Pendragon.

Yet he couldn't blame her for fearing the social repercussions of their union. Though she hadn't voiced any potential distress, he knew she must be worried. Once she became his wife, her place in Society would be forfeit, her life as she had known it gone. The Ton thrived on rules and exclusivity, and many of her so-called friends and acquaintances would cut her the instant they discovered she had wed him.

But he could prevent her disgrace, or at least minimize its severity, if he purchased a title.

Personally, he didn't give a flip for Society's dictates, nor did he care about being a lord, content to remain exactly who and what he had always been. But Julianna would care. She would be hurt and isolated, left to dwell on Society's fringes. Members of her own family might even decide to disavow her, shamed by her fall from grace.

He couldn't do that to her, would not do that to her, particularly knowing he possessed the means to see to it she could remain in the Ton.

"Why now?" Rafe said, repeating his friend's question. "For one very simple reason, I suppose. Congratulate me, Tony; I am getting married."

The duke's eyebrows winged toward the ceiling. "What! When? How did this happen? I had no idea you were even in the market for a bride. I thought after Pamela . . . well, forgive me, but I had some doubts you would ever decide to take the plunge."

"I could say the same of you, my friend, and I don't have a dukedom to perpetuate," Rafe said in a dry tone.

"Don't start with that. I get enough grief as it is from my grandmama, who never seems to tire of the subject of brides and babies. But we aren't talking about me, are we? So how did this all come about?"

Rafe drew in a measured breath, thinking it best to leave out the majority of the details. "I decided it was time, and the lady agreed."

After a few well-made threats.

A smile spread over the duke's handsome face. "By God, but you are full of surprises today!" Standing, he rounded his desk, then reached out to clap Rafe on the shoulder and shake his hand. "Well, congratulations, and I wish you every happiness. So who's the girl? Anyone I know?"

"Very possibly. It's Julianna Hawthorne."

Tony's eyes flashed with obvious recognition. "Hawthorne? You mean Lady Hawthorne, the widow?"

Rafe nodded. "Exactly."

The duke whistled. "Good God, she's been an impossible catch for years. How'd you manage it? Come to think upon it, how do you even know her? Not to put too fine a point upon the matter, but the two of you don't exactly run in the same circles."

"You're right, we don't. And for the sake of the lady, I have nothing more to say on the subject."

His friend gave him an arch look but obviously decided to keep further questions to himself.

"At least that explains your sudden about-face on the issue of titles," Tony said after a moment. "Is she insisting on your ascension as a condition of the marriage?"

"No. Julianna knows nothing of my plans to buy a peerage. She agreed to wed me just as I am."

A slow smile curved the duke's lips. "A love match. I am truly happy for you, my friend."

Rafe forced himself not to react. If only Tony knew the truth, he mused wryly, Julianna's words reverberating in his head.

"If you do this, know that I will hate you."

No, he thought, *ours is far from a love match.*

"I want to do this for her and our future," Rafe said, knowing that statement was honest at least. "Which is why I came to you. We wish to be wed soon, very soon, and I was hoping your connections at court might speed matters along."

Tony's brows furrowed in consideration as he moved back to lean a hip against his desk. "Well, under normal circumstances such legalities take months, even years. But since you are already well known to the Crown, I suppose it's possible the wheels of bureaucracy could be coaxed to move a bit faster. They'd have to be generously greased, however."

"I thought half a million pounds. Will that do?"

Tony barked out a startled laugh. "Yes, I believe it will do brilliantly. For that kind of money I think you can safely count on success. They'll be falling all over themselves to accommodate you."

"Good. Set it in motion, Tony, if you would."

"I'll ride back to London with you today."

"My thanks. I have one more favor to ask."

The duke reached for his port and took a drink. "Of course."

"I need a best man. I would appreciate it if you would accept."

"Surely. I would be honored. But what of Ethan?"

"I've asked him to stand with me as well. He's in Suffolk at his estate, though, so I don't know if he'll make it back in time."

"He will. When is the wedding, by the way?"

"Two weeks."

"No rush there," the duke quipped dryly. "You never do anything the easy way, do you?"

Rafe laughed. "I try not to, if I can help it."

"Dearly beloved, we are gathered together here in the sight of God, and in the face of these witnesses, to join together this man and this woman in holy matrimony . . ."

As the minister continued to speak, Julianna averted her gaze, unable to bring herself to look at Rafe now that the ceremony was under way. But then, she didn't need to see him to recall how breathtakingly handsome he looked in his formal wedding attire, his dark blue tailcoat and light gray breeches molding his splendid masculine physique to perfection.

When she'd started her walk up the aisle of the small London church, her heart had hammered so loudly she'd feared for a moment the others assembled might be able to hear. But no one seemed to notice, not even Harry, who escorted her to the altar, then silently handed her over to the man who would soon be her husband.

Over the past two weeks she'd tried to find some way out of this marriage, but realized all avenues of escape were futile. So here she stood in her finery of pale peach watered silk with short capped sleeves and a gossamer overskirt of the best white tulle. Dyed-to-match satin slippers graced her feet, their narrow golden buckles winking in the morning light, while a tissue-thin tiffany veil spilled from her head to just below her waist.

She'd wanted to wear black, believing the color more in keeping with the true spirit of the day. In the end, though, she had decided such a rebellion unworthy. Her difficulties with Rafe were private ones and not for the consumption of others, not even her own family. She might resent Rafe's actions, but to the world she vowed to present a cheerful front—or at least as cheerful as she could manage.

Luckily, the number of guests were few. From her own family, only Harry was in attendance. Maris and William were still on their honeymoon, and she knew Cousin Henrietta was too far away to travel on such short notice.

Needing an attendant, she had asked her friend Beatrice, Lady Neville, to act as her maid of honor. Understandably, Beatrice had been stunned when she had broken the news, full of questions that Julianna had managed for the most part to elude.

Having no family of his own, Rafe's side of the guest list was equally sparse, with only two friends to serve as groomsmen. And what friends, she'd thought, catching herself staring for a long moment when she recognized the Duke of Wyvern and the Marquis of Vessey waiting at the altar next to Rafe. She didn't know either man well, but their reputations preceded them, since they were generally considered two of the Ton's most eligible and infamous bachelors.

Suddenly the minister paused and Rafe began to speak.

The deep, solemn cadence of his voice drew her thoughts back to the present. And then it was her turn, everyone waiting in expectation for her response.

Her heart fluttered like a cornered hare, her fingers turning as cold as icicles in January.

This is it, she thought, *my last opportunity to refuse. Once the vows are said there will be no going back, not ever.*

As she well knew, marriage was for life. Once she pledged herself to Rafe, they would be man and wife until death parted them forever. She'd known one loveless marriage; how could she possibly face another?

And this time will be far, far worse, she thought.

As lacking as her first marriage may have been, she'd had the comfort of knowing herself heart whole. Her union to Rafe would in no way be the same. As contrary as it seemed, she loved and hated him both, emotions that would surely tear her apart over time.

How will I ever manage to cope?

In the next moment, a small tingling quivered deep in her womb, a sensation that was as odd as it was astonishing.

Is that the baby? she wondered.

Waiting a moment, she felt it again, the strange fluttering like the brushing of tiny wings.

Then she knew she must not waver for the sake of her child. She might resent Rafe, but she would never resent this baby the two of them had created.

Drawing a deep breath, she squared her shoulders.

And, as if from a very great distance, she heard herself say, "I do."

"A toast to the happy couple!"

Rafe leaned back in his chair and gave a nod of appreciation for Ethan's warm salute. The others raised their champagne flutes and murmured best wishes for Rafe and Julianna's future health and happiness before they all took a drink.

Seated together at one end of the Duke of Wyvern's extraordinarily long dining room table, their small group was making merry, or as merry as possible under the circumstances. As part of Wyvern's wedding gift to Rafe and Julianna, Tony had offered to hold the wedding breakfast at Black House, the duke's elegant Grosvenor Square residence. Although only six of them sat at the table, Tony had in no way stinted on the celebration.

In addition to champagne and fresh hothouse strawberries, they dined on salmon and lobster patties, shirred eggs, Westphalian ham, and a Beluga caviar that had been delivered all the way from Russia.

Julianna's complexion had paled a bit when one of the footmen offered her a spoonful of the roe. Knowing the scent might be making her nauseous because of the baby, Rafe had quietly suggested the servant move on. Her color improved soon after, and she managed to eat a few bites of the excellent fare.

He thought of Ethan's toast and wished it were true, wished he and his new bride really were a happy couple. He thought back to a moment at the altar when he'd wondered if Julianna was going to refuse to wed him, after all. His throat had squeezed tight at her prolonged silence, wondering what he would do if she decided to bolt. But then an odd expression of amazement passed over her face, followed by a soft little smile. Seconds later, she had proceeded with her vows.

He thought about this evening, and the celebration of their marriage, and wished he could take her on a honeymoon trip away from the city. But now that he and Julianna were wed, St. George presented a greater potential threat than ever.

From all accounts, the viscount remained in Lancashire, but Rafe refused to take any chances with his new wife's well-being. Over the past two weeks, he'd stationed men to guard Julianna's townhouse in Upper Brook Street. Without her knowledge, her new bodyguards had accompanied her on her various errands and excursions as she prepared for the wedding. Now that they were married and she would be living in his house, he knew he could even more effectively guarantee her safety.

He would die before he'd let anything happen to Julianna or their child.

Wyvern stood, interrupting Rafe's musings. The duke raised his glass. "I, too, wish my good friend Rafe and his beautiful bride every happiness. But there is news of another sort I also wish to celebrate."

Rafe paused, a sudden scowl furrowing his brow. He hoped Tony wasn't going to say what he thought he was going to say. Opening his mouth, Rafe started to interrupt him. But Tony, having imbibed a healthy measure of his own fine champagne, could not be stopped.

"Join me, everyone, in welcoming England's newest peer."

Beside him, Julianna grew still, her rosy lips parted, her dark eyes fixed on the duke with rapt attention.

"For his generous aid to the nation, the Crown has decided to grant Rafe a title. He had an audience with the Regent only two days ago and was duly accorded the honor. The new title will be gazetted and the Letters

Patent prepared, but those are no more than formalities at this point. So raise a glass with me and drink to Lord Pendragon, the new Baron Pendragon."

A marked silence followed, Allerton and Lady Neville clearly astonished, while Ethan openly grinned his approval. As for Julianna, Rafe couldn't tell how she felt, her face utterly devoid of expression.

He knew Tony assumed he'd already told Julianna the news; it was his own fault, he supposed, for not warning his friend to keep his mouth closed. But with the hurried wedding arrangements, there simply hadn't been time—or at least a good time—to tell her. Except for a few brief minutes here and there, he and Julianna had barely seen each other in the days leading up to the ceremony.

Even so, gaining a title was an important event and he'd wanted to be the one to tell Julianna, had wanted to watch her face brighten with surprise and pleasure and happiness. She would be a baroness, her position secure as the wife of a nobleman—even if he had come to the peerage in a manner sure to cause comment and the occasional haughty sniff. But with the support of a duke and a marquis, their acceptance in Society was virtually guaranteed. Julianna should be smiling. She should be happy.

So why isn't she?

Reaching out, Julianna curved her hand around the wine flute's delicate base and lifted it into the air. "To Lord Pendragon," she murmured.

The silence shattered, the others raised their glasses. "To Lord Pendragon," they repeated in unison.

Despite having initiated the toast, Julianna did not drink, quietly returning her glass to the table.

And as the wedding breakfast continued, so did his bride's near silence, her smiles never actually reaching her eyes.

Chapter Twenty

"WILL THAT BE all, my lady?" Daisy asked, as she helped Julianna into her favorite green silk robe.

Daisy, bless her heart, hadn't said so much as a word about the fact that Julianna was wearing her usual nightclothes on this, her wedding night. In the two weeks leading up to the ceremony, the only new garment she had purchased was her wedding gown. New night attire seemed ridiculous under the circumstances, she had decided.

"Yes, thank you," Julianna said, crossing to her rose-wood dressing table, one of the few familiar pieces of furniture in the bedchamber. "How is your room, by the way? Is it to your liking?"

The girl bobbed a curtsey. "Oh, yes. It's quite comfortable and larger than my old one. I worry, though, that I won't sleep tonight with it being so new and all."

Yes, I suspect I may have the same difficulty, Julianna thought, wishing she was back in her own townhouse instead of here in Rafe's.

Yesterday, he'd stopped by her home in Upper Brook Street for a brief visit, instructing her to choose whatever possessions she would like moved into his house in Bloomsbury Square. With a single sentence, he had quashed any lingering hope she'd harbored that he might allow her to continue living in her own home. Without stopping to think, she'd suggested he relocate to her Mayfair townhouse. Jaw stiff, he'd informed her that as of tomorrow her home would be with him.

"A wife belongs in her husband's house, wherever that house may be."

And so this morning, while she and Rafe were at the church being married, the servants had loaded her wardrobe, personal belongings, and a few select pieces of furniture into carts and moved them across the city. By the time she and her new husband had arrived at his townhouse this afternoon, all her belongings were installed.

What a peculiar experience it had been walking through the front door, her mind crowded with memories of her first and only other visit to the house. The first time she'd met Rafe.

So much had transpired since then, so much had changed. Nevertheless, she felt like a stranger tonight as she sat here in her new bedchamber. Attractive though it might be, with its white walls and deep blue draperies, the room carried none of the soothing qualities of her old room. Already she missed the delicate cream and jonquil–striped wallpaper, and the big scroll-armed chaise that had provided the perfect spot upon which to read or relax.

The windows here were in all the wrong places. The armoire was inadequately large. And although the bed was bigger than her own, it was not nearly as soft as her comfortable eiderdown mattress at home.

Over a very awkward dinner, Rafe had told her she had his permission to change any of the décor she wished. Another woman would have leapt at the opportunity, and the open pocketbook. Yet she wasn't certain she wished to change anything. Once she began putting her own touches on the place, it would be an admission that this was her home. And futile as it might seem, she wasn't ready to accept that fact.

Not yet, anyway.

"Pleasant dreams, Daisy," she said. "I shall see you in the morning."

The girl dipped another curtsey. "You as well, my lady. If you're needing anything just call me, no matter the hour."

Julianna gave her a smile and a grateful nod. "Good night."

Once her maid was gone, she sank down on the stool in front of her dressing table and picked up her brush. Slowly, she drew the bristles through her hair.

Her thoughts turned back to the moment Tony Black had made his startling announcement, back to her sense of shock—and hurt.

Rafe should have told me, she thought not for the first time.

Obviously, he'd had time to tell his two friends, but he couldn't take a few extra minutes out of his day to share such momentous news with her. Could not be bothered to mention that he'd met with Prinny and received the Regent's sanction for a peerage.

And at what price, she wondered? Just how much had it cost Rafe to buy himself that title?

Of course she'd known instantly why he'd done it.

The baby.

The son he apparently wanted at all costs, even at the expense of his own freedom.

As she'd sat at the duke's elegant table with its lovely wedding breakfast, she'd realized how little she mattered to Rafe. As the mother of his child, she had a place. As his wife, well, he would never have wed her for herself alone, and she would be wise to remember that fact.

She supposed she should feel relieved that she would

be a baroness, feel happy in the knowledge that she would not be driven from Society as she had feared. Instead what she felt was anger, and even worse, pain.

Squeezing the brush handle hard inside her palm, she fought off her tears.

No, she vowed, *I am done crying.*

With a heavy sigh, she set down her brush, then stood and crossed to the bed.

A good night's sleep will calm my mind, she mused. *Everything will seem a bit more tolerable come the morning.*

Slipping out of her robe, she draped the garment across the foot of the bed, then climbed between the sheets. With a sigh, she plumped the pillows and settled back.

She was about to snuff out the candle on her nightstand when she heard the door open.

Has Daisy returned? she wondered.

But when she glanced up, the person she saw was most definitely not Daisy.

Magnificent as a Greek sculpture brought to life, Rafe stood framed in the connecting doorway, a doorway she had erroneously thought to be locked.

Pulse quickening, she couldn't help but stare, his large body draped in a black silk robe that hugged the taut contours and mouth-watering angles of his masculine physique. Above the tie at his waist, she caught a V-shaped glimpse of his powerful chest. Below lay his firm, naked calves with their dusting of black hair, and lower still, his long, elegantly shaped feet.

When they'd been lovers, she'd seen him in far less. But somehow the sight of him in a robe was more seductive than nothing at all.

Forcing her heartbeat to slow, she averted her eyes and scooted upright against the pillows, smoothing the sheet and blanket across her lap. She was grateful now that she'd worn a modest nightgown, the buttoned placket covering her breasts, which had grown even larger since the start of her pregnancy.

He's probably come to talk. A few minutes, she thought, *and then he'll go away.*

"Yes, what is it, Rafe?" she asked in a crisp tone. "Do you need something?"

He quirked a brow. "Hmm, now there's a question." After a long pause, he continued. "How are you feeling tonight? Not queasy or anything? I couldn't help but notice you didn't eat much at dinner."

Oh, so he is worried about the baby. I should have known.

She repressed a sigh. "I am fine. I wasn't very hungry tonight, that's all. This day has been long and tiring."

There, she thought. *I have told him what he wanted to know. Perhaps he will take the hint now and leave.*

Instead, he strode farther into the room.

"I'll ask Cook to make more of your favorite dishes," he said, "so you'll be tempted in the future. After all, it's important that you eat and stay healthy."

She frowned, then frowned harder when he walked up to the bed and stopped. Leaning down, he folded back the covers on the unoccupied side.

"What do you think you're doing?" she demanded, her heart kicking inside her chest.

His vivid gaze locked with hers. "What does it look like? I'm going to bed."

For a moment, she couldn't speak.

Her eyes widened as his hands moved to the tie at his waist.

"Oh no, you are not. Get out!"

"You're my wife. I will sleep in here."

Clutching the sheets higher, she shook her head. "Sleep in your own room. You have a bed; I suggest you use it."

"I may have a bed but I prefer sharing with you. Anyway, it's our wedding night. Did you really expect me not to come to you?"

"Frankly, yes. The last time we were together you informed me you were bored."

An arrested look passed over his face. "I changed my mind."

"Well, so have I. I no longer want you. Now, leave my room."

His eyelids lowered and he shot her a smoldering look that made her bare toes curl with heat.

"Are you certain of that?" he murmured. "Why don't I join you so we can find out whether you still want me or not."

"I don't. Go away, Rafe."

He reached again for the silken belt and freed it. But when he shucked off the robe, she saw he wasn't naked—at least not completely, his lower extremities covered by a pair of snug, knee-length drawers. The cotton did nothing to hide his erection, though, the material tented out in an explicit display of male arousal.

Just because he's stiff as a truncheon doesn't mean he really wants me, she admonished herself. *Likely any woman would do in his present state, and I happen to be convenient.*

When he set a knee on the mattress, she flung back the covers and leapt out of the bed. Putting several feet between them, she waited, spine straight, her arms crossed over her breasts.

Stretching out on his side, he sighed. "What's this, now? Running from me? I know it cannot be due to a case of wedding-night nerves, since this is far from our first time together." He held out his open palm. "I know you are angry with me, but I'd like to make it up. Come to bed and let me pleasure you. I promise you'll like it."

Oh, I'm sure I would like it, she thought, which was

precisely the problem. She also knew that if she let go of her anger and resentment toward him, the only emotion remaining would be love. She wouldn't be able to bear it then, not when she knew his affection was no more than skin deep.

Silently, she shook her head no.

He paused. "Are you sure? Perhaps you just need a bit of coaxing."

Before she knew what he meant to do, he was up and off the bed. Catching her in his arms, he rocked her against him.

"Now, doesn't this feel nice?" he murmured in a husky voice that gave her delicious, shivery chills.

"Let me go," she replied with a calm she in no way felt.

"I will, *after* you give me a kiss. A man deserves at least a kiss on his wedding night, wouldn't you agree?"

"No."

"You used to be kinder. It's just one kiss. What harm can there be in one simple kiss?"

Plenty, she thought, *when Rafe is doing the kissing.*

Still . . .

"One kiss and then you'll go?" she questioned.

He nodded. "If that is what you want."

Warning bells clanged inside her head, her instincts telling her to refuse, to hold steady and make him walk back out the way he'd come in.

Another little voice began to whisper, urging her to take the tiny scrap of pleasure he offered. His arms felt so wonderful curved around her, his scent and strength everything she remembered. Everything she missed.

How could she deny herself?

As he said, what harm can there be in one simple kiss?

Besides, it might be a nice bit of revenge. Grabbing a handful of delight for herself, then pushing him away.

"All right, but only one," she said. "And we stop when I say."

His lips curved, eyes darkening like a forest at twilight. "Of course."

Without further preamble, he bent his head and placed his lips upon her own.

On a shivery sigh, she let the pleasure take her, his touch even better than she remembered, more erotic than her most heated fantasies, more delectable than the finest satin or the choicest wine.

Breathing him in, she gave herself over to the kiss, knowing there would be only this one, knowing suddenly how much she needed it, how deeply she craved Rafe's touch. Refusing to stint, she closed her eyes and let him draw her deeper, relishing every fiery taste and silken sensation.

She shuddered, her body suffused with heat.

God, it's so good, she thought, *so wonderful. How can I possibly stop? But I have to and now, while I still have the strength.*

Yet even as she began to move away, Rafe shifted her in his arms and angled his head. Slanting his mouth across hers, she felt him take the kiss deeper, careful never to break contact as if he hoped to stretch this single kiss into infinity. And as she floated on a cloud of bliss, she wondered if he just might manage the trick. And if she would let him.

The world narrowed, growing smaller and smaller until there was only herself and Rafe.

His hands began to move, gliding and caressing, stroking her curves and gently kneading her flesh. Arching like a cat being pet by her master, she turned into his embrace, welcoming it, welcoming him.

She didn't know when or how, but suddenly her feet were no longer touching the floor, her body aloft as Rafe carried her across the room.

The soft feather tick enveloped her as he bore her down onto the bed, his mouth amazingly still fastened to her own, making her quiver as his tongue swirled around her own.

She could barely think as he lay over her, so big, so powerful, his touch an imprint that went all the way to her soul.

Then, when her thoughts were starting to turn muzzy from lack of oxygen, he freed her lips. Her mouth throbbed, hot and swollen from his thorough feasting. Aching and hungry for more.

Kissing her cheeks and temple, her ears and neck, he kept her enthralled, even more so as his hands glided again over her frame, seeking and finding all her most sensitive spots.

A draught of cool air brushed across her skin as he unbuttoned her nightgown and peeled back the garment to expose her breasts. She nearly jumped out of her skin, tensing when he covered one of her nipples with his mouth and began to draw upon her.

"Oh!" she cried out, stiffening as a disturbing mix of pleasure and pain radiated through her.

His head came up. "What?"

"It hurts. I . . . I'm sore."

He paused. "The baby?"

She nodded, that single word enough to drive some of the passion from her mind, to clear her foggy senses.

What am I doing? How could I have let things go so far?

She didn't want to stop, the deep ache between her legs begging to be assuaged. But if she let Rafe stay now, she would have to let him stay again tomorrow night and the night after. She would have to let him come to her as often, and for as long, as he had need.

And what if his need ceased? What if he once more grew bored and turned his back? If she let him into her bed and into her body, only to watch him discard her yet again, she knew some part of her would break, and perhaps even die.

He had used her once. She could not afford to let him use her again.

"Stop."

Rafe cocked his head. "What?"

"Stop. You've had your kiss, now go." Aware of her naked breasts, she reached down to cover herself.

He caught her hands before she could close the bodice. "I couldn't have heard right. Did you say *stop*?"

Unable to meet his gaze, she looked away. "Yes. I've had enough."

His expression turned dark. "I know you want me. If I reached under that skirt, I'd find you wet and more than ready. And as for me, I'm hard as a freshly dug tuber."

Bending down, he tried to kiss her.

She turned her head so that his lips only grazed her cheek. "You said you would stop."

His jaw tightened. "I did, but surely you're not going to hold me to that promise now. You are my wife, Julianna. You belong in my bed."

"I am sure many would agree, just as they agreed we should be wed. You forced me into this marriage. Are you going to force me to service you as well?"

She shivered, recoiling at the fury that blazed in his eyes. For a moment, she imagined she saw more, glimpsed hurt and disillusionment shimmering in his gaze. Then the look was gone.

With a growl, he flung himself away and off the bed. "Have it your way, madam, and don't imagine I'll be back. I hope you enjoy your cold, lonely bed."

Stalking toward his room, he walked through the connecting passageway and slammed the door, the wood rattling so hard she thought the frame might crack.

Shivering, she curled on her side.

I did the right thing. She thought. *So why do I feel so empty? Why does it feel so wrong?*

Closing her eyes, she started to weep.

An overly large blot of ink bled into the foolscap beneath Rafe's pen, obliterating several of the words he'd already written above.

Hell and damnation! he silently cursed, reaching out to crush the ruined paper in his fist. Flinging it toward the fireplace, he watched the wad roll, then bump up against another trio of previously discarded attempts.

With deliberate care, he set down his pen. *I can't concentrate,* he thought, *and it is all her fault.*

To his recollection, he couldn't recall ever being so angry, at least not with a woman. But after Julianna's heartless behavior, how could he be otherwise?

He'd gone to her room last night with the intention of gently wooing her, showing her with tenderness and care that despite his past words and actions his desire for her remained strong. The passion between them had always been explosive, and he'd been counting on using mutual need to rekindle their relationship and forge what he hoped might be a new, and even deeper, bond. After all, they were now husband and wife. Last night but the first of countless evenings to come.

Yet she'd been skittish and defensive from the start, ordering him from her room before he'd even had a chance to get near her. After an admittedly slow beginning, however, he'd thought things were going well.

Even now, he could feel the almost concussive delight of having her lips moving under his once again. Experience the heady bliss of holding her close in his arms, so warm and lush, so Julianna.

Once he'd carried her to the bed, he'd lost himself in the moment and in her, savoring each sensation, relishing every touch. And she'd been enjoying herself, too. He knew she had.

Yet abruptly, she'd turned cold.

He'd been dying for her, his body diamond hard and throbbing with need when she'd told him to stop. The effort to comply had been wrenching. Yet it was the venom of her words that had bitten most deeply. Accusing him of forcing himself upon her, of attempting to violate her with no regard for her feelings or wishes.

That had hurt worst of all.

Grinding his teeth, he shoved back his chair and stood. Crossing to the fireplace, he bent down to retrieve the ruined balls of paper. Slowly, he fed them to the flames, his thoughts still centered upon his wedding night.

Wedding night, hah! More like wedding *nightmare.*

After he'd slammed his way out of her room, he'd come downstairs for a much-needed drink. But the liquor hadn't helped. If anything, the spirits only seemed to increase his ire, to fan the flames of his outraged emotions and sexual frustration even more.

Nearly two hours later, he'd returned to his bed-chamber to climb beneath his solitary sheets, and there he'd lain, utterly unable to sleep. At five, he'd given up any attempt at rest, dressed and shaved himself, then gone out for a ride.

The exercise did little to alleviate his mind, but at least he'd worked up an appetite by the time of his return.

He'd just been finishing breakfast when Julianna appeared, her face guarded and a bit pale. Without a word, he'd tossed down his napkin and left, retreating to his study.

He'd hoped to work, hoped to bury himself in dry financial matters that would drive all thoughts of her from his thoughts. And though he'd managed to accomplish something, it had been a very little something indeed.

Growling now under his breath, he tossed the last ball of paper into the fire.

Instead of remaining here at the house for what was sure to be a torturous dinner, he ought to send around notes to Tony and Ethan to see if they would like to join him for an evening on the Town. But doing so would be tantamount to admitting that his marriage was a disaster after only one day.

The same would prove true if he went out to find a convenient and willing partner to satisfy his lust. Taking another woman to his bed would serve Julianna right. But despite his anger, he knew he couldn't humiliate her that way.

Besides, he didn't want another woman. He wanted his wife, who happened to be upstairs in her bedchamber right at this very moment. But he'd sworn not to touch her again, and he wouldn't.

Gripping the edge of the mantelpiece, he wondered what he was going to do. *How can I bear living in the same house with her,* he pondered, *wanting her yet knowing she is out of reach?*

The same way he'd done without her all the time before their marriage, he supposed.

He'd given her up to protect her. He'd married her to do the same. He would honor his vows. He just hoped it didn't kill him first.

"Yes, my lady. I will see to it immediately."

"Thank you, Martin," Julianna said.

Seated in the morning room, she and her butler were finishing one of their twice-weekly meetings concerning the running of the household. "Is there anything further?" she added.

The older man straightened his already straight shoulders and cleared his throat. "Well, ma'am, though I do not like to trouble you with such things, there is the matter of a certain *large* individual. Despite my many admonitions that he not do so, he is still opening the front door to callers. Yesterday he scared poor Lady Neville when she stopped by for a visit, and then he had the bad manners to leave her waiting in the foyer."

Heavens! Julianna thought. No wonder she had found Beatrice waving her bottle of smelling salts beneath her nose when she had entered the room.

"I left instructions that one of the footmen is to answer the door when I am unavailable," the butler continued, "but *that person* does not listen. And he intimidates the footmen so they haven't the nerve to gainsay him."

That person, of course, being Hannibal, she realized without needing further explanation.

When she had moved into Rafe's house five weeks ago, she had brought along several of her own servants. In general, the adjustments in the household had gone smoothly with one notable exception. Stubborn and independent to a fault, Hannibal deferred to no one.

Except Rafe, of course.

She knew the easiest way to remedy the problem would be to go to Rafe, explain the situation, and ask him to put an end to Hannibal's cantankerous behavior. Unfortunately, she and Rafe were not on comfortable speaking terms these days.

In fact, despite living in the same house, they saw very little of each other. Occasionally they would share a meal, during which Rafe was always unfailingly polite. First he would inquire after her health, wanting to know if she was feeling well and if there was anything she required to make her pregnancy easier. Once she assured him she was well, the conversation would turn to mundanities—the weather, events around Town, or perhaps some interesting story one of them had heard.

Although she did her best to participate, to be equally polite and equally attentive, the encounters always left her drained and despairing afterward. Everything between them was surface now, without an iota of genuine warmth or intimacy.

We might as well be strangers, she mused.

Her fault, she supposed, since she had sent him from her bed. True to his word, Rafe had made no further attempts at having sexual relations with her. Lately, he barely looked at her, and never with anything close to passion gleaming in his eyes.

I should be relieved. And I am, she assured herself.

Yet she couldn't deny wishing things might be different, wishing by some miracle that Rafe loved her.

But he does not, she scolded, *and I am only torturing myself by entertaining such idiotic thoughts.*

She would endure the next few months and at the end of them have her reward.

Her baby.

She couldn't wait to give all her love to her child. Once her little one was born, she would be content. She would be happy. At least she would try to be.

For now, though, she must deal with life as it was, including resolving tensions among the staff.

"Thank you for bringing the matter to my attention, Martin. I will see what I can do."

He nodded his gray head. "My sincere appreciation, my lady." With a smart bow, he excused himself and departed the room.

Nearly an hour later, dressed in a warm but stylish blue velvet gown and a gray woolen cloak, she made her way downstairs. In need of a few more winter dresses that would accommodate her ever-increasing waistline, she was on her way to visit her mantua-maker. She planned to take Lady Neville up in her carriage so the pair of them could shop together.

At nearly the same instant she entered the main foyer, so did Hannibal. Seeing him reminded her of her earlier promise.

Drawing in a fortifying breath, she decided there was no time like the present. "Hannibal, I would have a word with you, if you please. Shall we adjourn to the drawing room?"

He peered down at her from his towering height, clearly deciding whether or not to obey. With a barely perceptible shrug, he moved down the hallway.

Once inside, she shut the door behind them. "You are scaring visitors who come to the front door and I wish you to stop," she began, cutting straight to the point. "You are also upsetting certain members of the staff, and I wish that to cease as well."

When she paused, he stood silent, crossing his ham-sized arms over his chest.

Swallowing against her own nerves, she forced herself to continue. "I realize that this was your home for a long while before my arrival, and that you have been used to doing things a certain way. However, those ways must now change. I am mistress of this house, and as such am in control of the household. I trust you will comply with my requests."

"Why have you kicked Dragon out of your bed? That don't sound very wifely to me."

Her mouth dropped open as hot color rushed into her cheeks. A long moment passed while she collected herself.

"My relationship with your master is none of your business," she said in a chill voice, "and I will thank you to mind your impertinent tongue. If you do not, you may find yourself looking for alternate employment."

"Dragon won't sack me. We've known each other since our days on the docks."

She shivered, knowing he was likely right. But she couldn't allow such defiance to go unanswered.

"Perhaps so," she said, "but you would be wise not to test my mettle. If you push me, we'll see which one of us prevails."

With eyes as black as tar, he stared at her for what seemed like forever. Then suddenly a wide smile split his mouth. "You've got pluck, missus. I like that. I like that a lot. All right, I'll leave off his nibs the butler and those jelly-kneed footmen of yours. They all need to grow a new backbone. Won't be near the fun around here not being able to needle them no more."

So he has been doing it deliberately, she thought. *I suspected as much.*

"My thanks for your sacrifice," she said.

He laughed. "You're welcome, missus. I know you're carrying a little Pendragon so I won't cause you more trouble. Expectant mothers need to stay calm."

Then you shouldn't have put me through the last few minutes, she retorted silently.

"Still, you ought to let Dragon back in your bed. He's touchy as a bear and ten times as cross these last few weeks."

Is he? she wondered. Around her, Rafe never seemed anything but cool and composed. Did it mean anything that Hannibal saw something different? *No,* she decided, shaking off the notion.

"That will be all, Hannibal."

With a salute of his chin, he strode from the room.

Slowly, she followed. As she approached the front door, she discovered Martin and the two footmen hovering, anxiety plain in their gazes.

"Is everything all right, my lady?"

"Quite well. You have sole custody of the door from now on."

Amazement lightened their expressions.

"Now, my coach, please."

Immediately, all three men sprang to do her bidding.

A few hours later, the bell jingled as Julianna came out of the milliner's shop, a small package containing a length of cherry-red ribbon clutched in her hand. With her mind still on the bonnet she planned to retrim for the holidays, she didn't notice the gentleman striding up the sidewalk until he was nearly upon her.

With a quick hand, he caught her by the arm and steadied her before she could take a tumble. "My pardon, ma'am, are you all right?" he asked.

Glancing up, she saw a familiar face. "Lord Summersfield! Good heavens, forgive my clumsiness. I nearly ran you down."

He smiled. "I believe *I* was the one in danger of running *you* down, but I am relieved you are unharmed."

Drawing her to one side, out of the way of other foot traffic, he released her. "So, you are shopping, I see. Are you on your own?"

She shook her head. "No, I am here with Lady Neville. But Beatrice always has a frightful time making up her mind about which trims to buy, so I decided to wait for her out here. I was headed for my carriage when we had our near miss."

Nodding in the direction of her equipage, she noticed the coachman and footman watching them. Having been observed, the servants discreetly turned away.

"What are you doing in Town this time of year?" she said. "I thought you generally went west to your estate."

"Yes, you're right, but I'd had enough grouse hunting and the partridges are thin this year, so I thought I would force myself to do my duty and actually attend a few sessions of the Lords." He broke off, then smiled. "And what of you? I understand felicitations are in order. Best wishes on your recent marriage."

She glanced away for a moment. "Oh, yes, thank you."

"Pendragon is a lucky man. I'm not sure how he won you, nor how the pair of you came to meet, but he caught himself a true prize."

"My lord," she said, once again meeting his gaze, "have I not told you before I have no need of such flattery?"

"And have I not told you, dear lady, that I am only being honest?"

Oh, dear, she thought. *Did I misjudge him? Were his proposals in earnest after all?*

But when he gave her a fresh smile, without so much as a hint of regret in his gaze, her qualms subsided.

Summersfield tucked a hand in his greatcoat pocket. "I hear as well we are soon to have a new peer. There's scarcely been talk of anything else since word came out that the Regent is granting your husband the rank of baron. Pendragon has been summoned to appear before the Lords in only two weeks hence so that he may take his seat."

"Yes, and we have both been called to appear at Court as well. Shulz is tailoring Rafe's attire for the occasion."

Julianna thought about the feathers and tippets as well as the full hooped skirt with train that she would be required to wear, glad that the cumbersome gown would thoroughly conceal any signs of her pregnancy. Not that she was showing yet—a benefit of the current fashion for high-waisted dresses—but she suspected all that would change in the very near future. With each week that passed, she felt the baby move more often as he grew bigger and stronger. But for now, she preferred that Society not know of her pregnancy, or the mental arithmetic would surely start to fly.

The shop's little bell rang again as Lady Neville

emerged, a bandbox swinging on a small string over her arm. "Well, good day, Summersfield," she said, curtseying to the earl. "Have you been keeping poor Julianna entertained while I dallied over choosing just the right bonnet?"

He bowed. "Yes, I had the happy chance to stumble upon her. Quite literally, I might add. We have been having a merry conversation ever since."

"Oh, do tell."

He did and more besides, making both Beatrice and Julianna laugh.

Soon, Julianna realized they were taking up rather too much room on the sidewalk, a few passersby beginning to give them looks. "Well," she said, "I suppose it is time we were on our way, my lord. It has been a pleasure seeing you again."

"Indeed it has," he agreed, giving them both a pleasant smile. "I have an idea. Why don't I take you ladies out for something warm to drink and a pastry? Surely you can both spare a few minutes more to drink a dish of tea and rest your feet?"

Julianna frowned. She had been out for several hours already and was expected home soon. But tea and a treat sounded lovely.

She thought of Rafe, knowing he wouldn't like her going anywhere with Lord Summersfield. Then again, perhaps he no longer cared. It wasn't as if he would be jealous.

And there could be no conceivable harm in such an outing. Married women appeared in public with single men all the time, many flaunting their cicisbeos with the same casualness they used among their women friends. Besides, even if Rafe did hear of the outing somehow, how could he object with Beatrice along?

"Yes, my lord," Julianna said. "That sounds like a splendid plan. Beatrice, do you not agree?"

Lady Neville nodded her blond head. "Oh, completely. You know how susceptible I am to a sweet."

"Shall we then, ladies?" he asked, offering each of them an arm.

"Then what did they do?" Rafe demanded, his brows lowered like a pair of daggers over his eyes.

Julianna's bodyguard—one of three who kept her under constant surveillance—cleared his throat before continuing. "She and the bloke talked for several minutes right there on the street. Her friend, Lady Neville, finally came out of the shop and the three of them started nattering on."

Rafe turned his letter opener over between his fingers. "Yes? What then?"

"Well, after that, they all went to a tea shop on Bond Street. Sat inside for more than an hour eating and drinking, happy as a flock of canaries. Laughing, too, as if they hadn't a care."

"And did you find out this man's name?"

"I did, guv'nor. Once the ladies climbed back into their carriage, John followed after them while I trailed the gentleman back to his home. A pretty little kitchen maid I chatted up told me the bloke what lives there is an earl. The Earl of Summersfield."

Rafe's grip tightened on the silver blade, hard enough that had it been a real knife, he would have drawn blood. After a long moment, he forced his fingers to loosen.

"Thank you, Pointer. Continue watching after Lady Julianna."

The other man gave a nod. "Like she was me own sister. And we all have the sketches of that other fellow, that Viscount Middleton. If he pokes 'is head back in the city, we'll spot him straight off."

Yes, Rafe thought. *With the runners I've hired, plus*

Hannibal and his own handful of men, St. George's return will not go unnoticed.

The bodyguard departed. Rafe leaned back in his leather chair, alone again in his study. Exhaling, he worked to calm his temper. Of course, the exercise did him little good, his efforts now no more successful than all his earlier attempts to end the frustration and discontent that had simmered in his gut for the past few weeks.

Julianna was his wife. They lived in the same house and yet they scarcely saw each other.

Hades, he cursed, *I spent more time in her company when we were sneaking off for assignations in Queens Square! And we were certainly closer then, since I was at least welcome in her bed.*

But not anymore.

His thoughts returned to the information he'd gleaned from the bodyguard, and Julianna's meeting with Summersfield, his fingers toying with the letter opener.

What had she been doing openly chatting with the earl? She'd given her word she would not encourage the man. Of course that had been earlier. Did she imagine she no longer needed to honor her promise? That he wouldn't mind her flirting with a rake like Summersfield?

Flipping the blade up, he poked the tip into his leatherbound blotter.

The man had nerve, sniffing around Julianna's skirts like some randy hound when he knew she was newly married. Perhaps he hoped to lay a foundation for later, counting on his luck turning, and her agreeing to take him as her new lover some months in the future.

Still, Rafe's more rational side realized that today's encounter was likely innocent, especially with Beatrice Neville along as an inconvenient third. The news that Julianna had enjoyed such a merry time over tea with Summersfield grated, though.

She never smiled here at home—not at him, anyway. He missed that, her glorious smile, and the pretty little twinkle that shone in her eyes when something struck her as funny.

It was not only the smile and the twinkle, he thought. *I miss her.*

Ironic that marriage had driven them apart. The rift between them seemed to grow wider by the day, but for the life of him, he did not know how to overcome it.

With a heavy sigh, he reached for the stack of financial inquiries on the corner of his desk. Needing something, anything, to take his mind off Julianna, he forced himself to read.

Chapter Twenty-one

LORD AND LADY Pendragon."

As the butler's announcement rang out across the ballroom, the eyes of every person present shifted their way.

For a long moment, Julianna and Rafe stood poised at the entrance to Lord and Lady Chipford's grand ballroom. With one hand resting atop Rafe's elegantly tailored black sleeve, she was careful to keep her mask of regal indifference from slipping, her insides a battlefield of nerves.

They had arrived late, thus avoiding the strain of standing for an eternity in the reception line. Julianna had deemed it the best strategy for making an easy entrance into Society—or at least as easy as could be managed under the circumstances.

Tonight would be their test.

Prinny may have granted Rafe a title, which only yesterday the House of Lords had grudgingly confirmed, but neither of those acts could make the Ton accept him. Or her, for that matter, since she was his wife.

But as Rafe moved the pair of them forward, he did so with an easy confidence that belied his newly minted status as baron. Looking every inch the nobleman, his demeanor was such that any casual observer might have assumed he attended such gatherings all the time, when tonight was actually his first.

Their host and hostess moved through the crowd to greet them. Luckily the entertainment was a small one by Ton standards, with scarcely a hundred guests in attendance. With it being early December, Society's numbers remained thin, only die-hard parliamentarians and devoted city-dwellers still in residence within London's borders, all the rest having long ago departed for the country.

Yet no matter the time of year, people always loved a party, especially one that could boast of having as guests the source of this year's most scintillating *on-dit*.

Will they succeed or fail? That was the question buzzing on everyone's breath. Julianna wished she knew the answer, not yet certain how the evening would unfold despite all her earlier optimism.

"Welcome, my lord and my lady," Lady Chipford said, a determinedly cheerful smile on her face.

Julianna had met her many times before and knew instinctively that Maude Chipford had not suggested the invitation. Her husband must have twisted her arm to gain her compliance. Chipford had aspirations at Court and with the prime minister as well. Obviously, he wished to support their newest selection to the peerage.

Both Chipfords were quite pleasant, particularly so when the Duke of Wyvern sauntered up and gave Julianna and Rafe an exuberant greeting.

"Glad to see you arrived," Wyvern said, a slight gleam in his vivid blue eyes. "I was beginning to think you had decided not to come."

"No," Rafe drawled. "We merely had a late start. Julianna could not decide whether to wear the sapphire satin or the gold."

What a whopper! she thought, realizing Rafe might be far better at Ton games than she had imagined.

"Well, I, for one, am glad of her choice." The duke reached out and took Julianna's hand, bowing over it. "May I say you look radiant in gold, Lady Pendragon. You made a very wise choice."

In a gesture that appeared both tender and possessive, Rafe covered her right hand where it still rested on his sleeve. "I'll remind you she is already taken, Tony, and suggest you look elsewhere. I am sure there must be a few eligible ladies here this evening who would value such attentions, even yours," he finished, softening his words with a smile.

Lord and Lady Chipford's eyes widened as they waited for the duke's response, plainly unaware of his close friendship with Rafe.

Wyvern tossed back his head and laughed. "I daresay you are right. But haven't you heard it isn't fashionable to dote on your wife in public?"

"Perhaps, but when have I ever cared about such things, particularly not when it comes to my own dear Julianna."

Turning his head, he gazed down upon her, his eyes filled with intensity and warmth. Catching the look, Julianna's pulse gave a wild leap, and for an instant, she lost herself inside his eyes. If she hadn't known better, she would have believed the expression sincere, believed he truly did care for her and that she really was his "own dear Julianna."

But then he looked away and the moment was gone, fading along with her weakness and her gullibility, her heart slowing as it returned to its normal rhythm. *He is playing a part for the crowd,* she reminded herself. After all, it wouldn't do for anyone to realize the truth about their marriage.

Apparently Lady Chipford believed the fairy tale Rafe was weaving, a soft, indulgent smile curving her thin lips. "I forget the two of you are still newlyweds. How very charming you are together!" Reaching out, she tapped her fan playfully against Rafe's arm. "Still, my lord, I simply cannot allow you to monopolize your bride for the whole of the evening. You shall have to let her be whisked away for a few minutes here and there."

Rafe returned his hostess's smile with a smooth one of his own. "Maybe a few, here and there, your ladyship."

Lady Chipford laughed, the sound as light as a girl's.

Not here ten minutes, Julianna thought, *and Rafe has already gained a conquest. Perhaps his acceptance in Society won't be so difficult after all.*

"Yes, Pendragon," Lord Chipford said, further confirming her supposition. "You must join me in the library for a brandy and some talk about the economy. Once you've had your dance, of course."

Rafe inclined his head. "Of course."

"Of course what?" the Marquis of Vessey asked as he joined their group. Bowing, he offered polite greetings all around.

"Pendragon has agreed to join Chipford for a brandy and talk of the economy," Wyvern explained. "I'm sure there'll be many fellows interested in your perspective, Rafe, myself included."

"Well, I, for one, prefer to remain out here with the ladies," Vessey declared. "In fact, if you are not otherwise engaged, I would be most happy to stand up with both of you ladies, though not at the same time, you understand," he finished, giving a humorous wink.

Lady Chipford laughed. "Thank you, my lord, but I am afraid I do not dance. Lady Pendragon might welcome the offer, though, so long as her husband has no objection. He is most possessive, you know."

The marquis raised a golden eyebrow. "Is he? I am glad to hear it. Lady Pendragon, would you care to take a turn this evening?"

"Yes, my lord, that would be most pleasant, and I am sure my husband can have no objection."

"Not at all," Rafe agreed, "so long as it's only one dance."

"In that case, I shall take this opportunity to request a dance as well," the duke stated, his deep blue gaze alive with friendly good humor. "Lady Pendragon, what do you say?"

She couldn't help but return his smile. "Thank you as well, Your Grace. I would be delighted."

Another couple soon joined their group, offering congratulations to Rafe on his ascension to the peerage and best wishes to Julianna on her and Rafe's marriage.

Without entirely realizing it, the two of them began to mingle, conversing with a variety of ladies and gentleman, all of whom seemed more than willing to chat. Some were merely curiosity seekers, hoping to collect a few tidbits of gossip to pass around come the morrow. Several others were friends and acquaintances of Julianna's who wished to meet her new husband. There was a small number who refused to come near at all, their disapproval of Rafe clear. Despite their snobbery, however, none of them were willing to give him the cut directly.

And all the while, as she and Rafe moved slowly around the room, Rafe kept her hand tucked securely beneath his own. To all the world, one would imagine them to be a devoted couple.

Nearly an hour passed before the music began, signaling the start of the dancing. Rafe led her forward to take their places for a contra dance, where the men lined up on one side of the room and the ladies on the other. Facing one another, each couple would come together, then move apart again as prescribed by the dance, gracefully threading their way in and out of the line.

For an instant, as she and Rafe stood among the fifteen other couples waiting for the music to begin, a nervous tingle ran over her skin. She and Rafe had never danced before. What if they made a poor showing?

But seconds later, he proved her worries to be groundless. Not only did he know the steps, he executed them with fluid skill, as confident and commanding on the dance floor as he was in everything he did.

Knowing they were being observed, Julianna took care to keep a smile on her lips, conversing quietly with Rafe whenever the dance brought them near. They spoke of nothing significant, simple pleasantries that could have been shared by anyone.

Toward the end of the set, she ran out of conversation and so did he. Moving to the elegant music, she let herself take what pleasure there was to be had, enjoying the necessity of touching Rafe, even if it was through the barrier of gloves. Coming together then apart again, she savored the way their bodies came so tantalizingly close before being drawn away once more.

And then the dance was through.

Swallowing down an admittedly foolish sense of disappointment, she allowed Rafe to escort her off the floor.

"Are you feeling all right?" he inquired, bending his head downward so they would not be overheard.

"Yes, I am quite well."

"If you should discover yourself otherwise, you have only to say and we will leave."

She was about to express her thanks when they were interrupted by another couple.

Five minutes later, Rafe departed for the library and its promise of brandy and economic talk, leaving Julianna alone. Deciding she ought to sit for a few minutes to conserve her energy, she found a comfortable chair, rather glad for a moment of quiet. But her moment did not last long as a familiar gentleman approached.

Tipping back her head, she met Lord Summersfield's affable gaze.

"How do you do, Lady Pendragon?"

"Very well, thank you, my lord." She paused for a moment, casting a quick glance across the room to see if Rafe had returned. He had not.

But why am I worried? she asked herself.

Rafe might play a good game of appearing madly in love with her, but she knew it was all an act. Besides, she liked Lord Summersfield and they were at a party in full view of Society.

She gave him a smile. "Please, will you not have a seat?"

A little over an hour later, Rafe strode back into the ballroom. With hunger tugging at his belly, he wondered if Julianna might be in a similar condition, eager to join the couples who were beginning to wander into the Chipfords' dining room. On his way from the library, he'd stopped to take a quick peek at the supper buffet, the foodstuffs as plentiful as they were sumptuous-looking.

Of course, considering the late hour, Julianna might very well be tired. Perhaps rather than indulging in a meal, she would prefer to call for their carriage and make their way home. Fully prepared to do whichever activity she preferred, Rafe cast his gaze around the room.

At first, he didn't see her. But on a second pass, he not only saw her but saw her companion as well. His eyebrows shot up, then crashed down again before knitting into a scowl.

She was dancing, and from all appearances seemed neither famished nor weary. Of course, he might not have minded so much but for the identity of her companion.

Blasted Summersfield, Rafe cursed. *The man should get his damned hands off my wife!*

Allowing Julianna to dance with Ethan or Tony was bad enough, since both men were well-known rakes who could charm a woman with nothing more than a look. But despite their reputations, Rafe knew he could trust both of them implicitly; Julianna was as safe with either of them as she was with her own brother.

But Summersfield was an entirely different story altogether.

Does the man care nothing for the fact that Julianna is married? Then again, for some men, marriage only increased a lady's allure. In the Ton, as Rafe well knew, the majority of couples married for wealth or social position. To their way of thinking, love and passion were to be indulged in later, emotions to be discovered outside the sanctity of the marriage vows.

Despite her earlier refusals to wed Summersfield, it was plain she enjoyed the man's company. Could she be forming a serious attraction to him, a bond that might one day turn to love? A sick lump formed in Rafe's stomach at the thought.

Grinding his teeth together, he watched Russell Summersfield whirl Julianna across the ballroom floor, the dulcet strains of a waltz floating like honey drops in the air. With a smile on her rosy lips, Julianna seemed to be having a grand time, her gown of guinea gold satin a perfect foil for her dark, silky hair and luminous brown eyes.

Although a good eight inches separated her body from the earl's, the space between them was far too close in Rafe's estimation. *A foot would be more acceptable,* he thought. *Or better still, the entire length of the ballroom.*

Fingers curling into fists at his sides, he strode forward. He didn't care how it might appear; he was going to cut in. But after only five steps, the musicians played a final flourish of notes, then brought the dance to an end.

Rafe kept walking.

By the time he reached the pair, Summersfield had Julianna's hand settled atop his arm. "Shall we make our way to the dining room to enjoy a bite of supper?" the earl inquired.

Julianna nodded. "Yes, that would be lovely, thank you."

"Why indeed, thank you, Summersfield," Rafe declared, maneuvering himself so that he blocked their path. "But that will not be necessary. I shall see to my *wife*."

Surprise lighted Julianna's features. "Rafe, I did not know you were returned."

"No, I am sure you did not. But seeing that I am, I shall take you in to supper."

Summersfield raised a brow. "Actually, that privilege should fall to me. By tradition, the man sharing the supper dance with a lady has the right to escort her in to the meal."

Arrogant ass! Rafe thought. *Does he think I don't know that?*

"And you," Rafe said, uncaring what Summersfield or anyone else might think, "have the right to release her and keep your teeth in your head."

Julianna gasped, then did so again when Rafe reached out and grasped her hand, transferring it with deliberate firmness to his own sleeve.

Holding her hand beneath his, he pinned the earl with a look. "One more thing. I would take it as a personal favor if you stopped chatting up Lady Pendragon in public places. I don't much care for you taking her for tea, either, so do not do it again."

Julianna's eyes widened, plainly appalled by his rude behavior. "Rafe!"

Ignoring her, he fixed his gaze on his rival. "Do I make myself clear?"

The earl returned his gaze. "Yes, perfectly."

Shifting on his heel, Summersfield turned toward Julianna and executed a bow. "My lady, a pleasure as always."

Then he was gone.

For a long moment, neither of them said a word.

"Julianna—"

"Don't," she hissed in a low tone. "Do not even speak to me." As he watched, she fixed a smile on her face. "Now take me in to supper."

"We can go home if you would prefer."

"I *would* prefer leaving, but you've made that option an impossibility. If we are to salvage the situation and put to rest what is otherwise sure to be prime fodder for tomorrow's gossip mill, we *have* to go in to supper. You will procure plates for each of us while we will pretend to be happy and cheerful for the next hour. After supper, I will take to the floor for one more dance and then, and only then, can we go home."

Does she also imagine I do not know the rules? he wondered, anger flashing in his system. *I just don't give a fig about them, that's all.*

He stiffened. "Madam, I do not care for your tone, and if I say we are leaving, then we are leaving."

She shot him a suddenly imploring glance.

"But in the interests of peace," he said, relenting slightly, "we shall go in to supper. Another dance, however, is out of the question."

With her hand still held beneath his own, they made their way to the dining room.

*   *   *

Nearly two hours later, Julianna allowed Rafe to assist her from the coach. She said nothing, just as she had said nothing to him during the long ride home. He too had been silent, staring broodingly out the carriage window.

Weary and out-of-sorts, she entered the house, murmuring a soft greeting to the footman before making her way up the stairs. All she wanted was to change into her nightgown, brush out her hair, and climb into bed, where she hoped sleep would make the dreadful evening fade away.

Supper had been an ordeal, but she believed her and Rafe's efforts to feign newlywedded bliss had achieved the desired effect. So long as Summersfield said nothing about the confrontation—and she very much doubted he would—the incident would be quickly forgotten. Remembering back, she didn't think any of the other guests had been close enough to overhear the exchange between Rafe and the earl. Otherwise, all anyone would have seen was the two men exchanging a few words.

Even now, she could scarcely credit Rafe's abominable behavior, nor his unforgivable rudeness to poor Lord Summersfield. *There is simply no understanding that man*, she grumbled to herself, as she let Daisy unfasten her gown.

All she and the earl had done was share a dance. True, Rafe had once been jealous of Summersfield, but what cause did he have to be now? She suspected his barbarian tactics were merely a case of territoriality. He might not want her, but he didn't want any other man to have her either.

Not that she was interested in another man. For goodness sake, she was five months pregnant! A woman that far along would either have to be madly in love or in need of a quick trip to Bedlam in order to consider starting an illicit love affair. Besides, as much as she liked Russell Summersfield, she had never felt more for him than friendship, and she knew she never would.

Raising her arms, she let Daisy slip a nightgown over her head, then help her into her a warm, ruby-colored velvet robe. Shooing her sleepy maid from the room to find her own much-needed bed, Julianna took a seat at her dressing table and reached for her brush.

Regardless of her feelings for the earl, she mused as she pulled the bristles through her hair, Rafe had no right to treat her or Summersfield in such a shabby manner. He'd acted rudely, embarrassing both of them, and for no good reason. Not to mention the fact that Rafe had warned the other man off, as if she had no say in her dance partners nor her friends.

She set down her brush with a sharp click.

Whomever I choose to like or dislike is my business and none of Rafe's, she thought. *He may be my husband, but he doesn't run my life—well, not all of it anyway,* she amended, thinking how he'd gotten his way in nearly every confrontation they'd had since their marriage, and even earlier than that, come to think of it.

Before she had time to reconsider her actions, she rose to her feet and walked across the room. Twisting the key to unlock the connecting door, she rapped her knuckles briefly on the polished wood, then, without waiting for his reply, shoved open the door.

Just a few steps past the threshold, she stopped.

Spacious yet comfortable, the room held a distinctly masculine flavor, trimmed in warm browns and deep reds that resurrected long-ago thoughts of dragons and shadowy lairs.

Having never before been in the room, she couldn't help but glance at the huge tester bed with its burgundy hangings and satin counterpane. Nor could she fail to see the massive mahogany chest-on-chest that stood against the far wall, its top cabinet doors opened to display a double row of books and a crystal decanter of brandy, the round stopper lying next to the bottle.

With only a lone candle on one nightstand and the mellow illumination from the fire burning quietly in the grate, she didn't immediately see Rafe. Seconds later, she spied him seated in a wide leather wing chair not far from the fireplace. Still dressed in his white evening shirt and black breeches, his throat lay bare; his discarded cravat piled in a heap on his dressing table, his waistcoat draped over the back of another chair. A lock of raven hair curled against his forehead, a faint shadow of whiskers riding his cheeks. With his legs stretched out in a negligent pose, he looked the part of sin personified.

Her pulse quickened at the sight of him, her breath growing momentarily shallow.

Having been caught in the midst of taking a drink, he swallowed a mouthful of liquor, then lowered his glass.

"I would have a word with you, my lord," she declared, stepping farther into the room.

He raised a single, inquiring eyebrow. "About what?" he drawled. "Unless you have come to apologize."

Her mouth fell open, breath catching in her chest. "Apologize! If anyone needs to apologize, it would be you. Your behavior tonight at the ball was inexcusable. You were unconscionably rude to Lord Summersfield, to say nothing of myself. I have rarely been so mortified."

"And what of your own behavior, madam?" he countered. "You are hardly without fault in this matter, cavorting around the ballroom in full sight of everyone."

"I wasn't cavorting, I was dancing. Or do you not know what dancing looks like?"

"Of course I know. And that"—he paused, circling a pair of fingers in the air—"whatever it is you were doing, displayed a far greater resemblance to the former than the latter."

"For your information, the dance is called the waltz, and it is all the rage."

"I'm sure it is, since it allows a libertine like Summersfield to put his hands all over a lady. He ought to keep his blasted hands to himself."

She stiffened. "The earl is not a libertine."

Rafe gave an impolite snort.

"And that is quite beside the point," she continued, moving closer. "He and I did nothing wrong tonight. You are the one who barged in and created a scene. A scene, I might add, that could have damaged your brand-new reputation among the Ton. You should be glad Summersfield isn't the sort to talk, or else he could make a great deal of trouble for you."

A muscle ticked in his jaw. "Believe me, I am not worried about Summersfield so long as he stays well away from you."

She took another few steps forward. "And that is another thing. You had no right warning him off. I will choose my friends as I please."

His eyes narrowed. "You may choose as many *female* friends as you like, but not men, and especially not Summersfield. Perhaps other members of your set don't mind being cuckolded, but I am not one of them."

Her mouth nearly dropped open again, unable to believe what she was hearing. "Is that what you think? That I am having an affair?"

"No. At least not for the time being. But I will not like it later any more than I would like it now. As I recall, I once told you I don't share what is mine. And you, my dear wife, are mine."

She blew out a breath. "Why do you even care? You don't want me except as something you can manipulate and control."

An intense gleam sparked in his eyes. "Who says I don't want you? As I recall, you are the one who banned me from your bed. I will be happy to return anytime you like."

A quiver rippled over her skin.

Rafe, back in my bed?

A part of her longed to say yes, a strong part. Inwardly reciting all her reasons against allowing such a thing, she forced herself to shake her head. "No."

He tossed back the last of the spirits, then set the glass aside. "Are you sure? You don't look entirely certain to me."

"I am," she assured him, wondering why her words didn't sound convincing, not even to herself.

"Mayhap we need to test the matter," he continued.

"Test it how?"

Before she could think to evade him, he reached out and captured one of her hands, pulling her forward to gently tumble her onto his lap.

"Rafe, what do you think you're doing?"

"What does it look like I'm doing?"

She squirmed. "Let me go."

"Shh, quit that now. You'll only hurt yourself. Anyway, you know you have nothing to worry about. I'll release you if that is what you truly wish. After our last less-than-satisfactory time together, you surely can have no doubts as to my trustworthiness on that subject?"

He has a point there, she conceded. He'd been as primed for sex as a man could possibly be, hard and ready, and yet he had forced himself to free her and leave the room. If he could summon that kind of willpower once, he could do so again. Particularly since as far as she was concerned they were not going to get anywhere near a bed.

Anyway, he is probably just baiting me, she decided, *determined to teach me what he thinks will be some sort of lesson.* Well, he was in for a surprise, since she planned to rebuff him yet again.

Tired of wiggling—especially given that her figure wasn't what it used to be—she fell still.

A moment passed.

"Well?" she asked. "Are we just going to sit here?"

His gaze moved to her waist, his fingers reaching to untie her robe. The velvet folds parted, revealing her thin lawn nightgown and the slight roundness protruding beneath.

Lifting a hand, he laid his palm against her belly, slowly tracing her shape. "I had no idea you'd grown so much. It certainly doesn't show beneath your gowns."

"Not yet. By next month, I suspect there will be no concealing anything."

A fierce expression crossed his face. "Good. I don't want you hiding our son."

There it is again, that possessiveness, she thought.

She was just about to climb free of his lap when the baby shifted.

"What was that?" he questioned.

"You felt it?"

He splayed his hand wider. "Is it the baby?"

Seeing his eager excitement, she couldn't refuse to share. "Yes. *She* is moving around. She'll settle down again in a minute or two."

"So this has happened before?"

She nodded. "More and more often. She'll be giving me full-fledged kicks soon, I suspect."

Gently stroking her belly, he waited, clearly hoping to feel their child move again. When a minute passed and nothing happened, he lifted his hand.

But he wasn't finished.

A gentle gasp escaped her lips as he reached for her hem and pulled the material upward. Shifting, she tried to stop him. "Rafe!"

"Hush, it's nothing I haven't seen before. I just want to feel."

"You've *been* feeling."

"Not like this."

Bunching the cloth beneath her breasts, he exposed her naked belly. Tingles shivered through her as he pressed his big, warm palm against her bare skin, slowly caressing the slight curve. She held back a tremor, an odd lassitude creeping through her, along with a pleasure she could not deny.

And then it came again, the visceral flutter of sensation that accompanied the movements of her child.

Their child.

Glancing up, he smiled, his eyes alive with delight. Holding her secure, he leaned forward and dropped a kiss onto her belly.

"Hmm, you smell so good," he said.

She quivered, knowing she should leave.

Breathing against her, he kissed her belly, once, then twice more. Gently. Reverently.

Her eyelids drooped.

Shifting her slightly again inside his strong arms, he straightened. Before she could think to say a word, he bent and captured her lips.

From the instant his mouth touched hers, her mind turned to mush, every lucid thought evaporating beneath the power of his kiss. Her toes curled, the flesh of her stomach warming beneath the easy, soothing strokes of his hand.

Humming in the back of her throat, she opened her lips to let his tongue delve inside, hot and slick and delicious. Teasing and tempting, he urged her to join in, coaxing her to play with him as he was so delightfully playing with her.

And she did. Sliding her fingers into his soft hair to hold his head steady, she matched the dark, wet wonder of his kiss with an undeniable need of her own. Within seconds she was lost, Rafe filling her senses, consuming her so that all she could feel was him and her own explosive response.

Her conscience whispered something in her head, but she brushed the warning aside, suddenly unable to remember exactly why it was she'd been holding Rafe at bay. What was the point in denying him? Not when his touch felt so right, so good.

Oh so good.

His caresses moved lower, his fingers trailing across her naked thighs. Easing her legs slightly apart, he traced the ultrasensitive flesh there but stopped short of touching her in the most intimate place of all.

His movements drove her crazy, each controlled stroke akin to torture of the most exquisite kind. Fine tremors rose beneath her skin, vibrating through her flesh and blood and bone.

Growing bolder and more demanding, his kisses challenged her to match his ardor with a raw passion of her own. As she strove to rise to the task, her breath grew ragged, her body turning hot, skin damp as if she were in the throes of a raging fever.

Curling her fingers against his shoulders, her nails bit into the cloth of his shirt. She clung, needing the safety of his strength as a thousand sensations whizzed and whirled through her like Chinese fireworks blazing in a dark summer sky.

Nuzzling beneath her ear, he strung a line of kisses down her throat before returning to her nape to give her a gentle bite. She cried out, her eyelids fluttering closed in a rush of bliss. Angling her face, she rubbed her cheek against the faint roughness of his own, before leaning closer to take his mouth in another sizzling mating of lips and tongues.

His growl of pleasure made her smile, his hand tightening for a moment against the tender flesh of her inner thigh. Feeling suddenly shameless, she spread her legs a little wider, hoping he would touch her where her desire burned the hottest.

Instead he kissed her before sliding his arms beneath her legs and back. Holding her secure, he rose to his feet, their mouths still fused as he carried her across the room.

A rush of cool softness enveloped her for a moment as he lay her against the sheets, his bed seeming as big as a sea around her. Then she didn't have time to think about beds or sheets or anything else but Rafe as he came down beside her and once again claimed her mouth in a fervid kiss.

Needing to touch his bare flesh, she slipped her hands under his shirt, delighting in the play of warm, smooth skin layered over taut muscle and hard bone. He seemed to approve, moaning low in his throat at her increasingly bold strokes. Exploring further, she slid her fingers beneath his waistband to tease the slight dip where his back merged with his hips. He pulled in an audible breath, shuddering beneath her touch.

Leaning up, he reached for her nightgown and tugged it to her waist. With one hand, he stroked her thighs again, caressing her sensitive flesh until she truly thought she might go insane.

Legs shifting, she whimpered, desperate for him to take her. Obviously aware of her heightened need, he spread her legs and slid a finger into her wet heat.

She arched and moaned, lifting her hips to urge him to stroke deeper, harder. But he kept his touch light, teasing her so that her desire built in ever-widening spirals. Shivering, she waited, her body poised on the very edge of completion. She knew she was close, that all it would take was a single stroke in just the right spot to send her over into oblivion.

But suddenly his hand grew still.

She shifted in restless hunger, needing him to continue.

"Do you want me?" he said, his mouth against her ear.

"What?"

"Do you want me?" he demanded, his voice a mixture of velvet and steel. "Tell me you want me, Julianna, or we stop now."

Stop? Oh God, we can't stop now.

And then she realized what he was doing. How he'd slowly led her to this place, playing on her hunger until he literally held her on a razor's edge of need, his will alone the difference between bliss or agony.

He wants me to beg, she thought. *Wants me to humble myself and admit my need for him.*

Pride insisted she refuse. Passion told her not to be a fool.

For a long moment she lay torn, then he moved his fingers again, just enough to taunt her. And suddenly her body gave her no choice.

"Yes," she cried, "I want you."

"Say it again. Tell me you want me in your body and in your bed."

Closing her eyes, she silently cursed him. "I want you inside me and inside my bed. Now, take me, Rafe, please."

Moving hastily to unbutton his falls, he did as she asked, removing his hand to sheath himself inside her. Reaching between them, he flicked his fingers and sent her hurtling, the pleasure flooding through her glorious as a starburst.

But he wasn't through, setting a pace that refused to let her desire cool, that urged her to climb up the precipice and jump over with him again.

And no matter what he'd done, she couldn't deny the beauty, the sheer wonder of his touch, the pure, unadulterated heaven of being held again in his arms, their flesh joined together as one.

Despite his obvious need, he was tender, stroking inside her with controlled power, making sure she was with him every step of the way as each of them drew closer to the ultimate satisfaction.

She wasn't prepared when the climax slammed into her, sensation rushing upon her so fast she screamed against the shattering burst of ecstasy that threatened to break her. But she rode the wave, awash in heat and light, and yes, love, as Rafe found his own completion.

Holding him, she didn't let herself think, didn't let herself regret, knowing there would be plenty of time for such things come the dawn.

Curling against him, weary and replete, she slept.

Chapter Twenty-two

THE NEXT THREE weeks passed slowly, life falling into a new pattern now that she and Rafe were lovers again.

After Rafe's skillful seduction, where he'd literally made her beg him to take her, Julianna had known the battle between them was lost. Despite her lingering sense of hurt, she found herself unable to do more than offer a token resistance when he came to her room and climbed into her bed the next night. And once he kissed her, there'd been no use at all trying to deny his need or her own.

Still, in many ways her situation seemed hopeless. She loved and wanted him, yet she existed in a constant state of anxious misery, waiting to see how long his desire for her would last this time. His passion for her would end, she knew, maybe sooner rather than later considering how large she was beginning to grow with their child.

He loved the baby, of that she had no doubt, Rafe apparently fascinated by all the changes occurring to her body. Often she would wake to find his hand on her belly, as if he craved the connection. But she feared the link he sought was to his son and not to her. He might make love to her but he never said a word about his feelings, his silence on the subject telling her everything she needed to know.

Out of bed, their lives were much as before. He worked during the day while she saw to the household. They shared meals and the occasional outing. To all outward appearances, they were a typical married couple.

Only she knew they were not.

So when Maris wrote asking her and Rafe to join them for the holiday, she'd been delighted to accept, hoping the visit would lift her spirits.

Now, alighting from the coach at Waring Keep, she knew she had been right.

"Maris!" Julianna exclaimed, smiling as she hurried across the pebbled drive and into her sister's welcoming embrace.

She and Maris exchanged hugs and kisses, laughing to be once more in each other's company after so many months apart.

"Oh, it's so wonderful to see you!" Maris said, her face wreathed in smiles. "I'm so glad you could spend Christmas here with William and me. I suppose we could all have stayed with William's parents at their estate, but the house is so very full of family and I thought it would be cozier this way. The four of us will drive over tomorrow for a fine Christmas dinner and games afterward."

Maris broke off, darting a glance toward Rafe, who stood not far from the coach. "But la, listen to me rattle away. Come, introduce me," she urged, threading her arm through Julianna's. "I still cannot believe you are married. Your letter gave me such a shock when it arrived."

"I can well imagine," Julianna said as she let her sister lead her forward. "Maris, this is Rafe Pendragon. My husband."

Releasing Julianna, Maris reached up and welcomed Rafe with a familial hug, which he returned with a gentle pat against her back.

"A pleasure to meet you, Mrs. Waring," Rafe said.

"Gracious, you must call me Maris. We are siblings now and cannot possibly stand on ceremony."

A genuinely warm smile curved over Rafe's lips, his face brightening to devastating effect. "Of course not. My apologies, Maris."

A small frown settled over Maris's slender brows. "Have we met before?"

Rafe cast a quick glance toward Julianna, then shook his head. "Not to my knowledge, no."

"You seem familiar somehow . . . Oh, good heavens, the bookstore! He's the one, isn't he, Jules? The handsome one we saw?"

Count on Maris to remember such a thing, Julianna thought.

"Is that how you two met?" Maris clapped her hands together. "Did you see each other again another day, and couldn't resist the chance to meet? How divine! You must tell me everything."

Julianna refused to look at Rafe. "Yes, well, perhaps we might do so inside. It's a clear day but still cold."

"Forgive me, I'm just so excited to see you both. Come in and we'll have hot tea before you go to your room. And William should be along any minute. He is down at the stable. One of the horses is in foal."

As if her words had spurred him on, boot heels crunched against the paver stones, Major Waring emerging from around one of the large hedgerows that sheltered the house on the north side.

With his appearance, another round of introductions was made.

"How is Marigold?" Maris asked as the four of them walked into the house.

William grinned. "She's a proud mama and doing well. The colt is gorgeous and strong. You must come down later to see them both."

Removing her cloak, Julianna took a moment to look around.

Though not nearly as grand as Allerton Manor, Maris and William's two-story Georgian house was both pleasant and pretty. A fine home, the interior was already showing traces of Maris's touch in the new entry wallpaper and in the large Meissen vase filled with bittersweet, the plant with its striking orange berries a favorite of her sister's.

When Maris let out a small squeak, Julianna turned to find her sister staring. *At her stomach.*

"Jules, is that . . . are you . . . well, are you increasing?"

As she'd predicted, the baby had grown considerably in the past few weeks, so there was no point in denying it. Besides, she had planned to share the news with Maris anyway.

With a little smile, Julianna nodded. "Yes."

Maris raised up onto her toes. "Oh, that's wonderful! But why did you not tell me?"

"You did not give me a chance."

"Well, you have time now." Taking Julianna's arm, Maris steered her toward the sitting room. "Come have a seat so you can share everything."

Only a few minutes after entering the drawing room, William took Rafe back out to the stable to see the new foal, leaving the women to talk in private. Once they were gone, Maris set in with questions, bubbling with excitement over the idea that she had been witness to Julianna and Rafe's first encounter and the start of their life together.

Deciding it was easier not to spoil her fancies, Julianna allowed her little sister to assume what she would. She didn't tell Maris everything, but enough to keep her satisfied and leave most of her romantic notions intact.

Though Julianna never like prevaricating, she couldn't bring herself to reveal the truth of how she and Rafe had *really* met, nor the fact that she'd been his mistress long before that fateful day in Hatchard's bookstore. When it came to her pregnancy, though, Julianna was far more honest, admitting that she had already been expecting at the time of her marriage. Maris's eyes widened slightly at the thought of her respectable sister engaging in an illicit affair, but soon enough she smiled and declared it was just too tremendously romantic for words.

After hearing Julianna's explanation, Maris admitted that she felt vastly relieved, since she'd been feeling rather hurt at having not been invited to the wedding.

"But you were on your honeymoon," Julianna countered.

"Yes, but until now I couldn't fathom why you could not have waited a few more weeks until our return. Now I know why, so all is well."

When the men returned, tea and sandwiches were served, all four of them sharing a convivial bit of conversation over the satisfying snack.

During the meal, Julianna learned one thing: Maris was very happy in her marriage, her little sister sending frequent, smiling glances toward her new husband, who returned them with equal affection and intensity. *If only Rafe and I had that kind of bond,* Julianna mused. For in spite of the fact that Rafe was once again sharing her bed, little else about their relationship had changed.

But she would not dwell on that now. She had this visit and the holiday to enjoy, and she planned to do so with enthusiasm.

Christmas day proved to be a delight, with an array of delectable foods and unbridled frivolity. William's family welcomed Julianna and Rafe with an easy manner, making only a brief comment about Rafe's recent ascension to the nobility before quietly accepting him into the fold. As for Julianna's ripening figure, any suspicions remained unspoken, leaving her to share the news about the baby in her own way and time. With everyone in a festive mood, she let herself relax and make merry, content to pretend for those few hours that everything was right in the world, and that her cares and worries were far, far away.

Over the week to follow, she and Maris spent hours catching up on all they had missed during their time apart, while Rafe and William either rode out across the snow-dusted fields or else retreated into the warmth of William's office to talk about the war or the economy.

Meals were exceedingly pleasant, filled with fine food and interesting talk, the evenings taken up with singing, charades, and card games.

At night, Julianna and Rafe shared a room, sleeping contentedly in each other's arms. Infinitely gentle, Rafe made love to her, taking care not to be overheard as if he knew how uncomfortable it would make her feel there in her sister's home.

Twelfth Night came and went, and with it arrived the end of their sojourn to the country. Yet on the last day before their scheduled departure, Julianna found herself wishing they might remain longer. Or at least that *she* might remain longer, since she knew business matters awaited Rafe back in London, matters that could not be indefinitely delayed.

Alone in their bedchamber before dinner, she waited for the right moment to speak.

"Shall we go down?" Rafe asked, tugging at the sleeve of his tobacco-brown superfine coat as he strolled from the adjoining dressing room.

Trailing the tip of a fingernail across the top of the polished walnut dressing table, Julianna shifted in her seat to face him. "Yes, in just a moment. First, I thought we might have a word."

He met her gaze with an inquiring expression. "Oh, about what? And may I say that you look especially lovely this evening. That color becomes you."

She cast a quick downward glance at her vibrant sapphire shot-silk gown before forcing her eyes upward again. "Thank you, my lord. I am glad you approve."

"I do, most wholeheartedly," he assured her with a smile. "Though I don't know if I will ever get completely used to hearing myself referred to as 'my lord,' particularly by you."

"You will, since that is who you are now." Hugging her blue-and-gold patterned shawl closer around her shoulders, she continued. "We have had a fine time these past several days, I think."

"Very fine. It's been a good holiday."

She nodded. "I know you cannot delay your return to the city. I realize you are quite busy."

"Busy enough, though the time away has been manageable."

"I am not constrained by any such restrictions, however, which is why I thought I might remain here a while longer."

"What?" His voice lowered to a graveled rumble.

"It is so peaceful here in the countryside, so relaxing," she rushed on, playing her fingers over the edge of her shawl. "I love being with Maris, and she would be a great comfort to me as my confinement draws near."

"Your confinement is three months away."

She dipped her chin. "Yes, which is why I thought I would stay through the spring."

A glower as black and formidable as a rain-soaked thundercloud descended over his brow. "Out of the question. Now, we'll be late if we do not go below for dinner."

"But Rafe—"

"But nothing, madam. The conversation is over."

Straightening her back, she laid a hand over her gently rounded middle. "It is not over. I wish to remain with my sister."

"You mean you wish to be separated from me. Well, I will not permit that, so put the notion out of your mind. We will return to London tomorrow as planned. Both of us."

"You are spinning this all out of proportion. I merely wish to stay here until the baby is born."

"Do you? And will you return immediately after the child comes?"

"Yes, I . . . well, yes, after I recover my health."

"And how many months will that take? Three, six, a year? No, Julianna, you are my wife and your place is at my side. If your sister wishes to visit you in London, she is most welcome."

"She is a newlywed. She cannot be away from William that long. How would it look?"

"How would it look for you, since you are also newly married?"

She bit the corner of her lip, realizing he had a valid point. But he was mistaken about her wish to leave him; such an idea had never entered her thoughts. All she wanted was a little time to relax in the comfort of her sister's companionship, to allay her fears as she prepared for the birth of her child and all the momentous changes the baby would bring to her life.

All she had succeeded in doing, though, was to make Rafe angry.

"I simply need some time," she said, trying to explain.

He raised a critical brow. "Yes, we've established that, I believe. Once the baby comes, should you still find yourself needing *time,* perhaps other arrangements can be made."

The breath left her lungs. "What do you mean?"

"You will always be my wife and nothing will change that save death. Couples separate, however, and if you find you cannot stand to dwell under the same roof as I, then you may go. Our child, of course, will remain with me."

A pain burst inside her chest at his threat, radiating outward like an exploding star. "I will never leave my baby."

"Then I suggest you find a way to continue our cohabitation." His spine unyielding, he extended an arm. "We are most definitely late now. Let us descend before your sister and brother-in-law come in search. And smile unless you wish them to know something is amiss."

Half numb and no longer the least bit hungry, Julianna stood. Laying a hand on Rafe's arm, she forced her lips to curve upward, when what she really longed to do was cry.

An icy sliver of wind crept beneath the collar of Rafe's heavy, many-caped greatcoat, making him wish he was inside the coach instead of riding beside it. But at present he preferred suffering in the cold to being confined in the landau with Julianna.

So she wants to leave me, does she?

His jaw clenched at the thought. Despite the fact that nearly a day had passed since her announcement that she wished to remain behind with her sister, her words still had the power to slice him to the marrow. Oh, she claimed their separation would only be temporary, but weeks apart had a way of turning into months and even years.

And here he'd thought matters between them were improving. Imagined—erroneously it would now seem—that Julianna was taking pleasure in their marriage.

Their union had not been an easy one from the start, he conceded, but with her return to his bed, he'd been convinced she felt something more for him than mere duty.

Lately he'd been toying with the notion that she might even be coming to love him. But last night's blunt declaration had swept away any such illusions. His hands tightened on the reins for an instant before he forced himself to relax, concerned he might unsettle his mount.

Casting a glance toward the coach window, he let his gaze rove over Julianna's regal profile, a pretty ermine-trimmed hat framing her dusky cheeks. A hard knot squeezed in his chest, struck as he always was by the dark allure of her beauty. But his reaction went far deeper than the surface, since he knew the woman who lay beneath. The soft, sweet, gentle being who possessed a core of indomitable strength and bravery, who fought for her beliefs and wasn't afraid to stand up and protect those she cared for in spite of the consequences.

A woman to be admired. A woman to be loved.

And I do love her, he realized.

After Pamela, he'd never expected to feel deeply for any woman again, but quite without his knowledge, the emotion had crept upon him and taken his heart unawares.

Sighing, he dipped his head against the wind. *What a sorry pass,* he mused, *loving a woman who does not love me.*

Perhaps he should have let her stay with Maris and William, since that had been her wish. But until his plans for St. George came to fruition and the man was rendered harmless, he could not risk Julianna's safety. She might chafe under his restrictions, but she and their child must be protected at all costs.

Nor was he about to let her take their child and move away after the babe was born. He remembered how much he'd longed for his father when he'd been a boy, how he'd had to content himself with infrequent visits and moments together that never seemed long enough.

My child will know both his parents, he vowed, *no matter the difficulties between Julianna and myself.*

Gazing at her again, he sighed and rode on.

Chapter Twenty-three

❦

"Oh, those look darling!" Julianna declared, taking a step back so she could get a better view of the cheery, sunshine-yellow draperies that a pair of housemaids had just finished hanging over the nursery windows.

With careful planning and patience, the new space was finally nearing completion. In the two months since her and Rafe's return to Town, Julianna had devoted herself to converting the dark, musty third-floor attic into a haven for the baby who would soon enter their lives.

Having received Rafe's blessing to make any changes she wished, she'd hired a crew of skilled carpenters, craftsmen, and painters to create a nursery, bedroom, and a playroom that any child would love. Following her direction, the men had done amazing work, literally transforming the old, drafty environs into a connecting trio of warm, sunny, yet infinitely cozy rooms.

Now, all that remained was seeing to the final details, little things such as hanging the last of the curtains and storing blankets, toys, clothes, and nappies. As for the furniture, a wide, exquisitely made rosewood cradle occupied a place just far enough from the fireplace to keep the baby warm without overheating him, while a walnut changing table and cane-back rocking chair were arranged atop a pair of nearby Aubusson carpets.

In the playroom, a huge hobby horse stood at the ready in one corner. When the toy had first arrived, she'd shaken her head at its impracticality, knowing it would be a pair of years at least before the baby was big enough to enjoy the gift. But Rafe insisted that his son or daughter would love looking at the horse, even if the child couldn't ride it for a while. And in that, she knew he was right.

Laying a hand on her protruding belly, she surveyed the nursery with its soothing peach walls and wide, sun-filled windows. The baby kicked, tiny feet pummeling beneath her ribs for a long minute. Despite the discomfort, the baby's increasingly frequent movements reassured her that all was well.

With less than a month of her pregnancy left, though, she found herself battling back worries about what was to come. After all, she'd watched her mother die in childbirth and knew all too well the terrible things that could occur.

But everything will be fine, she told herself. *For me and my child.*

She wished she had someone in whom she could confide, but she didn't want to unnecessarily alarm her friends or her sister by voicing her fears. And talking to Rafe these days was out of the question.

Since their return to London after the new year their relationship had grown increasingly strained. Rafe had even stopped coming to her bed at night. He claimed he did not wish to disturb her sleep, but she knew her personal comfort had little to do with his withdrawal. After their disagreement about her remaining in the country, he'd become more and more distant, until they once again found themselves living as virtual strangers.

Part of her wished to go to him and repair the rift, but

his threats had chilled her, had kept her silent when she might otherwise have lowered her pride enough to ask him to come back.

"You may go," he'd said. *"But our child will remain with me."*

The words had stayed with her all these weeks, gnawing at her like a rat at a rope.

He cares naught for me, she thought. *For all I know, he's taken another mistress.*

Nausea rose at the idea, scalding the delicate lining of her throat. Wrapping an arm around her heavy middle, she forced her thoughts back to the task at hand.

"Be careful," she warned as the housemaids stepped down from their ladders.

Once again on solid ground, they curtseyed and smiled. "Yes, my lady, and thank you."

Returning their smiles, Julianna watched as the two young women moved to another set of windows to hang more draperies.

At least Maris will arrive next week, Julianna thought.

Of course, so would most of the Ton, returned from their country estates to partake in the frivolity of a brand-new Season. Yet while the nobility danced and drank and cavorted until all hours, she would be here inside the townhouse readying herself to give birth.

Another bone of contention between herself and Rafe.

Last month, she had gone to him and asked if they could travel to his country house in Yorkshire, explaining how she longed for a bit of peaceful solitude. After a brief pause, he'd refused, telling her he had too much business in the city for them to leave.

"Besides," he said, "you will receive better medical care here in London."

And that had been the end of that.

She sighed. As much as she loved the new nursery and had her every need seen to here at the townhouse, she would have much preferred a respite in the countryside. If she closed her eyes, she could almost smell the spring-sweet air in her nose, her shoes crushing the greening grass as she strolled through the fields, birdsong playing like a symphony on the wind.

But such was not to be.

If only there were somewhere to go, even for a few hours!

Of course, there was her townhouse on Upper Brook Street. She still owned it, even if it was locked up, the furniture shrouded in dust sheets.

But what was the point?

No, she decided, she would content herself by keeping busy with preparations for the baby. She had hats and booties to knit and embroidery to finish on the christening gown she was sewing from a length of delicate white moiré silk.

I will be fine, she assured herself. *I have nothing whatsoever to fear.*

Where has he hidden them?

Blood thundered in Burton's temples, fury burning like a brand in his chest as he rifled through the contents of Hurst's desk. He'd already been through the man's bedroom, study, and library twice, searching every conceivable location for the fool's journals.

Yet nothing.

In the past four hours he'd searched every room in the townhouse, to no avail. The blighted things simply weren't here.

When he and Hurst arrived back in London earlier in the evening, Burton had set to questioning his old friend. Besotted as usual, Hurst had told him to look for the latest journal in his bedroom nightstand. The rest were stored in a trunk, he claimed. When they didn't turn up there, he'd suggested his study.

By the time Hurst began to seriously question Burton's interest in the diaries, it had been too late for him—the poison Burton put into his wine already beginning to paralyze his limbs and restrict his breathing. When Burton stopped by tomorrow and "discovered" his friend dead, the authorities would conclude Hurst had died of a heart seizure brought on by a life of excess and overindulgence.

Good thing for him Hurst didn't keep staff in the house when he was away, Burton thought. Bad thing for Hurst. The dolt hadn't even sent his valet ahead on this trip, he and Burton having traveled alone in Burton's curricle despite the wet March weather.

The idea had been to dash into Town, then dash out again, no one the wiser. Then they were to have continued on to Devonshire for a bit of seaside air. At least that's the plan Hurst had envisioned.

Privately, Burton had envisioned another scheme, one that included eliminating Hurst and destroying the written records the idiot had left behind. But his plan had contained a slight miscalculation. He'd already started Hurst drinking the poisoned wine before he realized the blasted journals were missing.

While Hurst was wheezing out his last few breaths, Burton had interrogated him again.

"Where are the journals?" he'd demanded, striking Hurst across his blue-tinged face.

"I d-don't know," his friend had sobbed. "Th-they ought to have been wh . . . where I left them. Hel . . . help me, pl . . . please." Gasping hard, he began to claw at his own throat.

Moments later the convulsions set in, a wet stain forming on Hurst's trousers as he lost control of his bladder. Burton crinkled his nose as the odor of fresh urine rose upward, creating a repulsive stink in the air.

He left Hurst a twitching heap on the study floor and returned to the man's bedroom to search one more time.

Yet he'd found nothing.

Nothing!

Now, once again in the study, he glared at his old
friend, at the staring blue eyes that no longer saw anything. Walking close, he took out his frustration by giving the body a pair of swift, punishing kicks.

Useless drunkard! Burton raged. *Bacon-brained lout!
What has he done with those bloody journals?*

More to the point, what had Hurst written inside
them? If it was nothing incriminating, he could relax.
On the other hand, if Hurst had written down enough
detail about Eleanor's death to be convincing, it could
cause him trouble.

His late wife's family had never truly believed his explanation that she'd fallen down the stairs while sleepwalking. Her father in particular had found the story
suspect, but hadn't possessed the evidence to refute him.
With Hurst's statement, he now just might.

I have to find those damned diaries, Burton thought.
Hurst had to have hidden them somewhere and gone to
his grave refusing to reveal the truth. But remembering
his last few minutes of life, and how he'd blubbered like
an old woman, perhaps Hurst hadn't been lying. And if
he hadn't been and the journals truly were not in the
house, it could mean only one thing.

Someone else had taken them!

But who?

The thought made his stomach churn, his knuckles
clenched into bone-popping fists at his sides. A scream
bellowed from his lungs, shaking the walls and reverberating against the ceiling.

Whoever it is, he vowed, *I'll find him. And when I do,
only God will be able to help the miserable bastard.*

*   *   *

"St. George and Hurst 'er back in the city," Hannibal announced without preamble as he crossed into the breakfast room where Rafe was eating a solitary meal. "But what's really interesting is that Hurst turned up dead this morning. Heart seizure, or so it's bein' said. St. George found him and is—how did I hear it—most distressed."

Hannibal pulled out a chair opposite Rafe and sat down.

Rafe quirked a sarcastic brow and set the fresh orange he'd been peeling onto a plate. "Oh, I'm sure he's beside himself with grief. No doubt been that way ever since he stood over his old friend and watched him turn blue."

"Ye think he done him in, then?"

"Undoubtedly. After what Hurst wrote in those journals of his, I'm surprised St. George didn't kill him ages ago."

"Perhaps he doesn't know about the journals."

Rafe ate a slice of orange, the fruit bursting sweet and tangy on his tongue. He swallowed and wiped his sticky fingers on a napkin. "Oh, he knows. It has to be the reason Hurst is dead. Weak hearts, as I recall, have never run in Hurst's family. He was far more likely to die of jaundice and a failing liver than from a heart disorder."

"Well, if St. George knows, then he'll be wantin' those journals back."

"Good thing, isn't it then, that I took the liberty of copying the salient pages and forwarding them to poor Eleanor Winthrop's father? Anonymously, of course. No doubt the marquis will find the account of his daughter's death quite enlightening."

Rafe drank some coffee, then returned the china cup to its saucer. "Considering the marquis's position in Parliament, this evidence will allow him to put pressure on the right people and see St. George brought to justice. I would pursue it myself, but considering my connection with St. George, his former father-in-law will be a far more effective advocate than I."

"Murdering bastard ought to be hanged twice," Hannibal said. "Once fer his wife and once for our poor Pammy. Won't say he ought to swing fer Hurst. That poxmonger deserved whatever it was he got. Guess he's down in Hell by now with the devil warming his feet but good."

"Let us hope so, Hannibal. Let us hope so."

Rafe paused, waiting silently for some kind of satisfaction to sweep over him. Three of Pamela's tormentors had now received their punishment, two of them dead. And the last one—the worst one—would soon receive his comeuppance if everything went as it ought. Eleanor Winthrop's father would be out for blood and if Rafe could arrange it, he would give the authorities reason to rethink not only her death but Hurst's as well. With the journals, it wouldn't be difficult to turn their inquiring eyes in St. George's direction.

Instead of pleasure, though, Rafe felt nothing but a lingering sadness. Pamela was dead, and nothing he did would ever change that fact. Revenge, he realized, was no longer his goal. Only justice would serve now. Justice and a freedom from the threat St. George still posed to himself and his family.

His stomach muscles tightened at the thought that Julianna might be in more danger now than ever. St. George certainly must have learned about her marriage to him, and if he found out Rafe was behind the disappearance of the journals . . .

No longer hungry, he pushed aside the half-eaten orange. "I want you to personally watch Julianna until this is over. She is to be guarded at every moment, is that clear?"

"Completely. But it might not be easy to watch her that close and not be seen."

Rafe shrugged. "Then let her see you. Follow straight on her heels and if she confronts you about it, have her come to me."

A twinkle sparked in Hannibal's gaze. "She won't like it a bit. You'd best polish up your strongest armor."

"Very amusing."

"Weren't meant to be amusin'. Just givin' you fair warning, is all."

"So noted." Rafe lifted his cup to his mouth again and drained the last of the coffee. "I believe you should also tell Appleby to pack his things and lie low for a while. Obviously Hurst has no further need of his services as a footman, so his sudden disappearance from the city won't look odd. Chances are good St. George won't peg him as the man who liberated the journals from Hurst, but if he does, then Appleby's life is in grave jeopardy. Tell him I'll take care of his expenses until St. George is firmly under lock and key."

"Man's got family over in Margate. I'll suggest he pay 'em a nice, long visit fer the spring and summer. He'll be right happy with that, I'm certain."

"Good. Now you'd best be going; you've got work to do."

Julianna rushed into the townhouse.

Or rather she waddled fast, since she didn't "rush" anywhere these days. At the moment, however, her current physical limitations were not uppermost in her thoughts—Rafe was.

I have a few choice words for him, she mused, *and I'm going to say them. What does he think he's doing, anyway? Having me followed, and by Hannibal no less!*

Over the past three days, she'd started noticing the man anytime she came within the vicinity of the front door. At first she hadn't thought a great deal about it but this morning there'd been no mistaking the matter when she'd ordered the coach for a trip to Bond Street to visit some shops.

Bold as you please, there he'd come, the big behemoth following her out of the house, only to climb up next to the coachman with the obvious intent of going along for the ride.

After arriving at her destination, she'd said nothing as he'd trailed her down the street. But when he'd actually had the nerve to walk into the linen drapers and stand behind her, well, she knew she'd had more than enough. Turning, she had confronted him with every intention of sending him on his way. But he'd stunned her, first by openly admitting that he was following her, and then again by telling her he was doing so at Rafe's behest.

"If you've a problem, my lady, you're to take it up with The Dragon," he told her. "Otherwise, I've orders to be your new shadow."

When she demanded to know why she was being trailed, Hannibal crossed his beefy arms over his chest and shook his head. "Talk to Rafe."

Oh, I'll talk to him all right, she vowed as she quick-waddled her way across the main foyer and down the hall to Rafe's study. Even her longtime butler, Martin, had held his tongue as she'd come through the door, no doubt glimpsing the martial glint in her eye.

As she approached the study she heard voices, but she didn't care. Whoever he had in there with him could wait. Her business took precedence.

Rapping her knuckles in a fast staccato against the door, she shoved it open, not waiting to receive permission to enter. "Pardon the interruption, my lord," she declared as she crossed into the room, "but I must speak with you. Now, if you please."

The room grew abruptly quiet, Rafe and his guest turning their heads to look at her. With her attention focused squarely upon her husband, she didn't at first pay heed to the individual seated across from him.

Her breath caught on a surprised inhale, however, when she did, taking in the woman's ethereal blond beauty and lithesome figure—so slender compared to her own body, now heavily rounded with pregnancy.

From his seat behind his desk, Rafe rose to his feet.

"Julianna, is something wrong?"

Her gaze darted between him and the woman.

Who is she? she wondered. *What's more, why is Rafe having a private conversation with her?*

"No. Well, yes. We need to talk," she repeated.

Rafe's dark brows twisted. "Can this wait a few minutes?"

She stared again at the woman, who gave her a small, conciliatory smile.

Highly aware of their audience, she nearly backed down and agreed to wait. Instead, she straightened her shoulders. "I would prefer that it not."

Who is she? Julianna wondered again. *Dear God, surely not his mistress? But Rafe wouldn't invite such a woman to his home—to* our *home—would he?*

The blood drained from her cheeks at the idea.

He crossed to her and took her elbow in his hand. "You look pale. You are not unwell, are you?"

Recovering slightly, she pulled away from his grasp. "I am fine."

He tossed the blond a quick glance. "Excuse us, will you?"

"Oh, but of course," she answered, her French-accented voice every bit as pretty as the rest of her.

Julianna preceded Rafe out of the room, cognizant of the fact that he had made no effort to introduce her to the other woman. *Are my suppositions correct? Has Rafe taken a mistress and is she even now sitting only in the next room?*

Opening her mouth, she nearly voiced the question, part of her desperate to confront him. Then she stopped.

What if the answer is yes, she asked herself. *If it is, do I really want to know?*

"So what is this about, Julianna?"

Letting the sense of affront over her original complaint return, she lifted her chin and met his gaze. "As if you do not know. Hannibal is following me around Town, and on your orders, I am given to understand. I want him to stop."

He tucked a hand into his trouser pocket. "Oh, that."

"Yes, that. Call off your dog, Rafe."

"Sorry, but I'm afraid I cannot comply. I suggest you learn to ignore him."

Her lips parted. "Ignore a giant? Impossible. Everyone will be whispering, wanting to know why I suddenly have a bodyguard trailing my every step. Frankly, it's mortifying."

"I don't see why. Women often have servants accompany them."

"Ladies take footmen and maids with them. No one will mistake Hannibal for either one of those."

"You aren't keeping an active social schedule this Season, and with your confinement all but upon you, you'll scarcely be out in company enough to be noticed. I fail to see the difficulty."

"The difficulty is trust, and your lack of it in me. Why is Hannibal following me?"

An inscrutable expression settled over his face. "I have my reasons."

"And pray tell what are those? Surely this is not because Lord Summersfield has returned to Town?"

A scowl lowered across his brow. "No, but you are to stay away from him nevertheless."

Her mouth firmed. "I told you once before that I choose my own friends."

"And I've told you to have a care in your choices."

And what of yours? she wanted to ask. *What of the woman waiting just beyond your closed study door?*

She straightened her shoulders. "So if not Summersfield, then what? I deserve an explanation at least."

A long moment of silence descended, as if Rafe were debating how to respond. "He is there for your protection, yours and the baby's."

"The baby and I are fine. We have no need of a guard. Or would jailer be a more apt description?"

For an instant, an expression of hurt strained his features. "You are free to come and go as you like, but Hannibal will remain."

"So you will not call him off?"

Rafe gave her an inscrutable look. "No. Now, are we done?"

Tears pricked behind her eyes. Blinking quickly, she willed them away, sorrow settling like a chunk of ice in her breast.

He turned, wrapping his fingers around the doorknob.

"God above, I wish I'd never met you," she murmured under her breath.

He paused. "Of that, madam, I am well aware."

Turning as fast as her figure would allow, Julianna sped away.

Rafe stood motionless, the brass knob forgotten beneath his fingers. Closing his eyes, he fought to steady his emotions. He supposed he could have handled the situation differently, explained his concerns about St. George to her. But he hadn't wanted to frighten her, not with the baby's arrival so close at hand. Better she be angry with him for a time than afraid to step foot outside the house. Or worse, that she dismiss his fears as groundless and take unnecessary risks.

She spoke of trust. What of her trust in him? She should know he had only her best interests at heart.

Taking a deep breath, he opened the door and stepped back inside the study.

Yvette Beaulieu looked up at his entrance and smiled. "Is everything well with your wife?"

"Yes," he lied, crossing to his chair and settling in. "Quite well."

"I can see now why you wish me to make a portrait of her and the baby. She is exquisitely lovely, as I am sure your *petit enfant* will be when he comes. I cannot wait to return for the commission. But I will be careful not to say a word, since it is to be a secret."

"Yes, just so."

Rafe wasn't sure there would be a commission. Once Julianna heard of his plan to have her and the baby's likeness painted, she might not wish to proceed. But he couldn't voice his concerns to Madame Beaulieu, not after he had contracted for the work.

The widow of an old friend, Yvette depended upon commissions, such as his own, to supplement her meager jointure and support her four children. Well aware she would not accept charity, he had thought the portrait a fine way to aid her, and at the same time do something nice for Julianna. He'd seen the expression on Julianna's face when she had noticed Yvette, however, and wasn't sure now that she would accept the gift.

Unlocking his top desk drawer, he counted out a stack of coins. "The first half down. I will pay the remainder upon completion of the work."

He would have paid her the entire sum now, but knew her pride would not let her take the money.

"Oh, this is far too generous. A third would have sufficed."

Yet as he watched, her small hand reached out and

took the coins, trembling slightly as she dropped them in obvious relief inside her reticule.

"Well, I should take my leave, monsieur . . . oh, *pardonnez-moi*, my lord, it is now."

He smiled. " 'Rafe' will do fine, just as it always has done. Take care, Yvette. Give my best to the boys."

"*Mais oui.*" With a laugh, she stood.

He escorted her to the door, Yvette leaning up to give him a Gallic buss on both cheeks. She laughed again as Martin held open the door.

Turning, Rafe noticed a movement overhead and glanced up in time to catch a flash of Julianna's skirts on the landing above.

With a sigh, he returned to his study.

Julianna peered out the window of the upstairs drawing room and watched the world pass by—ladies and gentlemen, nannies and children, maids, footmen, and street vendors all going about their normal routine. She wished she could join them, but after yesterday, knew she would not be able to go anywhere without being tracked.

Why is Rafe having me followed? she pondered again. She'd spent a near sleepless night with that question and others disturbing her thoughts and shaking her emotions. *Does he have so little trust that he must have me watched? Or is it something else?*

His silence on the subject infuriated her.

More than ever, she needed time away. She could always visit one of her friends here in the city, she supposed, but doing so would serve little useful purpose. Doubtless they would sympathize with her present unhappiness, and yet she had no wish to reveal the details of her failing marriage.

Pain squeezed in her chest at the thought, memories

flashing of the willowy blond as she'd reached up and kissed Rafe good-bye.

Is she his lover? The evidence would certainly seem to suggest she was, though Julianna couldn't truly believe Rafe would be so crass or so cruel as to bring the woman into their home if that were the case.

I need time to think, she decided, *away from this house. Away from Rafe.*

Yet could she escape Hannibal's surveillance?

Taking a seat on the sofa, she began to formulate a plan.

Nearly two hours later, Julianna slid the key into the lock of her Upper Brook Street townhouse, her pulse beating with relieved satisfaction. Closing the door behind her, she crossed the familiar entry hall, the house utterly silent in a way she had never before heard it.

Her plan had gone perfectly. Despite Hannibal's vigilance, eluding him had proven far easier than she had imagined it might be. Of course, her escape would not have been possible without the sharp-witted help of her modiste. Yet all it had taken was a few words into the woman's understanding ear in order to procure her assistance.

And so while Hannibal waited in the front of the shop as she supposedly tried on a dress, Julianna slipped out the back and into a waiting hackney. A short ride through Mayfair had deposited her at the door of her old home.

Walking into her sitting room, she pulled back the curtains to let in a rush of crisp spring sunlight. Removing the dust cover from her favorite chair, she settled herself comfortably, or as comfortably as she could with the baby drumming his tiny feet against the inside of her stomach. Hoping her touch might prove soothing, she rubbed her palm in large, easy circles over her belly. A couple of long minutes later, the baby finally began to settle, shifting one more time before falling still. Leaning her head back against the wing chair's high back, she closed her eyes.

My time here is limited, she mused. Already, Hannibal would be searching for her, and reporting her disappearance to Rafe, if he had not done so already. So she owed it to herself to enjoy her freedom, to revel in the pleasure of being home again.

Yet as she continued to sit and to think, she realized that as reassuringly familiar as her townhouse might be, it was no longer where she belonged. For good or bad, her home was now with Rafe. Whatever trouble lay between them, she could never go back to the past, to the way her life used to be. To the way *she* used to be.

She stroked her hand over her belly again.

When she'd told Rafe yesterday that she wished she'd never met him, she hadn't meant it. After all, if she'd never known him, she would still be living her old life, pleasant but passionless, each year melting into the next in a kind of innocuous haze. What would have become of her? Always a sister, an aunt, and a friend, but never more. Certainly never a mother.

Rafe had given her a child, and in that regard she had no regrets—the baby was, and always would be, a genuine blessing. But what of her love for Rafe? Did she regret that?

A tear dampened her face. With the back of her hand, she wiped it away. She ought to regret her feelings for him, she supposed. Lord knows everything would be simpler that way.

And yet she could not. Loving Rafe was part of who she now was and she wouldn't change that, not even to save herself the pain.

But what of the future, their future, assuming they had one together? As he said, their lives were now irrevocably entwined, their marriage one that, no matter how disastrous, would continue for the rest of their lives.

Given that, perhaps she should do more to reach out to him. Maybe she should put aside her fears and insecurities and admit her feelings, humble herself enough to confess her love and pray he felt some glimmer of warmth in return.

But what about the woman in his study yesterday? What if she was indeed Rafe's mistress?

If she was, the blond was soon to be gone. Julianna would insist he end the relationship and make the effort to rekindle one with her.

And if he refused?

Well, she would deal with that if it happened. She would also deal with Rafe's ridiculous edict that she be watched every second of the day. Did he honestly not trust her? Or did he imagine he was protecting her? And if so, from what?

Her escape today proved he had nothing to fear. She was perfectly fine and nothing untoward had happened.

Taking a deep breath, she rallied herself to return home.

The sound of the front door being opened and closed echoed through the empty house.

So, she thought, *I've been discovered. Is it Rafe or Hannibal who has found me?*

Footsteps reverberated against the polished marble floors, moving slowly up to, then past, each room. Straightening her skirts, she prepared herself for the confrontation to come.

The footsteps fell silent and a tall male figure filled the threshold of the sitting room. But instead of a pair of familiar green eyes, she met blue ones. Their expression both icy and terrifying.

Opening her mouth, she screamed.

Chapter Twenty-four

ᙢᑐᑐ ᑐ᙭

"N° LUCK?"

Rafe gave a quick shake of his head to Ethan as he strode across his study. Reaching for the brandy decanter, he splashed a draught into a tumbler and tossed it back, the amber liquor leaving a numbing heat against his tongue and throat.

Unfortunately the spirits could do little to numb his fear and worry over Julianna. Nearly two days had passed since she'd slipped away from Hannibal at the dressmaker's shop, and since then there'd been no sign of her.

After raking fingers through his already disheveled hair, he let his hand fall to his side, where it curled into a fist.

Most likely she was staying with a friend, still angry with him for ordering Hannibal to follow her. He would have been far less concerned and far more irritated by her disappearance were it not for the fact that he'd checked with all her friends—discreetly of course—and none of them appeared to be harboring her. Nor had any of them seen her in the past few days.

He'd also questioned her modiste, who denied any knowledge of Julianna's whereabouts since she had left her shop and climbed into a hackney cab. Hannibal, shamed at having been given the slip by a woman—and a tiny, pregnant one at that—set himself to the task of tracking down the hack driver. When he finally located the man, the driver said he'd taken her to a house in Upper Brook Street.

Her house.

"We checked the townhouse again," Rafe said, crossing to lean against the fireplace mantel. "It's obvious someone was there, since one of the dust covers is gone from a chair. But whether Julianna was there alone or not, I couldn't tell."

Nor could anyone tell if she'd left the house of her own volition, or at someone else's.

What if St. George has her?

The very idea twisted his gut into knots. Given the failure of her guards, though, he couldn't discount the possibility. Not only had Hannibal been unable to keep her in his sights, the runners had as well. He supposed their only excuse was the fact that they had been watching for an outside threat, never anticipating that Julianna herself would be the one to flee.

And while they'd been busy searching the nearby shops and streets for her, they'd lost track of St. George as well. In a fit of anger, Rafe had sacked the runners, and given Hannibal a dressing-down he wouldn't soon forget.

Still, the fault was his own.

Did I drive her away with my silence? he wondered, recalling their quarrel. *How will I live if something dreadful has befallen her?*

"She will be all right," Ethan said as if he'd read Rafe's mind. "Do not lose heart."

Rafe nodded without enthusiasm. "You're probably right. Maybe she went to visit her sister."

But he knew she hadn't. For one thing, Maris and William were supposed to be traveling to London in the next couple of days. Julianna wouldn't have left for fear of passing them on the road. Plus, being so close to giving birth, it was unlikely she would have undertaken such a long journey, even if she had been angry and upset enough with him to leave.

"I can ask a few more people if they've had contact with her," Ethan volunteered. "I know the Nevilles a bit better than you. Maybe Beatrice wasn't being honest when you asked her about Julianna."

"Maybe, but I don't think Lady Neville was deceiving me."

Yesterday morning Vessey had paid a friendly call only to discover the household tense with anxiety, and Rafe bleary-eyed from lack of sleep—sleep he hadn't done well to get last night, either. Once apprised of the situation, Ethan had offered to help, asking around the city in search of Julianna.

"Still, you might discover something if you inquire again," Rafe said, willing to do anything to find her.

A knock sounded at the door, Hannibal striding in with a half-grown boy held in his grip. "Sorry to interrupt, my lords, but this 'ere whelp insists on seein' you direct-like." The big man paused, turning a fearsome glower upon the boy, one that made the youth struggle against the hold the giant had on his grimy collar. "I told 'im to leave 'is message wit me, but he refused."

Rafe frowned. "You have a message for me?"

The boy nodded.

"Let him go, Hannibal."

Huffing out a disapproving breath, Hannibal prodded the boy farther into the room. The skinny, underfed youth stumbled slightly but managed to keep his balance. Nervously, he cleared his throat. "You Pendragon?"

" 'Course he's Pendragon," Hannibal barked. "*Lord* Pendragon to the likes of you."

The boy's eyes widened in obvious fear, but he held his place. Reaching inside his frayed tan jacket, he pulled out a letter, crumpled from having been tucked inside his clothes. "I was told to put it straight in yer hand an' none other. The man wot gave me this said you'd give me half a crown if I delivered it."

"What man?"

"Don't know. Never seen him afore."

"Was he dark-haired or light?"

"Dark. He paid me first to watch the lady, then after to keep this letter fer a couple days and give it to you."

Ethan sprang to his feet, while Hannibal let out a curse.

The brandy churned inside Rafe's stomach. "What lady?"

"Don't know. Pretty she were, but pregnant-like. Near big around as my ma just afore she birthed my little brother."

A stultifying silence fell over the room.

"He weren't lyin', were he?" the boy questioned, his worried eyes darting between them. "About the money, that is?"

Refusing to let his fingers shake, Rafe reached into his coat pocket and withdrew a coin. "No, he wasn't lying. Now, the letter, if you please."

The boy handed over the missive, then just as quickly snatched up the coin. Biting the corner to check the metal for authenticity, he thrust the money deep into his pocket. Before any of them could say a word, the child ran. Hannibal started after him.

"Let him go," Rafe ordered.

"But Dragon, he might have more information."

"Unfortunately, I fear all the information we need will be in this letter."

Crossing to his desk, Rafe picked up a silver letter opener and slit open the wax seal. He said nothing as he read the words inside.

"Well," Ethan asked. "Is it him?"

A black sickness rose within Rafe, all his fears having come to fruition. "St. George has her. He wants the journals and money in exchange for her life and the baby's. He's given instructions. We ride as soon as the horses can be readied. There is no time to lose."

Julianna shifted in the hard cane-backed chair in which she sat, trying to find a more comfortable position. Tugging her woolen mantle closer against the damp chill that permeated the narrow two-room cottage, she watched Lord Middleton pace to the window, stare out for a long minute, then pace back.

"It's cold in here. Perhaps you ought to go out for more wood," she suggested.

The flames in the room's single fireplace were burning low, producing little heat against the persistent spring chill outside.

Middleton turned toward her, a sneer on his face. "And perhaps you should shut your mouth."

She folded her hands over her belly and huddled deeper into her cloak. As she'd learned during the four days since he'd kidnapped her and brought her here, Middleton was wound like a short piece of thread on a large spool, capable of snapping at any instant.

He'd exploded once already when she'd refused to cook meals for them, giving her a savage slap across the face that had convinced her to change her mind. After that, she'd done as she was told, striving to be patient as she prayed for herself and the safety of her unborn child.

He paced to the window again, an annoying habit grown worse over the past couple of days. He was increasingly anxious, she'd noticed. The confinement and stress of the situation were beginning to take their toll.

They were taking their toll on her as well. She knew Rafe would come for her, if for no other reason than the fact that he would never allow harm to come to their child. Nor to her, she admitted, no matter the current state of their marriage.

Until he arrived, though, she had to stay strong, for herself and the baby. Despite the fear that had become her constant companion since this ordeal began, she refused to give in to its crippling effects. She'd also sworn to herself that she would not be worn down by Middleton's threats, subtle and otherwise.

During one of his more talkative moments, the viscount had told her how he'd hired a few street children to keep watch of her comings and goings. At first, he'd been stymied when Hannibal had begun to shadow her every step. But fate had taken a turn in his favor, he'd told her, when she'd slipped free of her guard and shown up at her townhouse alone. He'd chuckled as he recalled his moment of victory, as he liked to call it. She'd played right into his hands, a perfect little dupe.

So Rafe was trying to protect me all along, she realized. *If only I had listened.* Of course, it might have helped had Rafe seen fit to express his worries over her safety to her. Then again, she knew herself well enough to realize she might have discounted his concerns, and done as she pleased regardless of the danger.

So now here she was—wherever *here* might be.

Based on the length of the coach ride and the rich, loamy agricultural fields she'd glimpsed out the window on the way, she suspected he had taken her northeast, perhaps to his home territory of Essex, or maybe nearby Suffolk. She couldn't be certain, though, her surroundings giving her few clues. The cottage he'd chosen was certainly isolated, so much so that she hadn't seen or heard a single sign of human activity since their arrival.

As she knew, the chance for escape was slim, especially given her current physical limitations. But if an opportunity presented itself, she'd promised herself she would take it, no matter how unlikely success might be.

Until now, Middleton had been incredibly vigilant, his eyes fox-sharp as he kept track of her every movement. During the day he watched her, making sure she had access to implements, including knives and kitchen tools, only when she was cooking. The remainder of the time he kept such items securely out of her reach. When she needed to venture outside, he would bind her wrists with rope and tie her to a chair. At night, he locked her inside the cottage's only other room, a windowless chamber so tiny the single bed and washstand barely fit inside.

But his diligent attention was beginning to show cracks in its foundation, worry and a lack of proper sleep setting him on edge. Perhaps a subtle bit of goading might nudge him over that edge just far enough to make a mistake. Despite the risk, she supposed it was worth a try.

"He's not going to come, you know," she declared boldly. "If Rafe was planning to race to my rescue, don't you think he'd be here by now?"

Middleton spun to face her. "Oh, he'll be here. He wouldn't abandon his wife, especially not with you swollen big as a sow with his brat."

She forced herself to give a casual shrug. "Ordinarily that would be the case, but you mistake the real circumstances of my marriage to him."

"Really? Do tell."

"We took pains to keep it a secret, but I suppose it makes little difference now. Last year I agreed to be Pendragon's mistress. My brother owed him a great deal of money, you see, gambling debts and such, and well, Rafe and I struck a bargain. My favors in exchange for payment of the debt."

An amused gleam came into the viscount's eyes. "Finally, the truth. I did wonder about your unlikely liaison with a mongrel of Pendragon's ilk. How the two of you . . . er . . . came together, so to speak."

"It wasn't out of personal desire, I assure you," she lied. "It was an obligation, no more, no less."

"Then why the marriage, if he was already getting the milk for free?"

"This . . . mistake"—she paused, motioning toward her belly—"would be the reason. When he discovered I was with child, he saw his chance to force his way into the nobility. Using my lineage and his wealth, he knew he would be able to procure a title that would otherwise have been denied him. To him, the child and I are irrelevant, since he already has what he wants—a place in the Lords and a peerage."

"Privileges that cur does not deserve." Middleton growled, spitting out a curse. "Prinny is nothing but a greedy fool, sullying the greatness of this nation by inviting ill-bred rabble like Pendragon to join the ranks of true peers. It positively disgusts me to think of honorable noblemen being forced to countenance such as he in their midst."

Of course it isn't a problem for honorable noblemen to associate with titled rapists and murders, she reflected with an inward shudder. *At least not to Middleton's twisted way of thinking.*

Glancing toward the sputtering fire, she used the moment to steady her nerves. "So you see, he has little incentive to chase after me. If you are wise, you'll cut your losses and let me go. If you release me, I'll promise to say nothing of this . . . misadventure."

"Will you indeed?" He barked out a laugh, his voice rife with sarcasm. "How gracious of you, my lady. But you see I have a vested interest in holding you, since I'm in rather desperate need of funds at the moment. If Pendragon won't pay, then your family will."

"My family will hunt you down and kill you," she spat in sudden anger.

"Then they'll have to stand in line to do it." His

hands curled into fists at his sides. "Just before we left London, I learned that I am being sought for questioning by the authorities. My bloody former father-in-law has gotten hold of some documents that implicate me in the death of my wife. If he has his way, there will be a trial. A murder trial."

He began to pace. "Of course no one will believe Hurst's drunken rantings, but there will be enough dust stirred up to make my life quite difficult for a time. How dare they think to jail me, to humiliate me in public? How dare they, any of them, question a man of my stature? *Me,* Burton St. George, Viscount Middleton."

He ended by thumping a hand against his chest in obvious outrage, his eyes closed in a struggle to regain control of his emotions. When he opened them again, his gaze was a placid blue.

"No," he said, "should I have need of payment from your family, they will pay and be able to do naught about it. Once I've collected the ransom for you, I plan to be on a ship headed for France. I figure I'll take my chances with Boney, maybe travel on to Austria or Italy. I hear it's always sunny and warm in beautiful *Italia.*

"But despite your doubts, I know Pendragon will come," he continued. "Today or tomorrow at the latest. Like it or not, you are his wife, and that whelp growing in your womb, his spawn. He'll come, if for no other reason than pride." He lowered his gaze to her stomach. "Of course, if you'd prefer, I could try to help rid you of that . . . thing."

She shivered, more convinced than ever that Middleton was not quite sane. Instinctively she cradled her arms around her unborn child, shielding it from the monster that stood before her.

He laughed aloud, visibly enjoying her fear and revulsion.

"Thank God Maris found out what you were before it was too late," she said.

His laughter died, his expression turning nasty. "That's another matter I always wondered about. Why your innocent little sister took such a sudden aversion to me on the eve of our engagement. She was to be mine, you know. She *was* mine until someone whispered stories into her tender little ears. Was it you? Did you warn her off? Or did Pendragon tell you some sad tale?"

He sauntered closer. "I can see by your face he did. What did he say? Did he reveal what I and my fellows did to that pretty little tart of his? The one he was going to marry? Believe me, she wasn't worth it, though I did enjoy seeing Pendragon suffer. He actually cried, did you know that? Imagine a grown man weeping over a worthless trollop like her."

Julianna shuddered, unable to hide the involuntary reaction.

"Bastard's been set to ruin the lot of us ever since, though I didn't realize it soon enough. Challoner, Underhill, Hurst, and now me. Well, he won't win; I'll make sure of that."

"What do you mean?" she asked, her voice quavering.

"I mean that once I have his money I am going to kill him."

She sucked in an audible breath.

"I've already selected a spot for his grave." He moved closer and bent over to grab her chin between his hard fingers. "If you don't watch yourself," he whispered, a cold smile on his lips, "I'll do the same for you."

She suppressed the whimper that rose in her throat.

He studied her for a long moment, his gaze moving over her the way a snake slithered over prey.

Finally he turned away, releasing her chin. "Too bad you've grown so disgustingly fat. Otherwise, we could have found far better ways to occupy our time to-gether."

She shivered, sending up a small prayer of thanks for her pregnancy weight. If she lived through this, never again would she complain about having put on a few extra pounds.

He moved across to the window once more and stared out. A long minute ticked past before he turned, thumping his hands against his sleeves. "Christ, it's freezing in here and the fire's nearly out."

Julianna goggled at the statement, since he sounded as if he were only now noticing the cold.

"I will get some wood," he declared, crossing to pick up the rope he used to bind her. "I'll feed and water the horses, too, while I'm out," he mumbled beneath his breath as he approached.

She tensed in anticipation, hating it when he tied her to the chair, leaving her utterly helpless and alone. She nearly begged him to reconsider but knew her protestations would only make him enjoy the process more. Biting her lip, she remained silent as he secured one of her wrists to the arm of her chair, wound the rope twice around her body, then secured her other wrist to the opposite chair arm.

Then he swept the cutlery off the table and secured it where she could not reach. Tossing his greatcoat over his shoulders, he let himself out of the house without another word.

The baby kicked, as if to protest their confinement. "I know, little one," she murmured, comforting herself as much as her child. "I know."

Willing herself to relax, she leaned fully back into the chair. As always, she tested the ropes in the unlikely hope she might find a millimeter of give. Her heart gave a double thump when her bindings moved, if only fractionally. To make certain she wasn't letting desperation

cause her to imagine things, she tugged again, and discovered definite movement in the rope.

Her pulse leapt with sudden hope and renewed determination. She had assumed her rash conversation with
Middleton to be completely ineffective, but now she
realized it had been more successful than she had imagined. Still, had she distracted him enough to make a real
mistake, one that would allow her to gain her freedom?

Only time and effort would tell, and she knew she
needed to hurry if she had any chance of success. He
would be back soon, likely too soon, and if he found her
on the verge of escape, heaven knows what he would do
to her.

She quaked at the thought but pushed her fear aside.
Straining against her bonds, she ignored the discomfort
the ropes caused as they bit into her body, working to
force as much slack into the bindings as possible. The
gap wasn't enough to slip through, not without some
measure of genuine suffering involved. Realizing there
was no other way, she gritted her teeth and concentrated
on freeing her right hand.

The rough hemp dug into her tender flesh as she
fought to yank her hand through the loop. Pain streaked
up her arm, nearly unbearable as the rope scraped away
the top layer of skin. Closing her eyes, she gave one last
tremendous tug, knowing she would not be able to endure the agony for much longer.

Her hand popped free.

Ignoring her bleeding wrist, she lost no time loosening
the rope from around her body, tearing frantically at the
last knot that held her in place. The tips of three of her
fingernails snapped off in the process, but she barely noticed, dumping the rope on the floor. Climbing to her
feet, she hurried to the door, but stopped seconds shy of
reaching for the knob. Prudently, she detoured to the
window to check for Middleton. When she saw no sign

of him, she wrenched open the door and ran out, racing across the yard as fast as her legs would carry her.

She hadn't gone far when a pain stabbed through her middle, bringing her to a halt. Panting, she bent forward, arms wrapped around her swollen stomach. Almost immediately the agony began to subside, but the discomfort was a sharp reminder that she was in no condition to push her body too far or too hard, not without risking harm to herself or her child.

She was about to start forward again when her pulse leapt at the sound of horse's hooves pounding in the near distance.

Is someone coming? she wondered. *Oh, lord, please let them stop and help me. On second thought, since I'm praying, please let it be Rafe!*

Moments later, a familiar dark-haired rider rounded a curve in the rutted country lane.

It is Rafe!

Her heart pounded fast as tears of joy stung her eyes. Beside him rode Ethan Andarton, the two men galloping toward her.

She met Rafe's gaze, reading the relief in his intense green eyes. Smiling, she took a pair of steps forward.

Without warning, his expression changed, alarm flashing over his face. He opened his mouth and shouted something to her, but the erratic March wind swept his words away. Scowling, she fought to understand, intuiting an instant later what he must be trying to tell her.

Middleton! How could she have forgotten about him, even for a second?

As she turned and tried to sprint away, an inflexible arm curved around her waist, locking her within his grasp. Straining, she fought to break his hold, but his arm clamped down tight, squeezing until pain shot through her ribs.

"It'll hurt more if you don't stay still," he told her, his voice cruel with menace.

Fearing he might harm the baby, she ceased her struggles.

"Let her go, St. George!" Rafe shouted, he and Ethan bringing their mounts to a halt only a few feet away. Rafe moved to leap off his horse, but Middleton's next words froze him in place.

"Stay where you are, Pendragon," the viscount warned. "And don't come any closer, not if you want her to live."

A click sounded near her ear, the cold barrel of a primed pistol set against her temple. She trembled, closing her eyes for a long moment as she fought the urge to scream. Only when the need passed did she let herself look again.

"You know me well enough to realize I'll shoot," Middleton said. "You don't want me to shoot, do you?"

Rafe shook his head. "No. Just tell me what you want."

"You obviously received my note, so you know what I want. Twenty thousand pounds and the journals. Give them to me now."

"I will, once you release Julianna."

Middleton increased his grip. "Not until I have the items. You brought them, did you not?"

"Of course. Just as you outlined."

"Then let's see."

Rafe shifted in the saddle. "You'll forgive me, but I have reason not to trust you, St. George. I thought it wise to take precautions, so before my arrival I stopped and buried the money and the books."

The viscount stiffened in obvious irritation. "Buried them where?"

"Not far. Let Julianna go and I'll show you. You can keep the gun if you like."

"Rafe, no!" she cried.

Both men ignored her, their interest focused squarely on each other.

A long moment passed while Middleton weighed his choices. "You." He took the gun off her long enough to wave it at Ethan. "Get down from your horse. Before you do, though, give me your weapons. You too, Pendragon. Open your coats so I can see what you have."

Ethan glanced toward Rafe. "Are you sure?"

"Do it," Rafe ordered. "We've no other choice."

"That's right," Middleton said. "You don't have a choice unless Pendragon there would prefer becoming a widower."

Slowly, both men withdrew the guns from their pockets, then unbuttoned their greatcoats, each revealing another brace of pistols a piece.

Julianna wanted to tell them not to comply, not to give up the only protection they had, but she stayed silent, knowing her pleas would be brushed aside as before.

"Vessey. The saddlebags, put the guns inside," the viscount demanded.

Moving carefully, the marquis dismounted and did as he was instructed, opening the leather pouch on his mount and sliding the guns inside.

"Now, come forward and leave it. Close, but not too close, if you take my meaning." Middleton renewed his threat by pointing the pistol at her again.

Ethan gave her an apologetic look, then walked forward as far as he dared and set down the bag.

"Move away."

As soon as the marquis stood several feet distant, Middleton urged her forward, his fingers biting into her flesh in a bruising grip. Only when he drew close enough to touch the saddlebag did he act, giving her a rough shove to the right as he bent down to snatch up the pouch.

His push sent her staggering, feet hurrying as she fought not to lose her balance. A new pair of arms wrapped around her, catching her before she could fall. Steadying herself against Vessey's reassuring strength, she glanced around to check on Rafe.

With a sinking heart, she saw that Middleton was already seated on the other horse, his weapon pointed straight at Rafe.

"Take care of her, Ethan," Rafe said.

Turning their mounts, the men rode away.

"Oh, God, Rafe." A shudder went through her, shock and fear making her whole body quake. "Middleton will kill him."

"Rafe will be all right," Ethan said, though by his tone she could tell he only half-believed his own words.

"We have to go after him."

"I can't leave you. Rafe would have my head."

"Then don't. There are horses in the stable and a coach. If we start now, we'll only be a few minutes behind."

"Out of the question."

Pushing herself from his hold, she planted her hands on her hips. "Then I'll do it myself."

Turning on her heel, she headed toward the barn.

Behind her he uttered a low, muttered curse. "Women!"

Moments later, she heard him follow.

Chapter Twenty-five

H OW MUCH FARTHER?" the viscount demanded, his weapon trained on Rafe as their horses proceeded up the road.

"Not much now," Rafe said. "It's just a little ways ahead."

Of course, "a little ways" was as near or far as Rafe chose to make it, since his statement about having buried the money and journals was nothing but a ruse.

Knowing how imperative it had been to convince the viscount to release Julianna, Rafe had relied on deception to lure Burton away. Clearly, his improvised plan had flaws, such as the possibility of getting himself shot and killed, but at least St. George was no longer a danger to Julianna and the baby.

The truth was that Hannibal had the ransom, the funds and journals, stored safely inside a locked chest in a room at a nearby inn. But Rafe knew he would never have been able to talk St. George into releasing Julianna, then accompanying him to a public inn. The viscount, quite rightly, would have seen it as a trap.

Besides, Rafe had never had any intention of giving the money or the journals to St. George. He'd only brought them along as a kind of last-resort insurance policy in order to win Julianna's release.

Now all he had to do was lead St. George to a likely-looking spot in the woods, then find some method of distracting him long enough to wrest the gun from his possession. Once he had the viscount under control, he would march him back so St. George could be turned over to the authorities.

Of course, excellent as that plan might seem, actually making it work was not going to be easy. He would, he knew, have to stay alert and think quickly.

Aware of St. George's rapidly waning patience as the minutes passed, Rafe scanned the countryside for a stopping place. So long as the land wasn't too muddy, he supposed any location would serve. As they rounded the next curve, Rafe saw a heavily wooded area that showed definite promise.

"Here, this is it." Rafe pointed toward a large tree. "This oak is the one. I walked inland just there for several yards."

"You're sure?"

"Of course I'm sure. I'm not likely to forget where I buried twenty thousand pounds. You don't mind if I dismount, do you?"

St. George motioned his agreement using the business end of his pistol. "Lead the way. But I'm warning you, Pendragon, no tricks or I'll shoot."

St. George would shoot anyway, he knew. Once the viscount had what he'd come for, St. George would make sure to rid himself any potential liabilities— namely him. Dead men, as the saying goes, tell no tales. Although considering Hurst's journals, that wasn't strictly true, he thought wryly. Hurst had told a considerable amount even from his grave.

Boots sinking lightly into the half-thawed spring ground, Rafe began walking into the woods, St. George close at his heels. Overhead, naked tree branches spread outward like thick gnarled fingers, green buds still held snug in their cocoons, nearly ready to unfurl.

Imperceptibly, Rafe drew a deep breath to steady his pounding heart, aware that he required all the calm he could muster. When the right moment came, he would have to recognize it and act without hesitation. If he failed in the first attempt to free himself, he would not be getting another.

"I've been wondering," Rafe said, hoping a little conversation might divert St. George's focus, "how did you know I had the journals?"

St. George gave a laugh. "I didn't know for certain, but I decided to take a chance and assume you did. I figured even if it wasn't you, kidnapping your wife would be good for squeezing money out of your pockets. Besides, who else could it have been? Who else bears me such a deep and abiding grudge?"

"Oh, I'm sure there must be several others. Eleanor Winthrop's father, for one."

"Annoying old fool. Even with the so-called proof he believes he has, his claim against me will come to naught in the end. Once I destroy the original journals, those copies will appear as nothing but a fraud, manufactured to disgrace me. The marquis will look like exactly what he is—a grieving father unable to let go of his loss."

"And what of Hurst? Bow Street knows you poisoned him."

"Do they? His death was ruled a spasm of the heart. If he was poisoned, it was by drinking far too much for far too long."

"So you're staying with that story, hmm? Why bother when we both know the truth? You are planning to kill me as well, are you not? Why bother with secrets now?"

"Keep walking, Pendragon." St. George prodded the gun against Rafe's shoulder.

"No, really. I'm just wondering why you feel so confident about getting away with murder."

"Why wouldn't I? I've done it before."

"Your wife, you mean?" Rafe questioned as he led the way down a small incline.

"Perhaps, but there's another. In fact, since we're sharing confidences, it's someone near and dear to your heart."

A chill ran through him. "What do you mean?"

"Haven't you ever wondered at Papa's death?" the viscount drawled. "How he went so suddenly, and at such a young age?"

"It was a seizure."

"And so it was. Poison is an interesting thing. I've made a bit of a study of it over the years. Some varieties are completely tasteless, did you know? While others need the addition of something stronger to conceal the flavor. Alcohol is a good medium, especially when the recipient is in the habit of drinking a particular variety. Papa preferred brandy. He drank a snifter every night after dinner."

It took all of Rafe's fortitude to keep walking. *Mother of God, St. George killed our father!*

"It was simple, actually. Murder is, once you get up the nerve to do it the first time. He didn't even realize what I'd done, not until the last, when I leaned over and whispered it into his ear. I can still remember the look in his eyes, the horror of knowing he was going to die and by my hand."

"Why?" Rafe asked, his voice low and strained. "Did you hate him that much?"

"Hate him? Of course not. I adored him. No one was more devastated at his death than I. But he said unforgivable things to me, said I wasn't suited to be the future head of our family. He claimed I was selfish and unfeeling, cruel to those I do not deem my equal. He told me he wished *you* were his heir, wished *you'd* been the one born legitimate so you would one day hold the title. He said of the two of us, you were the better man."

He prodded Rafe again with the pistol. "Who's the better man now? Which one of us, I ask, is going to walk out of here the victor?"

Not you, Rafe thought as he reached up to push aside a mass of low-hanging branches. And that's when he knew.

Now!

Sweeping the branches aside, he paused for a fraction of a second so he could hurry under, then he let them fly.

The tree limbs raced backward, striking with an impact Rafe knew had to be painful.

St. George howled, beating at the rough tangle of branches as he fought to free himself from their clutches. As the viscount spun and slapped his way clear, Rafe lay in with his fists.

Pain shot through Rafe's right hand as his knuckles connected with St. George's jaw. He barely noticed the discomfort, though, too focused upon his goal of wrestling away the pistol. Clamping his fingers around the viscount's wrist, Rafe squeezed, flesh grinding against flesh, bone against bone, as each of them struggled for possession of the weapon.

Seconds later, the pistol popped free, soaring through the air for a long moment. A muffled thump echoed as the gun landed at the base of another tree.

Rafe dove for it, satisfaction roaring through him as his fingers curled over the wooden grip. Rolling, he brought the weapon up and aimed it straight at St. George's chest. Keeping the gun steady, Rafe regained his feet.

The viscount stopped, frustration and hatred shining in his sky-colored gaze. He spat out a curse but made no further move to retake the pistol, obviously knowing he was bested.

"Go ahead, Pendragon. Shoot me," St. George said. "You know you want to."

"You're right. I do. But that's the difference between you and me, St. George. I don't kill in cold blood, not even when I know the world would be made a better place by the act."

"Coward." The viscount spat.

"We'll see who the coward is when the hangman slips a noose around your neck. With my testimony and the rest of the proof against you, the Lords will give you death for sure."

St. George blanched, but said nothing further.

"Get going," Rafe commanded. "You lead the way back this time."

The return walk seemed shorter, the horses whickering a soft greeting as Rafe and the viscount emerged from the forest.

"Wait here and don't move," Rafe told St. George as soon as both of them were once again standing on the road. Before he and the viscount began the journey back to the cottage, Rafe planned to make sure St. George had no further means of escape.

Keeping the gun leveled, Rafe moved to his horse to retrieve a length of rope from inside the saddlebag. With the binding in hand, he approached St. George.

He was about to order the viscount to place his hands at his back when there came a rumbling of coach wheels and horses' hooves plodding quickly against the dirt road.

Glancing up, Rafe felt his eyes widen as he recognized the driver.

With a soft command, Ethan drew the team to a halt. "Well, this is a fine sight. I'm relieved to see you are the one now holding the gun."

"I managed to resolve the situation. But why are you here? You're supposed to be with Julianna."

"He is," Julianna declared, lowering the coach window and leaning out. "We came to help."

Rafe's heart gave an uncomfortable double beat.

Ethan had the grace to look sheepish. "She insisted."

"Well, I insist you take her back now, out of harm's way. St. George and I will be along in just a few minutes."

"We're not leaving you alone with him," Julianna said, plainly aghast at the idea. "Lord Vessey, assist Rafe."

"Ethan, stay where you are."

"No," Julianna said.

"Yes," Rafe answered back.

"Maybe I *should* help you, Rafe," Ethan began. "I don't trust him to—"

In an unexpected flash of movement, St. George shifted, slamming his elbow into Rafe's stomach. Pain shot through Rafe's belly, but he ignored it, fighting to keep the gun away from the viscount.

Suddenly a jolt reverberated up Rafe's arm as the gun discharged, the bullet whizzing harmlessly off into the woods. Realizing the weapon was now useless, Rafe tossed the pistol aside and prepared to use his fists.

Spinning away, the viscount bent down and reached into his boot. Metal flashed, silver glinting with wicked intent as Middleton straightened to display a knife clasped in his hand. Yelling a profanity, he charged at Rafe.

From inside the coach, Julianna watched, breath trapped in a painful bubble inside her lungs.

The two men circled, Middleton doing his best to stab and slash at Rafe, while Rafe managed to leap clear. Coming forward again, the viscount struck out wildly in an attempt to draw blood, the lethal blade missing Rafe by mere inches.

Above her on the coachman's seat, Julianna saw Ethan reach for his gun. A faint snick sounded as he cocked the trigger. But even as the marquis took aim, he held his shot. The men were too close and moving too erratically, Julianna realized, for Ethan to fire without risk of hitting Rafe instead of Middleton.

Rafe barreled forward, catching hold of Middleton's wrist and bending it inward. Locked in a furious scuffle, the men fought on, each move vital, each one possibly the last.

Down they went, striking the earth like a pair of enraged bulls. The men rolled, adding punches and kicks, the blade now lost somewhere between them.

The fighting continued for another long minute. Suddenly Rafe jerked and fell still, Middleton sprawled above him.

Julianna's heart stopped for a full beat.

No, it can't be! she cried silently. *Rafe!*

Without conscience awareness, she pushed open the coach door and started down. Stumbling as her feet hit the ground, she steadied herself against the vehicle.

Then she saw movement, catching a glimpse of Rafe's hands as he pushed Middleton up and off him, the blade buried to its hilt in the viscount's chest. Gleaming wetly, blood was smeared over both men, Rafe's hands and clothes soaked red.

Hurrying forward, she fell to her knees beside him. "Are you hurt? Did he cut you?" Frantic at the sight of so much blood, she ran her hands over him, searching for wounds.

Rafe shook his head, panting for breath. "No, I'm fine."

A deep groan rose into the air, making her jump. Glancing over, she met Middleton's eyes, the blue irises cloudy with shock and pain. Shifting his gaze, the viscount fixed a hate-filled look on his half brother. "May I see you in hell, Pendragon!"

A last harsh breath rattled from his lungs, a crimson line of blood trickling from his mouth as his body went limp in death.

Wrapping her arms around Rafe, Julianna closed her eyes and burrowed close. A shiver raced through her, together with a sense of relief that the ordeal was finally at an end. Rafe's arms came around her, holding her close as he rocked her against him.

"Are you all right?" he asked, brushing his lips against her forehead. "Did he hurt you? Your wrists—I couldn't say anything before, but—"

"I did that to myself when I was trying to escape. Otherwise, I'm fine, just scared, I—Oh! *Owwwww.*"

Pain jabbed through her middle as if she'd been pierced with a blade, the agony bending her forward even though she was huddled within Rafe's arms.

"What? What is it?" he questioned, alarm plain in his voice.

Unable to speak, she could do nothing but wait and hope the misery would pass.

"Is she all right?" Ethan stepped forward, leaning over in concern.

"I don't know."

"Maybe it's the child. Is she in labor?"

"Labor!" Rafe repeated. "But she's not due for another three weeks."

"Babies rarely care about schedules. They come when they want."

As she listened, the pain began to ease, muscles she hadn't even realized were clenched relaxing as the spasm subsided.

"Julianna? Talk to me. Is it the baby?" Rafe's eyes were deeply green and filled with a kind of anxiety he'd never displayed before, not even when he'd been battling the viscount.

She nodded. "I think Lord Vessey may be correct. This isn't the first pain I've had today."

Rafe released her long enough to climb to his feet.

Reaching down, he gently lifted her up to stand beside him. "Can you walk?"

"Yes, I think so."

"Let's get you into the coach." He turned toward the marquis. "Ethan, do you think you can deal with St. George's body? If not, we'll have to leave him here and return later."

"I should be able to get him up on one of the horses. Don't worry about me. Go on."

"Julianna and I will see you at the cottage, then."

"Oh, no, you won't," she stated. "I am not going back there."

Rafe's brows furrowed. "What's that?"

"I spent three miserable days in that cold, awful place and I'm not spending another moment. I most certainly am not giving birth there."

"I can understand you not wanting to return to the cottage, but you can't give birth here." He set a fist on one hip in thought. "I'd take you to the inn where Hannibal is waiting, but it's rough and isn't much better than the cottage. Ethan, what about Andarlly?"

"Certainly you are more than welcome to go to my estate. No one is expecting us and the house won't be prepared, but my housekeeper is a good woman; she'll know what to do. The trip shouldn't be much above an hour from here, assuming Lady Pendragon can make the journey."

Rafe bent his head toward Julianna. "What do you think, Julianna? Do you think you can wait that long?"

"Chances are good I'll be fine. It'll probably be hours yet before I deliver, and Ethan's home sounds wonderful."

"Then let us pray you don't give birth in the coach," he murmured. Sliding an arm beneath her knees and back, he swept her off her feet. As gently as he could, he settled her inside the coach. "Yell out, if you need me."

She gave him a small smile and a nod, watching as he shut the door.

A new pain lashed her as he vaulted into the driver's seat and set the horses in motion. Biting her lip, she rubbed a hand over her belly and urged the baby to wait.

Chapter Twenty-six

Y OU ARE GOING to wear a hole in the carpet if you don't cease that infernal pacing."

Rafe ignored Ethan's comment as he continued to stride up and down the marquis's sitting-room floor, exactly as he'd been doing off and on for the past fourteen hours. Dread tightened like a fist inside his gut.

She's been up there too long, he thought, *and still the baby isn't born.*

When Julianna had said it would be some while before she gave birth, she had not been exaggerating. But what at first had seemed only natural was now beginning to take on worrisome proportions.

The midwife, who had been called to attend his wife, had come down a few hours ago to inform him that Julianna's labor was progressing, albeit slowly.

"Some babies," she'd told him in an echo of Ethan's earlier remark, "like to take their own sweet time before making an appearance into the world. Nothing yet to trouble over," she'd reassured.

But that had been four hours ago. Hadn't he the right to be just a bit troubled now?

A rippling wail rang out from upstairs, sending a fresh shiver of apprehension down his spine. Julianna's cries of pain had reverberated throughout the house for hours now—all during the endless afternoon and evening and on through an interminable night. The first rays of day-light were just beginning to peek through the windows, sunshine rising to replace light from the candles that were even now guttering out, burned down to nubs.

She moaned again, the sound loud enough to drift down the stairs.

Dear Lord, how much more can she endure?

Dragging his fingers through his already tousled hair, Rafe stepped out into the hall and cast his eyes up the staircase toward her bedroom. "Perhaps I should go to her?"

"And do what?" Ethan asked from his seat on the sofa. "The women have things well in hand without any interference from you or me. Come, why don't you have a bite of this breakfast Cook made us before it goes cold."

"I'm not hungry."

Ethan gave a snort of disbelief. "You haven't eaten a decent meal in days, nor have you slept more than a handful of hours since well before we left London. The strain is beginning to show. Frankly, you look like the very devil."

Rafe supposed he did look rather worse for the strain—his cheeks rough with stubble, his hair standing on end, his cravat gone, flung aside hours earlier along with his bloodstained coat. But what did it matter how he looked? Whether or not he'd eaten or slept? His wife was lying upstairs, in torment as she tried to bring their child into the world.

What will I do if she dies? How will I ever go on with-out her?

Of course he knew he mustn't think like that, but still, what a tragic irony if he had saved her from St. George only to have her die in childbirth!

And I've never even told her I love her.

He wanted to rush upstairs and say the words, tell her

how much she meant to him before it was too late, but he held himself back.

She will be fine. She has to be fine.

Turning, he found Ethan at his elbow. "If you won't eat, then at least have some tea." He held out a cup.

Reluctantly, Rafe took it and forced himself to down a swallow, then another before crossing to take a seat. Silently, he set the beverage aside.

"Hannibal arrived not long ago," Ethan said. "He had my note and came directly. Since we brought Middleton's body with us, I had to send word to the local magistrate. Cobb is a decent sort, and given that the viscount's death is a clear-cut case of self-defense, there'll be no difficulties from him."

"Nor in London, I assume," Rafe said, linking his fingers together, then letting them hang between his knees. "No doubt there will be questions, but considering everything that has transpired, I suspect most everyone will be relieved by the outcome. Gentlemen never like a trial against their own."

"No, not even for a lord as obviously guilty as Middleton."

A new round of wailing sounded from above, all thoughts of the viscount abruptly wiped from Rafe's mind.

Is it my imagination, or are her cries growing weaker?

Springing once more to his feet, he resumed his pacing.

Seconds later, a shrill, heart-wrenching scream pierced the air.

God in heaven, she is dying!

Knowing he had to go to her, he rushed out of the room and bounded up the stairs, taking them two at a time. Flinging open the door to her temporary bedchamber, he charged inside.

Four women turned to look at him, including Julianna, who lay in the center of the bed, her nightgown folded up over her mounded stomach, leaving the lower half of her body exposed. Her dark hair was plastered against her head, damp with perspiration, her pregnant frame contorted in obvious pain and distress.

From her position at the foot of the bed, the midwife pinned him with a reproachful look. "My lord, what is the meaning of this interruption? You cannot be here. I must ask you to leave."

Ignoring the older woman, he strode forward, his gaze locked on Julianna. "I heard you scream. I came to see if you are all right."

Julianna gave another sharp cry, arching upward as she strained and panted against the pain. He watched the muscles in her spread thighs and calves flex, her belly rippling visibly as the contraction took her in its unforgiving grip. Tensing, he felt her misery as if it were squeezing deep in his vitals as well as hers.

"Lady Pendragon is giving birth and must not be disturbed." The midwife motioned with an impatient hand, silently ordering her assistant and a young housemaid to eject him from the room.

Rafe planted his feet, holding firm against the women's not-so-gentle shoves. "She's been giving birth for hours now. I've been downstairs listening to her. I'm not leaving until I know she's not in danger."

"She's in no more danger than any other woman bringing a life into the world. The baby is coming. I must insist you remove yourself from this room."

"What do you mean the baby's coming?" An arc of surprise flashed through him as her meaning sank in. "You mean now?"

"Yes. I mean *right now*."

Another contraction arrived, traveling fast on the heels of the last. Julianna screamed and rose up for a moment on her elbows before falling wearily back against the sheets.

Realizing his presence might be causing more harm than good, he allowed the women to shove him backward a step or two.

Julianna rolled her head toward him and stretched out an arm, her dark eyes luminous and beseeching. "No, Rafe, don't go."

Her plea stopped him.

Without hesitation, he shook off the women's hold and hurried to her side. Dropping to his knees, he grasped her delicate palm in his own, then stroked a comforting hand over her head. Fingers trembling faintly, he smoothed damp tendrils of hair off her hot forehead and cheeks.

"I'm here, sweeting. I'm here," he murmured, gazing into her eyes.

"It's hurts so badly." She inhaled sharply as another contraction hit, teeth clenched as she did her best to hold on through the agony that threatened to strip away the last of her tenuous strength.

Slipping an arm beneath her shoulders, he did what he could to support her, her body quivering from the exertion. Seeing her this way, in such misery, tore him apart.

How he wished he could bear her pain himself. He would gladly trade places with her, if it were possible. But this was a woman's burden, a torment only she could endure. All he could do now was stay by her side as she'd asked, and see her through it.

"My lord, I really must insist you go," the midwife ordered. "This is no place for a man."

"Place or no, man or no, I am staying."

He focused again on Julianna.

"I'm scared," she confessed, a tear sliding down her cheek. "I can't do this. I can't."

"Of course you can," he said in a stern voice. "Any woman courageous enough to do the things you've done can do this. You're my brave girl. You can do anything. Now squeeze my hand and squeeze it hard, hard as you like, when the next pain comes. I'm with you, sweeting. I won't let you go."

Moments later, she did as he'd told her, gripping his hand so tightly he feared she was cracking a couple of bones inside. He dismissed the pain, knowing his damaged hand was nothing compared to what she was suffering.

"I see the head," the midwife called. "Just a couple more pushes and the baby will be out. Don't bear down until you feel the next pain come on you, my lady."

"Nearly there, darling. Nearly there," Rafe encouraged.

Julianna screamed through the next pair of contractions, clinging to him like a lifeline. He felt her entire body shake as she forced the baby from her body in a slick rush of agony.

When it was done, she crumpled against him, weeping weakly from the strain.

A baby's furious cry filled the room.

Lowering Julianna gently back against the pillows, he leaned up to peer at his child, the tiny body red and wrinkled and shiny.

"What is it?" Julianna asked, voice faint with exhaustion.

"A boy," he told her, heart hammering in jubilation. "It's a boy!"

"You're crying," she murmured, lifting trembling fingers to touch his cheek.

"Am I?" he asked in happy surprise, blinking at the wetness. He bent close. "If I am it's because I love you so much," he whispered. "Thank you for our son."

Then, uncaring what the others in the room might see,

he pressed his mouth to hers and shared a kiss of grateful relief and profound joy.

Julianna passed the next two days in a weary haze.

The ordeal of being abducted by Middleton, combined with the physical and emotional toll of giving birth, had left her suffering from an exhaustion that seemed to penetrate all the way to her bones.

Sleeping in snatches, she would awaken to feed her new son, then drift back to sleep again. The baby had shocked her the first time she'd fed him, his tiny mouth latching onto one of her tender, milk-swollen breasts with an astonishing eagerness for a child only a few hours old. Soon, though, she'd grown accustomed to the novel sensation, finding it oddly pleasant, even comforting. Often during those moments she would stroke his tiny head with a single finger and marvel at the puff of downy black hair adorning his head.

The marquis's housekeeper—a sweet, motherly woman with a no-nonsense way about her—had taken on the role of temporary nursemaid, tending to the baby even as she tended to Julianna. This included encouraging Julianna to eat.

"You need nourishment, my lady, if you're to keep that young one strong," the older woman said as she pushed a dish of hot beef broth upon Julianna only an hour after the birth. Despite her exhaustion, the housekeeper refused to take no for an answer. And so Julianna ate and slept and slowly regained her strength.

As for Rafe, she had seen little of him since the delivery. Mrs. Mackey told her that he stopped by often to check on her but refused to stay, knowing Julianna needed her rest.

When it came to the baby, however, he was far less reticent. She remembered rousing slightly one afternoon to find Rafe rocking the baby in his arms as he murmured soft words into his son's little ears. Dropping a kiss upon the infant's head, Rafe had returned him to his cradle before departing on silent feet. She'd fallen back to sleep, waking later to wonder if the memory had been a dream.

Another memory she questioned was the one of Rafe telling her he loved her. Had he truly said the words, or had he only imagined what she'd wanted to hear during those final, pain-filled moments of the birth? She wasn't sure, her uncertainty only made worse by his absence.

On the third morning, with dawn just sliding over the horizon, she awakened. Without even opening her eyes, she realized she felt stronger, her mind clear for the first time in days. Turning her head on her pillow, her pulse danced to find Rafe seated in a chair next to her bed. "Rafe?"

"I'm sorry. I didn't mean to wake you," he said, his voice low.

"You didn't, I awakened on my own. It's so early . . . what are you doing here?"

A faint smile crossed his lips. "Just watching you sleep. This is the first time you've caught me."

A warm tingle spread through her. "You've been here before? I didn't know."

"You were too exhausted. How are you feeling?"

She shifted slightly against the pillows. "Better. A bit sore."

From across the room came a small grunt, then a cry.

"He must have heard us," Rafe said.

She nodded. "It's also nearly time for his feeding."

When she moved to toss back the covers, he stopped her. "I'll get him. You stay there."

A moment of shyness engulfed her when he returned and she had to open the bodice of her nightgown to his view. But as soon as the baby settled in her arms and began to suckle, her reticence fell away. *How right it feels having Rafe here to share this,* she realized.

"A little glutton, isn't he?" he commented, reaching out to skim a finger over one translucent cheek, his hand huge beside the infant. "What shall we call him?"

It was long past time they gave their child a name, she realized. "What would you think of Campbell? Cam? It was my maternal grandfather's name. He was a kind and wise old man. I remember the silly stories he used to tell when I was young. He always made me laugh."

"It seems a fine, strong name. Campbell, it shall be."

Gazing down upon their son, she traced the shape of his beautiful face, and the tiny features that grew more discernible by the day. Strong forehead, square chin, shell-shaped ears. His eyes were blue, though already showing marked tinges of green. Would they turn fully green or darken later to a shade more her own? Would he have his father's eyes? There was no mistaking the fact that he already looked like Rafe, a small replica in the making.

"I had a note from Maris and William," Rafe said, leaning back in his chair. "They send their congratulations on the birth. Maris wanted to come, but I wrote to say that we'll be in London again soon enough."

"Yes," she agreed. "As comfortable as this house is, I would like to be home again. It will be wonderful to see her and William when we arrive."

His stomach full, the baby stopped nursing and dozed off to sleep. Lifting him to her shoulder, she carefully patted his little back to expel any trapped air. Once done, Rafe reached out and took the baby, carrying him back to his cradle.

After buttoning her nightgown, she settled against the pillows.

Rafe returned to her bedside. Leaning over, he straightened her sheet and blanket, then reached out to smooth a curl off her cheek. "I should let you get some more sleep."

"Don't go. I . . . I'm not tired—well, not much, anyway. You could stay and . . . talk."

He hesitated, his gaze meeting hers for a long moment before he nodded and resumed his seat.

"All right."

A thick silence fell between them, broken only by the lilting melody of birdsong issuing from the trees beyond the windows.

She swallowed against a sudden tightness in her throat.

Now that I've persuaded him to remain, I can think of nothing to say. Stupid when there is so much to tell him, so much to ask, so much between us that needs repairing, if it can indeed be repaired.

Her eyebrows furrowed.

Rafe frowned as well, his dark brows dipping low over his eyes.

"Julianna, I—"

"Rafe, did y—"

They spoke at the same moment, their words crossing over one another in a clumsy rush. She laughed and he smiled, her pulse galloping with sudden, awkward nerves.

"My pardon. What were you going to say?" he asked.

"No, you first. I can wait."

"Are you certain?"

She nodded, rubbing her fingertips over the blanket, the wool both scratchy and soft.

His smile faded, a solemn expression taking its place. "Very well, I . . . Julianna, I wanted to tell you that I am sorry."

Her gaze flew up. Of all the things she'd been expecting to hear, it hadn't been that.

"For what?"

"For so many things, but most recently for St. George. I never meant to put you through that ordeal. You must have been terrified and . . . God, did he hurt you? Did he do anything that you haven't wanted to tell me? You can, you know."

Reaching out, he covered her right hand where it lay next to her hip. Gently, he stroked her wrist and the strip of white cloth that was neatly bandaged around her abraded skin.

"There is nothing to tell," she said, "not really. I was frightened, of course, and worried for the baby, but this"—she moved her wrist slightly—"this was my own doing. Remember, I told you about it already. It's fine. I'm fine."

He pinned her with a searching look. "Nothing else. He didn't harm you in any other way?"

"No. I think he was far more obsessed with confronting you than in paying much attention to me. But he's dead now and it's over. Let it go, Rafe. Let it finally be done."

Rafe bent his head and gently squeezed her hand inside his own, her flesh warm and smooth and alive. *Blessedly alive,* he thought.

Lifting her hand, he pressed his lips against her palm and breathed in her honeyed sweetness. She was right. It was time to bury the past and move on, to live for his future, for *their* future, assuming she still wanted to share hers with him. He'd come so close to losing her. He would do anything not to lose her now.

Dropping another kiss onto her palm, he released her hand. "I should have told you."

"Told me what?"

"About him. About St. George and my fears for you. Arrogantly, I thought I could handle the situation, take precautions to keep you safe without worrying you with my suspicions. That's why I had Hannibal following you and a set of runners as well."

Her eyes widened in clear surprise. "You had runners watching me? I never saw them."

"You weren't supposed to see them. I wouldn't have ordered Hannibal to keep you under such a tight watch either, had it not been for St. George's return to Town. I realize now what a colossal mistake that was. Instead of expecting you to meekly do as you were told, I should have been honest and warned you about my suspicions. If I had, you might not have felt the need to run, to expose yourself to danger."

"I didn't run. Well, I did, but not in the way you mean. I just needed a little time, a bit of breathing room in which to think."

"Room you didn't feel capable of taking in your own home because of me. I drove you away, Julianna. I forced you into his path."

She gave a gentle shake of her head. "I would likely have gone no matter what you told me. I possess an obstinate nature and would have done as I chose despite your warnings. I am to blame for my abduction as much as you."

"Perhaps, but I gave you reason. You obviously felt the need to leave, formulating a simple but extremely effective plan for eluding Hannibal and the other guards, and all to be free of me." He gazed into the dark beauty of her eyes, emotion settling like a lump of granite inside his chest.

He didn't want to ask the next question, but he knew he must. Steeling himself, he forced the words past his lips. "Are you so unhappy, so miserable, that you cannot bear to live with me any longer? I know I . . . refused to let you go when you asked at Christmas. Is it . . . still your desire to stay with your sister?"

He glanced away, unable to bear seeing the answer in her eyes.

"If I said yes, would you take the baby from me?" she asked in a strangely quiet voice.

A harsh shudder ripped through him, pain spreading as if she'd taken up a dagger and thrust it into his chest. With difficulty, he drew a breath. "No. A baby should be with his mother. I would never keep our child from you."

Julianna exhaled, tension easing from her shoulders as an unsteady rush of warmth and optimism flowed through her veins. "And I would never keep him from his father. Did you mean it, Rafe?"

He cast her a puzzled look. "Mean what?"

Her pulse thundered. *What if he says no?* she worried. *What if I'm wrong and he doesn't care, after all? What if he really does break my heart this time?*

But she had to know, one way or the other. She couldn't go on living her life, their life, the way it had been before.

"When I was delivering Cam." Twining her fingers together, she stared down at her lap. "You said you loved me. Is that how you truly feel or did you say it in the moment, because you were excited about the baby?"

He leaned forward. "Is that what you think?" His tone was rough with emotion. "Julianna, how can you not know?"

"Know what?" Her heart pounded harder.

Raising her chin with his finger, he lifted her face until her gaze met his. "That I love you to distraction, and have loved you for such a very long time."

"You do? But you never said—"

"I should have done, another lamentable omission on my part. My only excuse is that at first I didn't know, or at least if I did, I refused to admit the truth even to myself. I didn't want to be in love, you see. And then, well, I wasn't sure how you felt in return. I know you only married me because of the baby, because I forced you to take vows you did not wish to make—"

"I married you because I loved you," she interrupted. "I only refused your offer because you'd made it clear you didn't want me. You had, if you'll recall, cast me aside."

Dropping down to sit beside her on the bed, he drew her into his arms. "I didn't want to end our affair. The only reason I did is because of St. George. After I found out about his interest in you and your sister, I knew I could not go on seeing you. You would have been in danger had he discovered you were my mistress. I lost Pamela; I wasn't about to take that same risk with you, so I lied about my feelings to drive you away."

"Well, you did an excellent job. I thought I was nothing but a burden to you."

"No, never that, never ever that."

"But why didn't you tell me? Why did you let me believe you only wanted the baby and not me?"

"Did I? I thought spending half a million pounds on a title so you could be Lady Pendragon showed some measure of affection."

"But you did that for Cam and for your legacy."

He shook his head. "No, love. I did that for you. Believe me, I've had ample opportunity over the years to acquire a title for myself had I wished, but such trappings were never important to me. Once we were to be wed, though, I knew I could not see you disgraced, could not bear to watch you shunned by your friends and family, not when I had the means to effect a far different outcome. It was my gift to you, though apparently rather clumsily done."

She slid her arms around his back. "Oh, Rafe, I had no idea. And so much money. You shouldn't have done it. My family would have stuck by me, and my true friends as well."

"Perhaps, but I didn't want to put you through the pain."

"And here I assumed you didn't love me, only the baby."

"I love our son," he said, brushing a kiss over her cheek. "But I love you more. I have to confess, though, that the baby gave me a good excuse to do what I'd wanted to do all along. To take you as my own, to claim you as my wife, so I could love you as I pleased. It nearly killed me when you kicked me out of our bed."

"It killed me too. Oh, we've been such fools!"

"We have, haven't we?" He skimmed his lips across her jaw. "When St. George abducted you, I feared I'd lost the chance to tell you how much you mean to me. But I'll never make that mistake again. I love you, Julianna, now and forever."

In the next breath, his mouth claimed hers, kissing her with a fervor that made her senses grow giddy with pleasure and her spirits soar. Holding him closer, she poured all her love, all her life, into their embrace, knowing she never wanted to be separated from him again.

He was starting to ease her against the pillows to deepen their kiss even further, when she suddenly remembered something.

Turning her head, she broke away. "What about that woman?" she demanded, her breath coming out in a pant.

"What woman?"

A scowl creased her forehead. "Your new mistress. The beautiful blond."

"What blond? I don't know who you're talking about, I . . . oh, you mean Yvette Beaulieu."

"Is that her name? *Yvette*." Drawing in a deep breath, she prepared herself to forgive him, no matter what.

"Yes, and she is *not* my mistress."

Hope flared in her breast but she tamped it down, still not quite willing to believe him. "Then who is she?"

"The widow of an old friend, who is in need of a bit of cash. I hired her to paint your portrait—yours and Cam's."

"What!"

"It was going to be a surprise, but given your suspicious nature, I don't think I should make any further attempt to keep it a secret."

"You're sure? She's awfully pretty."

He chuckled. "Quite sure. Madame Beaulieu may be attractive but she'll never compare to you, my love. You are the only mistress I've had since the day we met, and you're the only one I'll want for as long as I live."

A smile stole over her lips, growing wider and wider. "Well, in that case, you may kiss me again."

With an exuberant laugh, that's precisely what he did.

Epilogue

West Riding, England
May 1813

SEE THAT THESE are included in today's post," Rafe said, handing a small stack of correspondence to Martin.

The butler bowed and accepted the missives. "Of course, my lord; I'll send a boy with them now."

"Thank you, Martin. Have you seen my wife? Is she still in the garden?"

"I believe so. Her ladyship took master Campbell outside about half an hour ago and they were still there last I noticed."

Rafe nodded, then turned, walking down the long hallway that led to the rear of the house. Anticipation bubbled in his blood, effervescent as champagne, his every step seemingly lighter than the next. He shook his head at his eagerness, unable to contain the grin that spread over his mouth at the thought of joining his wife and son. Foolish since he'd seen Julianna at nuncheon only three hours earlier and spent time with Cam that morning as well.

He was glad he'd let Julianna talk him into leaving London and spending the spring and summer at their country estate. The rolling Yorkshire dales were magnificently green as they stretched out as far as the eye could see.

Opening a side door that led to the gardens, he stepped through, his shoes crunching on the pebbled path. As he walked, he drew the air deep into his lungs, enjoying the scent of clean earth and burgeoning nature. He'd been here many times, but could not recall a more glorious May, the sky a vivid symphony of blue, trees unfurling their leaves like young girls preening for a ball, while flowers bloomed in explosions of fragrance and color.

Despite the love I felt for my mother, I've never fully appreciated all this until now, he realized. *Until Julianna. She makes everything she touches brighter, most especially me.*

Warmth hummed in his blood, his smile widening as he came upon her and Cam. The pair of them were settled atop a blanket beneath the wide, sheltering limbs of a giant oak, a tree he'd called his friend as a boy.

As Cam grows larger and stronger, I will show him how to climb that tree, how to sit in its sturdy branches and dream the way I used to do. But since the boy is scarcely two months old, Rafe reminded himself, *I suppose I will have to exercise a bit of patience.*

Julianna looked up and saw him, a happy smile parting her lips, her velvety eyes alight with pleasure. "Have you finished your work?"

Nestled on a separate baby quilt at her hip, their son lifted a small fist and waved it as if to say hello.

Rafe restrained the impulse to waggle his fingers back in reply.

Dropping down beside Julianna, he leaned over and pressed a kiss to her mouth. "Not all of it, no, but I couldn't stay inside a moment longer, not with this glorious day and the two of you waiting for me outside."

She caught his hand inside her own. "It is lovely, just

the right temperature, neither too hot nor too cold. The baby likes it. He's been laughing."

"Laughing, hmm? You know his nurse will say it is only a bit of trapped wind."

"Mrs. Bascom is a kind and wise woman, but she is wrong in this instance. Cam is definitely laughing. Watch."

Placing her palms over her eyes, she bent over the baby, who watched her with rapt fascination. "Peek-a-boo!" she exclaimed in an exuberant voice, opening her hands as quickly as she could to once again reveal her face.

The baby paused for a half second, then let out a high-pitched giggle. After a moment, he grew still, watching.

Julianna hid her face again, then sprang the surprise. "Peek-a-boo-boo-boo!"

Cam giggled again, his infant laughter rippling into the breeze.

"See," she said, turning to Rafe in delight. "He *is* laughing."

"He certainly is." Rafe grinned and made a funny face at his son. Cam chuckled, meeting his gaze with eyes that had turned nearly as green as his own. "Isn't he amazing?"

Julianna nodded, her gaze turning solemn. "He is. Our little miracle."

He slipped an arm around her waist and nuzzled her neck. "I can't wait until you feel well enough for us to try for another."

Although they were sleeping in the same bed every night, they hadn't made love since well before the birth, a situation that was wearing on them both, especially him.

"Actually, the doctor stopped by this morning while you were out inspecting the tenant farms," she said.

Rafe raised a hopeful brow. "Oh, and what did he say?"

"He said I'm very healthy. So long as I feel like it, I can resume relations anytime I wish."

He paused. "And do you—feel like it?"

Her cheeks flushed a light pink. "Yes, I do, quite strenuously, in fact."

If they hadn't been outside in full view of the house with the baby next to them, he would have laid her down on the blanket and had his way with her right then. Instead, he had to content himself by other means.

Cupping her jaw, he crushed her mouth to his, pouring every ounce of his passion and adoration into the kiss. Julianna trembled and moaned, threading her hand into his hair as she parted her lips wider to invite his tongue inside. Intoxicated by the pleasure, he took them both deeper, his senses afire in a way that made him shake.

Only by sheer force of will did he find the strength to pull away, breath shallow in his lungs. He and Julianna stared at each other for a long moment, then turned together toward the baby.

Cam was sleeping, peacefully unaware.

"That got a bit out of hand," she murmured.

He nodded. "Just a bit."

In unison, they sighed, then laughed.

"I love you, Rafe."

"I love you, too. More each day, if that's possible."

"It is," she said. "Because I feel the same."

He kissed her again, careful to keep the embrace light. "You know, it is time for Cam's nap. We could take him upstairs and let his nurse see to him for a while."

Her eyes gleamed with interest. "I suppose we could. I sometimes take a nap in the afternoon as well. No one would remark if I stayed in my room for a couple of hours."

"And there is a book I've been meaning to retrieve from my bedchamber. I could come upstairs and stay for a bit."

Slow smiles curved over both their mouths.

Standing, he gently picked up his son. With the baby nestled in his corner of his arm, he reached down a hand to Julianna.

"Shall we, my love?"

"Yes, Rafe."

Placing her hand in his, he lifted her to her feet. Together they strolled toward the house.

Read on for a sneak peek at

The Accidental Mistress

by Tracy Anne Warren

Coming from Ballantine Books
Available wherever books are sold

※ ⁂

April 1814
Cornwall, England

ONLY A FEW more yards, Lily Bainbridge told herself. *Only a little while longer and I will be safe. I will be free.*

An icy wave struck her dead in the face. Gasping for breath, she pushed on, arm over arm as she fought the unrelenting drag of the rough, rolling sea. Above her, lightning flashed against a viscous gray sky, slashes of rain hurtling downward to sting her skin like a barrage of tiny needles.

Arms quivering from the strain, she put the discomfort out of her mind and kept swimming, knowing it was either that or drown. And despite the suicide note she'd left back in her bedroom at the house, she had no intention of dying, certainly not today.

Many would call her insane to plunge into the sea during a storm, but regardless of the danger, she'd known she had to act without fear or hesitation. Delay would mean marriage to Squire Edgar Faylor, and as she'd told her stepfather, she would rather be dead than bound for life to such a loathsome brute. But her stepfather cared naught for her wishes, since marriage to Faylor would mean a profitable business deal for him.

Slowing, she scanned the jagged shoreline, and the waves that crashed in thunderous percussion against the rocks and shoals. Although she'd swum these waters for nearly the whole of her twenty years, she'd never done so during such a seething tempest. Alarmingly, nothing looked quite the same, familiar vantage points distorted by the dim light and the churning spray of the surf.

Treading fast, she fought the clinging weight of her gown, the sodden muslin coiling around her legs like iron shackles. Doubtless, she would have been better off stripping down to her shift before taking to the sea, but her "death" had to look convincing, enough so that her stepfather would not suspect the truth. If she lived through this and he discovered she was still alive, he would hunt her down without an ounce of mercy.

With her heart drumming in her chest, she swam harder, knowing she dare not let herself drift and be swept out to sea. A knot formed in the base of her throat at the disquieting thought, a shiver rippling through her tired limbs. *What if I've miscalculated?* she worried. *What if the storm has already carried me out too far?*

Her apprehensions evaporated when a familiar sight came into view—a narrow fissure, black as coal, that cut its way into the towering cliffs, which lined the shore. To the casual eye, the opening appeared no different from any of the other sea caves in the area, but Lily knew otherwise. For beyond its foreboding exterior lay protection and escape.

Giving an exuberant pair of kicks, she continued forward, crossing at an angle through the waves. With the tide now at her back, the surf pushed her fast. For a second she feared she might be dashed to pieces against the rocks, but at the last second the current shifted and washed her inside with a gentle, guiding hand.

Darkness engulfed her. Tamping down a momentary sense of disorientation, she swam ahead, knowing better than to be afraid. The cave was an old smuggler's pass that had fallen into disuse, a secret retreat that had once provided a perfect hideaway for inquisitive children, and now a truant, would-be bride.

With seawater eddying around her at a placid lap, she glided forward until she brushed up against the cave's perimeter wall. A small search soon revealed a ledge that told her she was in the right place. Dripping and shivering, she hoisted herself up onto its surface, then paused for a moment to gain her breath before rising to her feet. Careful of each step, she followed the cave's gentle bell shape until the interior gradually widened to provide a pocket of natural warmth and dryness. When her foot struck a large, solid object, she knew she had arrived at her ultimate destination.

Teeth chattering, she leaned over and felt for a wooden lid, opening the trunk. Her fingers trembled as they curved around the lantern she knew lay inside and the metal matchbox set carefully to one side. With the strike of a match, light filled the space, flickering eerily off the rough walls and low stone ceiling. Stiff with chill, she stripped off her clothes, then reached again into the trunk for a large woolen blanket, wrapping herself inside.

Thank heavens she'd had the foresight to secret away these supplies! After her mother's death six months ago, she'd known she would eventually have to flee, aware that as soon as the mourning period ended, her stepfather, Gordon Chaulk, would likely decide "to do something about her," as he'd been threatening to for years.

And so, while out on her regular daily walk, she had slowly filled the smuggler's chest with necessities, including money, food, and a set of men's clothes she'd altered from an old one of her father's. As for boots, she'd had no choice but to steal a pair from one of the smaller stable boys. Not wanting the lad to suffer for his loss,

she'd anonymously left him enough coin to purchas
new ones. He'd grinned about the odd theft and hi
propitious windfall for weeks.

To her knowledge, no one but a few old-time smug
glers knew about this hide-out, despite the thriving busi
ness of sneaking contraband tea and French brandy pas
the noses of the local excise men. Certainly her step
father wasn't aware of the caves. To most Cornishmen
he was still considered an outsider, despite having lived
here for five years—ever since marrying her mother and
taking up residence at Bainbridge Manor.

Five years, Lily sighed. *Five years to wear the life ou.
of a good woman who'd deserved far, far better tha*
she'd received.

A familiar lump swelled in her throat, a single tea
sliding down her cheek. Ruthlessly, she dashed it away
telling herself that now was not the time to dwell upon
her mother's untimely demise. If only she'd been able to
convince Mama to leave years ago! If only she'd been
able to keep her mother from falling prey to the bland-
ishments of a handsome charmer, who'd turned out to
have the heart of a poisonous viper! But having been a
child at the time, her opinion had not been sought, nor
heeded.

Toweling dry the worst drips from her hair, Lily
crossed to a pile of kindling stacked against the far wall.
Using some of the wood, she built a small fire. Blessed
heat soon warmed the space, calming the worst of the
shivers that continued to rack her body. Returning to
the trunk, she dressed in a shirt, trousers, and coat, the
masculine attire feeling strange against her skin. *At least
the clothing is warm, and—even better—dry,* she mused.
*And until I reach London, I had best get used to being
dressed like a boy.*

She wasn't so foolish as to imagine she could journey
to London on her own, at least not dressed as a woman.

A female traveling without escort would invite comment, but worse, she would be subject to all manner of predators wishing to make her their prey—out to steal her reticule, or, shudder the thought, her virtue. And in addition to providing her some measure of safety, the ruse would allow her to leave the area without detection. Rather than accept help of any kind, she planned to make the long walk to the coaching inn at Penzance. That way, should her stepfather question anyone later, they would have no cause to remember a redheaded girl matching her description.

Nerves made her wish she could leave now, but until the worst of the storm subsided she would be better off staying here inside the cave. Pulling on a pair of long woolen socks that eased the cold from her toes, she reached once more into the trunk for a cloth-covered wedge of cheese. Belly growling, she broke off a chunk and ate, enjoying the sharp, satisfying flavor.

Minutes later, her meal finished, she prepared to complete one last task—an act she had been dreading. Just the thought of proceeding made her cringe. *But the deed must be done.*

Locating her ivory comb, she drew the teeth through her damp, waist-length hair, careful to remove every last tangle before tying it back with a thin, black silk ribbon. Drawing a deep, fortifying breath, she lifted a pair of scissors and began to cut.

Three days later, Ethan Andarton, Fifth Marquis of Vessey, swallowed a last bite of shepherd's pie, then set his knife and fork at an angle onto his plate and pushed it away. Reaching for the wine bottle, he refilled his glass with a dry red of questionable vintage—apparently the best The Ox and Owl in Hungerford could provide.

Crowded full of men come to town for a nearby boxing mill, the public room hummed with noise and the occasional raucous burst of laughter. Drifting in spirals near the ceiling lay an acrid blue cloud of pipe smoke combined with the yeasty scent of ale and the heavy aroma of fried meat. With the inn's only private parlor already occupied, Ethan had decided to sit among the locals, tucking himself into a surprisingly comfortable corner table. From his vantage point, he could see all the boisterous goings-ons. But such matters were not on his mind as he quaffed another mouthful of wine.

It will be good to get back to London, he mused. *Good to return to my usual amusements and haunts now that I've taken the necessary first steps to see my future arranged.*

Not that he was eager to *have* his future arranged, but a long span of serious reflection on the matter had convinced him he could no longer afford to put off his duty. At thirty-five, he knew he had to wed. He had a responsibility to his lineage, an obligation to sire sons who would carry on the family name and title. And in order to do so he needed a bride—whether he truly desired one or not.

Of course, were his older brothers, Arthur and Frederick, alive, he wouldn't be facing this particular dilemma. Arthur would be marquis now—no doubt long since married, with children of his own. But by some cruel twist of fate, both of his brothers had lost their lives during an attempt to save a tenant's child from drowning in a storm-swollen river. Frederick had dived in first; then, when his brother failed to emerge, Arthur had followed. In the end, all three had perished, both men and the child.

Ethan had often wondered what might have happened had he been home that fateful day instead of traveling on the Continent. Would he have been able to save them? Or would he, too, have lost his life? He knew he would gladly have traded places, gladly have died in order to save the life of even one of his brothers. Instead, in an instant, he'd gone from third in line to being marquis, a position he had never once craved for himself.

After the accident, he'd arrived home raw with grief over the loss of his brothers only to find every eye upon him—family, servants, and tenants, all looking to him for guidance and reassurance. Feeling his old, carefree life slip like sand from his grasp, he'd done his best to step into Arthur's shoes and honor what his older brother had left behind.

In the twelve years since, Ethan had risen to the challenge, learning what he had to, meeting each expectation and every demand with determination and fortitude. There was one obligation, however, upon which he had long turned his back, stubbornly retaining that last bit of independence—until now.

He remembered his friend the Duke of Wyvern's reaction when he'd mentioned his decision last week.

"You cannot mean it," Anthony Black had said, his brandy snifter frozen halfway to his mouth. "Why on earth do you want to go and get leg-shackled? Especially when you've a surfeit of beautiful, willing women climbing in and out of your bed. Women, I might add, who have no expectations of achieving a ring out of the deal."

Leaning back in his chair at Brooks's Club, Ethan met his friend's midnight-blue gaze. "Because it's time, Tony, whether I want it to be or not. I can't put this off forever. I need to think to my future, the family's future. It's my duty to set up my nursery and father an heir or two to assure the title."